"Distinguished by wonderfully evocative descriptions of the Western landscape, *Mountain Time* is sure to strike a chord with readers who have struggled with the past and won the freedom to embrace their own lives."

—Beth Duris, *BookPage*

"If any writer can be said to wear the mantle of the late Wallace Stegner, Doig qualifies, as a steady and astute observer of life in our Western states. Infused with his knowledge and appreciation of the Western landscapes, his novels are a finger on the pulse of the people who try to reconcile their love of open spaces with the demands of modern life, particularly the form of 'progress' that threatens the environment. . . . This is an honest and resonant portrait of idealists facing middle age and learning to deal with past issues that shadow their lives."

—*Publishers Weekly*

"Invigorating . . . exhilarating . . . this is quintessential Doig."

—Robert Allen Papinchak, *Chicago Tribune*

Praise for *Mountain Time*

"A serious story from the reigning master of new Western literature . . . *Mountain Time* will not dissuade those who rank Doig
among the best living American writers, and one might even begin
making comparisons to some of the best *dead* ones, too. Faulkner
comes most readily to mind. . . . [Doig is] bigger than the Big Sky.
He stands upon the shoulders of Wallace Stegner and A. B.
Guthrie, taller than Edward Abbey and Tom McGuane, and sees
much further. He looks homeward, and he sees a place in all our
minds, not just in those who live in and write about the West."

—Ron Franscell, *San Francisco Chronicle Book Review*

"[Doig's] abiding love for his home ground carries the day in
Mountain Time, as it almost always does in his work. . . . He
understands his characters well, and manages to make them all
the more interesting not in spite of their flaws but because of
them. . . . He lets the story tell itself, which is what stories are
supposed to do."

—Jonathan Yardley, *The Washington Post Book World*

"A rich, resonant read, crafted out of Western talk and terrain.
It deals with the history we're given and the history we make for
ourselves. . . . Doig is a writer who deserves wider recognition.
Mountain Time is for readers who admire novelists who treat the
landscape with as much affection as their characters (think Stegner or David Guterson)."

—Bob Minzesheimer, *USA Today*

"There is much to admire in *Mountain Time,* especially in the
relationship between its protagonist, Mitch Rozier, and his can-
tankerous dying father. . . . In [the] conflicts between father and
son, Doig has found a plausible marriage between theme and
character, setting and sentiment."

—Michael Frank, *Los Angeles Times*

Mountain Time

A Novel

Ivan Doig

Scribner Paperback Fiction
Published by Simon & Schuster
New York   London   Toronto   Sydney   Singapore

To Liz Darhansoff
for all the safe safaris through the fine print

SCRIBNER PAPERBACK FICTION
Simon & Schuster, Inc.
Rockefeller Center
1230 Avenue of the Americas
New York, NY 10020

First Scribner Paperback Fiction edition 2000

SCRIBNER PAPERBACK FICTION and design are trademarks
of Macmillan Library Reference USA, Inc., used under license
by Simon & Schuster, the publisher of this work.

Designed by Brooke Zimmer

Manufactured in the United States of America

3   5   7   9   10   8   6   4   2

The Library of Congress has catalogued the Scribner edition as follows:
Doig, Ivan.
Mountain time : a novel / Ivan Doig.
p.   cm.
I. Title
PS3554.O415M68   1999
813'.54—dc21   99-14324
CIP

ISBN 0-684-83295-X
0-684-86569-6 (Pbk)

The
Coast

One

LEXA McCASKILL RAN BOTH HANDS THROUGH HER COPPERY hair, adding up appetites.

Non-wedding for 50, the job slip on the refrigerator door read. But fifty, when it came to party food, in her experience meant either forty grazers or sixty, depending on whether last-minute lightning strikes of invitations offset the no-shows. She still marveled at how people treated guest lists like poker hands, panicking when their hole cards sent regrets and then bluffing wildly to try to fill out the room. The last occasion she did the catering for, she had overheard the host introducing his tai chi instructor.

Now she remembered that tonight's was a lakefront techie bunch, whose style was to balance their plates with a dab of this and an atom of that while comparing the latest paraphernalia of their health clubs. Go strong on dip dishes and let them eat their treadmill hearts out if the smoked salmon and the Swede balls run short, she decided.

While she religiously jotted down today's chores on stickits, a habit picked up by osmosis from Mitch, she was restless to head outside. Out the kitchen window the beaming morning weather was almost enough to make a person forget Seattle's rainblotter reputation. In celebration, the jazz jockey on KPLU played the Eckstine-Vaughan cut of "Ain't It Clear." The window-high bush of sunlit white rhododendron blossoms nodded along in the Puget Sound breeze. She hoped the sun would hold for Mitch while he flew back up the coast. He seemed to need all the warming up he could get, these days.

Lexa, at forty, long since had adjusted to a lot of life's double talk, but modern living-together still took some tiptoeing through the terms. When they started at this—when she and Mitch Rozier swallowed away what they had done to Travis—she and for that matter Mitch had to get used to being called a Significant Other. Then along came the census takers, who slapped on them the information that they had become POSSLQs, Persons of Opposite Sex in Same Living Quarters. Now all of a sudden the expression for what they were to each other seemed to be Spousal Equivalent, which possibly was one reason Mitch looked so furrowed up lately.

Earthly mischief in every Sarah Vaughan note, *"and ain't . . . it . . . clearrrrr."*

Lexa killed the radio, went into the backyard to the herb bed and started gathering burnet to flavor the vegetable dip. From his garden patch next door where he was bent over from the waist to stab slugs with a trowel, their landlord Ingvaldson watched her suspiciously. He was possessive of Mitch, and as yet Lexa's presence—now six years—was something he preferred not to acknowledge.

"Morning, Henry," she called over to him. "Your slug supply holding out okay or should I send over some of mine?"

"Yah, I got plenty," Ingvaldson said moodily, and eviscerated a six-inch-long banana slug.

A bit of grin twitched on Lexa as she snipped stems of burnet while Ingvaldson went back to pretending she was nowhere in sight. There was an ocean between the crabby old fisherman and her, literally. He liked to fill Mitch full of tales of the North Pacific because Mitch did not know a bowline from a bulkhead, but Lexa most definitely did, having cooked on fishboats out of Sitka and Yakutat and Kodiak. A woman who had trawled farther north than Henry Ingvaldson was always going to be grounds for consternation.

Back in the kitchen, whistling to herself for the company of it, she pulled out her next-to-largest mixing bowl. This was on the early side to be making the vegetable dip, but she had learned that no one at a catered shindig could tell that the dip had been sitting in the refrigerator most of the day. Whereas if the carrot sticks tasted more than a minute old, there would be Handel choruses of whining. So, stir now, chop later, always a sound policy. She spooned globs of yogurt and mayonnaise into the big bowl, followed those with judicious sloshes of buttermilk and began to whisk the mixture, her square rugged hands liking to be doing something.

Every so often she caught one of her customers staring at these hands, attention snagged on the glaring white swaths of scar across the base of both palms. In the territory of suicide try, yet not quite on target across the wrists, which caused the uncertainty in those stares. Barbwire was responsible, she never bothered to tell the customers. She had put all her weight on the lever of the wire stretcher, one last notch, her father rummaging in the Dodge Power Wagon they used for fixing fence when he thought to call out, "Hey, petunia, I think that's about enough," but the barbwire already snapping with a murderous *twang* and

IVAN DOIG

sharp metal whipping across the bottoms of her clenched hands, the next thing she knew was the white face of her father as he tore apart a grease gun and globbed grease onto her slashes to stop the flowing blood. She was thirteen then and, scarred for life, was mad only that she would have to forfeit the entry money for her and her roan Jasper in the barrel race at the Gros Ventre rodeo the next week.

Up from those hard-used hands, Alexandra Marie McCaskill—married name, Lexa Mudd; she knew that last name was not Travis's fault, but it hadn't helped—was what her parents' generation liked to term "presentable" and she herself had always calculated out as no more than a C+. To start with the plus side, there was the family flag of the McCaskills, that hair, an enviable royal rich red mane on her sister and a shading toward burnished copper in Lexa's pageboy cut. Another McCaskill attribute, though, Lexa could have done with less of, the expansive upper lip which must have come from generation after generation of ancestors' pursed expressions at their circumstances back in stony Scotland. The handsome gray eyes of that musing clan had *not* come down to her, only a faded sea color. Face a bit too square and unplaned. Nose a bit saucy. It all added up to what she ruefully knew was a permanent kid-sister look, which had not been made any easier by growing up alongside someone who possessed the power to cloud men's minds. The pair of sisters weren't even in the same contest on figure, Mariah lanky and shouldery as the McCaskill men had been, while she was more sturdily consigned to their mother's side of the family, chesty and puckish. So far, Lexa had managed to stay a few judicious pounds away from stocky even though, to Mitch's constant wonderment, she ate whatever presented itself.

Including now a contemplative tablespoonful of vegetable dip at eight in the morning, as she tried to figure out why it tasted so blah.

Right, whizbang chef, remember the trip into the backyard?

She cut the frilly shamrock leaves of the burnet off the stems, minced the tiny pile with a butcher knife, then stirred their green flecks mightily into the bowl of dip, the better to have the catered-to ask, "Ooh, what gives it that cucumbery taste?"

With the dip stowed on the bottom shelf of the crammed refrigerator, she consulted its door again, the thicket of cartoons, snapshots, and other clutter there that served as the almanac, calendar, account book, album and footnotes of life in this household. Here was a young, young Mitch pictured as a college sophomore, grinning rather queasily amid the fallen cornices at the University of Washington after the '65 quake. And there his favorite shot of her, on a rocky shore: copper hair against the salal, rubber boots and a yellow rain suit, her arms full of beach find; peeking around her hip was the square of duct tape that reinforced the seat of the rain pants. Next, tucked alongside a forest of grocery coupons, the latest postcard from Mariah on her Fuji Fellowship to wander the world for a year and do her photography. The Bay of Naples this time. *Shooting the ash outlines of the long-gone in Pompeii today,* Mariah's handwriting on the back a slanting rain of ink. *Makes a pair with the shadow burned into the wall at Hiroshima. Scotland next for, you guessed it, lighthouses. Then home, Brit A'ways #99 on the 12th. See you at SeaTac, honeykins. Sibling love, M. McC.* Okay, Lexa told herself with a mix of pride and rue when those postcards came winging in from the storied corners of the world week after week, one McCaskill sister has it made. One to go.

She arranged today's stuck-on chores down the door in the order she ought to get to them: pick up smoked salmon and salad makings, prepare the meatballs, prepare the vegetable trays.

Prepare Mitch, for that matter. Her regular pourer, Brad,

who like three-fourths of the males in Seattle dreamed of making his living by playing music, rarely got gigs, but he had one tonight. So Mitch did not know it yet but he was going to have to tend bar. From Lexa's point of view he was perfectly fitted to the job, since he didn't indulge in alcohol. But he never liked taking orders, even if it was only "White wine, please." And tonight's catering job was way over east of Lake Washington, in the land of software that he called Cyberia, so that was not going to be popular with him either. *Could be quite a night in the food field,* she warned herself.

It about blew her mind sometimes, the long arithmetic of chance that had delivered her here, to this, to life with him. Her father would have said she took the uphill way around. But a hilly day at a time, sometimes bumpy minute to minute, she and Mitch had been sorting out living together, right from the morning when it occurred to both of them that her stay under this roof seemed to be more than temporary.

They hadn't made it out of bed yet, skin still peeping at other skin, before Mitch broached, "This takes some getting used to, you know."

Did she ever. Here she was under the sheets, more or less, with a guy big enough to eat hay but who hung around with holy ghosts like Thoreau for a living. One minute Mitch was Mr. Love Handles of Steel and the next he was a sponge for language. Lexa's heart was, so to speak, still trying to catch its breath.

"What," she'd retorted, kidding but not. "Getting laid without dating?"

"That I can probably adjust to," he allowed, small wry smile on his big face. "I meant, more like playing house. Who's going to do the laundry?"

"Mmm, I see what you mean." They eyed each other across the love-mussed bedcovers. After a moment, Lexa said, "How about you do it for the first year, then it'll be my turn the next."

"A *year*?"

"You've been doing it practically forever, haven't you? A year is shorter than forever, last I knew."

"Can't argue with that. Weekend breakfasts?"

"I'll do Saturdays. No, wait, *Sun*days," she hurriedly amended and got from him the smile that said *right guess.*

So was it always going to be guesswork? she had to ask herself these days.

TWO

"PEOPLE WHO GET THEIR NEWS FROM *DOONESBURY,*" THIS Halloween refugee who was his grown daughter made fun of him—Mitch had to hope it was fun—as the pair of them put on blades. "What happens when you and Lexa run out of refrigerator magnets?"

"Boopsie will have a Web site by then," he said, trying to catch up as Jocelyn began to coast on her Rollerblades.

Around them the horde on wheels kept thickening as more skaters pumped across the Embarcadero and glissaded onto the sidewalk in front of the Ferry Building. Several hundred, Friday-nighted to their pierced eyebrows and gaudy fingernails, already had congregated beneath the building's clock tower and were milling around in various states of balance. "How rav!" and "Dressed for excess!" sang this tribe of recreational outlaws. In khaki slacks, rental black knee pads and a messageless yellow T-shirt, Mitch felt next thing to naked. One or another of Jocelyn's hues—orange tank top, chartreuse leotards, knee pads painted a disturbing fleshy pink—flared in the corner of his vision as he and she rode their skates around clumps of waiting bladers. Not that he couldn't have kept track of her just by the way she jangled. Wherever Jocelyn got her fashion news from, it dictated a wristwatch with an industrial-strength expansion band, deliberately too big so that it slid up and down her arm, and a bracelet made of what seemed to be links of an old tire chain, to blockade the watch from flying off. Time clanking ominously Mitch did not need to be reminded of.

"Whatever. Advertising was so, you know, not me. I'm jacked on marketing now," Jocelyn drawled her way back to where they had been in the conversation before he brought down on himself that accusation of hopeless Doonesburial. (On himself and Lexa, which doubly smarted. So much for nonchalantly reporting on your current household partner to the child of your ex-wife's spiteful loins.) All he'd done was confess he had never heard of Jocelyn's latest employer, something called Juice Up, then step in it deeper by asking if she had written any juicy ads lately.

"Juice Ups are freestanding health drink kiosks," she severely recited for his benefit, although he still couldn't tell whether this mantra was advertising or marketing. "They're kind of Starbucks out on the sidewalk, only citrus. Hey, really, you never've tried one?"

"Jocelyn, I don't want to seem anti-citrus or anything, but . . ." This marked her fourth fresh occupation that he knew of. Hers the not-yet-molded face of a growing girl there behind the swaying hank of reddened hair that fell past her left ear to her collarbone, she nonetheless had turned twenty-five, the same age her parents had been when they tripped into marriage and produced her, and she already was a couple of careers ahead of Mitch (even if he counted college football) and four ahead of her mother. Mitch wondered whether Jocelyn's generation kept some kind of family album of their jobs.

"*We rolling!*" someone bellowed in echo of the tower clock's first deep note, and by its eighth chime, were they ever. In one single accelerating commotion the massed Rollerbladers let themselves loose, each of them a polymer marble in the spill that rolled toward Fisherman's Wharf. Tourists in rental cars wildly pulled over at the sight of this meteor shower of get-ups, the closets of San Francisco airborne on low-flying naiads and masquers, leftover Wavy Gravys and incipient Courtney Loves, seasoned exhibitionists and heart-in-throat first-timers alike borne on boots speedy as midget locomotives. Skating the rim of the city, the rolling multitude hung a left at Bay Street and aimed its thundering wheels toward Fort Mason.

Carefully matching Jocelyn stride for stride, finding the push-and-glide rhythm of the exercise laps he'd lately been taking on skates, Mitch one more time told himself to quit worrying. Hadn't he biked across Iowa, kayaked Glacier Bay? As much of Mitch as there was, he needed to keep fit or watch himself inflate enough to leave the earth.

So, when he called Jocelyn about getting together before he flew home and she pleaded this weekly habit of skimming through the city (grooved San Franciscan that she was, after a half year here), he had been able to say he did some Rollerblading, too.

"That'll work," she replied, which it had taken him a moment to decipher as an invitation to skate along with her. Or a challenge.

On the long straight glide past the marina, where necklaces of lights out in the bay showed off the Golden Gate Bridge, a bare-shouldered young man in salmon-colored overalls scooted up between Jocelyn and Mitch. Asian lithe and American friction-free, he seemed paused even as the three of them rocketed along side by side by side. "Primo outfit, Joss," he yelled above the *chunga chunga chunga* sound of urethane wheels. Appraising Mitch and their family resemblance, he gave Jocelyn a knowing look. "Be your blades!" he said, and sped ahead like a breakaway hockey player.

Of the next many minutes of pushing and gliding, pumping and striding, Mitch later could summon only a blur as the skating swarm honed in on the Palace of Fine Arts, a hundred bladers at a time peeling into its rotunda and joining hands to form a whirling roller snake there beneath the odd old umber orange-squeezer-of-Caesar dome. Then, centrifuged out to the columns around the rim of the rotunda, Mitch propped gratefully beside other bladers catching their breath (in his case, there was a lot of breath to catch) as bottled water popped into every set of hands, Jocelyn chugging down copious glugs of hers (*Eat your heart out, Juice Up*, registered on Mitch) before the final six miles through this lovely mischievous city which from Lombard Street onward was, God help the beginning blade skater, a labyrinth of hills.

Ahead of Mitch and Jocelyn as they made the turn off Lombard, the little red reflectors on the back of skaters' helmets straggled up, up, up in the night like Christmas lights strung too thin. A vast apprehension sucked into Mitch. The conference he had been covering in Berkeley was called "Thinking Like a Mountain: The Place of Nature in a New Millennium." If he thought like the ski-slope street rearing in front of him at this instant, the mental result could only be a hideous subterranean giggle at how much trouble humankind still had with uphill.

While he clambered up the slope in imitation of Jocelyn's short, digging strides, what he tried not to think about was how many times his pounding heart had already beat, in fifty years.

Huffing and puffing, he floundered to a halt at the first

plateau of intersection when Jocelyn called over to him, "Ready to skitch?" She grabbed on to the rear bumper of a bread truck, Mitch following suit, each sitting back on their skates for the hitchhike. They passed row houses of all pastel flavors, the corner of every block given over to coin laundries or tiny exorbitant restaurants. Oh, San Francisco, dear and doomed, stacked so prettily on tectonic fracture. Mitch knew he ought to be writing in his head, tucking away fragments for his piece about the conference. But clinging to a truck bumper took a surprising amount of concentration.

At the top, where they and the truck gratefully let go of each other, lay a sane few level blocks before the route crouched and dived underground. The Broadway tunnel, a third of a mile of amplified skate-wheel sounds and infinitely repeated yellow tiles, not to mention unamused car traffic, disoriented Mitch a bit.

"*EEEEhooo!*"

Halfway through this treacherous echo chamber, the shriek Jocelyn let out scared him half to death.

Lurching to look around at her, Mitch was met with a moon of grin that informed him her whoop had been for the absolute ki-yi kick of it. Right. Drive another stake into old Dad. He managed a pale smile and floundered into stride again as she tore along ahead of him like a catapulted pumpkin. Once more he felt an obscure genealogical guilt that instead of Marnie's fine-boned features, Jocelyn had been handed his bulk.

They swooped out of the tunnel into a garlic precinct of North Beach.

"Hey, wait."

Breathing heavily, very heavily, Mitch managed to halt Jocelyn at the first street corner. "Let's watch, a minute."

Skaters shot out of the tunnel in platoons, Mitch saw, a sorting of some kind occurring for this passage. Here came pairs of women in shimmy dresses holding hands, and now men in sequins line-dancing.

And next the half-Asian young Nureyev in overalls again, impossibly coasting sideways, even more impossibly each foot pointing an opposite direction in line with his spread-eagled arms, a human parallelogram from shoulder blades down to rollerblades as he drifted by like a beautiful winged statue. "Go ninja, Joss!" he called out as he cruised around their corner in an effortless lean and set sail through Chinatown for Union Square and the stretch turn toward the Ferry Building.

Jocelyn gradually stopped twirling on her blades and settled into watching beside Mitch. Knowing better, he still couldn't help but seize the moment as a hope, maybe, that she was putting away the arsenal of resentment. This made twice that he and she had got together this year, Seattle and here. He would need to think all the way back to be sure, but twice seemed to him a new record in the twenty years since Marnie catapulted herself and the kids to Key West. ("Why'd you stop there?" Mitch had howled down thousands of miles of phone line at her. "Wouldn't they let you behind the barbed wire at Guantanamo?") Before that there had been a determined try at split custody but it turned out to be cruelty to small creatures, the bewildered kids never with either him or Marnie long enough to know where their next beddie-bye would take place. Mitch, knowing he would be condemned but quite used to it from life with Marnie, gave over daughter and son, and away she went with them as far as she could and still have the U.S. mail deliver child support checks.

Jocelyn eyed Mitch, wondering why he felt he had to do this, make like he wanted to connect at last, after everything.

You're some late, Dadspace. You and Moms hit this time where you couldn't stand each other, way back there. So now I'm supposed to what? Just say, "No prob, I never did want a father around anyway, Momso's hairball sailboarders did just fine"?

But chill as she tried to be, she kept noticing his sopping wet T-shirt, the sheen of sweat rolling out of his wavy hair crested with a little gray, the seismic rise and fall of his chest. He looked buff enough, for his age. But taking some more time here on the corner probably wouldn't hurt. She didn't want him going dead in the midst of this. She thought she did not want that.

He heard Jocelyn rattle a bit beside him. Joss, the kid in overalls called her. Chinese for *idol,* something like that? What, Mitch wondered now, had he and Marnie been thinking of when they picked a name as breakable as Jocelyn? Or, for that matter, when they christened her brother Laurits and almost before he was done teething stuck him with the nickname Ritz?

But it wasn't nicknames that nicked a family to death, was it. He closed his eyes a moment against the record of domestic misadventure brought closer to him again with Jocelyn's move to his coast. Bad tempers and worse sighs, Marnie's toy store of a brain versus his infatuation with whatever story he was working on that week, the mattress the only surface in the house they put any effort into, the two kids too soon—he could read it off like an old traffic ticket: *Speeding into marriage while under the influence.*

Three

WHETHER THESE PARTICULAR MOUNTAINS WERE THINK-
ing or not, they were showing unclouded brows as they
paraded past the right-hand wingtip when Mitch flew back to
Seattle in the morning.

Lassen and Shasta, Jefferson and Hood, Adams and Rainier,
the fire alps of the Pacific High Country shone in the sun one
after another, dormant pyramids of glacier and snow higher
than hell and once upon a time as potent. He knew that on a day
this drastically clear even the lonesome cone to the north, blue-
white Mount Baker, would be out and waiting to make its
appearance when the plane hooked above Lake Washington
into the SeaTac landing pattern.

More than willing to be seduced by every blessed one of them rather than tackle the Berkeley conference lurking in the laptop on his tray table, Mitch discovered over Shasta and Lassen he could catch a rare good look at each volcano's birthmark, its frozen scar of crater, by craning over the woman in the window seat. Elderly and teak-colored, Indonesian to judge by her head-to-toe batik garb, she watched him with the flat attention of a sentry, which he was used to. Particularly on airplanes, people seated next to Mitch reacted as though they were being forced to share their picnic blanket with a St. Bernard.

It was on the tip of his tongue to tell her he had a son teaching English in Jakarta, but even if she understood, there were dead ends immediately ahead in that kind of conversation. Where in that city did Ritz live? No idea. Was he married? Not by last secondhand report. If Jocelyn was icy about Mitch taking himself off the battlefield of their childhood, Ritz was the silent Antarctic. No, the Rozier version of fatherhood would not do anything much for international relations. Mitch gave the woman a smile that turned out not to be worth the effort either, and went back to peering down at the restless earth below.

Edgy and rapt, shifting in the constraint of the plane seat, he could not escape the feeling that he was in suspension in more ways than one. He had been writing "Coastwatch" every week for more years than he dared to count. Had tried his utmost to grope his way among all of it sprawled down there— the sea-bent coastal capes, the snake routes of rivers, the strangely serene cliff-faces of dams, the faltering forests, the valleys going to suburbs, the slumbering but restless earthquake faults, the cloud-high mountains made of internal fire. So how about, for a change, this chance to actually watch the coast, peep from thirty-five thousand feet down onto the wreath-green lovely untrustworthy Pacific littoral, the jagged edge of America. The Left Coast. Home for him ever since he had left home.

(In one of his fights with his father, the old combatant had jabbed: "They call it the Coast because that's what people do there?") So what if Bingford was going to give him freckled hell for not finishing up the Berkeley column by the end of today. He knew *Cascopia*'s deadlines at least as well as Bing. Mitch shifted savagely in his seat again. A *Cascopia* deadline was the one instance he could think of, anymore, where time was not truly lethal.

With a grimace, he faced his laptop.

Scrupulously he logged in the $3.95 that a cup of terminal coffee had cost him in the San Francisco airport. Even before the laptop computer, Bingford accused him of being the only person on the paper whose expense account was carried out to the third decimal place.

As he started scrolling his Berkeley notes up onto the miniature screen, something like glazed panic set in. What he had from the various speakers sounded like quotes from parrots who had been eating dictionaries, *biome* this and *paradigm* that. Maybe he was growing jaded, but the Berkeley sessions seemed to him one more case in the raging epidemic of conferencitis. *The place of nature in a new millennium,* you bet. What would conference throwers do without the year 2000 on our cosmic odometer?

He tried tapping out a glom graf:

Four hundred and fifty-two of this land's leading theorizers theorized tooth and claw over the meaning of nature when they gathered last week in . . .

Deleting that, he started searching the storage of his laptop a bit frantically for something more melodic to lead with.

TLM, he punched up, and there it materialized on the little screen, *"thinking like a mountain,"* Aldo Leopold after wiping out wolves in New Mexico, turning himself around to preach holy caution in messing with things of the wild. *"Only the mountain has lived long enough to listen objectively to the howl of a wolf."*

He scrolled on through his laptop Leopoldiana:

"*. . . Reached the old wolf in time to watch a fierce green fire dying in her eyes. . . . I was young then, and full of trigger-itch. . . .*"

Been there, too, thought Mitch, at least the young and itchy part.

He hunched, uneasily transfixed, thinking about the sainted Leopold trying to murder the last wolf. He had once interviewed a plant geneticist, a bitter-mouthed elfin woman tucked away in a federal agency for thirty-some years, who told him the human brain had been the equivalent of a nuclear catastrophe for all other life on earth. "Ours is the journey of the worms through the wormwood but on a planetary scale," she had said in a teaching tone that he greatly resented at the time. "We, the unfeathered bipeds, amount to a worldwide epidemic that causes extinctions. Smallpox was nothing compared to our effect on other species." Mitch had tottered out of that bilious government green office realizing he would never be able to translate that into print. You can't go around deploring brains.

He sneaked a look at the sky-cutting outline off the wingtip now. Mount Hood, the mainsail of Oregon's mountains, standing there spanking white. Beneath the plane would be Portland, green salad of a city, and the pewter beauty of the Columbia River.

Mitch felt himself tensing, dreading what was coming again. Where were clouds when you needed them?

He forced himself to wait a minute. Another. One more.

Then abruptly lifted his eyes to see Mount St. Helens, the blown cone, under the wing now.

Mitch stared in sick fascination at the broken crown of St. Helens, the gaping bowl of crater and the ragged blown-out north half of the volcano. The lateral blast of the eruption had leveled forests for seventeen miles, sandblasted the soil off Coldwater Ridge six miles away, put up an ash cloud that blotted the

sun all the way to Idaho and churned out rock, mud, and lava in
a gray delta of debris that now fanned out from the ladle of the
mountain like molten lead gone cold and ended in those distant
ridgefuls of flattened silvered trees like metal splinters.

Juanita Trippe was still under there.

The two of them had been taking turns at the camp on Coldwater Ridge; the simmering volcano was naturally Mitch's beat,
but Trippe was goofy for the mountain. She liked to brag that
she had been in the first Girl Scout troop to trudge up this most
perfect and gentle of the Cascade cones, America's convenient
Kilimanjaro. The spell held. The mountaineering that Juanita
Trippe later did with like-minded female climbers who called
themselves WOT expeditions—Women On Top—she always
trained for on St. Helens.

When the mountain started acting up in the spring of '80,
Trippe took it personally. She shed the oxymoronic title of *Cascopia*'s business manager and demanded in on the volcano story.
Mitch didn't know a base camp from a bassoon, so it made sense
for Trippe to set things up for them on Coldwater Ridge where
they could monitor the monitors, the put-upon feds and excited
university scientists just outside the "red zone" that had been
evacuated when the mountain's harmonic tremors and burps of
ash started getting interesting. Trippe more than pulled her
weight in the watch on the volcano and she was a proven outdoors photographer, had a climber's alert eye for shifts of light
on the face of a mountain. The Vesuvius Bureau, they called
themselves, and Mitch would remember those weeks as a sweet
streak of writing, no environmental *on the other hand*s about a
rumbling ten-thousand-foot peak.

He also was frankly relieved that his and Trippe's two or
three after-party forays into bed together, years before, had not

led anywhere. Juanita was muscular, spoiled, bawdy, rich, cold-blooded, and indefatigable, and she reminded him of a big-hat halfback he was glad enough to play beside but could stand to be without after the season.

She cheerfully bossed him off the ridge that last night. The volunteer Lighthawk pilot who was going to help Mitch tally up clearcut logging on the timberland around St. Helens could only fly early the next morning, Sunday. "We can swap back at noon," Trippe instructed. "Weather's good. I want to climb out early for some dawn shots anyway." That brilliant May morning Mitch and the Lighthawk pilot scoped out clearcuts—Mitch knew with satisfaction that it would make a good gruesome "Coastwatch" piece after the shaking mountain resolved itself; portions of the forest were so chopped up it looked like the earth had the mange—and when they were through with that they buzzed St. Helens, mosquitoing for twenty minutes or so around the cone, before flying back to Seattle.

He and the pilot were barely out of the Cessna on the landing strip at Boeing Field when they heard the boom. It signaled Pompeii in the forest.

At observation posts and in campgrounds and on logging roads and at picture-taking perches like Coldwater Ridge, vigil keepers caught in the same moment with Sunday larkers, they died and they died. Died they all who were encamped along the north rim of the red zone as the power of Mount St. Helens welled over it, to a sum of fifty-seven.

The place of nature in *what* new millennium?

Ask Juanita Trippe, Mitch could not help but think, down there buried a millionfold with her camera in her mummified hand. Times like this, as he stared out at the blast from the past that was Mount St. Helens and then the giant fire kettles named Adams and Rainier and next the inchworm traffic of Seattle on freeways and bridges underlaid with earthquake faults, site after site where the old brute physics of the planet someday were going to have their say again, he had the terrifying suspicion that he was beginning to understand extinction, from the inside out.

Four

At least an hour a day Lexa walked, prowling the city, a compact Stetsoned woman in blue jeans and a teal rain jacket, gathering miles under her feet as a kind of ransom against the routines of living with other people's walls all around her.

This was her most regular route, down past the Ballard taverns favored by Henry Ingvaldson and the other old vikings of drink and then across the ship canal locks and up through a shoreline neighborhood to a grove of alders along the railroad tracks where great blue herons nested. This she had figured out for herself, that the gorgeous featherduster birds populating the waterways of Seattle must have a heronry not too far, and she had watched their flight patterns to find the spot.

She had her binoculars on the treetop stick nests and the floppy young birds—*Come on, Junior, poke your head up a tad more*—when the seaplanes started going over. Nine A.M. sharp, Lexa knew without having to check her watch, the Lake Union float-plane fleet launching. A minute apart, they laboriously skied the sky, following the ship canal out to Puget Sound and then purring off northward to weekend places in the San Juan Islands. Seattle wasn't as overrun with seaplanes as Alaska, but close.

You did love those floating goonies, didn't you, Travis. You were trained in birds but you were quite a plane man.

She was competing at Cheyenne when she met Travis Mudd. That season on the circuit, in her third and winningest year at barrel racing for the college rodeo team, she was cruising through Colorado State U. majoring in beer and high times, already wistful that her elementary ed degree was waiting on the far side of the Fort Collins haze of fun. As usual at big-deal Cheyenne, the brass band for the grand entry played on and on, but this year each batch of riders into the arena was greeted with a skin-prickling bullfight solo from the trumpet, the giddy ascent of notes putting the crowd in a whooping mood. With the kind of buzz on that she always got from competing, everything slightly slow motion and sharp edged, she naturally took notice of this trumpet player, the type of all-legs Western kid called a long drink of water.

When she rode, her horse Margarita shied off slightly at the first barrel, costing them the shade of a second and any prize money right here. To teach malingering Margarita a lesson, Lexa leathered the mare without letup around the next two barrels and across the line in a steaming finish.

She reined up hard and heard, lofty but with that Jimmy Buffett trace of flirty wooziness to it, a trumpet riff of "Margaritaville."

Of course she looked up the trumpet player. As shy as he was tall, but shoulders broad enough to eat off of, and a face like a puppy's that invited nuzzling.

"Pretty funny," she commended his razzing tribute to Margarita.

"Pretty good ride," he had ready, "except having to drag that horse along under you."

"She knows how to be a real shy whore," Lexa said conversationally.

Travis's grin slipped a little. Then and as their courtship heated up, he looked at Lexa as if he couldn't get enough of her and listened to her in continual mild alarm.

Travis finished his wildlife management degree at Northern Colorado the next year, and Lexa, who would have come at you with a hammer if you had hinted she was in college to land her M.R.S. degree, found herself married to him the week after graduation. The education of Lexa McCaskill began then.

As the last of the seaplane flock droned into the distance, Lexa headed back along her route, trying to calculate how long she could stretch the outdoors part of today and yet not have to end up handing around Snickers bars for tonight's dessert. She resolved to drive rather than walk to her docent hours at the zoo, and use the car phone to remind her crew when and where to show up. *And leave Mister Mitch the news that he's been elected bartender.*

Now that she'd given herself the guilty pleasure of a little extra time, she stopped to play tourist at the ship canal, where the big lock was lowering several work-stained fishing boats to meet the tide of Puget Sound. As usual Lexa drew a lot of looking from the fishboat crews—that hat and the unfeigned ranch-born way she parked her hands in the top of her front pockets, only the thumbs out. Cowgirls need love too; wasn't there even a song to that effect? She knew that if she was aboard with any of the leering crews there would be no such reckless eyeballing, no suggestive kidding, and above all no touching: those were the sea rules that protected her when she had cooked on the *Bella Hammond,* the *Arctic Dancer* and other trawlers of the Sitka fishing fleet, her and half a dozen men in close quarters for weeks at a time in the lonely Gulf of Alaska. And husband Travis had never said anything, Travis and his blind trust in rules.

Perhaps men weren't meant to be heard from. Mitch hadn't called from the Berkeley trip. Telephones disagreed with him, he claimed; they were absolutely full of stuff that his ear found hard to take. So he never called from out of town, or much of anywhere else. You could draw up quite a list of Mitch's nevers, Lexa knew by now.

The sonofabitch, I love him.

That thought spun her on her heels, her hiking boots resounding on the steel walkway of the lock gate as she crossed back over and headed to the fish ladder.

Lexa fully knew—Mitch had told her *this* enough times— that the fish ladder was a public relations plaything. Ninety-nine percent of the migrating salmon and steelhead into the rivers feeding Lake Washington rode up through the canal locks as the boats made their passage. Still, she liked to visit the one percent, the fish that had fought their way up the stair-step rapids.

The glass-walled viewing area was dim, grottolike, which meant she could walk right up to the fish in their transparent channel. Today it was the spring run of steelhead, silver dirigible trout hanging there in the greenish water, seeming to pant, to muster themselves.

So why am I losing him, the sonofabitch.

Only a bit at a time, and there was more than a handful of Mitch left, for sure. But as a spousal equivalent, lately, he seemed to be evaporating, coming home edgy instead of eager, in a cat-kicking mood. She herself did not know why, in this loose jangly era of dosie doe and everybody change partners again and again, she thought a ceremony would bring a more sturdy commitment to each other. (Mariah had considered it cause for congratulations when given the news merely about her moving in with Mitch: "Finally going to try shacking up, huh?") Or was commitment overload his malady already? He was the kind who waded into his work up to his neck, then was always surprised when some rogue wave tossed unpleasantness up his nose. She could imagine other cutouts of life Mitch once could have fit, running a bookstore in Missoula or teaching high school English in Moab, working the job to death in sorrowless surroundings. But "Coastwatch" had been his existence ever since environmental reporters were thick on the earth.

She stayed longer than she intended watching the exhausted steelhead, survivors paused behind the glass wall.

Five

"SEEN MITCH?"

"I thought he's in Birkenstockley, doing the green thing."

"He's supposed to be back for this morning." Bingford retracted his head into his office impatiently.

The *Cascopia* building was in Seattle's Fremont district, where the Sixties still roamed. The hempen necessities of life were available there, as were cafes with good rowdy names such as The Longshoreman's Daughter, plus deluxe junk shops, plus bars that were museum pieces from the days when hair was *Hair.* Indeed, the neighborhood merrily ran the gamut from Lennon to Lenin, a twenty-foot-high bronze Eastern European clearance sale item depicting Vladimir Ilyich forging into the future with rifles stacked slyly beside him, but now peacefully surveying traffic at a particularly funky Fremont intersection.

In such environs, employment at the weekly newspaper *Cascopia* was a lot like manning the drawbridge against the slick downtown Seattle skyline to the south, for the building squatted at the north edge of the old steel bridge over the ship canal; only the bridgetender, making the twin halves yawn open by means of counterbalances, sat closer to the moat. Both Bingford and Mitch liked the racket of the Fremont Bridge's traffic gates clanging down and its girdered halves groaning and humming as they labored upward, on the best days many, many times. Others on the staff either quit in a hurry or made a major aural adjustment; the "Cityscape" columnist, Moira Mason, had been wearing earplugs for ten years now.

At the moment the bridge was up on its haunches, letting a single sailboat putter through while cars stacked up, and Mitch was killing time and dietary intentions at the Espresso A Go Go stand, waiting until he could stroll across to the office. He was in the fetching mute company of Trixie, the mannequin in her powder blue miniskirt and white go-go boots lounging with the stand's *espresso!* sign bandoliered across her shapely form. Mitch would gratefully have spent the rest of this day hanging out with Trixie.

Thinking and frowning, he sipped coffee and tore into a bagel; he was going to have to work through lunch. Distill something out of the Berkeley conference vapors. His mind sometimes sneaked up on an idea for his column while he did other things, so now he studied the familiar upended bridge and the views east and west of it, the white froth of mountains cresting over the streeted hills of the city. As Mitch had written so many times even he was tired of hearing it, Seattle in its rapid career had spread itself as a freehand Brasilia, a capital of enterprise installed in the middle of a timber jungle. The two-hundred-foot cedars and Doug firs originally prickled so thick along Puget Sound that the first sawmillers made their fortunes right there on the shore. By now enough of the great forest had been thinned away to let in a metropolis of two million people, and still coming. Seattle, the consummate doodler on the margin of America. The place had given the world some dervishes of the electric guitar, connoisseur lessons in coffee, *The Far Side*, airplanes by the stratosphereful, and now the alchemies of software. Twenty-five years ago it had given him "Coastwatch" to write, then ever since yawned, "So what?"

Mitch fired a bank shot of his crumpled coffee container into the recycle bin, the ghost chorus of his trade keening at him. Ed Abbey smoldering in his grave in the slickrock desert, Stegner magisterially whopping the nail on the head in every sentence of his hallowed "wilderness letter." Feverish Bob Marshall, the Thomas Wolfe of the Forest Service, writing and hiking himself to death in the mountains he so adored, his epitaph theirs: "How much wilderness do we need? How many Brahms symphonies do we need?" And back beyond them the sweet ponds of Thoreauvia. The whispering pines of Muirland. St. feathered Francis, if you really want to go back. Whatever all else Spaceship Earth was running out of, it didn't lack for old soaring planetary anthems. Although, in Berkeley, in this time on the cusp of the next millennium, academic bigfoots had just spent three days in airless rooms arguing about the nature of the word *nature*.

Clanging announced that the drawbridge was going down. Mitch headed across, envying Trixie her job.

Wishing himself on a mountain wall of granite somewhere, Bingford looked down at Mitch through his office window. Huge color photos of mountain climbers spidered onto crags covered the office's other three walls. Look closely and in every case the wiry dangling man with a flaming sunburned face was Bingford. Successions of *Cascopia* staffers, where a generation amounted to around three years, had been stunned to see their editor/publisher arrive back from Denali or Aconcagua or Everest with a face like a camp-stove victim. Gradually the effects of sun glare, cold, and wind at extreme elevations would peel away, and the freckles would crop out again. Watching this over the years, Mitch had wondered if Bing added a freckle for each conquered mountain, the way fighter-plane aces painted downed opponents on their cowlings.

At this moment Bingford hesitated, not something he was used to. What good would it do to call Mitch in? By now the two of them knew each other's lines of argument like sailors knew rope knots.

Still, something kept him at the window, unable to tear his eyes from Mitch coming across the bridge in that peculiar tender-toed floating way he moved. Heft trained into grace, like the Lippizaner stallions Bingford had seen perform in Vienna during his trip to climb the Eiger. *He's always had some moves,* the editor in Bingford speaking now. At his best, Mitch could write a column with a skateboarder's eye for odd angles and fast surfaces. But he was a considerable way from his best, these days.

"Old times, guy," Bingford said quietly.

Spired and wooded and not a little stoned, the campus sprawled amid the 1960s like a disassembled cathedral. The University of Washington, thirty thousand students strong and restive as a mutinous barracks, was the upper left corner of the battle banner that was writhing through Berkeley and Madison and Morningside Heights and a hundred other bastions of learning, wafted by the highs of drugs and dorm sex and soon to be blown jetstream-high by the storm of opposition to the Vietnam war.

Mitch Rozier had come for football.

He was raw then, but he knew it and figured there might be a cure for it in a place like Seattle. His athletic scholarship had come like a bingo jackpot—the big kid from a small town playing his one card in life and having it pay off at the Shrine game, the high school all-stars on the other side of the line strewn like train-wreck victims in the wake of Mitch's three touchdown runs. In the stands was Washington's most junior assistant coach, assigned to recruit the longshots, and even though this fired-up running back was from some dinkyville, he liked the kid's unexpectedness on the field, the quicksilver quality you didn't often see in a fullback. So Mitch arrived to the green-and-gray city, the Elysian campus, and the boot-camp-like football practices of the Washington Huskies. The industrial brand of football played in the Pacific Coast Conference was savage compared to what he was used to, but he did not back off from it. Mitch was very sizable, and as determined as he was large. He knew a free ride to a college degree when he saw one.

After where he had come from, college was Coney Island. As best Mitch could determine, he was undergoing something like hourly evolution. Hurrying from class to class, he would have sworn he could feel one part of his brain grow, then another. He was like that example of the chickadee they talked about in Biology 101, able to expand one lobe when winter came and a greater number of feeding spots had to be remembered. For a while it surprised him every time, and then the surprise became reliable, that he all at once could stretch his mind around some bigger thing. Just then the UW campus had some hot departments. History—God, man, over in History one of the profs had kicked William F. Buckley's fancy butt in a debate over Vietnam. And in English, to his and the department's mutual astonishment, Mitch found home. The white but Afroed instructor for his writing skills section openly winced when he bulked into her classroom, but as soon as she discovered this was one football jock who seemed incurably curious about the insides of sentences and would rework a piece of writing until the paper gave out, she fed him books. A nature freak herself, she turned him on to Thoreau, inspector-general of the seasons: *"I once had a sparrow alight upon my shoulder for a moment while I was hoeing in a village garden, and I felt that I was more distinguished by that circumstance than I should have been by any epaulet I could have worn."* To the tidal force of Rachel Carson: *"I tell here the story of how the young planet Earth acquired an ocean . . ."* To the University of Washington's own just-dead nova, Theodore Roethke, who had held forth in this exact classroom; greenhouse ghost that he always was—it did not hurt that he had been a father fighter, too—Roethke ranted great whispers of poems through the windowpanes to Mitch's tuned-up ear. *"At the field's end, in the corner missed by the mower/where the turf drops off into a grass-hidden culvert"*— Mitch knew that field. And to the human hawk of Big Sur, Robinson Jeffers—Mitch practically groaned sexually when he encountered the lines *"the old voice of the ocean, the bird-chatter of little rivers. . . . Love that, not man apart from that."* It was a time when zinger sentences walked the earth.

Football, though. What the University of Washington coaching staff wanted at fullback was a kamikaze short-gainer and what they rather quickly realized they had in Mitch Rozier was an excess of IQ for that role. Kranski, the starting fullback, was barely organized enough to put his socks on, yet turn him loose on third down and short yardage and he would ram into the line like a runaway ox. The second-string fullback, Buford, ran those plunges in his own can't-hurt-me-if-I-don't-think-about-it fashion. But Mitch, to his own revelation and certainly the coaches', always tried to fine-tune that situation of fighting for inches of gridiron; his timing was *too* fine, hitting the hole over left guard with precision, but if the defensive line delayed the guard any—if an atom of dirt delayed him—the guard would find Mitch running up his backbone in the pigskin equivalent of a rear-end collision. It became apparent to all concerned: the only chance for the name Rozier to be inserted in the University of Washington starting lineup was if Kranski and Buford collided in the shower room and both fractured their tibias. For precisely such a possibility, of course, a major football program needed a battalion of bodies, and nobody much minded Mitch being kept on the team as backup to the backup fullback, especially Mitch.

Busy lighting up in every way he could think of, came the day when he went to football practice after his first experience with marijuana half scared to death that it would somehow show on him, he'd be singled out of the warm-up drill by one of the assistant coaches screeching, "Hey you, dope fiend, outta here!" When no such thing occurred, it quite rapidly dawned on Mitch: these old white-socks guys were *afraid to know*! Within days he confirmed this by showing up in the locker room wearing a Levi's jacket with a peace symbol painted on the back and the coaches stared very hard but not one of them said a word to him.

There he sat, then, on into his junior year, all-conference scholastically and benchwarmer into eternity, until the pivotal Saturday afternoon when the Huskies were playing at home against Southern California. Much to the disappointment of the mud-oriented Washington coaching staff, no drop of rain was falling on Seattle, the world capital of H_2O. On the dry field Southern Cal tailbacks were taking turns romping around the end of the elephantine Washington line. Bored, the Husky third-stringers were sneaking peeks at the cheerleading squad, envying the yell leader, a gymnastic imp named Mancini whose duty was to put his hands under the purple pleated skirts of the female cheerleaders and boost their pretty butts onto his shoulder.

Mitch in particular was engrossed in watching this activity

when Bingford, the freckled and notorious editor of the *UW Daily*, detached himself from the sidelines press and said something at length into Mancini's ear.

Lit up like a jack-o'-lantern with inspiration, Mancini grabbed his bullhorn and yelped:

"All right! Listen up, everybody. Just had a request to do a 'Go' cheer for an institution that's dear to us all—North Dakota Agricultural and Scientific! Got it? Go, N-A-D-S!"

Even before the student section woke up brightly to the opportunity to roar "GONADS!" Mitch was laughing fit to rupture and lurched up off the bench. He dashed over, picked up Mancini under the arms, and held him in mid-air like a squirming cat, and shouted:

"Now let's try S-P-E-L-I-G! SPELLING!"

He had barely set Mancini free when the backfield coach Jacobson boiled up beside him. "Rozier, are you in this game?"

"Not that I've noticed."

"Are you high?"

"Six foot five, same as always."

"You know what I mean, boy—are you on something?"

"Twenty Questions does beat the crap out of this." Mitch jerked his head toward the scoreboard showing *UW o VISITORS 27* in bright buttons of light. "But Jake, Coach is going to think both of us lack T-E-E-M S-P-I-R-U-T."

Mitch unsnapped his helmet, tenderly took it off with both hands, then reached back and slung it, sailing end over end, high into the ecstatic student section. It was the longest University of Washington pass of the day, and it concluded the football career of Mitch Rozier.

Not long after, he stood in a field carpeted with several thousand other zonked-out souls. When yet another of those funny-looking cigarettes made its way around to him, the hand that offered it was supremely freckled.

"You're the fringie fullback," said the possessor of the hand and the joint. "Or were."

Mitch took a drag, the better to contemplate Bingford.

"And you're the rich mountain climber's kid. No cure for that so far, though?"

"Famous in our own time," Bingford said with a world-weary sigh. He scanned the air. "Where's that mothering piano?"

Chords of the Mothers of Invention's "Freak Out" jangled out of the earnest but challenged band that had set up on the flatbed of a sod-hauling truck. The platform of piled-together logs where the piano was to hit loomed like a sacrificial altar. The crowd splashdanced in the creek or cavorted in the farm fields, green pastures of pharmacopia.

Still staring into the sky, Bingford asked: "They take away your jock scholarship yet?"

"Does a bear go in the woods?"

Bingford cocked his head. "What're you doing for spare change?"

"Washing dishes at the House of Pancakes. And I hump big stuff for a moving company, Saturdays."

Speculatively Bingford made a bicep, à la Charles Atlas. Mitch wanted to swat him one and at the same time had the urge to giggle at the hopeless little muscleman pose.

Now the helicopter approached, whacking the air frantically. Beneath it the piano swung like a pendulum. The crowd scattered like chickens under a hawk, except for an unshirted young woman on acid who loped along under the swaying Steinway, arms uplifted as if to hug it. She let out a sound between a moan and a wail when she was held back.

Mitch was finding he couldn't decide whether the idea of a

piano drop was the greatest thing yet or plain silly. Either way, here he stood, at this particular spot of existence taken over by this spontaneous tribe, a breed all their own, shaggy, loose limbed, barefoot and more than a few rousingly naked. Present and accounted for, at the dawn of a time when a piano would plunge from the sky. Margaret Mead—she was still alive, wasn't she? Then where the hell was she, if not here watching this? If she wanted to see a cargo cult, bigfella-in-sky-him-come-let-piano-*drop*, if she wanted to see Coming of Age in America Right Now, if she wanted real *anthro*, here it was. Okay, maybe some little bit of what he was feeling was the marijuana starting to cook in him, but the greater cause for exhilaration, Mitch was convinced, was himself, here, now. If this wasn't something new in life, that you could stand out here with grass tickling your toes and holy smoke up your nose and feel giddy and perfectly sane at the same time, he didn't know what was.

Mitch inhaled deeply, air this time, and felt his brain settle back into his head a little.

Side by side he and Bingford contemplated the laboring helicopter, close now. For no particular reason, Mitch heard himself pop out with:

"My old man always calls the thing a heli-copeter."

"My old man owns a couple," Bingford confessed in return.

Fathers, the ghosts of dead wars. Neither Mitch nor Bing, nor all the sons and daughters in the skin-plaid fields that day and in the hairy ranks they would form against the war in Vietnam, needed to name their names, those spent shells. Antecedents always think they still own the combat zone. Lyle Rozier, who to hear him tell it had the time of his life in the jungles of World War II. Jerry Bingford, fighter ace in Korea and cocky toward earthbound mortality ever since. Young in their time, but too many turns of the world ago. While the news that counted now hovered here.

The chopper noise flooded over the pasture, tingling in

Mitch the way the thunder of a football crowd always did. Used to. He glanced sideways at Bingford, who seemed similarly swallowed in the blissful storm of noise.

The roar of the helicopter drowned out something Bingford said. Mitch cupped an ear at him.

"Come by the *Daily* office," Bingford repeated. "You can be our aviation reporter."

Having lifted its burden into bomb-run position a couple of hundred feet up, the helicopter now honed in on the log bull's-eye where the piano drop was to occur. Businesslike, the helicopter seemed to brake in the air. But the piano kept going. As, now, did the helicopter. Panicking at being towed by his cargo, the pilot let the piano loose.

Far overshooting the log platform, it plummeted to the earth with a dead thud. Not a chord, not a note, not so much as a plink.

"Encore," Bingford said softly.

Mitch could not have told why, but that decided him to show up at the *Daily* office.

After Mitch's sidelined but bylined final years of college and a few more on a well-intentioned but criminally underpaying community newspaper, he latched on as a rim dog on the copy desk at Seattle's morning daily, the *Post-Intelligencer.* Not the most sensational of jobs, and he still wasn't sure he even liked newspapering. But he liked being around people who liked newspapering. Accordingly, there he sat each day, fashioning the three sentences for the front-page weather box and boiling down wire copy into bite-sized stories called "Quicklies"; Marnie had taken to giggling and calling him Mister Quickie.

He was hunched over his keyboard trying to think of some fresh way to say *"rain later today"* when the call came that someone wanted to see him down in the lobby. He never liked eerie stuff, but somehow he had the prickling feeling it was going to be Bingford.

The last time Mitch saw him, Bing was in a Rocky Mountain high period, off to climb the fourteeners of Colorado and then goof around the Grand Tetons for a summer. That had been, what, considerably more than a year ago, Mitch realized, an evening spent parked below the runway approach to SeaTac airport while the two of them smoked some reminiscent dope and let the roars of jets take them over as plane after plane waddled down a scant hundred feet overhead. Between the soul-emptying flushes of noise and the good weed, they gradually slid off philosophical deep ends. After what must have been an exceptionally potent puff, Bing revealed to Mitch his nearly paralyzed moments of fascination on rock cliffs sometimes at being suspended there by the double-sure piton his old man had invented and patented: he was hanging there by a combination of genetics and contrivance that just seemed awesome in those moments. Mitch in turn confessed his own latest source of awe, *A Sand County Almanac*—it singlehandedly had almost sent him back to do a master's degree in English. Hell, you could opus-pocus your whole thesis on Aldo Leopold's rhythms, the old boy *wrote* like the coming up of the sun and the going down of the sun and the stopless turning of the seasons . . . but then along had come Marnie and marriage, and Mitch had chickened out on going back to school, but who knew, maybe eventually he would. It had been one of those funny warped nights, much too much said in sloppy circumstances, and Mitch and Bing had both ended up a bit embarrassed by the time the last jetliner swept its cone of thunder over them. You couldn't really base a gut-spilling friendship on aeronautical decibels, could you? Now Mitch headed down to the lobby decidedly on guard.

"How's life in the Quickly lane?" Bingford said as hello.

"Salaried," Mitch answered, steering him out of the building. One never quite knew with Bing, whether he was simply stopping by to visit between conquests of tall peaks or whether he was here to unload on establishment journalism.

"Happy under the big crapping bird?" Bingford resumed when they were outside, eyeing scornfully up at the *P-I*'s massive revolving globe with the Hearst eagle the size of a pterodactyl squatting atop it.

"Close enough. Why? You curious about getting on a paper again? They probably won't let you start right in as editor here, you know."

"I figured I'd start my own."

"Why don't you save time and just wad that money up and throw it out a window?"

"This is one window people are going to throw money in. Remember *'Hip spade wants to dig you'*?"

Mitch had to laugh. All of them on the *UW Daily* staff had gone bug-eyed when somebody brought in one of the underground weeklies with that first barrier-exploding personal ad. After that crack, the deluge. "The wanna ads, Bing? Hey, even we at the *Pee Eye* are running those these days. Kind of late to the orgy, aren't you?"

"Not if I gather ads from enough places out here and put them in enough corner boxes in all the good towns. People move around. The I-5 corridor—think about it, Mitch." It actually didn't take that much thinking. Bingford's scheme was based on the long skinny freeway archipelago from the Canadian border to the foot of the Willamette Valley, a day's drive to the south. That Interstate stretch alongside the Cascade Range took in the campus towns of Bellingham, Corvallis and Eugene; it took in both state capitals, Olympia and Salem, with their burgeoning staffs of young guerrilla bureaucrats; it took in the hip metropolises of Seattle and Portland: in short, the Pacific Northwest confederacy of beardedness and bralessness, ready to set out to explore the new back-page alphabet of desire.

The cute little bastard, Mitch thought with a shake of his

head, he's going to be able to buy his own mountain. But said only: "Could pay off."

"Trippe is coming in with me," Bingford mentioned as if it was the wildest of coincidences. Mitch could not have been less surprised. She had been on the *UW Daily* with them and in and out of mountain climbing with Bing. Trust-fund daredevils, two on a rope. Hers was a branch of the Pan Am fortune. This was another thing about Seattle that Mitch could never get used to: these pockets of polite wealth. Neither Bing nor Juanita would say *family money* if they had a mouthful of it. "And—"

"You came by to give me the first subscription."

"—we have an opening," Bingford went on undeterred. "You'd fit, big guy."

"Hey, here I get to write the weather every day. Wouldn't quite be the same in newspaper camp." Their old *Daily* phrase for various counterculture once-a-week-maybe excursions into print made Bingford wince. *"This past week, we had weather again,"* Mitch teased. "Nope. Thanks anyway."

"Come on, Mitch. This isn't you. We'll even scrape up the same salary for you the Big Bird there does."

"Bing, I'm married and got a kid on the way, all right? Marnie already thinks my working for a newspaper is next thing to picking up tin cans along the road. What's she going to say if I throw in with you just because we smoked some grass together at the U Dub?"

"Most of the time, you'll be out where you can't hear her," Bingford said helpfully.

In spite of what he knew ought to be a fire wall of guilt and shame, those words of Bingford's sizzled up the back of Mitch's mind. He had already started half admitting to himself that Marnie was more of a flake than he'd bargained for back in their dating days, when she simply seemed turned on in innumerable entertaining ways. Her latest phase, one hundred percent wok cooking, had him sneaking meals between meals.

Trying not to sound tempted, he asked: "Out where?"

"Wherever." Bingford threw up his hands to illustrate *out.* "We want you to be our nature freak."

So much for history, that caravan route of distant spices. Out of the haze of cannabis smoke and freckles had emerged Jerome "Bing" Bingford III, editor/publisher of an urban weekly newspaper for people concerned to know the difference between tofu and futon. From the shipwreck of a marriage and the raft he had sent his children away on and the shoals of a number of other major regrets had waded, big and drenched inside and out and environmentally the last of his kind, Mitchell Rozier, "Coastwatch" columnist and now quite late to work.

"I see we can call off the search party" was his greeting from Cynthia, the duplicitous receptionist and chief spy for Bingford. "At least you're back in time for the staff meeting."

"Right, Cyn," Mitch growled. "Wouldn't want to miss that just for the sake of getting my work done."

A pair of eyes permanently parked in neutral and an indecipherable murmur met him as he stepped into his cubicle. His cubemate was the new video reviewer, Shyanne Winters— monosyllabic and thin almost to the point of transparency. In his time, Mitch had shared the cubicle with drunks and brooders and at least one proven felon, but Shyanne spooked him. At her first staff meeting, Shyanne had gone on and on in an avid near whisper about corporately responsible non-lactic vegan dietary rules until it dawned on the assembled Cascopians that no milk in the office meant no lattes in the office, and she was rudely hooted down. Shyanne seemed to expect that the world was going to put nasty stuff on her. As a reviewer, she had the habit of tapping an instantaneous lead sentence into her computer, then dissolving into a sea of sighs. Mitch's attempts at sympathetic conversation during these longeurs only dragged him into her swamp of despond as well. Mystified but also royally fed up, he finally had gone to Bingford about her.

"How about getting me out of range of the Living X Ray there?"

"Oh, come on, Mitch." Instantly Bingford's management style, counterattack, kicked in. "Can't you goddamnit be a little fatherly—" Bingford caught himself. "Be some help to her, she's young, okay?"

Now Mitch matched Shyanne's more or less greeting with something equivocal and went directly to his computer. He had barely managed to enter *"Coastwatch/Berkeley gasbaggery"* when heads prairiedogging out of sundry other cubicles announced the staff meeting.

In the conference room the *Cascopia* staff was strewn on the edges of tables and windowsills. It struck Mitch that compared to Jocelyn and her Rollerblading cohorts—always with the Transylvanian exception of Shyanne, of course—these Seattle grungemeisters looked like an Amish choir.

They had unholy mouths on them, though. While Bingford and Cynthia conferred in the doorway to be sure everyone was on hand, the usual rabid factions went at it over whether staff meetings ought to be held oftener or never. By reflex Mitch pointed out that in the distant past when Bing panicked on every publication day and called a lunch-hour meeting to try to straighten matters out, they always managed to do something useful: eat.

"IM time," somebody droned. Institutional Memory was not a prized attribute among the younger Cascopians.

"Hey, now, not me," Mitch protested with a chesty laugh. "Not as long as Flatley waddles the earth." He cocked his head around to find the restaurant reviewer, who could recite what kind of sandwiches and pickles Bingford ordered for lunch in 1971. Then realized everyone in the room was staring at him, a gallery of faces masked in mockery, embarrassment and here and there shocking malice.

"Flats is no longer with us," Bingford called over to him. "He's doing a CD-ROM for Microsoft on Pacific Rim cuisine."

Bingford proceeded to the head of the table, holding a single sheet of paper. "One announcement. A biggie." He rubbed his cheek as if a freckle was bothering him. "The paper's going free."

Nobody said anything until Walmeier, who covered baseball, ballet, and brew pubs, asked: "*Scusi*, but how's that work?"

Our sinking captain didn't say it would work, Mitch mentally edited Walmeier; he merely said it would occur.

"Readership is dead in the water," Bingford was going on glumly. "Mailbox roulette"—the personal ads—"isn't what it used to be. People can feel each other up on the Internet now." Next he resorted to his lethal sheet of paper, trotting out the data. Free weekly newspapers—Mitch in his mind edited that, too: *giveaway* newspapers—were the national trend; it would build circulation and thereby hoist the advertising rates. "I've talked to them downtown," Bingford was saying, which always meant the rival *Seattle Week!*, also known as *Seattle Eek!* "They're going to have to go this same route. So are the Oregon guys, *Portlandia* and the *Eugene Scene*. And Bellingham, the *Bellyburg News*. They're all taking the price off the paper."

Bingford paused and went after that bothersome freckle again.

The room stirred, or rather, Mitch stirred it. He had sworn to himself, over and over during Bing's predestined announcement, that he was going to keep his mouth shut. What evil ventriloquist, then, was producing a voice exactly like his to suggest to Bing the next logical step: pay people to take the newspaper, why not? Rig up the vending boxes like slot machines: if a person grabs one copy of *Cascopia*, the box pays him a quarter; if the customer takes, say, three papers, make the payoff a dollar. "Circulation will go through the roof, Bing, I can practically guarantee."

"Mouth, Mitch." Bingford primly patted his lips as if reminding Mitch to employ a napkin there. "When I want my ass kicked in front of an audience I'll go on Letterman, all right?" Bingford crumpled his sheet of paper, signaling that the meeting was over. "This is where we are, people. Not easy times."

Back to his cubicle, Mitch settled himself into his chair but did not turn to his waiting computer.

He was half a century old, and working for a giveaway newspaper. Put that in your Institutional Memory and smoke it, Rozier.

"Are you, like, blocked?"

Mitch jumped as if goosed. Then spun his chair around to face the wraith in the doorway.

Shyanne's health mania was, it could only be said, incurable. Assorted natural purgatives and other herbs lay stuck away in every desk drawer at *Cascopia*. Wary of what vegetable matter she might foist on him, Mitch now checked:

"Are we on the topic of bowels here?"

"Writer's block," she specified eagerly. "I have it every time. I mean, I just walk into this building and I'm, 'Oh. There it is again. The block.'"

Mitch tried a smile, with the awful feeling that it was going to look sickly. "No, this is just a really hard piece to—"

"*Strictly Ballroom* was the worst," she broke in. "How can you write a review about something that's totally perfect?"

"Listen, ahm, Shyanne. I've got to start turning out this piece or—"

"If you won't spam it around? How I take myself past being

blocked?" Shyanne came to roost on the edge of her chair, her sharp knees inches from Mitch's. She looked intense enough to cut diamonds with. "I always go: 'Reader, I married him.' "

Mitch's brow furrowed massively.

She spun around to her computer and in the ritual keyboard flurry that Mitch recognized, he indeed heard her fingers make the keys conjure Charlotte Brontë's once deliciously inked words on her screen in up-to-the-instant pixels.

Shyanne sat back, wan but wired. "See, there's my lead, every time. I, like, borrow it awhile."

"Your *lead*? Isn't that more of an ending?"

"Sure, but it hooks up on the interpersonal level. 'Oh, hey, reader? Here I am again! Past the block!' "

"But Charlotte *Brontë*'s reader exists in England in eighteen-um-something," Mitch pointed out with a force that startled himself. "Out there ankle deep in the moors. Who has never laid eyes on a video, let alone the forgettable Joan Fontaine as Jane Eyre."

Eyes vast, Shyanne suddenly was emulating the old Procol Harum song "A Whiter Shade of Pale."

"Be joking," she said very low.

"I kid you not, those people were video deficient. So, don't you think going interpersonal with *that* reader is kind of"— Mitch knew that if there were a referee on the premises he would be whistled for piling on, but he could not stop himself— "unnatural?"

"Be blocked, see if I give a zit!" Shyanne was vigorous enough in springing out of her chair. "I will not work in the same space with a destructive aura. I'm going to Bing about you—we are over being cubular together."

Six

"WAY COOL! YOU CAN HEAR IT *EATING* IT!"

The third-graders shepherded by Lexa were in ecstasy at the unscheduled feeding time they were witnessing. Squirrels are cats with the brains left out, she reflected, judiciously watching the long-tailed gray tidbit being feasted upon by the zoo's eagle invalid, Spike. A minute ago the squirrel was bounding along, bippity bippity, at the grassy verge of the injured raptors' perch area, and the golden eagle, dragging wing and tether and all, nailed it with a huge noiseless pounce.

"Yuck, gross!"

"SHHH. *Listen.*"

Indeed, the sounds of Spike ripping apart the squirrel with

his beak, tearing ligament from bone, could be clearly heard. Parents were in for twenty-seven graphic reports at dinner tables tonight.

Palmer wasn't even trying to hide his pride in Spike. Slipping the gauntlet onto his wrist, the raptor keeper said: "Little snack between meals there. But I don't want to see any of you attacking our squirrels with your bare teeth, hear?" The schoolkids moaned in adoration while their grim-mouthed team of teachers and field-trip volunteers, who were getting more than they volunteered for on this field trip, tried to quell the rampant bloodthirstiness.

"While Spike chows down," Palmer continued, winking at Lexa where she stood in front of the herd of kids, "let me introduce you to our other birds of prey."

The raptor casualty ward currently included a snowy owl, a kestrel and a red-tailed hawk, besides the feasting eagle, and Lexa had heard Palmer's spirited spiel about each bird enough times that her attention drifted off to the zoo's Northern Trail again. She had taken this pack of schoolkids there—she took all the groups in her weekly docent stints there—and naturally the bear enclosure wowed them. The two grizzlies, big and bigger, frolicked in the pond dammed by the transparent viewing wall. The grizzly male, six hundred pounds of bad attitude, in particular seemed aware of the audience. The kids delighted in scaring themselves by racing right up to the glassed-in bear, but Lexa, knowing she was being sappy about it, nonetheless always stood all the way at the back to watch the creature from as much distance as possible.

The summer she had cooked for the bear tagging team, the team leader Zweborg was forever saying *Gee gosh, I hate to see that* when the massive pawprints would show up on the trail between them and the camp.

The six of them and a hundred or two grizzlies were prowling the Kenai Peninsula. It was a great break for Travis, because on the research rungs of the Alaska Department of Fish and Game this was way up there, setting foot snares along streams choked with spawning salmon to catch huge and hungry bears. Then, when you caught an Alaskan version of grizzly, firing a tranquilizing dart into his shaggy hide and hastening (but not hurrying; Zweborg, the priss, always piped out *We must not hurry, people, for we have no time to waste*) through the procedures of fastening a radio collar on the medically controlled griz, taking its measurements, tagging its ear, and smearing blue tattoo ink under its upper lip and plier-pressuring a permanent identification number into there. The team looked like crazed surgeons air-dropped into the middle of the wilderness, their implements spread on the back of the bear. Souped up on adrenaline, but not *hurrying*, each of them performed some chore on the animal—the two that always made Lexa catch her breath were Ruthie's handling the needles of the bear dope called etorphine, deadly to humans, and Travis's count-your-fingers-first task of tattooing the inside of the griz's lip.

Blued, tattooed, and construed, the grizzly then had to be given the shot of antidote and watched awhile to make sure it woke up and went back to its bear ways okay. Quite a lot of sentry duty in tagging bears. Lexa noticed, though, that the paw prints across the trail at the end of the day—the bear that *wasn't* there—spooked the F&G team more than their tagging work did, and they would all erupt into yodeling or nervous yelps to announce their presence. Everyone was armed to the teeth and beyond, the men packing shotguns loaded with slugs and Ruthie the bear-drug dealer with a .375 Magnum revolver strategically on her hip. The times Lexa was out with them she was about as concerned over all the large-caliber weaponry in the hands of fresh-from-the-lab wildlife biologists as she was with the potential grizzly in the bush. Even Travis, who looked like Hunter Hank the minute you put him in the outdoors, was actually the genetically suburban son of a Phoenix airline pilot.

But the summer passed with nobody either eaten or shot, and Lexa looked back on it as a highly instructive season. Other than Zweborg, whose mind seemed to consist of a compartment labeled *Everything About Bears* and another labeled *Christian Thoughts for the Day,* she was the one among them who had any history with grizzlies. When they were barely big enough to see over the dashboard of the Power Wagon, she and Mariah had watched as their father shot a sheep-eating bear, the grizzly trying its mightiest to tear off its own trapped toe and reach the man. There had been other family bear encounters as she grew up along the Rocky Mountain Front in northern Montana. So she had already been where Alaskans were stampeding toward. The human population of the Kenai was multiplying as fast as the U-Haul trailers could be unloaded, and the idea behind the tagging team was to study how the bears were faring as their home range was encroached on. Lexa would not have said she was against science, exactly, but she was going to be mighty surprised if the data indicated anything but grizzly life eroding away.

Hers not to reason why, though. Travis seemed to thrive there in bear camp. He had charge of the floatplane, out at the trailhead, and the flying lessons he had cajoled out of his father back when he was a teenager looked pretty smart now. There was one other side of Travis she hadn't had a chance to see before, the elastic way he could fit himself around whoever was in charge. In no time at all, Zweborg was writing evaluations on Travis that were the bureaucratic equivalent of frankincense and myrrh.

Not overly surprising, then, when at the end of each week Zweborg would clear his throat and send Travis and Lexa out on the supply run. Everybody knew it made no sense to send the *cook* out of camp for the day, but gamely put up with sandwiches and dried apricots in Lexa's absence. So, armed and pack-carrying, the two of them would head out on the trail, Travis's cute flat cowboy rear end close ahead of her as they hiked fast and loudly announced themselves to possible bears. Travis's style was to caterwaul the Eagles' great song "You cain't hiiide yore lyin' eyes." Lexa adapted top-of-her-voice commands that had worked well on the McCaskill family sheepdogs. *Jump in the truck, bear! Bear, go lay down!*

Both of them would be thoroughly keyed up by the time they reached the lake and the floatplane moored there. Now at last came the conjugal part, the reason Zwee—bless his pointy old Jesus freak head—sent them out together. Nights in bear camp posed a marital problem, with four other people in sleeping bags a few feet away and half awake anyway listening for grizzlies outside. But the sleeping bag she and Travis were promptly into here—the emergency-landing bag, stowed in the cargo area behind the plane seats—was gloriously their own, in solitude. Those quick sessions in the back of the plane were only half undressed and makeshift and breathless and hard on certain parts of the body, but if you were young, newly wed and turned loose in Alaska, what more could you want? It was the best summer she and Travis had together. The one good summer.

"So our buddy Spike has had his snack." Palmer was hitting his usual crescendo, just as the corralled schoolkids were growing restless. "Now we'll show you a little aerial feeding of our other birds."

Pulling the impressive leather gauntlet onto his left hand and forearm, Palmer shouted over to the raptor house for his assistant keeper Suzette. An answering shout told him Suzette would be a while, she'd had to make an emergency run for veterinary supplies.

Lexa saw Palmer hesitate. Then he was calling to her, over the kids:

"Help me out with the food flight? You've seen how Suzette tosses."

Lexa bit a little inside corner of her lip, but ducked through the white rail fence around the raptors' perching area and walked slowly out to Palmer.

" 'Preciate this," he said, handing her Suzette's gauntlet for her wrist. "We'll start with the kestrel, work our way up."

The pair of them went over to the perch where the kestrel sat, a double handful of dignity and ferocity. Heart beating a little more than it should, Lexa focused on Palmer as he brought the hawk onto her wrist, letting it settle there, ruffling a bit, to accustom itself to her. His familiar unhurried way of moving, keeping the routine smooth, nothing to alarm the bird. Palmer, like Travis, was a natural at such handling.

To the audience beyond the fence Palmer pointed out the sideburns patterns of the kestrel, and the hawk's brilliant eye spoke for itself. The squirmy schoolchildren stilled when Palmer took the taut little hawk onto his own gauntleted wrist, stepped away from the perch area and paced off fifty feet before turning around to face toward Lexa.

She reached into the plastic bag of meat chunks and took out one the size of a vole. She held the morsel in her ungloved hand, tucked the meat sack out of sight on the side of her away from the hawk, and looked to Palmer.

"Ready on the right, ready on the left, ready on the firing line," Palmer called out. He launched the hawk, and a breath later sang out, "Toss!"

Lexa flung the piece of meat up and away with an under-hand toss, just enough loft to it for the bird in its springing swoop off Palmer's wrist to hurl itself onto the quarry in an eyeblink. The meat speared in its talons, the kestrel resumed its perch and began ripping at its meal.

Chuckling, Palmer strode back to the area of the perches, collecting Lexa on the way with a "well done" squeeze just above her throwing elbow. He steered her to the snowy owl, yellow eyed within its intense shroud of white.

"Now we'll show you some hunting that's more of a gliiide," began Palmer, smoothly playing out the word. "Casper here has a wingspan of more than three feet, and with that he's capable of floating real fast over the tundra until he sees . . ."

Lexa found she and Palmer had ended up quite close, practically touching, as he discoursed about the unblinking bird. A long sergeancy in the army and a determined slog through night classes had brought Palmer to this zoo career. He was published in his field, the care and repair of crippled birds of prey. He had a perfectly fine second marriage, to a wife who sold real estate, and they had a couple of kids. *Palmer's plate is full,* Lexa reminded herself for not absolutely the first time; *he doesn't need anything more on it.*

Fishboat rules, she savagely told herself and stepped well away from Palmer, looking only at the Arctic owl on its scarred perch.

Lexa had landed in Seattle during a foghorn Christmas, the *whoommm?* and *gimme roommm!* of freighters and ferries droning in from Puget Sound like dueling bassoon players. Each streetlight had its pyramid of fog, and fir trees lost their outlines near the top. Cars, their lacquers muted by all the gray, looked anonymous and mousy.

Alaska when she left was sunlit, mountain after mountain shining. Let it, she told herself. Some sonofabitch will find a way to put it in cellophane and sell it off.

As the cab crept from the airport to the half-erased city, she had this all worked out, how she would check into a motel, order in a deep-dish pizza, rent a car in the morning and head home. If the place where you go to announce your marriage has failed is home.. More like out at first base, she tried to joke to herself.

She was barely into the motel lobby before she shucked her Kelty backpack and stacked it against her one suitcase and phoned him.

"Hi, it's Lexa Mu . . . McCaskill. Fogged in."

"We get that some, this time of year. Hey, how you doing?" Mitch's surprise at hearing from her sounded genuine.

"Been better," she answered honestly enough. "Driving across the mountains tomorrow. I—wondered if you'd be, too. Going home for the holidays, like the shitty song."

"No, I don't do that anymore."

"Probably smart. I'm going to have to tell them Travis and I split the blankets."

"Ah. One of those."

She could hear him saying the next thing ever so carefully, but he did not hesitate with it.

"Wait out this weather, why don't you. I've got room here. I'm going to some people's for Christmas dinner. Come with, no reason why not."

Now he paused.

"Lexa? The divorce news will keep. Believe me."

Seven

SKY AS CLEAR AS A VACATIONING METEOROLOGIST'S CON-science, sailboats sprinkled on either side of the floating bridge across Lake Washington like white tepees on a vast blue prairie, Mount Rainier sitting passive and massive over Seattle's southern horizon, even the chain-link commuter traffic grinding along less glacially than during most so-called rush hours—Mitch could scarcely believe such a death spiral of a day could yield an evening like this.

As he drove east toward the suburbs beyond the suburbs, where Lexa's catering job lay in wait, he gingerly checked around on his body and found a place or two that felt better, some, for his having stopped at Gold's Gym and worked out vengefully on the weight machines. But the rest of him harbored one deep ache or another anywhere he cared to think about.

His mind kept returning to Bingford, that freckled rat. Give-away, right; they'd all been given away, with toe tags on, at the staff meeting. Bing might as well have folded up the whole business right there in front of them today, announced he was shutting down *Cascopia* or selling it off or giving it away to the Fremont bridgetender or whatever the inevitable disposal process was going to be. Now the next thing would have to be the *d* word, downsizing, and Mitch not so idly wondered whether Bing had enough guts left in him to go around from cubicle to cubicle saying *fired* instead. And if he was going to get around to saying it, Mitch fumed onward as he changed lanes and then changed back again in the thickening traffic at the Bellevue interchanges, he could have done so this morning and thereby relieved him, Mitch, of the rest of the day of stewing over the Berkeley conference piece, which had turned out to be a hash anyway.

In the fathoms of his bones, though, Mitch cringed at the thought of no more *Cascopia*. He felt entitled to fear; he was very nearly the only person he knew of in America who had been doing the same thing for the past twenty-five years. "Coast-watch" was the one long devotion he had ever been able to maintain in his life. Okay, sure, now there was Lexa, but—

Lexa. The unphoned.

He grabbed up the car phone that had been forced on him by Bing in one of his publisher moods, then realized. While he'd been busy writing down Lexa's phone message with the ring-around-the-rosy directions for getting to the party place, Shyanne tornadoed back into the cubicle to snatch up her cher-ished review video of *The Gods Must Be Crazy*, and he'd missed the phone number Lexa was giving. Nor, he found now, was directory assistance about to hand out the phone number of Aaron Frelinghuysen, latest cybernaire.

All Mitch knew was what everybody knew, that the guy had more money than most nations. Frelinghuysen had piranhaed his way into the techieville food chain with a bit of wonderware called ZYX, and from Silicon Valley to Silicon Alley, the deals had lined up for him.

But, tough luck for the man who had next to everything, the prime mansion sites along Lake Washington had been used up by the earlier generation or two of computer bigfoots. So now the mode was to pick a spot along the next woodsy body of water, Lake Sammamish, and build something whopping. Mitch drove and drove and drove in the tangle of lakeside streets that turned into lanes and less, stopping four times to decipher Lexa's directions. Finally he found the driveway where, amid vehicles that surely had cost big digits, sat her purplish VW van with *Do-Re-Mi Catering* standing out in firm white script.

When she'd first found that van, it was painted in a flowery fantasia with scarlet lettering rampant, reading LOLLAPALOSER.

"The guy gave me a deal on it," Lexa had marveled.

"I'll bet he did." Mitch had circled the vehicle, twice. "You know, Ingvaldson will have a stroke if he sees this in the driveway."

"Henry should visit the twentieth century before it's too late."

Carefully Mitch tried again:

"Are most people going to want their finger food delivered in something that looks like it's been orbiting the planet since nineteen sixty-seven?"

That struck home. "I'll paint it royal burgundy," she said.

The Frelinghuysen house much surprised Mitch. Cyber barons had been building their dreamhouses the size and decor of airport terminals, but this one, while extensive, was low and restrained, nestled under fine old undisturbed cedar trees.

He was let in by a physically perfect member of the household staff, all courtesy, who pointed him in the direction of the kitchen.

On Mitch's way down the hallway, though, a wall-size glass case of coastal Indian masks suddenly loomed. The fantastic oval eyes, the playful exaggerations of proboscis and incisor and claw and ear, the unquenchable life in the wooden grins and leers and anguished expressions floated like a sorcerer's séance. Haida, Tsimshian, Tlingit, the tribes of the greatest carvers were all represented in this hallway Valhalla.

Overawed by the art collection, he dawdled along from mask to mask until he came to a thunderbird headpiece with an imperious nose so hooked that it circled back on itself, abalone-shell eyes eternally wide awake and skull-top ears which had little faces in them.

"Thunderbird, old buddy, you're worth more than what I'm driving," Mitch muttered, meaning it.

"Thunderbird," echoed a rather too pleasant otherworldly voice.

Mitch spun, startled, as the wall behind him blued into a computer screen. The thunderbird mask appeared there for a moment, then dissolved. Outlines of templates, various sizes and shapes, revolved onto the screen until one descended into place and took form as the thunderbird's hooked beak. Then the template ghosted out of the beak and ascended, twice, and made the ears, the identical basic form as the beak. Ovoid templates spun into place and made the eyes, and then the equally mighty nostrils in the beak, and then smaller versions of the same template form made the littler eyes in the faces within the ears. White on blue, other lines formed themselves, the ceremonial mask inexorably growing in detail and power. Mitch realized he was watching a schematic of how the ancient carver had created the thunderbird head. For an instant the computer-modeled mask hovered there in the pleasant blue screen, then cedar texture sheathed over it, then paint applied itself where the carver had done so. It was as hypnotic as it was spooky. Mitch knew that the original peoples of the coast loved to play with transformations, have two or more of the creatures they carved meld with one another in the same space by sharing body parts. Now the computer was taking apart the art by which the carvers had taken apart time and space and being.

He got out of there, caught his breath and went on to the kitchen.

He found Lexa bossing her food help as if building the pyramids of Egypt. It always unnerved him, her flinty way of running a crew. He had known her to fire the most charming kid on the face of the earth, *kapow*: "Told you once already, Jason, learn to read your Mickey Mouse watch and be on time."

Now she leveled a look across the kitchen at Mitch and said: "Well, hello there. So, lucky, how was San Francisco?"

"Breathtaking."

He swapped quick greetings with the crew, Allison and Guillermo and Kevin, and went right over to Lexa, aware he was more than a little late. "Bridge traffic," he alibied reliably. "Anyway, hi." He inclined his head back toward the computer extravaganza. "Video night at Potlatch Acres, have we got?"

"Everybody shut your eyes while I make out with the bartender," Lexa directed. She stood on tiptoes and planted a gale-force kiss on him. "Mmm," she assessed in a voice low enough for just him to hear, "a person of your lip description used to sleep with me."

"Used to? I thought that came with this job instead of Social Security."

She looked serious. "You did get together with Jocelyn?"

"Approximately." Mitch seized a fistful of carrot sticks.

Lexa poked her hands into her apron pockets, her no-bullshit-allowed-on-these-premises stance.

"Gory details later, how about," Mitch bargained. He munched and tried to look semi-willing for her. "Reporting for duty. Honest. More or less."

She gave him one more testing gaze, then said:

"Okay, right this way. The bar setup is over by the windows. You'll draw spectators."

He followed her into a living room with a cedar-beamed cathedral ceiling and a glass wall out onto darkening Lake Sammamish, the lights of the other houses along the shore sparkling off the water like necklaces tossed down in tribute. Taking his station at the opulent bar and trying not to sound edgy, he maintained to Lexa: "No prob, boss. Let the sipping hordes come."

"Crowds are your life, right, footballer?" she teased like a chirpy cheerleader. "I never worry about penalty calls when the game is in the hands of the old Iron—"

"Don't get going on that, okay?" He hastily whirled into the work waiting behind the bar.

Lexa pretended to adjust the tail of his tent-sized white bartending jacket, surreptitiously pinched his butt, then headed once more for the kitchen to shake up the troops there. But she stopped at the doorway to glance back at Mitch, bulking there against the nightblack water, the big man she had traded Alaska for.

Sitka was still dark, she was still the lawful wedded wife of Travis Mudd when the call came, Travis on his side of the bed saying into the phone, "God, they got it stopped? They don't? Okay, I'll be there as soon as I can get hold of a plane."

Lexa rolled over toward him, batting her eyes as he snapped the bed light on and dove for his clothes on the chair.

"Got ourselves an oil spill."

He sounded like the usual Travis, apologetic and put out, but yanking on his pants in the sallow bedroom light he looked eager along with those. Lexa would think, after, of something her grandmother had said about men when they had a forest fire to fight: *They turn back into absolute boys.*

She had to ask Travis "Where?" twice before he glanced around from the vital business of tucking in his shirttail.

"Hnh? The worst. Valdez."

That dim Alaskan morning, everything that could go wrong at Valdez was racing to do so before sleepy-eyed officials could begin to catch up with the dimensions of the disaster—the thousand-foot-long tanker having daggered itself so thoroughly on a reef that eight of its eleven cargo tanks were spewing oil, the spill-response equipment too little and too late; then the next inevitable misfortune, the wind picking up and spreading the oil slick ninety miles down the shores of Prince William Sound. Estuaries went black-dead under the killing coat of muck, as did stream mouths where salmon spawned; fish, seabirds, eagles, the intricate food chain of the Sound was being smothered or poisoned as the oil bled from the tanker and kept on spreading. All those first nightmare days of the *Exxon Valdez* cascade, Lexa wanted to grab Alaska and shake it: *See! See! You and your fancy wages for that pipeline!* She was already packed and ticketed for Valdez when Travis called to suggest: "You might as well come on up. I'm going to be here a real while."

The emergency bird clinic by day, a swing shift of cooking meals to go for the fishboat crews who took it upon themselves to fight the oil away from the Port San Juan hatchery—Lexa had never worked harder nor more hopelessly in her life. The oil port was a crazyhouse, with money rather than mirrors bending everybody out of shape. Sky-high hourly wages for scrubbing oil-befouled rocks, boat jobs skimming the oil off the water of Prince William Sound, opportunities galore in provisioning the oil company's army of spill consultants and the stunned state agency honchos and the environmental feds and the media invasion; she vowed not to let the boomtown-of-catastrophe atmosphere get to her, but it constantly did. As did the tarred dead birds, the dead sea otters, the dead seals, the dead this and the dead that of Prince William Sound.

Feeling about half sick as usual, she was disposing of the floppy carcass of one more cormorant that she had tried unsuccessfully to soap-rinse the oil from, when Travis came around with the familiar man whose size made him unmistakable around town.

"Montana, right?" Lexa said the instant Travis introduced him.

"Does it still show that bad?" Mitch sounded none too pleased.

"We had Roziers in the Two Medicine country, where I'm from," she elaborated. Her eyes lifted to the black wavy hair, the rocky set of his face. "You look kind of like their kissing cousin."

With the barest of smiles he owned up to that, saying that his family in Twin Sulphur Springs had shirttail relations north there in the Two country, all right. "Probably they're the ones who got born with some sense."

Lexa held her tongue about that, and by now Travis was saying, "Giving him the full tour. Mitch's following this for his paper in Seattle."

A notebook was swallowed in Mitch's hand. "L-E-X-A, do I have it spelled right? Last name same like Travis's or . . . same, got it. You've been washing birds? How many of them pull through?"

The photo came then and there, Mitch of course asking if she minded but already cocking the camera as she collected the next oil-slicked cormorant against the chest of her rain suit. This one was a beach find, she gave Mitch the vocabulary, maybe not quite as far gone as the floaters they found flopping out there in the actual curd of oil atop the water. She would remember that he then had question after question for her, and a barrage of others for Travis in his capacity as the state's wildlife monitor of this mess, before the uproar broke out at the town dock nearby. A fishing boat had tied up, grimy and loaded with five-gallon cans of oil the fishermen had scooped up by hand. Photographers and reporters jammed around the fishermen, who claimed they were capturing as many gallons of oil as the fleet of fancy skimming equipment combined. Then the crowd surrounded an embarrassed oil company spokesman, who had to call over even more reluctant executives into the clamor.

All at once Mitch Rozier recited:

> *"When in danger,*
> *when in doubt,*
> *run in circles,*
> *scream and shout."*

Still watching the dock commotion, the three of them shared an unfunny laugh. "Sounds like what we work with every day, doesn't it, Travis?" Lexa couldn't help saying. "Where'd you get that?"

"Something my old man used to say about the army, is all. The pipeline"—Mitch was abruptly back to questioning—"were the two of you up here during the construction? What was that like?"

She could say of herself, later, that she had started off not particularly well-disposed toward a newspaper word merchant. She'd had one for a brother-in-law, an ungovernable piece of work named Riley Wright, until Mariah came to her senses and bailed out of that marriage. So Mitch the writing man did not win anything much from her at first except civility—not even any real Montana kidding, as he seemed to feel pretty far removed from where the foundations of the Roziers were poured. Of course, she was curious, as exiles everywhere are about one another, but not enough to make life tricky yet.

Meanwhile Travis and he chimed with each other, Travis keen to have somebody for once interested in the ins and outs of the whole coastal ecosystem instead of coming around for thirty seconds for the latest body count on wildlife. Out of that, she could later tell herself, came their pipeline flight.

They lifted off in a white and yellow Cessna 207 at first light that Sunday, Travis professionally laconic in talking to the tower. Stuffed into the copilot's seat, Mitch watched out the side window for the airborne moment from the times he had been up with the Lighthawk pilot—the plane wheel halting its spinning an instant after takeoff and sitting motionless in the air. He half expected to see Mount St. Helens rise beside the climbing plane.

Travis first circled out over Prince William Sound, the fleet of oil skimmers and collecting barges below like beetles on an oddly sheened pond, the filthy bathtub ring around Prince William Sound stretching toward the Gulf of Alaska beyond the horizon. Then he aimed the plane back over Valdez and the farm of storage tanks, and the silver worm of the pipeline stretched ahead.

Mitch no longer liked flying, and he never had liked having someone looking over his shoulder. The coppery presence at the corner of his eye caused him to glance back every so often.

Perched on the front edge of the jump seat behind Travis, Lexa thought to herself *Hey, bud, this is Alaska. Life is close quarters here,* and rubbed it in:

"I hope this is okay, me hitchhiking along?"

"Oh, sure, fine," Mitch lied. Couldn't say much else, with her husband doing the flying. He eyed Travis sideways, though, wondering how they sorted things like this out, how much Lexa mixed into his work. Stuck her spousy nose in, so to speak, although it did seem to be a fairly acute nose.

Wrapped in the sounds of the Cessna, the steady force of its engine and the vibrating thrum of the cockpit, they settled back for the long day of flying, the oil aqueduct of Alaska constantly there under them, the land threaded with forty-eight-inch pipe from its Arctic shore to Valdez's channel into the Pacific. Mitch's hands stayed busy with his notebook, trying to make the Alaskan earth say words. Here at the start of their route north every horizon was crazily corrugated, the mountain ranges like lines of icebergs off the end of the big one, Denali.

Lexa watched him work, trying to figure out what registered on a housebroken Rozier, writer no less. *Ones I knew, even our sheepherders thought were shagnasties. He got out someway.*

Eventually they were skirting Fairbanks, bush planes parked like pickup trucks along the airport runway in the middle distance, surprise suburbs claiming the ridges. Then the pipeline out in the open, climbing some ridges with a wink of gleam and disappearing into others.

They came above country now which was naked of anything manmade except the pipeline and the haul road beside it. At irregular intervals, a side road would run out a few hundred yards and turn into a flat graded oval—like a giant frying pan, with the side road the handle. Mitch puzzled over the pattern of this for a while before pointing and guessing, "Helicopter pads?"

"No, those're gravel pits." Travis raised his voice in answer. "Takes a lot of gravel to keep the haul road from sinking."

It all floats, Mitch's column began to form. *The pipeline and its road are levitated atop tundra and permafrost by the most expensive construction project since that orchard in Eden. Even before the Prudhoe Bay oil is pumped aboard a tanker at Valdez, it defies gravity and other concerns of earth for eight hundred miles.*

Travis was saying over the plane noise that the weather ahead wasn't the greatest, but he figured he could keep under the worst of the clouds.

"And above the ground, right?" Mitch answered, calculating the skimming landscape not very far below.

"Bear!" Lexa shouted then, sounding inordinately happy about it and pointing past Mitch's nose out the side window. To his further confusion, next she yelped something to Travis about getting out his tattoo kit.

Travis grinned at her like a boy given candy and yelled, "Let's go see him." He stood the Cessna on its right wingtip and zoomed the plane into a tight circle. The tundra fanned beneath them, little squib lakes appearing then quickly erasing, the three of them on their sides there three hundred feet in the air and Mitch concentrating on not giving in and reaching for the sick sack, until at last Lexa pointed to the wingtip and the galloping clump of fur under it. Travis made a couple of swoops so they could view the bear from each side of the plane, then he put the Cessna atop the piped path of oil again.

They flew across cockeyed rivers, channels bending back on themselves as if trying to make knots. One such set of kinks, unruly and silty, was the Yukon. And constantly the pipeline . . .

. . . *goes and goes and goes, tracing its bright solo strand across our largest state. It is true that it is a mere thread in the carpet that is Alaska. It is also true that this single thread has magically dyed the rest of Alaska to the color of oil money.*

Two-thirds of the way to Prudhoe Bay, Travis put down at a skimpy village for refueling. The wind coming through the pass in the Brooks Range ahead rocked the plane even on the ground. The three of them piled out laughing and doing *scissors, paper, rock* for first turn at the outhouse behind the trading post. Lexa lost to both men and complained that the laws of chance as well as anatomy were rigged against her. "You can at least both go at once and have some kind of a contest, can't you?" she urged.

By the time that was taken care of and an industrious native named Fred had raced out on a three-wheeler to gas up the plane with Travis watching, Mitch had ducked into the trading post. He bought apples for a dollar apiece, entertained at how Bingford's eyes were going to pop at this on the expense account and jogged back across the gravel runway.

Ululating howls of sled dogs rose from behind every house

in the village. Lexa, as if back at bossing ranch dogs, commanded over her shoulder: "Hush, you huskies!"

That made Mitch give her a smile, somewhat on the speculative side. Across certain stretches of the flight the sameness of the landscape and the mesmerizing drone of the plane had sent him daydreaming into Travis's life in this big land, a willing wife with him. It didn't take much bumpy air to jostle that drift of thought, though. Marnie would have gagged at setting foot on a fishboat or even into one of the scabby Alaskan towns. And he himself? He had grown up in not much of anywhere and had pulled out of there as soon as he could, too. He doubted he was Alaska material.

"Here." A little late, he thought to offer the apple sack. "Have some on my publisher." They huddled out of the wind next to a ratty-looking snowmobile shed and watched Travis go about his plane chores. Lexa dug into the apples.

Conversationally she said, "Guess you know you're in Bob country north."

He certainly did know that, but was surprised she did. Then put it together, that the Forest Service's Bob Marshall Wilderness Area lay just west of where she had grown up, along the same spine of the Rockies where Mitch had, far away there in the lower forty-eight. Up here Marshall, in his twenties and made of luck, had plunged into the Brooks Range and come back with a preservation paean to the colossal wild country at the gates to the Arctic. And a pipeline runs through it.

Brow corrugated with interest, Mitch studied off past the aluminum-sheet roofs of the village to the storied peaks all across the sky ahead of them. "Travis's work ever take him into the Brooks Range?"

"Only flying through Atigun Pass, like today." Lexa studied the apple in her hand as if it had just reminded her of something. "But I've been pretty far back in, on the headwaters of the Anaktuvuk River."

He felt major-league stupid. She cooked for all kinds of backcountry expeditions, Travis had made mention of that.

She showed him an askew smile, then contemplated the mountains. "Spent a solid week in a sleeping bag, back in there."

"May I ask, doing what?"

"Trying to keep from starvation."

She hadn't liked the setup from the minute the bush pilot dropped them off on the upper Anaktuvuk, a guide she'd never worked with before confidently insisting the camp be put up out on a gravel bar, right there handy to the river for his clients to flail their fishing lines at. One couple from Japan, the other from Florida, Dopey the guide and Lexa, then there they were at streamside when a cloudburst cut loose in the elevations of the Brooks and every drop of moisture on the North Slope started coming down the Anaktuvuk. They were lucky to flounder across the backwater to shore before the river took the gravel bar. They had managed to grab one tent and their sleeping bags and a provision pack that would feed six people for three days— Lexa knew it was going to be a long week before the plane could get back in to fetch them. The Floridians proposed hiking out. *Meet a bear in the tundra and it isn't going to go hungry,* she pointed out. Dopey made hero noises about thrashing his way downriver for help. *Right, bushwhack for a hundred and fifty miles to the Beaufort Sea and hail a passing iceberg?* Along with Lexa, the Japanese couple wasted no more time arguing in the rain but climbed into their sleeping bags to start saving their body warmth and energy. The other three gradually came to their senses and bedded in too to wait for the weather to lift and the plane to come. An eight-day week, it turned out to be before they heard the marvelous drone of the engine.

She gave Mitch only the quick version, but it was enough to knock his Seattle socks off. She shrugged and sent him a glance. Somehow demolishing her apple and managing to speak at the same time, she asked as if suddenly curious:

"Ever wonder if you're doing any good at all? The things you write, I mean."

"I don't have the world straightened out quite yet," came back from him. "But it maybe doesn't hurt for me to keep poking around at it."

"Lots of us poked at this pipeline project as hard as we knew how, and here the sucker came anyway."

"You're not big on oil, it sounds like."

"I'm not big on watching the spillionaires go at it. These are the same people Travis and I knew when they were milking money out of the pipeline construction."

Now Mitch was the one curious. "What keeps people like you and Travis in Alaska?"

"Travis loves it up here."

As if hearing himself cited, the long-legged figure across the runway gave them a thumbs-up sign and beckoned them back for takeoff.

City habited, Mitch glanced around for where to deposit his apple core. He noticed Lexa was empty-handed. "What'd you do with yours?"

"Ate that part, too." She shrugged. "Old habit. My grandfather got us to doing it," she said as they started back to the plane. "Most of his life he was a forest ranger, there on the Two, and when he used to have us kids out hiking or camping he showed us how to keep taking little tiny bites on our apple core until all that's left are seeds and stem." Lexa inclined her head to watch up at Mitch as she finished. "In the wilderness, you don't want to leave any more of yourself than you have to."

They had been back from the pipeline flight several days when Travis suggested to her at breakfast:

"Come on down the Sound with me this morning. Something you need to see."

At the first stretch of oil-smeared rocky beach, a bargelike craft with what looked like artillery aboard was moving in close to shore. Travis's boss from the Juneau office, Timmons, was on hand. There was much consultation, and then a cannonade of high-pressure water jetted onto the rocks, spray and crude-oil sheen flying.

It was like watching a powerful fireboat at work, only the target here was not fire.

"Whooee!" With the first hope she had felt in a long while, Lexa jiggled Travis in the ribs. "This is going to do it? They can just hose away the oil?"

"That's the deal."

Travis looked odd, taut. The two of them watched another blast of water scour away at the scummed-up rocky beach. After a minute he said as though thinking out loud, "We have to hope they don't get too much into your line of work with this."

Lexa gave him an inquisitive look. "The bird washing? Hey, they're not going to hose my sick birds with that thing. Over my deadly body."

"No, your other line of work," Travis said shortly. "We've got—there's still marine life under those rocks. Protozoa and micro-organisms, on up. Bottom end of the food chain, you might say." Travis inclined his head toward the hosing operation. "That water has to be hot to take the oil off. Scalding."

Lexa stared at the jet of water. Then at him. "It might *cook* anything that's still left alive under there?"

Travis tightened his jaw. "Timmons signed off on it. I had to, too."

"On—?" Lexa felt a little dazed. Alaska, oil, Valdez: were slippery answers all they ever had?

Neither of them said anything more, right then. Travis had told her just enough, then counted on her to cut him some slack; she knew the symptoms. She made it through the day, sneaking reluctant looks at the hosing operation, and at the pack of

$16.69-an-hour workers mopping up around the rocks that had been hot-blasted. She made it on through her galley shift on the fishermen's command-post seiner. When she got home, she snapped the bed light on in Travis's eyes.

"You're letting them kill the rest of the beach to clean it?"

He wrenched himself up against the headboard, his excellent shoulders and slimboy chest bare to her. Blinking hard a couple of times, he had it ready for her. All too ready, she thought.

"We don't know how to get around some biota loss from it, all right? But—"

She didn't say anything, waiting.

"Lexa, I am not a marine biologist. Timmons and I think this is the only way we can get a certifiable cleanup. Otherwise, what are we going to say—'No sweat, don't bother picking up that oil'? You can see where that'd put us," he practically pleaded. "We'd have the world on our necks for letting Exxon off the hook."

"Instead you're going to have a dead beach."

"A *cleaned* beach. Which is what Timmons and I are supposed to make happen. After that, we'll have to see how things establish again." Travis took a major breath. "There'll be studies then. They can second-guess us then, if that's the way things turn out."

His eyes quit meeting hers. "Some sleep might improve both of us," he said, and snapped off the light.

When she went to Mitch Rozier in the morning, the first thing he did was to mutter: "Why do these things always have to happen on deadline?"

Before he began phoning around to marine biologists he knew down the coast, he paused.

"Travis must've figured he didn't have any choice."

Lexa's eyes looked dull, but her voice wasn't. "That can get to be a habit."

Glancing at her as he made notes, Mitch spent the next hour cornering people by telephone. One way or another, all the researchers he could get hold of said they wished there could have been more research before the beaches were scoured, but none of them wanted to be quoted by name as opposing the oil cleanup. After the last one, Mitch hung up and told Lexa:

"You're right. They're flying blind on this, to get the beaches cleaned while the oil company is still hysterical enough to do it. Got one more call to make."

Bingford's voice in Seattle went rapidly up the scale:

"Are you in the same Alaska as everybody else? All they've been writing for weeks is Prince William Sound polluted to the max with oil, and here you come tra-la-la *against* the cleanup?"

"Only the hosing with hot water. The scalding part."

"Hot water, right, that's exactly what you're trying to get us into, Mitcho." Bing made him go over it again, then at last asked: "Who would we hang the story on?"

"I can't use the source's name."

"Mitch, guy," Bing began, which he always did when he thought Mitch was getting in over his head.

"But it's somebody who somebody blabbed to. It's solid."

"Only if you cover our ass—"

"You don't have to tell me that again, Bing."

"—every which way with—"

"Bing, you little craphead, I do know that."

"—reaction quotes from the poor bastards who signed off on the hot hosing."

"I was about gonna go do that," Mitch said, meeting the eyes of the woman whose marriage he was about to wreck.

I always knew, with Travis, that winters were going to be the worst. When we could get out, have some room around us, we didn't do too bad. But cooped up together, that's when we'd start biting the doorknobs.

Posted by the kitchen door, Lexa was keeping watch on the expressions of the guests starting to circle the table of food. A bit of peering and comparing was good; slow stares at, say, the curl of the lettuce leaves were not. This crowd seemed to be automatic grazers, and she at least could breathe a sigh of relief at that. The space of white jacket across the room was less easy to map.

Mitch would be the same season all year long, if the world would let him. That's a lot of if. I hope I'm not feeling winter coming, again.

Lexa pushed the kitchen door sharply with her hip and disappeared to cutlery duty.

Meanwhile Mitch, with a touch of panic, was finding out that bartending had changed dialects since the last time he filled in at one of Lexa's feeds. Somewhere a switch had been flipped and everyone who had been drinking bottled springwater that cost more than perfume now could not get along without boutique beer. He had finally mastered the dozens of water labels; now here was the new zoo of brew. Still, he managed to maul the requested brands out of the army of dark little bottles until a pallid guy with hair like a headful of quills came back to the bar complaining that he had been handed a Fort Apache Amber Ale when he'd asked for a Forklift Amber Ale.

"Time-out!" Mitch boomed to the waiting semicircle of thirsties, and clinked bottles around until he had them scrupulously alphabetized, Anchor Steam to Zyggurat Pale Ale.

While Lexa hovered at the table and trafficked this or that onto people's plates—she always had the urge to pat a party into shape—Mitch whipped beer out like a Las Vegas dealer. Tribal talk among the techies was of stock options, it seemed; Mitch wondered whether stockbrokers talked about computers at their parties.

Another spurt of beer aficionados, latecomers, and then the physically supreme specimen who had let him into the house came through the line, accompanied by an equally blonde and tawny woman. *Sheena @ jungle.com,* Mitch thought. They were so gorgeous together they practically hurt the eyes. Mitch handed them a matched pair of beers and they strode away like cheetahs.

Amid his collection of pangs, Mitch singled out hunger as one he could do something about. He slipped over to the food table while Lexa was there inspecting its remnants.

"What do you want devoured?"

"Celery sticks."

"How come you never say the Swedish meatballs?"

"Vegetables are healthy for my profit margin, Rozier."

He remembered to ask: "How's business been while I was gone?"

"Weddings up the wazoo," she said quite cheerfully.

"Really. In this day and age." Crunching away on the celery, he scanned the room curiously. "So where's our host? Off trying to morph himself into Bill Gates or something?"

Lexa gave him a funny look. "You just served him a beer, doofus."

"*That's* Frelinghuysen?" Mitch yanked his head around to stare after the blonde muscleman. "Life is unfair, I can take. But this guy has more going for him than Jesus did."

A series of blunt chords indicated the band was tuning up. Lexa rolled her eyes. "See you around," she said and fled for the kitchen.

Mitch went and settled himself in back of the bar while the black-clad band avalanched into its first set. From rock through grunge to ska, musicians seemed to be turning from butterflies back into cocoons. Driven by lots of horns, the music was very fast, very loud, very happy, very everything. Through that set and a bunch more, Mitch tried to keep himself tuned only to the industrial-strength music and dispensing an occasional beer.

Lexa sailed out of the kitchen only once and only long enough to snatch the last few slivers of smoked salmon away. She had on her hunkered-down-in-a-hailstorm expression. Mitch vamped a couple of dance moves for her benefit and she stuck her tongue out at him. He loved big helpings of sound and could not see why she clung to voovy-groovy jazz; "There's no whang to it," he kept pointing out. (On the other hand, musically speaking, more than once she had shown him, as Paul Desmond's make-out alto saxophone toyed with "Two of a Mind" on the CD player, that there is only one playful curlicue of vowel between *sax* and *sex*.)

Now the band reached the end of another musical peregrination, and silence rang out.

"Prime time," someone near Mitch said. "Fre's going to play."

The band looked sour as Frelinghuysen vaulted up to share the stage, but hey, it was *his* stage. They shuffled around wanly while he went to his musical weapon of choice, which proved to be the synthesizer. Cries of encouragement chorused from the guests, Frelinghuysen deprecatingly waving them off. Then, ten of the world's richest fingers flexed themselves once, twice, and began to caress the equipment:

Pling pling pling pling pling pling pling pling pling pling pling pling NEE-NYEE pling pling pling pling pling pling NEE-NYEE pling pling pling pling NEE-NYEE pling WAH DAH DAH DEE DAH DUH . . .

That *Chariots of Fire* theme suddenly conjured a wall of runners behind Frelinghuysen, the movie's familiar slow-motion frieze of British distance runners training on the beach for a flannel-era Olympics. Except, everyone in the room caught on within nanoseconds, these were not those ancient Brits in frumpy shorts; these were younger and Lycra-clad and led by a significantly familiar figure.

The guests roared and applauded as the golden head rhythmically bounded along at the front of the pack and its still-golden current version bobbed over the keyboard.

"Fre did cross-country at Lakeside," Mitch overheard. "High school state champion."

The theme music underwent another electronic metamorphosis and abruptly another wall turned into a stadium with a cinder track, this time a newsreel-gray figure striding and striding in gawky detachment. Roger Bannister at Oxford in '54, breaking the four-minute mile. But the runner at his shoulder nobly setting the pace for him was no longer Chris Chataway, it was Frelinghuysen. Fascinated and appalled, Mitch suffered the realization that he was the only person in the room old enough to remember when Bannister's historic mile happened, rather than having it cooked into his mind by television's backward glances. He peered as hard as he could at the spectacle playing out over Frelinghuysen's fingering, but the simulation, the templates or whatever they were—the mask of Frelinghuysen shouldering history along before he was born—looked utterly seamless. Just as Bannister burst his historic tape, a mountain came into the room and two figures were loping its African slope, Kip Keino training with the playful and predatory cyber-Frelinghuysen shadowing him up through the thin air of Kilimanjaro.

When that magnificent duo scampered into a mist, Mitch thought he had endured all, but the music reverted to the movie theme's plings of portent and another beach took over a wall, this time unmistakably the Oregon coastline, broadloom of sand between forested capes and haystack rocks with surf grandly breaking. At a distance, a shimmer of tiny figures was coming. As they grew ever closer, several dozen of them undulating in the satiny running, their track uniforms took on brightness against the tan beach and green bluffs; colors from a fever dream, maroon, lemon, vermilion. By now it could be seen that two runners were moving well out in front, like the quickest in a flock of sandpipers. The righthand one, of course, was the requisite Frelinghuysen. The other was longhaired and mustached and as intense as the shaped flame of a cutting torch. Steve Prefontaine, running the sand like the die-young competitive demon he had been.

"Pre!" the party guests shouted in media-reified recognition. Then began the chant:

"Pre! Fre! Pre! Fre!"

Ai yi yi, thought Mitch, and reeled to the kitchen.

Lexa was superintending the cleanup. Scraping, washing and pouting, Kevin and Guillermo appeared to be in agony at missing the music. She sent them a look that jerked them back to their chores, then turned to Mitch. "What in the name of Elvis is going on out there?"

"New group," he reported wearily. "Cyberman and the Synthetics."

Afterward, going on out to her van and his car, Lexa provided:

"That was different."

The mutter from Mitch sounded something like:

"We can hope so."

After a couple of tries they found their way out of the lakeside maze of streets and Lexa in the lead zoomed for home. She was the type of driver who gobbled up yellow lights like grapes. After three intersections in a row flashed red in the windshield of his Honda, Mitch grabbed the car phone and punched her van's number.

"Lexa, suppose you could slow down to the speed of sound, so we can talk?"

The van ahead shot along for most of another block, then out came an arm signal he hadn't seen since the driver's ed handbook; Lexa's arm right-angled down to indicate coming to a stop. Also downpointing was her extended middle finger. After the van jarred to a halt at the next stoplight, in went her arm and her voice came over the phone:

"I thought you were in a strong silent mode tonight."

"Just because a guy doesn't say anything doesn't mean he doesn't have anything to say."

"You lost me there in the *doesn't*s. So, what's to say that can't wait until we get home?" *He wouldn't dump me by car phone, would he?* The phone clapped to her ear, she peered into the sideview mirror, trying to glimpse Mitch past his headlights. The honk of the Honda's horn made her jump. The light had turned green.

"Make up your tiny goddamned mind!" she shouted into the phone and put the van in gear.

Mitch said mildly, "I only wanted to report that I missed you like hell."

"So much so that you call me about it now that you're finally back, huh?"

"Can't you think of it as call waiting?"

"Never mind!"

They drove in silence until the VW van and the Honda sailed in file onto the Evergreen Point floating bridge, watery heavens of shoreline lights reflecting toward them on Lake Washington. As they neared the western shore, Mitch inquired: "Is this a fight?"

"It'll do until one comes along," Lexa said. "What *is* eating you?"

What could he answer—the bowels of the earth? the traitorous incisors of Bingford? his daughter the serpent's tooth? the golden gullet of ZYX?

"Been a day of win one, lose about a dozen, Lex." To start somewhere, he recited to her Bingford's scheme of turning *Cascopia* into a freebie paper.

"Wuh oh, sounds wrong from here." Commiseration instantly came into Lexa's voice. "Our family motto always was, free stuff is that price for a reason."

"It's not just the freebie part," Mitch resumed after a moment. "It's—oh, hell, you name it. Too many times up and down the field, I guess."

They drove in silence, Lexa waiting him out. *It's his damned cell call.*

85

Finally Mitch's voice arrived again, with forced brightness:

"On the other hand, I get the deck chair on the *Titanic* to myself now. Shyanne grabbed her herbarium and jumped overboard."

Goodo, at least he's not cradle robbing. Lexa gunned the van toward the next changing light, remembered and reluctantly gave in to the brakes. As the Honda's headlights eased up behind her, she put to him:

"What, then, Mitch? If it isn't just Bing giving away the store, what's freaking you? Jocelyn give you a tough go?"

"Could say that, yes. It seems I've been awarded the permanent blame for trying to limit the damage, back there when her mother and I split."

"You knew that then. It'd take brain transplants to ever get those kids of yours to change their minds about that. Maybe that's what kids are for, one of life's little ways of telling you family trees don't come cheap either. Mitch? You still do know the blame was worth it not to carve up Jocelyn and Ritz, don't you?"

"Yeah. Yeah. I was just reviewing for the test, I guess."

The Ballard neighborhood was tucked into its bungalows for the night. The vapor lights at the ship canal locks glowed blue in their nightlong duty, and there was the salt scent of Puget Sound as they parked both vehicles, bumpers nearly touching in the skimpy driveway. As Mitch came up to help carry her catering gear in from the van, Lexa broke a laugh at him.

"What now?" He peered at her in the dimness outside the house. "Were you expecting one of those Fortune 500 geeks to follow you home?"

"Can't stand to quit work tonight?" She poked an indicative finger into the stiff white fabric still tented on him.

"Yeah, well"—he glanced down at the bartender jacket he had forgotten to take off—"if you want me to say bartending is beginning to grow on me, so could fungus. Come on, let's get this stuff in. I'm about to crater."

The phone message machine on the kitchen counter was blinking red-hot as usual. Lexa headed straight for it while Mitch arrowed up to the bedroom.

"It's probably my dad," she soothed. "Reporting in from the latest footprints of Lewis and Clark."

Shucking shoes and clothes right and left in the bedroom, all he could shed of the day, he felt a craving for sleep, geysering up out of his body's subterranean regions in the form of yawns. He made it as far as pajamas before Lexa came into the room.

"Mitch?" Something in her voice. "The phone message. It was *your* dad."

He closed his eyes as if to see what it was like. Then blinked them open, looking at her with his face gone bleak.

"It would be," he said.

The
Springs

One

"MITCH? GUESS WHAT, KID. AW, YOU'RE NEVER GONNA guess. I landed a buyer."

The old hated tone of voice. Lyle Rozier proclaiming he had the world on a towrope and a downhill pull at last. Rubbing his opposite ear as if the words had gone right through him, Mitch winced into the phone that next morning. How many times had he heard this, or something an awful lot like it? There had been his father's Geiger-counter period, when uranium prospecting was going to put him on Easy Street. Then the pipe dream of raising rabbits—*Think about it, Mitch, all they do in life is copulate and populate*—to supply dog food manufacturers. Somewhere in there, that genuine-Rocky-Mountains-rustic-gateposts scheme, which skinned a hillside and everyone involved. From the sound of it here came another one, some surefire and doomed deal, Lyle style.

"Imagine that, a buyer," Mitch held himself to. "For what this time?"

The voice on the Montana end immediately rose. "The property, what the dickens do you think? The Rozier Bench!"

Mitch might have laughed if he hadn't been concentrating so hard on heading off his father's latest fit of enthusiasm.

"Better start at the start, Dad, okay? Lexa's on with us. I asked her to be."

"Oh. How's every little thing, missy?"

"Swell, Lyle," Mitch heard her say in the kitchen and echo on the phone. And more than half guessed the part she was thinking: *Do I really want to be in on a Rozier family gut spill when I'm not any kind of a Rozier?*

"The Bench deal took a while," Lyle swept on, "but we're about to close on it. Why I'm calling." Mitch's wince was sharper. The benchland at the edge of his father's town of Twin Sulphur Springs was as speckled as a pinto pigeon egg: every dot a rock, or a clump of them. Some vagary of a glacier had left the elongated heap, topographical kin to the other low flat-topped buttes of that country but so stony it grew only stray tufts of buffalo grass. All those years ago Lyle typically had not out-right purchased the acreage from the XY Ranch; he had gained title in a shortsided swap by doing the ranch's haying in exchange for the useless bald bulge of ridge. Mitch, seven or eight at the time, could recall his mother's fury, her tight repeated asking what they were supposed to use for money that summer while his father was being paid off in dirt, *no, rocks, Lyle!* And every time Lyle had answered: *Adele, it's a chance to get hold of property.*

"What's your buyer want the famous Bench for?" his skeptical son asked now.

"What it's good for. Gravel."

"Since when does that country need any more—"

"Gravel's only the gravy part of the deal, of course. That's why you've got to get yourself back here and do some eye-balling. There's all these papers, with the place here in town involved and all. You have to be in on them. You're the heir, you know."

"Wait a minute. Your *place*. You just now said the *Bench*—"

"It's all gonna go. The house. The stuff. Unless there's any of it you want. I keep telling you, that's why you've got to come and eyeball—"

"Dad, where are *you* going to go?"

"Aw, I'll think of somewhere."

Oldtimer's, Mitch thought in a panic. "Listen, don't do any-thing—don't sign anything, understand? We've got to talk all this over, do we ever, but for right now whatever you do, don't—"

"Mitch, you been listening?" Lyle's sharpness of voice did not sound like a person coming down with Alzheimer's. "I sure as the devil am not signing anything by myself; you're the one who's got to come and be in on the paper pushing. Lexa? You still there? Is his hearing all right? And if he hasn't worn his fin-gers off driving a typewriter, he can come and dab his name on a little paperwork, right?"

"He's got enough fingers left for most purposes," Lexa attested, giving Mitch a lewd grin around the kitchen door-frame. Flushed, he produced a rigid digit to her, readily enough.

"Mitch? I know you don't like coming over here much." His father spoke now in that old rhythm—bluster and wait, boost some more and take advantage—that Mitch knew like elevator music. "But this is one time you've just got to." The significant pause, then the harpoon: "Never bothered you on any of this before, now did I."

Mitch believed he could make the case that *bother* was the name of the game between them approximately the past thirty-five years. But specifically this, bunching up everything in his possession and throwing it away—no, Lyle Rozier had not resorted to this before.

"I'll . . . I can get there sometime tomorrow if it's so goddamn life-and-death. But promise me you'll sit on your hands until I show up, all right, Dad?"

"Deal," said Lyle, and hung up.

Lexa was already coming into the living room as Mitch whammed down the phone receiver. "Not much for good-byes, is he."

"I hate this! Why can't people divorce their parents!?"

His outburst drew from Lexa a gaze postmarked San Francisco and Jakarta.

"All right, all right," Mitch said with a hard swallow. He rubbed his forehead as if trying to start things moving in there. "If I'm going across the mountains to stop that father of mine from screwing up royally, I need to call Bing for time off. If there's still anything to have time off from." But he turned back from the phone to Lexa. "I don't suppose you could come along? Ride shotgun down the avalanche?"

"Can't. Mariah."

Mitch blanked on that.

"My sister is flying in," Lexa said with red-letter enunciation. "Tomorrow."

"I knew that." He sneaked a glance toward the refrigerator message center.

"Only child." Lexa shook her head. "You guys always got the whole birthday cake to yourself."

She watched Mitch stand there as if gathering himself.

"Before I go," he announced. He held out his arms and tried to smile. His voice dropped. "Hey, lady, want to wrestle even if it's with clothes on?"

She puckered as if thinking it over, then stepped into the

hug, nuzzling under his jaw with the top of her head. *So we're both in for a dose of family.* Her mind lingered on that briefly as she breathed hot encouragement into the hollow at the base of his throat.

TWO

TIME ZONES FROM SCOTLAND TO SEATTLE BALLED UP within them, the zombied passengers of flight 99 from Prestwick were being gradually disgorged from the Customs area, dragging baggage and an air of serious expenditure as they made their way toward the concourse exit, where Lexa watched as keenly as though counting sheep through a gate.

Here came a milling Elderhostel tour group with fresh crushes on one another like eighth-graders, trudged after by ruddy Scotch-faced geezers who all looked like ex-Mounties, trailed by a cloned-looking Silicon Glen clan whose minds were plainly ahead on their software presentation in Redmond—

There. Announced by her hair.

"Mariah! Over here!" Lexa lifted her right hand from its pocket perch and wigwagged it as high as she could reach.

Mariah, all footwork and grin, cut a sharp angle through the concourse crowd. Bangles probably from Timbuktu flashing from her ears, and her gray eyes the quickest anywhere.

"Hey there, cowgirl. Aren't you the sight." They hugged the breath out of each other, *mmm-mmm*ing in near-identical timbres.

The sisters pushed back to arm's length, gazing with frank investigative smiles into the family mirror they provided each other. Mariah as ever wore her contradictions like a gorgeous breastplate: she was starting to look her years, but those were only forty-two and most of them devilishly flattering to her. Her narrow quick-fox face was tanner than tan from her year of summers in both hemispheres. The fetching mouth, between tiniest parentheses of wrinkles, was expressive in more ways than one. Nose, eyes, eyebrows were the full set that had come down to her from their regal grandmother Beth McCaskill, guaranteed to still hold beauty when Mariah was twice forty-two. *Looks aren't everything,* Lexa one more time tried on in self-defense. *They're a hell of a lot, though.* She would not have bet on how she herself was holding up, but knew for sure that she would have Mariah's reading on that soon enough. She felt the familiar stir, the forcefield of all the years of love and contention. Reuniting with Mariah always gave her a buzz on, a complicated one, heart and head kicking in at different times. There was nothing remotely like it, these first minutes back together with someone you have known as long and acutely as yourself.

"Brought you stuff," Mariah was already at. "Your little Norskie bungalow is going to look like the United Nations powder room before I'm done."

"Hey, all right. In that case I didn't absolutely waste the trip to the airport." Lexa poked her sister's ribs as best she could through the protuberances of photographic gear slung on

Mariah. "Come on, you walking camera shop, let's get you home. So how was the big silver bird?"

"Can you believe it?" Mariah's hair flung vividly. "We're flying over the North Pole, there's the ice cap and the sun out on the Arctic Ocean and every iceberg in the world, and what happens but those stews—"

"—flight attendants, Ms. Politically Uncorrectable."

"—those dumb-ass stews come around asking us all to pull down our shades to watch a rerun of some freaking television program. I wouldn't do it. Would. Not. Do. It. Told them that until television gets as rare as that ice cap, I'll look out the window I paid a junior fortune for."

"You didn't happen by any chance to be *shooting*, did you?" Lexa teased.

"Me? Shoot pictures in public? Which reminds me. Jesus, you look good, squirt. Your own catering must agree with you. I want to take a bunch of new shots of you while I'm here. You and Mitch looking domestic as canaries."

"No guy around the place at the moment," Lexa started to explain; "Mitch split—"

"The bastard!" Mariah's eyebrows were up like battle flags. "What, the curse of the McCaskill sisters strikes *again*?"

"No, no, no. He split for Montana for a few days of family stuff, that father of his, is all. He'll be back as soon as—"

"The *un*bastard!" Mariah momentarily dropped a couple pieces of baggage to make an erasing motion in the air. "Saint Mitch! *Good* Mitch!"

"Damn your sweet hide, though, Mariah," Lexa said, laughing but a little spooked at the Mitch sonata; "there's still no conclusion you can't broad-jump to from a standing start, is there."

Mariah gave her younger sister a glance so affectionate it all but ruffled her hair. "Now you're sounding like our own wild card of a father."

"Listen, you're going to take the big bed, upstairs. With Mitch gone, there's no reason—"

"No, now, I'm not going to run you out of your bedroom, and that's that. Tsk, Lexa, what would a shrink make of that?"

Arguing by rote until Mariah finally gratefully surrendered, the sisters then put their strenuous selves into wrestling her baggage collection up the stairs. As they clattered back down, Lexa asked over her shoulder: "So, how long can you stay?"

"Couple days to shake the jet lag, if that's okay?"

"You bet. I can stand some company; mooch your absolute damnedest. The wonders of Ballard are at your service, Ms. Fujiship, ma'am."

The silence from Mariah caused Lexa to look around at her.

She had followed Lexa to the kitchen and propped herself in the doorway, arms crossed, lanky but enough of her in all the right places, a figure pined at by half of Montana that Lexa knew of and probably now by a goodly proportion of the world. For once, she was not wielding a camera, and the absence showed. *Hey, what, she looks—distracted, abstracted, whichever word that is,* Lexa's mental antenna went up in surprise. Mariah always arrived anywhere like a cavalry charge, and to see her retreat into herself just like that was cause for concern. Watching her, those deft long fingers holding only herself in the arms-clasped pose, the alone look of someone outside her own country still on her, Lexa had to wonder what she ought to do next toward this particular out-of-kilter kin. Like all families these days the McCaskills sometimes could get as various as trail mix—the last occasion that had brought Mariah and Lexa under the same roof was when their father had married Mariah's ex-mother-in-law. But these two, growing up together in the peopleless miles of the ranch, had known each other like set habits. Now it was always a matter of trying to keep that going. Knitting her brow in what she hoped was a significantly sisterly way, Lexa probed:

"Sorry it's over?"

Mariah blinked and stirred. "It's not, by a long shot. My so-called job is sitting there; the paper wants me back doing it the minute I get unpacked. Then there's the photo show; the Missouri River Museum is already biting my rump about that schedule. I've got a gazillion prints I have to do. And then the—"

"Whoa there. The going-around-and-around-the-world part, I meant."

"Had my fill of airplanes, that's for sure. What's up here? You feeding one of your cash-flow multitudes tonight?"

"I'm going to feed *you*," Lexa stipulated. "Just a little veggie stir-fry? And Dungeness crab? And sourdough bread?"

"Oh yes." Mariah for once sounded reverent.

"Here, earn your keep, peel some carrots."

Mariah picked up the peeler so that it balanced delicately between her thumb and forefinger like a compass needle. "Which end do I use, again?"

Lexa swatted at her with a stick of celery.

Whittling away at a carrot, Mariah mused: "Riley said once, we ate out oftener than long-haul truck drivers. You suppose indigestion was the real reason we split?"

"What do you hear of Riles?"

"Still in California committing mayhem three times a week in that column of his. And wouldn't you know, he has a radio talk show now."

Lexa's eyes went mock wide. "Since when does Riley need radio for that?"

"And?" Mariah prodded, starting to destroy another carrot. "As long as we're doing *The Exes' Files*—"

"Yeah, well, old Travis," Lexa said reluctantly. A tender area, this. All the other McCaskills, Mariah and their father and mother, had been as fond of Travis as if he was the family mascot. All the other McCaskills hadn't had to look across the table at him at every meal and wonder when he was ever going to evolve beyond boyish charm. "He's sort of Travising through life. Been put in charge of another environmental assessment of Alaska, last I knew. You watch, he'll suck his way up to being head druid in charge of paper clips yet."

They left that and yakked on while Lexa cooked and Mariah kibitzed—*So where do you want to go back to?—Mmm, that's easy. Nineteen seventy-four. You, of course, were too wet behind the ears then to remember, but Nixon got a stake driven through his putrid heart, and the Eagles' song that year was "Take It to the Limit," and I was going out with Hal Busby, finally somebody who knew how to neck, and—Quit! Geography, worldgoddamntraveler, not your own old hornyography. What'd you see that you would go back to, first?—What really got to me was the Bell Rock lighthouse.—A Scotch rock? Your favorite thing in the whole world was a Scotch rock? The Fuji folks should get a refund on you*—then they ate lustily to the inescapable tune of family catching up—*So before I left I gave my old camera bag to our beloved new stepmom Leona, the one with* MMcC *branded into it (remember?), and told her I guessed she'd have to change her name to Meona now, huh? She gave me one of her damn smiles and said that really wouldn't be hard; the tough part had been changing to McCaskill. Anyway, where are our esteemed delegates to the Lewis and Clark Bicentennial Planning Committee by now?—Uhm, somewhere south of Mandan, last postcard said. Dad claims if Lewis and Clark had traveled by motor home along with forty-eight other committee members, their expedition would've taken a whole hell of a lot longer than three years*—and finished to Mariah's groans of satisfaction and Lexa's pleased glint.

"You of course saved room for—"

"Hey, no. *Lexa.* You scamp. You didn't—"

"Coming right up. Set your mouth for it." Lexa whisked to the kitchen and the refrigerator, to come back triumphantly bearing a glass bowl of black cherry Jell-O studded with tiny pink marshmallows.

Mariah giggled as if caught peeking in a Christmas stocking. "How'd you know I *dreamed* about this stuff, the whole time I was away?"

"Oh, just a shrewd guess based on the fact that we've been sisters for a combined total of eighty-two years, going on eighty-f—"

"Shush! I'm lifting my spoon."

"Not yet, you're not. Stand back from that Jell-O, lady." Reaching into her apron pocket, Lexa quick-drew a can of Reddi Whip, piling it atop the dessert dish like berserk cumulus clouds.

"Classic," proclaimed Mariah and dove her spoon in. "Ohh. Umm. Mmm *mmm*."

"Easy, girl." Lexa cocked an eyebrow at her. "The management takes no responsibility for runaway passion at the table."

"You know me, I can abstain but I can't be moderate." Mariah paused between iceberg-sized spoonfuls. "You're having some, of course."

"Sure."

"I was afraid of that."

They wiped out the dessert in no time, then flopped down in the living room for recuperation. Lexa watched Mariah without trying to make a point of it. *There's still something; she . . .*

"I'm going to crash pretty quick," Mariah announced, giving a lusty yawn.

Her eyes met Lexa's a moment, then went reflective again.

"The bod starts to go," she mused. "I can't pull the all-nighters doing my prints like I used to, and the eight-day weeks kept catching up with me on my trip—the International Date Line *means* it, did you know that?" She stretched her every inch, managing to look like a million damn dollars while doing it, her sister thought. "We're not bulletproof anymore, Lexa."

Lexa sat bolt upright. "No kidding? Then thank God I'm the younger sister."

Another fetching yawn caught up with Mariah. "This feels

like the cut-you-off-at-the-knees kind of jet lag coming. But it's not here yet. And until it is"—she rummaged in her camera bag until she found an airline mini bottle of Lord Calvert—"I'm going to have a Lord ditch with my favorite and only sister, how about."

"Jell-O and alcohol both in one night? What's next, rolling naked on the lawn?"

Mariah didn't even have to stop to calculate before she said laughing, "Hey, kid, we've both done worse."

" 'All the world's wayward except thee and me, and thee's a little wayward,' " Lexa dramatically burred one of their grandfather's mock preacher quotes.

Ice and tap water and the regal glug of Lord Calvert departing the midget plastic bottle, pop of Lexa's wine cork and purl of pouring, then the McCaskill sisters clinked glasses and in one voice toasted: "Here's at you." Lexa waited a second to ask:

"Mariah? Meet anybody?"

"Mate anybody, you of course mean? You coupled-up types just can't get that off your mind, can you?"

"Yeah, well, that part too."

Mariah took a sip of her drink and then owned up:

"There was a New Zealander, when I was shooting on the South Island there. But nothing lasting."

"Some big something temporary, though? Mariah, I don't mean to pry, but you seem kind of—"

"Romantically exhausted?"

"—splattered against the bug screen."

Mariah stared over her motionless glass at Lexa. Finally she said: "Bingo, sweetie. It was not nice, calling it off with Colin, but I couldn't see us long-term. Met him when I was doing the Mount Cook shoot." An earring detached into her long slim hand, then the other. She jiggled the bangles in her palm a moment, a little *chingchingching* sound, then dice-tossed them onto the coffee table in front of her. "He's a glacier guide, is he ever.

More like a souped-up sherpa, really—carries people's gear up while keeping them from falling into humongous crevasses. Talks like Hillary on Everest—after every trip up and down the glacier he'll say, 'Knocked the bastard off again,' and that'll be it for about an hour. But talk about a god bod—one look at Colin and you want to start eating him with a sundae spoon."

Mariah paused in a major way.

"Lexa, he was twenty-four."

Lexa twirled her finger in a little water-down-the-bathtub motion. "I guess they don't count years counterclockwise or anything down there so you could kind of reverse toward Colin's age?"

Mariah tried with no luck at all to smother a convulsive laugh. "Girl, you are so full of sympathy."

"Serious a *secundo*, Mariah. Are you sure you can't fudge the arithmetic there a little? I mean, guys seem to think they can flip back in the calendar and get themselves a Jennifer any frigging time they feel like—"

"Twenty-four and young for his age."

"Ow."

"Colin doesn't know diddly about anything except waltzing up and down glaciers. Doesn't care about getting anything done in life except that, either. I'd try to show him what I was up to with my photo work, or talk to him about all that was involved in the museum show or doing the book, and any of that left him cold. Subzero on the ambition scale, that was Colin. But he was a beaut."

Lexa studied the sister who had told her to always let the world see those wrist scars: *They show you've been through some life.* Lately Mariah had been through some herself, had she not, leaving Bambi on the glacier.

"Book," Lexa thought to prompt. "What's the book? You've always been a shooter, not a scribbler."

Mariah swirled her drink, peering down into it as if taking a look at her hole card.

"Got a contract, honeybunch. It grew out of the print show. I'm doing a photo book of the stuff I've been racing around and around the world shooting this past year, which is to say everything."

"Oh, everything," Lexa echoed after a considerable moment. She couldn't help a bit of mischievous smile as she asked: "Gonna take up the shelf space, isn't it?"

Mariah set her drink down as if it had turned too fragile. "Okay, earthly resemblances, how about. That's what I'm up to. *Think* I'm up to. Hope to bejesus I'm up to, and can get into my shooting."

Now one of her hands worried around in her mane of hair for a moment while she looked over at Lexa. "Wasn't happy in my work, before I landed the chance to go artsy-fartsying around the world. The usual midlife shitstorm, I suppose." She shrugged just enough to punctuate that. "It's not all the *Montanian's* fault—there Missoula is, growing like crazy, and not a damn one of the new folks seems to want to subscribe to a newspaper. So the management's got problems, but they've also got thumbs for brains. Their idea of a roving photographer is 'Here, Rover, go fetch us another picture of some politician cutting a ribbon.' One reason I went after the Fuji prize so hard."

Lexa listened as though there was going to be a snap quiz later on this.

"So there I am, the world to choose from." Mariah pantomimed deadly dart throwing. "But guess what, Lexa. The more places I went, the more I kept having this sense that I'd sort of seen it before. Not like I'd been there in the vasty past; I haven't gone Shirley. But I'd be taking a picture and think, Hmm, this is familiar. Desert dunes and ocean waves. How come they're alike in the shapes they take, when they're opposites in what they're made of. Or the same with places. There I'd be in Petra—"

" '*That rose-red city*—' " Lexa chimed in grade school poem-memorizing rhythm.

" '—*half as old as time.*' " Mariah joined her in the recitation, the two of them faking little high fives at each other when done. But Mariah sobered again promptly. "And I'd shoot this really old carved-marble building or that, and I'd think, God *damn*, I've had something pretty close to this in the camera before. Mesa Verde. Totally different place, different civilization, different everything—but a certain cliff with a building tucked under, say, it could be the same cliff half a world away. Or a *sister* cliff, how about. So I started shooting pairings. How one thing goes with another. It's christly hard to do, Lexa, but it's even harder to explain. Let me think a minute."

When she had, she started:

"You remember what Jick"—their father—"used to say about the Hebners? 'All the faces in that family rhyme.' There were a bunch of families like that when you think of it. The Zanes, that long horsefaced look on every one of them? Or the way you could tell that bowlegged walk of any of the Frew family a mile off? That's what I'm after, the resemblances, the natural family of forms. I—" Mariah stopped and grinned. "What're *you* grinning at, shrimp?"

"You wouldn't just happen to have any of these so-called pictures anywhere in your plunder?"

Mariah held out her arm, wrist bent. "Twist," she begged in a royally prim tone, then jumped to her feet and began digging out prints. "Stop me after a couple hundred, okay?"

Off Africa, waves trailing their spray like white shadows; in the Gobi, a settling sandstorm dusting oceanic dunes. The sky-cutting summit shard of the Matterhorn; within the cobalt blue ice face of an Antarctic glacier, the same sharp-tipped pattern like the ghost of a mountain. Paired likeness by paired likeness,

Lexa marveled, Mariah's photographs lived up to the contours of her mind. Now she heard her clearing her throat discreetly before saying, "Colin country."

A rampart of ice and snow on Mount Cook, milk moon lending whiteness.

"Then this."

A rampart of stone, as if carved from the first azure of dusk. Lexa drew in her breath. "Jericho Reef. Wooooh."

"Hey, who's letting herself run over in public now?" Pleased, Mariah told her there were going to be a batch of such pictures of the Rocky Mountain Front before she was done with the book. Lexa barely heard.

The remembered mountains. The month of June the greenest on the calendar of memory. Trailing the sheep up. The trails were carpets into the anteroom of the sky, up from Noon Creek and English Creek, past the falling-down homesteads, up across the foothills with their stands of spriggy timber, and then *up* that really meant it, the trails climbing the mountainsides, Jericho Reef and Roman Reef and the other stone shoulders of the Two Medicine country. Lexa felt a catch at the back of her throat, time's reflex. They went horseback, she and her father, sometimes Mariah, tending the sheep camps in what they thought of as their family mountains . . .

Lexa reached again for the Southern Hemisphere moon-and-mountain picture, brought it up within inches of her eyes, compared it with the Jericho Reef shot, and made herself frown. "You're slipping, though. I knew you should have taken me along in your baggage."

"Slipping?" Mariah's voice rose. "You along, why? What for?"

Lexa turned the Mount Cook photo around and shook her head disparagingly. "No goats."

"You would bring those up."

· · ·

The launch of Mariah's photography career had been from a point of rock on a mountain named Phantom Woman. She and Lexa had lately graduated to separate horses—*Two is a lot of girls on one horse,* their father had admitted after their three-day session of arguing and elbowing while riding double on the first camptending trip to Phantom Woman—and they were making the most of their new saddle freedom by exploring off a little way along the mountain slope while their father dealt with the sheepherder. The birthday camera practically burned in Mariah's hands, she was so eager to start working it. But already she had enough of a shooting eye to know that the mountain goats grazing idly around below that rocky reach of Phantom Woman were prime picture material, if they would just show more of themselves than they ever did.

"What would be neat," Mariah mused, "is if they'd get up on that rock, the saps."

"Make them," Lexa surprised her with.

"Oh, sure, herd mountain goats? Ninny, you can't do with them like a band of sheep, they're wild anim—"

"You don't *know?*" Lexa was ecstatic with secret knowledge. "Nancy told me!"

What Nancy Buffalo Calf Speaks, old and blind and murmuring out of her Blackfoot past, had passed along to Lexa worked like a charm. That summer the promontory rock turned into Grand Central Station for mountain goats, goats sniffingly curious, goats profoundly bemused, goats in winsome family groupings, goats in spectacular horned solo glory against the cliff line of the Rockies, roll after film roll of perfect posing goats. Mariah had pictures all summer long in the *Gros Ventre Gleaner,* the *Hungry Horse News,* the *Choteau Acantha,* and ultimately when the Associated Press picked one up, statewide.

The great goat success brought the girls attention from closer sources as well. Their father came home one day from paying a visit to the English Creek district ranger station and promptly paid them one.

Jick McCaskill looked down from under his everyday Stetson at his goat-tamer daughter Mariah and her probable accomplice Lexa. He said as if thinking out loud:

"Ranger McCaskill—your otherwise doting granddad— has the notion you young ladies are baiting his mountain goats." Jick studied from one picture-innocent daughter to the other. "Which upsets him all to hell. I am apt to get that way myself. Among other things, baiting goats is against about forty kinds of federal law."

Lexa could just feel the tug-of-war going on in Mariah, whether or not to make some smart crack about little sisters at least being good for goat bait. Loyalty, backed up by Lexa's warning stare, won. Mariah tossed her hair back over her shoulders to look up at their father and said:

"How would we? You mean, like with cheese?"

"That is what we don't know, Ranger McCaskill and myself." Jick inventoried them again. "Our best guess is rock salt. But how the two of you could lug a block of that up—"

Mariah and Lexa were shaking their heads in unison.

Oats? barley? cottonseed cake?—each commodity suggested by their father drew another synchronized head shake from the girls.

"Well, then, now," he said, at last out of list and patience both. "Lexa, whatever it is you've been up to, cut it out, hear? As for you, Mariah, you can figure that you've now got all the pictures of goats you're ever going to need in one lifetime, and it can remain a mystery why they like to prance right up and pose on that same one rock for you. Savvy?"

The girls did, although what their male forebears never did manage to savvy was that Lexa's formula for making mountain goats line up and sniff with curiosity consisted of squatting here and there on that particular rock and simply peeing.

. . .

"Here's the last thing I was working on," Mariah was saying. She handed over a solo print.

The ocean looked like cloud, with a tall turreted shaft planted amid it like a lordly summoning horn being stood in the corner between uses.

"Alexander McCaskill's lighthouse, my dear Alexandra. The Bell Rock."

The graceful slender implantation of stone a hundred feet high looked no less impossible in the glossy photo than it must have on the vellum plans drawn in 1807. The Bell Rock lighthouse, off the east coast of Scotland, had to rise from the slightest spur of reef, which vanished with each high tide; to build there was to steal firmament from the ocean. One of those stonemasons who had dared to lay granite on unwilling water at Bell Rock was their grandfather's *great*-grandfather.

"Our own family stuff in the album of everything? Pretty sneaky even for you, Mariah."

"You know what I was going to pair it with? The Black Eagle stack."

Lexa studied Mariah. "Maybe your body clock is farther out of whack than you think. They dynamited that—"

"—years ago. You bet your rose-red booty they did. It's even worse than that, Lexa—I was there taking pictures of that sucker when they blew it up. Umm, down."

The gigantic smokestack of the Black Eagle smelter would start to show above the curve of the central Montana horizon as you drove within fifty miles of Great Falls and its Black Eagle hill, a smoking beacon against the sky. Lexa well remembered the silly but disorienting sensation of missing that manmade landmark, pole magnet to the eye for an hour at a time on any car trip, the first time she went back to the Two Medicine country after the divorce from Travis.

Mariah was thinking out loud:

"I was going to use it as—I don't know, the runaway version of something like Bell Rock. Signatures on the horizons. The lighthouse sending its signals out to sea, all nice-nice . . . the Black Eagle stack taking over a piece of country about the size of Scotland and saying, Hey, we're the biggest furnace in the world here, we're smelting the copper guts right out of Montana. Anyway, so much for that pairing."

Highly cameraed up, their father had been known to say of Mariah's approach to life. *Taking on the whole world with it now,* Lexa mused. *That's Mariah for you.* With this flame-haired sister, when life wasn't heart heart heart, it was job job job.

Mariah's eyelids closed, then opened reluctantly as Lexa watched. "*Now* I'm crashing," Mariah admitted. "Where's that blessed bed you're forcing on me?"

Three

WHEN THE MIDDLE NAME OF YOUR HOMETOWN IS SUL-phur, there is not much you can do about the smell of your childhood.

Two generously pungent ponds burbling away at the temperature of warm soup convinced Mitch Rozier's forebears that the place would spawn an American version of Baden-Baden, but Twin Sulphur Springs turned out to be another teetery Western town, stunted by distance, regularly put upon by tough weather barreling down out of the Rockies, and to the sorrow of the first three generations of Roziers, devoid of earthly wealth except that pair of thermal swimming holes. By the time Mitch was blinking his way into his teens, his father Lyle was reduced to bossing a crew of rock pickers on the glacial benchlands north of town where hard sod had been cut up into grainfields. Out there on the rock pile it did not seem much of a debate whether Twin Sulphur Springs ought to be regarded as an unspawned spa with a healthy mineral aroma to it or one more West Nowhere with the added detriment of smelling like eggs gone bad.

So, Mitch took away with him a kind of bitter awe that his father never once wavered from that life, those stoneboats that you could heap high springtime after springtime and still have a world of rocks amid the alien grain, then the haying contract every summer at so much per ton but never as many tons as anticipated, then the mad dashes of trucking in the harvest each fall if the white combine—hail—hadn't claimed the grain first. Winter, though, when his father was cooped up in town, was the season hardest to get through. Mitch dreaded suppertime, coming home from scrub basketball practice and right away being dispatched by his mother to play fetch. Across town he would go, between the springs steaming side by side in Artesia Park, their aroma barely clearing from his nose by the time he reached the V.F.W. club. Fluorescent dusk in there, the men along the bar drinking with their hats on as Mitch edged in. Lyle Rozier holding forth, you could count on it.

"Wouldn't you know. Here's my heir apparent, with orders from headquarters. Hey, Fritz"—or Mike or Monte or whoever else had once had the fate of being shipped overseas; New Guinea was Lyle's own chapter of foreign war—"how do you think this kid of mine is gonna stack up? Needs another year or two and some pounds on him to really handle rock, but maybe he'll amount to a hay hand, what do you think?"

Supper ready at home, now to grow cold while his mother's temper heated up. Mitch tried, "Mom said—"

"I can pretty much guess what she said." Just the right tinge in his father's words to draw a general laugh along the bar.

He would not forget standing there, raw as a stripped willow, watching as his father didn't budge on the bar stool except to dig in the shirt pocket where his smokes were kept. Then the bright crack of a match against his father's horn-colored thumbnail, new sulphur whiff filling the boy's nostrils as Lyle lit up another Lucky and ordered another beer. "We'll go before you know it, son," Lyle Rozier was saying, while Mitch was already more than halfway to his own verdict of stay or go.

And the minute you come back, the Mitch of now was thinking to himself by way of his nose, you wonder how Proust could encounter the wafts of the past and get a butter cookie out of it.

As if by family mandate he had been driving the twisty old highway from Choteau somewhat too fast, but well ahead of time he braked hard for the bridge at the Soda Creek curve and its miserably unbanked turn where the half-dozen white highway fatality crosses had accumulated across the decades. This time of year the road was dry, and with the advent of antilock brakes the bad curve was not necessarily lethal anymore. At the start of the winter of 1962, however, his mother's big tail-finned Chrysler apparently had skidded like crazy before wrapping itself and her around the concrete bridge abutment. Barely two miles out of town, Adele Rozier had already built up speed on another of her impromptu getaways to the Sweetgrass Hills, three hours away on the northern horizon, to simmer down for a few days or a week with the accommodating aunt and uncle who had raised her. By the county coroner's estimation she was dead in the time it took for the noise of the crash to carry to the nearest farmhouse. Cause of death: black ice. Mitch had been sixteen when his mother's car wreck came on top of everything else, there in that strange set of years that still were the longest in his life.

Past the Soda Creek curve the highway drew a dead aim on

Twin Sulphur Springs, the yellow striped line a straight shot to the bumptious gazebo in Artesia Park at the far end of town. Beyond, as if keeping their wary distance, sat the Rocky Mountains. Now Mitch drove with excessive care—this section of road was unevenly patched from frost heaves—and used the time into town to let his eyes graze. The country here was ledger-line flat on both sides of the highway and yet not in sum; the bumpy edges of benchlands protruded everywhere like knees of reclining Gullivers. Grainfields whose more natural crop was cantaloupe-sized rocks had been farmed into all the bench tops but one, the hopelessly pebbly elongated rise showing above the park at the west edge of town, and that was the Rozier Bench.

Mitch glanced at it one more time and pondered, *Dad, why? And don't tell me, "Because."* The lone thing the family property supported was the high school's big white rock letters *TSS,* repainted springtime after springtime by senior classes of varying artistic temperaments. Mitch's father had always got a kick out of acting civic, particularly if it didn't cost anything or, better yet, paid off somehow. Among Lyle Rozier's endeavors had been the contentious term he served as county commissioner, long enough to get a number of roads paved at the Twin Sulphur Springs end of the county and coincidentally one of them right out to the Rozier Bench. Currently his chosen connived post was as county brand inspector. Mitch shook his head. One Rozier trotting around to ever-diminishing cattle ranches, another dedicated to the vanishing species called newspapers. *Stuff like that can't run in a family. Can it?*

As he pulled into town, it seemed to him even more shabby than the last time he had been here, no more than half a year ago. A fast-food delivery truck was backed up to its first port of call, the Town Pump, *Gas–Groceries–Videos–Electronic Poker.* The aquamarine post office, Uncle Sam's cinder block contribution, squatted next to the old community hall that was now the senior center, with a wheelchair ramp put on like a hasty patch. In the squeeze-tube line of enterprises that squibbed out toward visitors approaching any American municipality anymore, the only new business Mitch could spot was a small medical equipment supply store, there to supply oxygen for emphysema sufferers. Any other change in a town like this was probably something vanishing. Until the statute of limitations on athletic fame ran out how ever many years ago, there had been a weathered sign at the town line proclaiming STATE CLASS B FOOTBALL CHAMPIONS 1963. Mitch's last game here, the Class B play-off. It came down to the Springs wind and Mitch. The Forsyth Dogies looked stunned when a typical gust stalled their point after touchdown, the kick in mid-air, the football fading like a shot duck. In the ungodly weather, next thing to winter, all game long Mitch made yardage against them in that deceptive drifting style of his, running faster than he looked to be, then pouring on a bit more speed yet. The Forsyth Dogies got back on their school bus with the wind fanning their whipped butts.

At least they beat me out of here. All too aware that the downtown face of the Springs on a bright afternoon of this sort was like being in a stucco desert, he took the backstreet to his father's place. Even so he had to skirt Artesia Park on the way. The fume of the twin springs and the gazebo needing paint and the bald patches of what had been intended to be lawn were everything he remembered. *Well, what could you expect?* he addressed the convention of ghosts in his mind. Come out here and create an unnecessary town from scratch and that's what it was going to look like, scratch.

He pulled up in front of the house. His father's pickup was not there, but rolling stock of several other kinds abounded around the place—vestigial tractors and several generations of self-stacking hay bale haulers (none of which, Mitch recalled, ever worked worth a damn), and the power buckrake his father had driven before bale-stacking gizmos came into vogue, and the truck of all purposes called the Blue Goose, now mostly rust. Lyle Rozier's knickknack drawer was his yard.

The skeletal traffic jam aside, the Rozier place looked barely populated. The four wavery aspens out front that his father forever fed agricultural fertilizer were the thinnest of sentries. The house itself seemed gaunt, life only in its lower half; the upstairs, you could tell from the hazy unwashed windows, was a deck of unoccupied bedrooms. Downstairs, the ancient lacy curtains hung like doilies on a packing crate. Mitch climbed out of the Honda and walked down the gravel driveway toward the kitchen door. There was the large gray canker in the soil not many feet from the kitchen steps, where in the time before sewers and garbage collection reached this end of town his family tossed the wash water and stove ashes, and for that matter emptied the slop pail. The lye of the soap and ashes had killed the ground for good.

As if suspecting that kind of behavior, the Aronson house next door had a newly built bay window bulging like a vigilant eye. Whatever had got into the Aronsons, the paint on their place also looked suspiciously fresh. With particular wariness Mitch sized up the new fence of shellacked jackstays between the houses.

"Are you the son?"

The accentless voice across the fence belonged to a carefully maintained man of about forty, wearing a brushed-denim shirt which cost about the same.

He ducked adroitly through the poles of the pristine fence and whipped out an earnest handshake. "I'm Donald Brainerd. We're next door now."

"Mitch Rozier," Mitch reluctantly owned up to. He nodded toward Brainerd's spruced-up house. "When did the Aronsons pull out?"

"Last December. We came up from Boise in time for winter. I thought we should test that out." Brainerd seemed to be trying to do a fair assessment of Twin Sulphur Springs' brand of winter. "It wasn't as bad as all the predictions."

"One will be," Mitch forecast with no effort, "if you stick around."

"Oh, we're here to stay. I can run my consulting business mostly by E-mail and cell phone—FedEx when I have to. Nice to be able to do that and have all this, too." Brainerd indicated proprietorally toward the Rockies behind Mitch.

Mitch turned around to them, the distant but sharp-edged skyline up over the Rozier Bench. Mountain by mountain they took hold of his gaze. He knew them from boyhood and could still name each one, from southmost Cathedral Reef with its gray-blue upthrust calling on the sky, to the mammoth pachyderm lobe of Ear Mountain, to the distinctive stone ramparts north in the Two Medicine country, Roman Reef and Jericho Reef, with the profile of Phantom Woman Mountain presiding between. Mountains of an older order than the Coast's volcanic apprentices; folded, palisaded, scarped. And up there along the Divide of the continent extended the Bob Marshall Wilderness, named for that bat-eared Mozart of the national forests, roaming and rhapsodizing. Right now Mitch wished that more people had seen along with Bob Marshall that this neck of the earth was always going to be a country of great mountains and mediocre human chances.

Reluctantly leaving the sight of the mountains, Mitch turned around to deal with next door.

"Your father is something of a character."

Mitch glanced toward the hard-used Rozier house, then toward Brainerd's modernized little house on the prairie. "Everybody is, in a certain light."

"I have to tell you, we're concerned." Brainerd let his voice drop as if sympathetic to Mitch's plight. "I'm glad you're here; we thought we might have to call you."

"What about?—isn't he all right? I talked with him on the phone just—"

"I didn't mean healthwise. He tore out of here in that pickup as usual this morning." Brainerd frowned past Mitch. "It's the appearance of the place. Wouldn't a reasonable person say it's . . . overcrowded?"

Mitch turned and joined in Brainerd's appraisal.

"No," his rewrite instinct kicked in. " 'Junk laden' is more like it."

Brainerd cleared his throat. "Everything sits right there, out our window."

Mitch's eyebrows went up. "You're not telling me my father moved all his junk into view the instant you bought your place, are you? That'd have been the biggest sonofabitching deployment since Desert Storm."

"We were led to believe his collection comes and goes. It seems mostly to come."

Mitch put on an expression of sympathy. Ah, the troublesome life of the window Westerner. Those gorgeous purple mountains and the Lyle Roziers of the world in the way.

Already tired of changing sides—he had been in his father's teeter-totter of a town now for, what, fifteen minutes?—Mitch gave the neighbor a look with some shoulder to it. "Donald?" he said as if it was a guess. "I'm here to see about straightening some things up. Give me a little time with my father."

Brainerd ducked back through the jackstay fence looking unsatisfied but not surprised either, and Mitch went on into the house.

He knew that his father was no housekeeper, but the sludge of items had grown to geological proportions. Newspapers were stacked like hay bales. Amid the multiple months' worth of the *Great Falls Tribune* and the *Choteau Acantha*, Mitch was startled to spot past issues of *Cascopia,* then remembered that he long ago had sneaked his father's name onto the subscription list. Why on earth had he thought it was a good idea to give Lyle a weekly reminder of the gulf between their two lives?

Old machinery parts congregated comfortably on end tables and sideboards as if visiting from the backyard. Seasons of clothing were tossed onto hooks on the wall, Lyle's red-and-black plaid winter cap with earflaps mashed over his fishing hat.

Amid it all, a once-green easy chair showed a seat which sagged to the exact fit of Lyle Rozier's venerable rump. An almost as venerable bunny-ear television set, probably Ed Sullivan and Dagmar painted on the cave walls inside it, sat under a startling new VCR box no more than arm's length from the easy chair. Was his father's eyesight going, too?

Mitch unabashedly prowled. Christmas cards were still lined up in the bay of the window. The UNESCO one he and Lexa— all right, Lexa—had sent. A few with names Mitch recognized from around town. Then one with the shaky inscription *Wishing you another year on top of the ground, old Sarge. Your pal, Fritz.* Mitch made a mouth; Fritz Mannion, another single-handed winner of World War II, wherever he was now. *One time out on patrol old Fritz tripped, saved our lives,* Lyle's voice echoed from the past. *I of course went to help him up, and here's this movement in the jungle just ahead. Got my rifle around on it in a real hurry, but Ferragamo behind me beat me to it by about a trigger squeeze. He had that BAR going, the Jap never knew what hit him. I didn't even have to fire, Joe'd almost cut the guy in half already. Hadn't been for Fritz's big feet, though, that Jap would have ventilated us for sure.*

Fritz's scratchy remembrance, and a stamped greeting from the electrical co-op, and the few others: Mitch wondered if Lyle cared that the handful of cards was a sad collection, or even noticed.

His father's desk in the far corner of the living room—the "neutral corner"—was as laden but organized as ever. And unlike any other appurtenances in this household, the daybooks ranked on the long shelf above the back of the desk were kept free of dust. The ledgers of Lyle's crews, year by year.

1962 was inked on the spine of one in a hand different from the rest. For that matter, the teenage boy's hand that had so carefully written those numbers was different from the grown Mitch's now, was it not?

He felt the urge to pull out the daybook and flip through its pages, but why start that again. Names of crews, marching down the ledger lines, and their days of work tallied across the wide double pages of each month, that was all the thing held. Fritz and Ferragamo both were in there. Hayfield warriors, that indelible summer, still serving under old Sarge Lyle Rozier.

In spite of himself, Mitch drew down the daybook and opened it to the first crew of that year. *April: rock picking* recorded in his father's neat hand. Unlike everything else, the bookkeeping in the Rozier household had always been meticulous. Except.

He heard a vehicle crunching into the driveway. The pickup that ground to a halt outside the bay window was the latest in his father's succession of faded Smokey the Bear green rigs, bought every few years when the U.S. Forest Service auctioned off used surplus. Lyle Rozier despised the Forest Service and all other government agencies that kept people like him away from the big piñata of natural resources in this country, but the pickups were a bargain he couldn't pass up.

Mitch watched his father step from the pickup cab as if measuring the distance down to earth from his preferred automotive eminence, then hold the door open for his passenger, his deaf border collie Rin. Next, a groove of behavior Mitch would have recognized from a dozen blocks away—Lyle turned, lifted his head a notch and took a deep, deep sniff. So far as Mitch had ever known there was no physical reason for that habit, nothing wrong with his father's magisterial nose; he simply seemed to feel entitled to an extra share of the air every so often.

Looking around as if he had all the time in the world, Lyle eased back, propped himself against the fender, lit a cigarette, and took a deep drag. Mitch realized his father was going to wait there for him.

As he stepped out the kitchen door, Lyle peered up from under his battered brown Stetson. "You made it."

"Looks that way, doesn't it. How you doing, Dad?"

"Not bad for the shape I'm in." The identical answer he had been giving for the half a century Mitch personally knew of.

They shook hands, still awkward at it as if they had mittens on.

Of Lyle Rozier, many would have said *big-headed*, but to put it as neutrally as possible, his hat had a great plenty to rest on. The Rozier box of face, as his son all too ruefully knew, could not be called distinguished but certainly qualified as distinctive, full of surprising promontories. There was such a thing as a Rozier jaw, blunt and stubborn as the plows of the French peasants who passed it on; and definitely a Rozier nose; and cheekbones broad enough to substantiate the rest of the foursquare proportions. This one-man Mount Rushmore face had been Lyle's asset, if not yet his fortune. The worn lines even improved it, the way an Anasazi cliff dwelling seems more natural because it's ancient. (Not that his father was ancient, Mitch reminded himself. There could be an exhausting number of years of Lyle left to deal with.) The problem of the eyes, though.

The bluesteel eyes which Mitch met again, now as always, with a stir of resentment at the weight of presumption under those Roman senatorial lids. His father's drill-bit way of looking at you as if he had seen you before you put your clothes on this morning and knew just what you were covering up.

Crutches and a snowy new walking cast had been unexpectedly useful to Mitch as camouflage, that distant evening of the picnic supper in the park. After the monumental broken leg had kept him in bed all summer he at last was up and around and giddily aware of the new reaches of his body. Mitch did not yet know enough to put it this way, but he was finding it intriguing to be around himself: the growth spurt that would change him so hard he sometimes would ache out loud—change him from a sixteen-year-old inadvertent cripple into a seventeen-year-old who threatened the dimensions of doorways—was in full spate. And still thrumming in him too was the somewhat scary sense of apprehension (it all had happened too quick to be called fright; mortal instillment of awe, more like) at the fashion in which fate had idly snapped his leg in two places. But that was almost over-ridden now by this steady amazing tide of growing up: every day a strength of some kind that he hadn't known he had. The crutches of course were bastards to handle at first, but he had overpowered even them in a hurry, his shoulders and arms mastering the swing that carried the plaster weight of the leg along with ease, his hands calloused enough from the relentless squeezing exercises he'd done on the bedpost knobs to not be bothered by the harsh wood of the crutch grips.

His father and even his mother were determinedly socializing with the crew at the picnic supper that Saturday before haying was over; a Rozier family tradition, and there weren't many. The customary crowd of a dozen had the park to themselves there in the late-summer dusk and were visiting with one another almost as if they had not had every day of the haying season together to do so. But wives of the crew always came too, welcome additions, jolly Mabel Tourniere down from Gros Ventre, and up from Great Falls, Janine Ferragamo, a peaches-and-cream redhead beside her dark quiet husband Joe. The unmarried men were on their best behavior, handling everything like eggshells; as far as Mitch could remember, even Fritz Mannion stayed heroically sober for the duration of the picnic.

His walking cast, still fresh, invited everybody's autograph.

"Private Mannion!" his father teased Fritz. "Still remember how to make your *X*, do you?" Fritz whinnied a laugh, protested to his old sergeant that he was entirely capable of providing name, rank and serial number, and with laborious penmanship did so.

When it came her turn, Mrs. Ferragamo thoughtfully leaned over and scanned for an untaken place to write her name on the plaster. Mitch without even trying could see way down her summer dress to—surprise, surprise—twin treats of forbidden skin playing peekaboo with him from where they were barely hidden in a turquoise blue brassiere.

The time it took Janine Ferragamo to sign her name was all too soon over, and everybody began sitting up to the fried chicken and three-bean salad and all the rest. Each table had space for half a dozen, so his father joined in with the unmarried men and his mother presided at the table where Mitch sat.

His mother was at her best in a crowd like this. She always took care to ask each of the crew wives to bring a potluck dish of some kind, so they would feel in on the occasion, and she laughed readily, instead of seeming to examine every conversation for booby traps the way she did at home. Now she simultaneously kidded about how starved Mitch was all the time and made sure he did justice to his food. In the natural way of things, then, he could sit there propping his leg along the bench and look like he was following the yakking of Tom Tourniere and Joe Ferragamo beside him, and his mother's chitchat with Mrs. Tourniere next to her, all the while able to drift his gaze catercorner across table toward Mrs. Ferragamo.

Until this day he had not known there was such a thing as a brassiere the color of turquoise.

Here was another talent he hadn't known he had, these innocent tumbleweed glances, while he worked on the matter of how good-looking Mrs. Ferragamo—the *rest* of Mrs. Ferragamo—really was. Beyond pretty, he knew that much. Although he didn't think beautiful; Julie Christie in whatever the name of that foreign movie was, that constituted beautiful. No, Mrs. Ferragamo was, how could he classify it, cuter than was to be expected, sort of the way a cheerleader's looks improved when you realized she was a cheerleader, even though in Mrs. Ferragamo's case she had to be almost his mother's age and with Joe, of course, on the scene, very much a married woman.

All at once Mitch felt something riding him piggyback.

He turned half around to the load of his father's eyes on him. No frown behind them, no wink. Simply letting his son know that he had been caught at it. Mitch was pretty sure that look of his father's had brought him those sergeant stripes in the war.

He felt himself redden, and redden some more, burn from the knowledge of that gaze.

Unblushing toward his father all the years since, Mitch said now:

"So here I am, heir to the fortune in gravel. What's this about a buyer for"—he cast a glance around the ramshackle place—"the Rozier chateau and grounds?"

Lyle cleared his throat. "Kind of keep your voice down, okay? Not just everybody knows about this gravel deal."

"Like, say, Donald Brainerd?"

"Already met the improvement to the neighborhood, did you." Lyle tossed down his cigarette and ground it into the driveway. It always surprised Mitch to see work shoes on his father. His type of strut you would think could only spring from cowboy boots.

"Lexa said to tell you she's sorry she couldn't come and watch the gravel fly."

"I bet."

At last Lyle unmoored from the pickup fender. "Let me show you a little something interesting." Off he marched to the nearby shed. He was moving more slowly and stiffly than the last time Mitch had seen him, but he still went as arrowstraight as if on a parade ground.

Lyle threw open the double doors to the machine shed, which held a maze of metal but not a bit of it machinery. Skinny rods each about three feet long with exotic bends at their ends were in tangled iron pyres on the floor, in rust-streaked downpours on one wall and in dangling black stalactites from the rafters. The place looked like a case history of ferrous extrusion gone mad.

By the opposite wall stood a cheerful red barbecue grill, half a sack of charcoal beside it; into that wall were burned hundreds of sets of the hieroglyphics that once had been seared onto herds of cattle and horses, Tumbling T's and Walking 7's, Barbed Y's and Rocking O's, Dice 8's and Rafter S's and all the rest of what was evidently an entire capering glossary of this menagerie.

"Branding irons," Lyle pronounced in a remnant of his sergeant voice.

"I see they are." Mitch picked up a couple of the brands waiting to be heated in the grill, clattering a Quarter-Circle R against a Lazy A. "You've been hard up for a hobby, I guess."

"Hobby!" Lyle's voice cracked from indignation. "These're business. I sell them. Every guy new to this country is gonna want one, you just watch and see."

"And they're going to do what with them, swat snakes?"

"Mitch. It's not just the iron," Lyle said with terrible patience. "Think about it. I sell the whole brand, registration and all. Gives guys the right to call their ranchettes the Bar BQ or whatever the heck if they buy the brand, now doesn't it. They can legally put it on the kid's pony, paint it on their Jeep Cherokee, all that."

A familiar dread filled Mitch. "But you've been the county brand inspector, right?"

"Sure have. And I know just what you're going to yip about next. But this isn't whatchacallit, conflict of interest."

"Maybe not, but you can pretty easily see it from here." Mitch gaped around again at the metal mess, with an equal legal tangle doubtless somewhere behind it. "There can't be much of a living in selling branding irons."

Lyle's expression turned hedgy. "Sort of one."

Mitch gestured violently at the collection. "Where'd you come up with all these? What'd you use for money?"

"Oh, I see what you're driving at," Lyle said, lowering his voice. "Took out a mortgage on the place. And the property, of course," with a pleased nod in the direction of the benchland. "See, though, that's the beauty of selling the Bench. Pay off the mortgage and hang on to the branding iron collateral and still come out ahead." He studied the expression on his son, then admitted: "It's a little complicated."

Mitch could almost feel tentacle after tentacle of litigation and forfeiture wrapping around his knees. *Lawyer, banker, gravel man, grief.*

"Dad, the paperwork you want me in on." He was trying to fight off the perverse hope that his father *was* certifiably losing his mind; dementia might be the best defense, the way the case of Lyle Rozier versus the contractual world seemed to be going. "Don't you think I ought to start looking that over?"

"Sure, sure. Head on into the house, make yourself at home if you remember how. I have to detour by the pickup a minute."

Again in that first-floor attic that was the living room, Mitch gazed around for some spot clear enough to work. After the helter-skelter cargo of branding irons and the general strew outside, his father's desk looked more than ever like the unnaturally tidy bridge on a tramp freighter.

"I can still keep book, anyway," Lyle's voice came. He unhurriedly followed that commentary in from the doorway, hanging up his hat on one of the already full coat hooks without looking as he passed.

Mitch gave a grudging grin, or a grimace.

Lyle fussed around at the desk, moving this ream and that. Mitch watched this uncharacteristic bout of squint and dither, then glanced once more at the television set so suspiciously close to his father's easy chair. He had the sudden inspiration that maybe a lawyer could prove that his father had worn out his eyes on that electronic additive atop the TV, hundreds of video viewings of *The Sands of Iwo Jima,* most likely. Eyesight, Your Honor. He couldn't see well enough to read the fine print; our defense is this eye chart.

"Getting a lot of use out of your VCR?" Mitch casually asked.

Lyle seemed delighted to contradict him. "VCR, nothing. Ever heard of the Web?"

Gingerly he crossed the room and picked up the WebTV remote control, poised over it as if trying to remember the fingering on an accordion, then hit enough buttons to bring up a display of icons on the screen of the television.

Mitch was still staring at the pixelated portholes of the Internet when his father let drop:

"I talk with Ritz on there quite a lot."

My Ritz? Laurits? The vagabond of Jakarta? A pang shot through Mitch and quivered there, but he tried not to give his father the satisfaction of seeing it. "Is that a fact. What about?"

"Been keeping him up to date whenever I sell a branding iron. He seems to get a kick out of it. Way we got started, I just was curious what he thought of that part of the world—you know, I was out in some of those islands during the war. I thought it was sort of interesting he's over there, too." Noticing the look on Mitch, he further reported: "Can't seem to get connected with Jocelyn, though, at that advertising outfit."

"That was twenty minutes ago. She's, shall we say, rolled

along. Then tell me"—*you're the expert on the far-flung Rozier family all of a cybernetic sudden*—"how Ritz is doing."

"He sounds real good on the E-mail. Busy, teaching and all. Turned vegetarian, but I guess that happens anymore?"

Now Lyle hesitated, evidently trying to shape his next news. "Mitch? These days you can do a search on there, you know. Find just about anybody anywhere. Matthew helped me with it on Ritz. Brainerd's kid, although you can hardly tell it."

Of the making of terrifying contracts there was almost no end, Mitch found as he immersed himself in his father's accumulated sheafs. The stacks of gilt-edged conveyances of cattle brands to *aforesaid Lyle Rozier* appeared dismally irrevocable, Mitch finally deciding he would have to lug the whole smear off to the county seat, Choteau, and throw it all to the mercy of a lawyer. (Lyle meanwhile had done some reflecting on his claim of nonconflict of interest: "Most of those brands, Mitch, I bought outside this county. Some, anyway.") The proposed deal on the proportion of his father's worldly possessions that weren't branding irons took him a good while longer to parse through, but the half-inch-thick set of papers indeed seemed to add up to an offer from Aggregate Construction Materials, Inc., to buy the bench-land and what was called concomitant residential property. The money wasn't great, but it was better than might be expected for a rock pile and this badger den of a house.

Mitch sat back. As much as he hated to go near the legal jungle with anything as blunt-edged as logic, there was this to be asked:

"And what are they going to do with your glorious gravel?"

"Roads."

The Alzheimer's-has-got-your-daddy alarm went off in Mitch again. He took a long hard look at Lyle, then leaned around him to peer out at the trafficless street.

"Naw, not around town here." Lyle waved away his son's quizzical frown. "Up there." He inclined his head in the direction of the mountains, watching Mitch. "Aggregate's betting there's going to be gas and oil wells. Those leases along the reefs, you know. Could happen."

Mitch felt like he'd hit an air pocket.

"Can't pave into that country," Lyle was going on. "But they can lay down some gravel. Keep them from cutting ruts four feet deep, look at it that way."

"In the *Bob*? They're going to drill in a wilderness area? How the hell can they get away with that?"

"Of course not *in*," Lyle stipulated. "Next to, up against, I guess you could say. Alongside." Mitch goggled at his father, this walking dictionary of helpful locutions when it came to draining the life out of wilderness.

"Listen, Dad. Those so-called energy leases, don't get your hopes up. There's Forest Service hearings and environmental impact statements and fifty kinds of bureaucratic decisions to be made before anything like that can even begin to—"

"Those're being made. Else why is Aggregate so hot for our gravel?"

Point taken. Somebody besides Lyle Rozier was counting on gas and oil rigs trundling into the Rocky Mountain Front, or there wouldn't be this half an inch of legalistic blandishment sitting here on the table, would there. Every reporting hair on Mitch was standing at attention. He knew this was a "Coastwatch" natural, although geography would need a little amending—the Rocky Mountains as the sister shores of Malibu. But you think about it and that's absolutely what they once were, in glacial times: inland seas comparable to the Great Lakes pooled up on both sides of the Rockies in that era of massive freeze and melt. And where there had been vastnesses of water like that, of course there had also been reefs, the rock enfoldments up there along the Bob that had trapped the oil and gas deposits which

Aggregate and the energy speculators now were doing their damnable best to tap.

It abruptly came back to Mitch that "Coastwatch" and *Cascopia* were about as gone as the Ice Age. He drew what he hoped was a steadying breath. The other question presented by the Aggregate paperwork still gnawed, however. One more time he turned to his father, Houdini of deals:

"The wonderful world of gravel aside, okay? Why is Aggregate in the housing market for this place?"

"Because I told them no deal no way on the Bench property unless they took this, too. It's all got to go. We can make a clean sweep of it, Mitch, don't you see?"

"What I don't see is where you think you're going to *live* if you toss away this place, Dad!"

"Aw, something will come along," Lyle said as casual as a touring baron.

The fear he had not wanted to think about surfaced in Mitch. Did his father intend to come live with him? (And of course Lexa, who definitely had never signed on for shared occupancy with Lyle Rozier. And add in Ingvaldson, who was sourly suspicious of any fellow codger who didn't qualify as Norwegian.) Mitch could not help but remember the occasion, pre-Lexa, when Lyle had deigned to come to Seattle for a visit and, instantly bored, spent his time either using a metal detector to hunt for lost pocket change in the sand at Golden Gardens beach or sitting in on juicy cases in divorce court. Most of all Mitch recalled the kind of thing that had occurred when the young woman clerking at the Safeway made the mistake of complimenting his father on the gold-rimmed extra-green sunglasses he had on:

"*Why, thanks, missy. Know where I got them?*"

"*They're really rad! Where?*"

"*Off a dead Jap in the South Pacific.*"

"*H-h-have a nice day, sir.*"

In the here and now, Mitch resorted to a suggestion which many another hale geezer or geezelle out here had managed to hit upon for themselves:

"Were you maybe thinking of getting yourself a double-wide?"

An unexpected glint came into Lyle. "Now there's a real interesting choice," he commended, as if the idea of a retirement mobile home was major original thinking by his son. "Let's sort of deal with that as we go along, how about. First, why don't we get a pen going. Aggregate's already been itching to—"

"Let them itch."

"Oh, I don't think so," Lyle said slowly, drawing his head back against the veteran leather of his easy chair. "Thing is, see, a deal can always get away if you're not pretty speedy about clinching it."

"Takes two to clinch," Mitch tap-danced a pair of fingers on the Aggregate stack of paper to make his point. "The Bench and home sweet home here, it's all in my name, too, as well as yours. Mom's doing, in her will, remember?"

"Tell me something I don't know. Mitch, this dickering with Aggregate is as much for you as it is for me. You never wanted to take any of this on." Lyle indicated the household empire of odds and ends and the provinces of tractor carcasses and branding irons beyond. "Not blaming you, but you just never did want to pitch in here and try to make something of this—"

—this *family*, Mitch in amazement waited for him to finally own up to. His father's so-called life under this roof, walled into himself and his own schemes, had been mainly of the man's own choosing. Didn't use the GI Bill to go to college after the war. Didn't take the veterans' preference jobs that came up elsewhere. Didn't even try for the big wages on the boomer projects he rabidly approved of, such as the Interstate highway or the missile silos. In something like patient fury Mitch awaited the confession from the old man that his closed-in approach to life had added up to a half-dozen Christmas cards curling in the May sun.

"—this town. Son, here's your shot at walking away from the Springs for good and all. With no, what do they call them, encumbrances. Just takes signing your name a time. Well, okay, a bunch of times, but—"

"I came, I saw the paperwork and I don't concur. What's the hurry here? Aggregate doesn't have to lay its roads in the next five minutes, does it?"

"Mitch, for crying out loud, are you going to drag your feet about this?"

"I'm not going to be dragged into it without a chance to think it over, if that's what you mean, Dad." He mightily wished Lexa was here to hoot effectively at his father's grandiose gravel. *Her* father happily bargained his ranch into a buffalo preserve. Good God, the hopeless algebra of lineage.

Lyle swallowed with what seemed to be a lot of effort. "This takes more energy than it used to. I could sure stand a cup of joe." He made as if to get up, but first frowned toward Mitch. "You want some, or do you only drink herbal substances?"

"I'd better make it," Mitch said mildly and headed for the kitchen. "Coffee knows when somebody from Seattle is around."

The kitchen was somewhat more navigable than the living room, but only because of a central two-foot-high pack of paper plates. Plainly Lyle had dispensed with doing dishes and ate picnic style.

Locating the pot that looked as if the next perk might be its last, Mitch put in what he knew was twice as many measures of coffee as his father would and got it started. He hung on in the kitchen, trying to tend the stings of being the son of this father. All the old everything. That long-standing charge that he was AWOL from the life his father had set up for him. All right, then, what if he had come back to the Springs after college, then "married local," as they said in this town? Then had Springs versions of Jocelyn and Laurits. He still was as sure as anything that they'd be sailing through the streets of San Francisco and the lingual bypaths of Jakarta just the same. He was even surer he would have started off dead-ended in any career here. In that wonderful might-have-been life sponsored by Lyle Rozier, worked at what? Become his father's partner in seasonal muscle? Divvy a job that barely supported one person. All the rocks, hay and grain truck dust you could eat.

Behind him the back door shot open. A pale, pale teenage boy, wearing a Twin Sulphur Springs Salamanders basketball jersey and jeans that bagged out like harem pants, stood with hands in pockets and eyed him from under eyelids at half mast.

"You'd better be Matthew," Mitch said, holding a ready-to-tackle pose.

"He is, he is," Lyle called from the living room. "You can tell by his door manners." The pair in the kitchen watched each other with leery eyes, time lengthening between them while they listened to Lyle pulling himself up out of the groaning old chair and making his way to the kitchen door. "Mitch, Matthew. And I suppose vice versa."

The boy flicked a gaze as opaque as mica toward the living room and Lyle's WebTV screen and said, "I'll come back some other time and we'll do our search for a General MacArthur site."

Mitch watched the tall twig of boy hunch out the door, the back of his head pasty white beneath his buzz cut. Guilty visions of Shyanne suddenly swam to mind.

Lyle was saying, "Matthew sort of likes it over here. Nobody's on him to pick stuff up, I guess."

Mitch just about laughed. Of course! His father's shambles of a house was a teenager's hog heaven, accumulation without particular purpose but dangerous proportions.

Mistaking Mitch's expression, Lyle said: "I don't let him hang around too much of the time. He's got parents, they're there for a purpose. Although that father of his is a dud if there ever was one."

Mitch pursed up, but said only: "Coffee's ready."

This father of his accepted the cup, took a drink, made a face.

"Where were we?"

"Fighting."

"Wouldn't want to lose our place at that," Lyle fairly spat out. He gave his son a terribly tired look, then went to the table. Chair legs scraped in predictable protest. He sat down and pulled out his pack of cigarettes in the same motion. He took his time about lighting up, Mitch watching the old performance. But of all things, the next note out of his father sounded as nonbelligerent as the offered words:

"Mitch, you suppose we could postpone any more arguing for a while?" Exhaling smoke slowly as if to settle his nerves, he let out along with it: "It's harder and harder to get along with Luke."

Another war with some neighbor. Or the brother of his cyber-gospelist, Matthew? Mitch waited, but nothing resembling an explanation seemed to be nearing his father's blue-hazed horizon.

"Make me ask, why don't you. Who's this Luke character?"

Lyle sniffed. Then cocked his head as if he himself was interested to learn what he was going to speak out next. And only then uttered:

"Leukemia."

Mitch felt as if the skin on his face was suddenly too tight.

He stared at the older man as if trying to see into the box canyons of his mind.

"The doc says it's about got me. Why I called you."

"*Leukemia?*" Stunned as he was, now Mitch caught on: all

that pinballing around the place by his father, little tiny distances, pickup fender to the shed, back to the pickup, only then to the house, and only across bits of a room at a time, to the desk, to the chair, to the doorway. Resting places. That was what Lyle Rozier's life consisted of now. Whatever was left of it. "When did you find this out?"

"Aw, year or so. The kind I've got can go slow, you know."

"*Can't* be that long. I was out here to see you just last fall and you were perfectly fine—" Mitch stopped at the look on the other's face.

"No," his father provided as if he had it written down somewhere, "that's about what it's been, a year now."

"*Then why the goddamn hell didn't you tell me?*"

"You got your own life to lead, seems like," came Lyle's bland response. Put that way, it did not sound a particularly commendable fact.

"Dad, we have to get you going on the best medical help we can. I'll—"

"Mitch, I am bright enough to spell *doctor!*"

All of a sudden this was the hot-faced Lyle, the foreman who could fire a lazy hayhand so fast he would be a mile down the road before he knew what hit him. The father who blazed for years when a son defied him. The V.F.W. club veteran, revisiting his war with nightly ardor.

With old and awful familiarity Mitch watched this flare of temper, numb to its heat but trying to measure its light. *Choosing the ground to fight on one last time, old Sarge?*

"They've looked me over every which way, down at the Falls," Lyle was saying. "And called in their visiting guy from the Mayo Clinic, just to make sure. Chemo or marrow transplant or any of that, the odds they gave me didn't even add up to longshot. Told them I wouldn't go through that sort of a beating for nothing." He tried on a tough grin. "Everybody eventually catches something they don't get over, I guess."

On automatic, Mitch heard himself recite: "Nothing at all they can do for you?"

"Not the docs, no." Lyle was staying oddly reflective.

Mitch listened to his father pronounce *myelogenous* and *terminal* and other medical adjectives, but his true awareness was back there on the lightning-spike epitaph *leukemia*. One diagnostic word, all it took. The space of a breath had brought Mitch his turn in the gunsights of obligation. Bingford had buried his famous father in Aspen earlier this year. Ingvaldson's daughter the Unitarian minister had popped back from Duluth to frown compassion over his kidney stone episode last winter. Like the flyways of rattled birds, America's concourses were constantly crisscrossed with Baby Boomers trying to nerve up for the waiting bedside consultation, the nursing home decision, the choosing of a casket. Mitch could generally pick out the stunned journeyers home in airport waiting lounges, the trim businesswoman who lived by focus sitting there now with a doll-eyed stare, the man celebrating middle age with a ponytail looking down baffled now at his compassion-fare ticket. Targeted from here on, in featureless waiting rooms the color of antiseptic gloves, for the involuntary clerkwork of closing down a parent's life. The time came; it always came. The when of it was the ambush.

Four

"IT'S ME," REPORTED MITCH'S VOICE, AS IF NOT HAPPY
with that fact. Amid pie dough, Lexa was listening in to the
phone machine. "Deep in the heart of Artesia Park. Sharing a
phone booth with squashed beer cans, and the wind is blowing
in like a true sonofabitch. I've spent all day dealing with, trying
to deal with, my father. It's about five o'clock, Mountain time—
four o'clock *your* time, right?—and I need to talk to you, Lexa,
do I ever. Give me a call when you're back from walking or zoo-
ing or whatever, would you, please? The number at the house is
four-oh-six, nine-six-six—"

Really a shame to interrupt such a nice report. He must have rehearsed.
Lexa picked up the phone and with a floury thumb mashed the

answering machine button to off. "Mitch, hi. Sorry about the machine being on, but we voted to pig out on lemon meringue pie tonight."

" 'We?' "

"Mariah," she reminded him in three emphatic syllables. "I walked her all over Seattle today sightseeing, so she's resting her bod." Piquant alto *zzz*s trailed down from the upstairs bedroom. "How's it going there?"

"Uphill, Lex, every daddy-loving inch of the way. He's determined to get rid of everything, starting with, I don't know, the kitchen dishes. Him and his damn deals—it's going to take a deck of lawyers to figure it all out."

"Why're you calling from a phone booth?"

The rim of the Rockies faced Mitch as he stared across the scabby little park. "Lexa, he's about gonna die."

Lyle, who sounded like the healthiest bull in the world on the phone? Concern rushed into her tone. "Mitch, how come, what of?"

"I wish to hell I had answers to any of it except what of." He filled her in on his father's year-old onsets of leukemia and reticence. "The doctors laid it on him that it could be any time now, he finally came out and admitted to me, but God, it's hard to tell. One minute he's marching around as ornery as ever and the next he turns into a wing walker, never lets go of one thing until he has hold of something else. It's like"—the memory jumped up and surprised him—"watching Jocelyn and Ritz when they were learning to toddle. Only he's toddling in the other direction." Lexa could hear the wind whistling in on Mitch and the phone while he struggled for voice again. "But hey," he managed to resume hoarsely, "stop me before I babble more. I just called because I had to let you know I'm high-centered here until I figure out what to do with him. When I tried him out on coming to Seattle, he just snorted and said he'd rather have cashed in his chips in New Guinea than go bye-bye on the Coast."

She twiddled at the curls in the phone cord as if trying to decide whether to pinch off her next words. But they had to be offered.

"Want me there for immoral support?"

His relief was almost painful to hear. "How can you? You've got jobs lined up, haven't you?"

"Gretchen's outfit can fill in." Lexa by this time was ruffling among the refrigerator slips, rearranging the food circles of life. "We've covered for each other before. I'll need to tell her to kick butt on my crew every so often just to keep them in practice, but other than that, everybody will probably survive." She lifted her eyes toward the ceiling, already grinning a little at the chance to tickle Mariah in the ribs and bestow the news that the McCaskill sisters would be driving back to the Rockies together.

The street was longer than the town, back to the fanciful days when Twin Sulphur Springs was going to warm the toes of the world, and Mitch walked west from the park to where the thin old asphalt gave way to a stub end of gravel in a block of vacant lots. A solid snarl of tumbleweeds lay jammed against the barbwire fence of the nearest hay field. One geodesic weed evidently had skittered over the top of the others like an acrobat vaulting the backs of his cohorts, and it sat now against the gravel, rocking as it waited for the next ride from the wind. Mitch went over and thoroughly tromped it into milk-colored straw.

There. Had my exercise, at least. All else that was yet to be done, back down the street at his father's place, held him in a kind of disbelieving trance as he walked the return direction.

Call his father's doctor in Great Falls, try to find out what to expect.

Call Bingford and ask for further time off from one dying enterprise to tend to another.

Figure out how to tackle the swamp of household. Did the

place need a housekeeper or a nurse or what, and where could you get any of them in this skin-and-bones town?

The list went on like some terrible infinite timetable. He felt like a tourist to his own circumstances, not quite understanding how he signed up for this. The tired reviewing line of houses along the way, lived in by people he no longer knew or who had become poor fits to the faces in his memory, didn't help. Seattle and everything he had ever chosen for himself lay little more than a day's drive away, but as distant to this situation as the good ship *Lollipop*. He wanted not to walk back through that Rozier door, not be trapped again between those walls echoing with old family fights. Not have to become the rules-playing son when the contest was his father's medical gauntlet. And knew there was no escaping this street. You can't not go home again when someone is sitting there dying.

He crossed the lengthening shadow-copies of the aspens as he turned in at his father's driveway. Soon be suppertime. He cast a yearning glance toward Donald Brainerd's place and its ganglia of messagery and FedEx but told himself, *Forget it. Lexa will skin you alive if you have meals from Gretchen's outfit overnighted in here.*

On in to face reality or whatever currently passed for it, he was surprised to find his father standing stationed at the bay window.

"Mitch?" Lyle called over his shoulder as if taking roll. "Here we go. Come watch this."

Mitch joined the spectating. A gaggle of magpies, black and white and saucy as a masquerade party, had taken over the yard to try to boss Rin away from his dog dish. Their clamor was wasted on a deaf dog half dozing with his nose behind his paws. What must have been the drum major of the magpie flock had alighted out in front of the dish and was striding around cocking a look at the out-of-it dog. Confident in its reconnaissance, the bird now took a brazen hop to the dish. It commenced to gobble the food, Rin watching like a sleepy pensioner. All at once he put a paw out, pinning down the magpie's long train of tail. There was just time for a victimized squawk before Rin leaned his head forward and ended the magpie's dish-robbing career with one snap of his teeth.

"He gets himself a lot of magpie cutlets that way," Lyle said proudly.

"He probably isn't real keen to share with us, though." Mitch sent a wary glance toward the kitchen. "Any wishes for supper?"

"Dairy Queen. I get by pretty good on milk shakes. Butterscotch, if you want to be fancy about it."

Mitch could put up with most things if there was food attached. By the time he was back from his trip to the drive-in, his father had made his way to the backyard and settled onto the running board of the defunct old blue truck, a can of Coors in one hand and a smoke in the other. "Sure gonna miss these, dead," Mitch heard him mutter over his repasts of beer and nicotine. When Lyle became aware of him, he made room on the running board. "Might as well eat out here," he told Mitch. "Pretty evening and all."

Mitch's cheeseburgers and Lyle's milk shake barely outlasted the sun as it encountered the crags and reefs of the mountains. The purpling time, the Roziers had always called this point of dusk when the mountains turned plum. Watching the sunset procession of shades, the older man sat and smoked, the younger man simply sat.

"Mitch," Lyle said after a while. "We haven't talked over the disposing of."

Heirlooms by the dumptruckload, you bet. Mitch did not even bother looking around to tally it all, the equipment collection that overpopulated the yard, the branding iron warehouse, the no-account house chockful of borderline cases of rummage-or-garbage. "When the time comes, if I'm going to be your executor—sure, Dad, I'll naturally take care of getting rid of stuff."

Lyle took an audibly deep drag on his cigarette. Along with the cascade of smoke he let out:

"I meant me. What's left after the undertaker's stove gets cleaned out, anyway."

"As in *ashes*? Your *cremated* ashes?"

"Only kind I know of," Lyle said unperturbed, "unless you count these." He tapped the gray residue off the end of his cigarette.

Ten seconds ago Mitch would have sworn his father's final resting place did not matter to him. So why was he speechless?

When he did manage to make his mouth work, what came out came out stiffly: "Dad, sorry, but I just always figured you'd want to be buried—you know. Next to Mother." His father was the last person in the world he would have expected to let a bought-and-paid-for grave go to waste.

"Don't take this wrong, Mitch. Nothing against your mother, you know that." He shifted around on the running board and glanced at the ground. "But I decided I don't want to be down there."

Where, then? In a Mason jar on my mantelpiece in Seattle? Couldn't say that to a dying person, though, could you. Not even one full of dickering about his dying.

"If you really figure we've got to start thinking about, uh, arrangements, I'd better start keeping track." Mitch began to get up and go in the house for his laptop, feeling monumentally silly.

Impatiently his father put a hand on his arm and stopped him. "There's a fire tower on Phantom Woman Mountain," the older man said and flipped the still-glowing stub of cigarette toward that peak with the stone suggestion of a woman's face on the darkening mountain skyline. "I did the majority of the work building it, back in CCC times, Mitch. What I want is for you to toss my ashes from that tower." Lyle looked directly at his son. "Right in the old girl's eye."

They were eighteen and unkillable, that Divide summer of 1939. Inseparable, practically joined at their tanned rib cages, he and Ferragamo. The regimented life at the Civilian Conservation Corps camp was keeping them from either going hungry or going criminal, but the pair of young men had plenty of velocity left over after each day's labor. Lyle was local and knew just how to take advantage of that in hitchhiking rides for them into Twin Sulphur Springs. Anybody driving to town recognized him half a mile off as the Rozier kid. Joe Ferragamo, plucked from Paterson, New Jersey, was grateful for such a guide, a friend who didn't call him Joisey. And what Lyle liked right off the bat about Ferragamo was how swift he was at catching on to things. In his very first fistfight, there out back of the CCC barracks on Soda Creek, Joe didn't go in for the roundhouse knockdown style but instead concentrated on staying on his feet, the way the Western boys fought. Lyle could tell he'd been watching, soaking up. In no time the burly local kid and the weedy but improving East Coast youngster were a regular pair at "pal night" at the Saturday movie in Twin Sulphur Springs, getting in two for the price of one.

Joe Ferragamo thought Montana was the luckiest thing that had ever happened to him, which it was. From his first footstep off the train, the mountains took him over. There on the depot platform at Browning, surrounded by similar young guys from the East staring west at the halfway-up-the-sky wall of the Rockies with apprehension or in some cases outright fear, what Joe felt was excitement. The highest thing in Paterson had been the waterfalls that powered the silk mills, when there used to be silk mills.

Then when his company of boys and men—they were some of both—was being trucked south to the CCC camp and the highway climbed back up past the layers of cliffs at the valley of the Two Medicine River, he could see that there were more and more mountains ahead, blue-gray and constant, all the way to the farthest distance, where they'd been told this place called Soda Creek and their camp lay. Out here was the real it, Joe decided.

He and Lyle fell into the Phantom Woman job. Joe happened to be pickaxing a stubborn stony cutbank right at the new trailhead when the forest ranger came riding up the main trail with what looked to Joe like all the horses in the world strung out behind him, and asked if he knew where to find the crew boss.

Charging off up the slope and then tagging at the crew boss's heels on the way back down, Joe was there all ears when the ranger asked whether he could borrow a couple of the CCC lads for a week or ten days; there had been a foul-up at headquarters and he was short a couple of good workers to finish up the fire tower on the summit of Phantom Woman.

"Tell you what, I'm about to call lunch," came the reply. "Sit and have some with us and I'll go over my roster, see if I can find you a pair of working fools."

The instant of lunch call, Joe raced up the trail again, this time to Lyle. "Horseback and everything, we'd getta be!"

He was surprised that Lyle showed hesitation about volunteering. It meant no town, no pal nights at the movies, for a week or maybe two, but wasn't it worth it to be on top of a mountain—of the Continental Divide—and leave something built with your own hands?

"What the hey, why not," Lyle said finally, and away they went to offer themselves. Initiative counted with the crew boss, and for that matter, the young ranger, Paul Eliason.

By the time the rest of the jealous catcalling CCCers were putting away their lunch utensils, Joe and Lyle were riding up Phantom Woman Mountain like tickled cowboys.

When they eventually came up over the brow of the peak, there in front of them on the summit loomed the fire tower like a daddy longlegs standing at attention. Joe took one look at its cabin in the sky and started yearning to be a forest fire spotter.

Ranger Eliason proved to be a fussbudget of the first order. The minute they arrived on top of the mountain, he made it clear to them there was the right way, the wrong way and the Forest Service way. They barely were off their horses before the ranger was making the pair of them go up the fire tower and install the lightning rod. When the ranger's back was turned, Lyle gazed elaborately at the utterly clear blue sky and winked at Joe.

The real work started as soon as they clattered down the stair steps from the tower to the mountaintop again. The ranger led them over to the nearest of the rock formations surrounding the legs of the tower. Eyebolts, he explained, had to be anchored into the stone formations and tension cables strung to the tower to prevent sway in the high winds up here. "Now then, laddie bucks," the young ranger piped, "have you ever drilled rock before? No? Here's the procedure."

They slugged away with a sledgehammer, taking turns holding the drill bit and turning it a quarter of a revolution for each hammer stroke. The *spang* of the sledge striking resounded off the neighboring mountains, a godhammer of creation ringing in Joe's ears, an uninvited din of hard labor in Lyle's.

The boys survived the eyebolting and cabling and most of a week's worth of other unheard-of tasks before Eliason started fretting over the stairs.

"These will rot out in no time," he complained about the stairwork done by the framing crew that had put up the basics of the tower. The hefty floorboards on all three landings had been set flush against one another, instead of being spaced half an inch apart—the young ranger had checked the manual, twice—so that moisture would drain through, nor had the edges of the steps been beveled to encourage runoff.

"This just won't do," Eliason decreed and put Joe to trimming down the stair edges with a drawknife and plane, and Lyle, with his heft, to ripping out the stair landings with a pinch bar and a hell of a lot of grunted pulling of tenpenny nails with a hammer.

There was quite a kick to this work, a kind of steeplejack thrill as they progressed up and up the zigzag stairwell, ever farther into the air above the top deck of the continent. They seemed to be the only lucky ones permitted into the crow's nest while the ship of earth sailed without tremor through the blue weather. They had reached the third and highest landing, Lyle having just finished tearing out the floorboards and ready to nail in the new set and Joe tenderly shaving just enough off a stair edge a few steps below him, when the Forest Service bigwig unexpectedly swept through.

Even more surprising, the man was on foot, backpacking, rather than regally on horseback. Eliason, just then coming up the stairwell to mother-hen over Lyle as he spaced those floorboards, gawked, knit his brow and clambered down in record time. The boys could overhear the visitor claiming that he wasn't really inspecting anything but scenery, but from the hesitant way Eliason shook hands with him he was obviously somebody important. They truly knew Eliason was rattled when, though it wasn't even close to high noon, he called Joe and Lyle down for lunch. Hammer dropped and drawknife set aside, they descended to where Eliason was nervously rubbing his hands on his ranger pants and the first person from Washington, D.C., they had ever met was waiting with handshakes for them, too.

Eliason dug out the Forest Service's version of a treat, a can of tomatoes apiece to go along with baloney sandwiches, and the four of them sat on a couple of the tower's anchor rocks munching and slurping. The headquarters man made conversation like a house afire, asking Joe and Lyle this, that and the other about themselves and the CCC while he practically inhaled lunch.

Obviously he was in a hurry and and didn't seem to be giving the fire tower any particular going-over, but all through lunch, Eliason looked as if his diaper was being checked.

His sandwiches and tomatoes ingested, the visitor finally glanced up at the tower as if just now noticing it. "Really ought to see all the view there is," the man said genially. "May I?"

Eliason jumped to his feet and escorted Mister Important over to the tower. Watching them go, Lyle wondered in a sarcastic whisper to Joe how a guy landed a job like that, drawing pay for loping around on the mountains. Joe had been turning that over and over in his head too, not able to take his eyes off the Forest Service official as he daydreamed of maybe being in charge of mountains himself, someday.

While Lyle's attention shifted to the important matter of popping a blister on his hammering hand with the point of his jackknife blade, Joe couldn't get enough of the ceremonial visit and sat watching the two men ascend the tower. They had climbed the majority of the stairs, the bigwig talking over his shoulder to Eliason, when it hit Joe.

"Hey, mister, don't! Those boards aren't nailed!"

The man froze, a step short of the top landing and the teetery floorboards Lyle had left flush against the stair-tread beam but not actually on it so he could mark in the spacing, before he and Joe scampered down for lunch. Eliason was so close behind he nearly bumped into the other man's rump. In a flash he reached around and gave a testing push down onto the board where the visitor's foot would have put weight. It tipped forward off the center beam of the landing like the trapdoor of a scaffold, then sailed off into air, plummeting to the ground thirty feet below with a clattering hit.

Wordlessly Eliason reached again and yanked the remaining boards firmly into resting on the stair-tread beam, then grabbed Lyle's nail can and hammer and spiked each one down. Joe sneaked a look at the belated expression on Lyle, stunned and guilty. To the amazement of both boys, the headquarters man only gave them a chiding grin and made the schoolyard sign for *shame, shame,* one index finger whittling the other.

The instant the visitor vanished down the Divide trail, Eliason laid into the two of them. Joe figured he had good reason to; Lyle's lapse had come close to dropping the ranger's boss three stories on his head onto the rocky brow of Phantom Woman Mountain. "This just won't do. Don't ever walk away from your work without securing it," the ranger told them, then found ways to repeat it. It helped none that all three of them knew the lecture was aimed at Lyle.

Eliason sent the boys back to the stair work, then grimly disappeared into his tent to write up the visit from headquarters. Through the first hour of the afternoon Lyle steamed, then boiled over.

"*This just won't do,*" he mimicked. "Next thing, he'll be telling us how to blow our noses."

Joe checked him in alarm. He had been half expecting this, hoping against it.

"Say, Lyle, he *is* the top dog." Ferragamo, who had been bossed every which way by life in the slums of Paterson, found it a relief to be overseen by mere Paul Eliason. Besides, there was this chance-of-a-lifetime mountain.

"I don't care if he's the pasteurized Jesus," declared Lyle. "I've had enough of him."

Down went his hammer with a thud of finality. "Come on, let's tell him we want our walking papers."

"I'm sticking."

"What, and keep taking it from Paulie the Parrot?"

"Lyle, I—it's different for me. You're acquainted down in town, know your way around and everything. Where, me, if I mess up out here . . . it's a long way back to Paterson, and there's plain nothing waiting when I get there."

"Up to you. I'm heading down that trail."

Ferragamo's heart sank with each sound of Lyle's shoe leather going down and down the tower steps. He called out: "Say, Lyle?"

At the bottom of the stairs, Lyle turned and looked up at him.

"Catch up with you, first Saturday night when I'm down from this?" Joe tried out. "Go to the show together?"

Lyle gazed toward him through the zigzag of stairs and railings for an extended moment, then sent up a smile. "Sure. Sounds good. See you on pal night."

That held. The two young men gravitated back together on those Saturday nights, even after Lyle parted company with the CCC and latched on at a haying job on the ranch next door to the Soda Creek camp, and after Ferragamo came out of his mountain summer honorably blooded, struck by a falling snag during the big Flume Gulch forest fire. Across the next couple of years of jobs as young muscle in the Twin Sulphur Springs country, they stayed in touch, and when the war came in '41 went in together and, still together, were destined to a place which would do its best to kill them, the other side of the world from the mountain called Phantom Woman.

"In the old girl's *eye*?" Mitch stared at this fathomless stranger, his father.

"Kidding, Mitch." Lyle sniffed hard. "What do you call it in your line of work, a figure of speech? I mean it, though, about you carting my ashes up there and throwing them off. That's what I want done with myself. Hope you don't mind too much."

Dying man in front of him or not, Mitch couldn't help sounding confounded: "I didn't know Phantom Woman meant such a lot to you."

"Oh, you bet it does."

"Let's hear it, then."

"What?" Suddenly cross, Lyle grumbled: "It was way back there, doesn't matter any to you. Something wrong with me wanting that kind of thing?"

Lyle Rozier at one with the earth, mingled ash to dust? No, Mitch supposed, such miracles were capable of happening. Deathbed conversions, they were called. Still puzzled, he studied his father.

"Of course if it's something you don't want to do," Lyle was saying with just the right amount of infuriating solicitude, "they have these young guys in Glacier Park now who hire out as, what's the word, sherpas. We could maybe set it up with one of them to—"

"Never mind!"

Mitch whirled and went over to the vaguely green remnant of a John Deere tractor. One mitt-size hand against the rugged old corrugations of the tractor tire, he leaned there, eyes off toward the wilderness crest to the west, all the while Lyle watching him as if gauging a touchy fieldhand.

Lord, what a size Mitch was. It had surprised Lyle for thirty-five years now, his boy outgrowing the family line so. This was no time for the lump in the throat, though. He called over in his best negotiating voice:

"I know you're gonna think this is just another scatbrain idea of mine, but Mitch, I do need for you to promise. That you'll do right by me, on this."

"Okay, okay, *okay.*" Mitch turned around to him. "But I still don't get it. How you can want to gravel up to the eyeteeth of the Bob, and at the same time want yourself sprinkled over the top of one of its mountains."

It took obvious effort, but Lyle let that argument go by. He muttered instead:

"In memory of Ferragamo, let's just say. Joe was on that fire tower work with me."

Mitch pondered this. The last he could remember of Ferragamo and for that matter his notable wife was that final crew picnic. All right, the man did figure in that New Guinea blood-and-guts tale his father always used to tell. But that was long ago and far away. Particularly far from a Continental Divide fire tower. Nor was it like his father to turn sentimental. Stubborn, sly, exasperating and the rest, you bet, but—

Sounding satisfied on top of it all, Lyle now announced: "That's probably about enough of a day." He put his hands on his knees, pushed himself up off the running board and started his slow march toward the house. Mitch noticed he did not once look back at the mountains.

The burgundy VW van scrushed to an abrupt halt in the drive-way the next day at what would have been suppertime if there was any supper in the house.

Mitch all but vaulted over his father to get out of the living room and welcome Lexa. He was surprised to hear Rin, who never barked, give a series of rusty yips.

"He won't bite, but he might pull your tail feathers out," Mitch called to the figure bent over into the back of the van.

The figure reversed out of the bay of the van and, looking bemused, stood holding a handful of cameras swaying at the end of their straps like a collection of shrunken heads. The dark red mane of hair barely interrupted by her *Hard Rock Cafe—Beijing* ball cap would have bought and paid for Lexa's copper approximation several times over. From her lanky point of vantage she was now pensively regarding the off-key Rin at her ankles, and out of her came: "Ever hear the one about the dyslexic atheist who didn't believe in dog?"

"Mariah hitchhiked along," Lexa called out as if it wasn't more than evident, popping around the other end of the van carrying the Kelty backpack she still used as a suitcase. "You know how it is with these world travelers, they can't get enough of exotic locales."

"This one comes with hot and cold running arguments," Mitch said, a bit on guard although he didn't yet know why. He jounced down off the porch steps and swept Lexa to him with a bearlike arm, extending his other hand. "Hi, Mariah. Been some time, right? You along on work or pleasure?"

Mariah gave him a grin. "Both if I can get them. How's the hometown treating you, Mitch?"

"The Fuji jet-setter claims she has to get her newspaper shooting eye back," Lexa reported dubiously. "But I still think she's out of her mind to come here and target-practice on—"

"This town ought to be good for something besides going stir-crazy in." The first smile in days cropped out on Mitch along with his journalistic instinct. "No shortage of run-down stuff for photo features around here." Going to the van, he grabbed yet more of the photographic gear. "Need some room to spread out for a night or two while you're on your shoot? The bunkhouse isn't taken yet." He steered them past Rin and said, "Come on in, before my father deals the ground out from under us."

In the living room, Lyle stiffly arose out of his warren of a chair.

"Population's up around here all of a sudden," he observed. "Here's one I know, anyhow. How's the Lexa?" He said it with no inflection she could detect, leaving her to decide whether or not it was a greeting.

With no small effort she made nice and said back, "I thought the question is, How's the Lyle?"

He just laughed.

Mariah was gamely introduced by Mitch and her habit of wearing cameras explained; indeed, it seemed probable that much of her photographic output for the *Montanian* across the years lay in the stacks of newspapers in this room.

Lyle appraised Mariah at length, then turned back to Lexa. "Come to help out?" He had all the approach of a kindly card cheat. "How are you at forging Mitch's signature?"

"Let's just put our crayons away awhile, Dad."

"Mitch can't seem to stand the thought of prosperity," Lyle confided to the two women. "Makes it hard to leave him what he has coming to him."

Lips compressed, Mitch started clearing decades' worth of *National Geographics* off a couple of chairs. As he did so, Lexa analyzed the pair of jousting men. Together, the family likeness of Lyle and Mitch was inescapable: they were same song, second verse. The wavy hair, still a full head of it in pewter shade on Lyle, Mitch's black with wisps of gray around the ears. The faces like larger-than-life masks done by the same emphatic hand. How, she wondered, had they turned out so opposite inside those similar heads? *And how am I supposed to pitch in anything useful when they can't even get past hello without starting to fight?*

Mariah had been scanning the room, familiarity tickling at her from somewhere. The story of her lens life, déjà voodoo. Twin crinkles of concentration appeared between her eyes as her mind tried to frame when she had seen this particular layout of *Bad Housekeeping* before; that logjam of clutter in the far corner, the tipsy angle at which it reposed; the globe of metal rods about ready to teeter off the crowded sideboard . . .

"The Kobe quake!" she blurted.

Realizing three curious stares were fastened on her, she alibied with a little laugh: "Nothing, nothing. Last little tag end of jet lag, is all." Now it was going to have her photographic attention every time she walked in here, though, how much this hermit cave of a living room resembled the Japanese museum's tumbled exhibits that she had shot in the trembling hours after the great earthquake there.

"Some of us around here were starting to think about supper," Mitch issued to fill the conversation gap. Enlightened sharer of household chores or not, he had been deeply hoping Lexa would take charge of the forbidding kitchen. Instead she cast one glance into that disaster area and said, "Let's eat out."

He knew she did not have the Dairy Queen in mind, so that meant the Springhouse, downtown. "Dad, can we bring you something?"

Lyle the unbudgeable was reaching to where his hat was hung. "Thought I might step out with you," he said in a tone of grandiloquent hurt. "If you don't mind my company."

The Springhouse Supper Club was somewhere between unfinished and deteriorating. It was also extensive and yawning and empty, but no sooner had the four of them taken what appeared to be the cleanest table than they were in a line of traffic as black-clad Hutterite men five or six at a time began to find their way to the banquet area dividered off at the rear.

"Beats the dickens out of me, what they're doing in here," Lyle had to admit when Mitch, Lexa and Mariah looked the question to him. A population all their own across Montana and the Dakotas and up into Canada, the Hutterites dwelled in their farm colonies of a hundred or so people, talking German among themselves and following their Anabaptist communal religion. They had kept their way of life by avoiding things of the world that might infect it—television, radio, the camera's eye, public schools—and it might have been supposed that supper clubs would be prominent on that list. But the one thing the Hutterites were thoroughly modern about was their agriculture, and when the table of four saw a pair of civilians in knit shirts and high-belted trousers pushing video equipment into the banquet area where the Hutterite bearded legion was congregating, they caught the drift. Fertilizer salesmen or some such, come to preach the virtues of their product to an audience lured by a free supper.

"We may have to go in there and take religious vows"—Mitch resorted to yet another dry bread stick—"to get any food in this place."

"Those guys really are out in force," Lyle observed, recognizing white-bearded Pastor Jacob Stapfer from the Freezout colony east of town in the next covey of Hutterites trooping in. "How's t'ings, Lyle?" the brethren elder sang out.

"How you doing, Pastor Jake?" Lyle called back. The Jehovahlike figure was plainly doing top-notch, cruising into the banquet area just as if a Hutterite in a supper club wasn't as unlikely as soup du jour in the Old Testament.

"I can feel your trigger finger twitching from here, Mariah," Lexa teased.

At long last, as it seemed to Mitch, the waitress emerged from the kitchen and with a harried look gave them menus and the bulletin: "The special is pork chops and applesauce."

"Rib eye," Lexa said without touching the menu.

"Just the salad bar for me," Mariah decided just as fast.

"Milk shake," Lyle said, "but I'll live it up and have chocolate."

Mitch had started through the menu, but realizing it was his turn told the waitress before she could get away: "I'd like the special and I'd like it now, please."

"Rib eye," Lexa warned.

"Lexa, will you quit? I'm about starved. I want fast food, I mean, quick food." Mitch turned to the waitress to check. "The special is ready, right, sitting there cozy on the steam table?"

"Always is."

"Then bring it on."

Away the waitress went, and Mitch settled himself to determinedly not taking the last bread stick, while Lexa ragged Mariah about the brown lettuce and petrified carrot sticks she was doomed to at the salad bar and Mariah maintained she had eaten far worse specimens during her wanderyear. Through the divider between them and the Hutterite-filled banquet area an amplified voice took over:

"Those of us at Biotic Betterment are just real happy that you farm animal people could join us here tonight and listen to our message and get a free supper out of the deal, too."

Bacterial additives for health and heft in livestock, the sales pitch proved to be, or as it was intoned more than once, good bacteria used against bad bacteria.

Lyle sounded reflective as he swizzled the final bread stick, then put it down without tasting it. "It's getting so you need to be a scientist just to grow ham and eggs."

"In just a minute here we're going to be showing you a video on what our bug can do for your four-legged creatures," the knitwear voice was confiding. "But first we'll draw for the door prize we promised you gentlemen. Here it is, right here. This lovely mantel clock. Battery-run, no need for a cord. Terry, draw a name out of the hat, would you? There you go, thank you kindly, Terry. And the winning name is . . . Peter Zorn!"

There was a moment of collective contemplation among the Hutterites. Then a voice:

"So, vich Peter Zorn is t'at?"

The four eavesdroppers had to grin.

The microphone maestro, though, sounded unamused. "How do you mean, which?"

"Vell, I'm Peter Zorn from t'e Seven Block colony," the Hutterite voice answered.

"And I'm Peter Zorn from t'e New Alberta colony," another voice attested.

"And I'm Peter Zorn from t'e Kipp Creek colony," chimed in a third.

It plainly had escaped the bug prophets that the Hutterites get by with only a handful of family names—of the sixty black-garbed men in the banquet room, probably twenty were Stapfers, twenty were Liebknechts and twenty were Zorns.

"Umm." The microphone handler could be heard working his brain about the problem of the repeat Petes. "What I guess we better do is, umm, put the names of you three gentlemen and your colonies onto slips of paper and draw again."

"But t'at vill mean two Peter Zorns von't vin a prize. And you said t'e vinning *name* is Peter Zorn."

"Oh, for—Terry, go out to the van and bring in two more clocks."

Amid the tableful of chuckles, Lyle was practically bursting with neighborly pride at the Hutterites' ability to drive a bargain. "If we could cash in on our place like they do on farming, we'd be sitting pretty. Don't you think, Mitch?"

A clamped expression came over Mitch.

Lexa chipped in, "I'd sure never make it as a Hutterite"—she stopped hard, then finished the thought—"wife."

Another uncomfortable faceload overcame Mitch, but Lexa hurried right on:

"Those old bearded coots run everything except potato peelings and dirty diapers."

"They're tough sonsofguns, men or women, either one," Lyle maintained. "Look how they stick to that way of life of theirs. They raise a kid, that kid listens to them. They pass along what they can to that kid, that kid knows what to do with it. Mitch and I have been having a conversation along those lines the last couple of days, and I'd be interested to hear your take on it, Lexa and Mariah. You ladies have had parents. Don't you think then when they make you their heir, you ought to—"

"Dad, can't you drop this long enough to—"

"Hey, I think this isn't our war," Lexa spoke up, with a meaningful glance at Mariah.

"I'm just along for the ride," Mariah claimed. Then made a guilty U-turn out loud. "No, I'm not. Am I ever not."

Two sets of male curiosity and one of sisterly foreboding settled on Mariah. She looked Lyle in the face, then turned toward

Mitch, then full-on at Lyle again. "I've got a humongous favor to ask you."

Lexa, Mitch noticed, was industriously chewing a corner of her mouth.

His father, on the other hand, sat back with crossed arms and waited for Mariah as if he had all the time in the world.

"What it is," Mariah resumed, gesturing too casually with her water glass and slopping a little, "I'd like to—could I kind of hang around, do you suppose, and take pictures while you, mmm, go through"—she took a hard swallow of water and let the words out in a tumble—"whatever you're going to go through?"

Lyle squinted one eye as if peering through a rifle sight, then translated:

"While I gradually kick the bucket, you mean?"

"That's the idea," Mariah said fast. "I know it sounds a little gruesome."

"A *death*watch photo essay?" Mitch bit out. "You want to use him as a poster child for *that?*" By now he was casting a dumfounded look in Lexa's direction.

What can I tell you? She pulled into Seattle, her mood up and down like a yo-yo, we were just sistering away like we've always done, and then you called, and Mariah had to get back to Montana somehow anyway, so we hop in the van and along about Coeur d'Alene she comes up with this idea of wouldn't it be something to shoot Mitch's dad's last days. I had four hundred miles of telling her huh-uh. Your turn.

The majority of this he could divine just from the expression on Lexa. Mariah meanwhile was heard from again. "My editor gave the idea a shit-hot go, Mitch."

"Well, I give it—"

"These'd be in that newspaper of yours?" Lyle asked, frowning along with his squint.

"You bet, but *after*," Mariah specified delicately.

"Listen, shooter, points for effort, okay?" Mitch started in on

Mariah. "But we're going to have more than enough to handle around here while—"

"Rib eye," the waitress sang out as she slid a sizzling platter past him to Lexa. Conscientiously waiting for the rest of the food to land before further batting down Mariah's scenario, it took Mitch a minute to realize the meal deliveries had ended with Lexa's. He shot a look for the waitress in vain, then at Lexa. She dug into her steak.

Lyle's granitic head thrust a couple of inches closer to Mariah.

"What do they pay, on something like that?"

"Probably not as much as you have in mind. Nothing, actually."

Lyle was taken aback. "Hell of a note," he muttered, "when you can't even make a living out of dying."

"Lyle, you'd be—it's news, see. The story of"—Mariah took a breath—"how you face death is worth telling readers. There's this aging population, and a bazillion of us lint-free Baby Boomers who've never had to deal with anything more serious than burying the class hamster, back in first grade. I hate to say it, but people need to see your kind of situation." She stopped for a moment. "Lexa and I have been through this with our mother. Haven't we, kiddo." She laid a quick hand on Lexa's arm. "Lung cancer, that was. We didn't have a clue, before we had to watch her go. I guarandamntee you, my photo piece on you won't leave anybody clueless about life's last dance, Lyle."

"Wouldn't exactly be my best side, though, would it," came his dry objection.

"And the newspaper can pay Mitch," Mariah skipped right on. Mitch's head snapped around to her. *What, for my father? Like a bounty on coyotes?* "Not much, but some," she was explaining, as close to apologetic as she evidently could get. "It'd be on a free-lance basis for caption stuff of what I shoot. Oh, and the paper can put you on as Teton County stringer as well. The regular one in Choteau needs time off for a hip replacement."

"Just what I've tried to work my way up to in twenty-five years of journalism." Mitch spoke with ominous calm. "Second-string stringer. Such a deal, Mariah." He turned to his father. The silence from that quarter was saying all too much.

"Dad. You're not going to do this."

Lyle went back to his folded-arms pose. Then gazed off as if calculating and said:

"Ohhh, I think maybe so. Yeah."

The thought of his father being allowed to grandstand his way out of life, winking tragically at the camera eye in front of a statewide readership, appalled Mitch.

"Forty-eight hours ago I had to pry the fact of your sickness out of you! Now you're ready to parade it in front of a camera?"

"Hey, *parade* isn't a very nice way to put it," Mariah chided.

"Guess maybe I'm forty-eight hours older and wiser," Lyle speculated.

"You heard Mariah." Mitch could hear his own voice rising. "There's nothing halfway financial in this for you. You'll be giving yourself away." Although he wouldn't, would he, in the way that really counted.

Mitch stared across at his father, then over to Mariah. "Nothing against you and your camera, okay? But it's just a fact of . . . I was about to say life, but now it has to be *death* too, that the camera will be in the way—"

"Will not," said Mariah hotly.

"Since when?" Lexa said, chewing the last bite of her steak.

"—every time we try to sort ourselves out on anything, medical, family, the sonofabitching gravel, *anything.*"

"Tell you what, Mitch," Lyle broached abruptly. "I'll back off and let you think over the gravel deal if you'll go along with the picture taking."

"And I promise I'll get out of everybody's hair anytime there's heavy family stuff you have to deal with, how about?" said Mariah, all reasonableness.

Mitch rubbed his forehead as if trying to erase all this. "Lexa, what do you think?"

She felt Mariah's eyes on her, and from across the table the pierce of Lyle's. "What can I say," she slowly furnished to Mitch, "except maybe get it written in blood from both of them."

Lyle chortled from way down deep. "Didn't expect to be made famous for this, but you take what you can get." He held a hand toward Mariah. "Shake?"

"Shake." She gave him a squeeze of the palm firm enough it obviously surprised him. She aimed the same slim vise of hand out over the table. "Mitch?"

"Shake," he gritted out and shook hands with her and then, feeling doubly foolish, with his father. Lexa rolled her eyes and downed a final forkful of her baked potato. Looking beyond pleased, Mariah bounced to her feet and went off to raid the salad bar.

"Shake," announced the waitress, depositing a milk shake in front of Lyle. "Here you go, hon." Before whirling away again, she advised Mitch, "Yours will be a while."

"Wait a minute." He sounded between desperate and miserable. "We all ordered at the same time, I asked for the special because it was sitting there ready, right? Where *is* mine?"

The waitress bit her lip and peered nervously toward the kitchen. "Cookie is on a kind of a slowdown."

Mitch swiveled to join the waitress's perusal of the kitchen ready-window and was met with a glare.

"She's ticked off at the boss," the waitress confided. "For taking on this big feed tonight."

"The Biotic Betterment banquet?"

"Right, how'd you know? So anyway she's only doing one order at a time." Just then theme music swelled in the banquet area, announcing video time. *"Swine diseases are ever lurking."* The blare through the divider got right down to cases. *"Parasites, bacteria and viruses are always on the attack, and each and every pig in your swine yard is their battlefield. Erysipelas . . . leptospirosis . . . transmissible gastroenteritis . . ."*

An angry flick of the order slip ensued at the ready-window. "There, she's starting on your pork chop special now," the waitress said.

Fuming and famished and having told the waitress to tell the cook where to dispose of that pork chop, Mitch launched off to the salad bar for emergency rations. ("The garbanzo beans are your best bet," Lexa's advisory followed him.) He caught up with Mariah as she was trying to pick up slices of pickled beets the size of poker chips with recalcitrant salad tongs.

"You are some piece of work, you know that?"

"I don't think I hear the Hallelujah Chorus coming."

"What's up with this brainstorm assignment of yours anyway? Jesus H., Mariah, you waltz in here from the world at large, you vamp my father into—"

"Nobody's vamped anybody around here yet that I know of," she told him pleasantly.

"—turning himself into a photo album of saying *sayonara*. What in the name of hell is it you want with this? You're a roving photographer, aren't you? Why can't you rove into somebody else's family mess?"

She met Mitch's eyes with her own, gray and sharp as flint arrowheads. She kept her voice down. "Never pretty, is it, doing a piece somebody isn't happy to have happen. I want to do your father's story because it's going to be a chance-of-a-lifetime shoot, okay? I can absolutely feel that set of pictures waiting to happen out of his . . . circumstances. But Mitch, you really want to know what else I can get out of this?" She did a quick little toss of her head, storm of hair clearing away from the vicinity of her eyes, as if that would help her to sight in on him. "Some mountain time, even if this half-assed excuse for a town did manage to miss the entire Rockies by about twenty miles. At least I can sneak out to them from here, early mornings and in between doing your dad. It's a job thing; you of all people ought to be able to savvy that. The paper will keep sending me to snap the same old Rotary lunch speakers in every weinie place like this in the entire state, if I don't think up better shoots. While what I really want to work on is my photo book, and I need these mountains for that." She checked on him with another straight-on meeting of the eyes. "Any of this give me a passing grade?"

"I was way off. You're *twice* as tricky a piece of work as I thought."

"Get a grip of yourself, can't you?" *Rrr*s rolled in Mariah's admonition like the wheels of Scottish war wagons. "What I'll be doing on this assignment, full livelong working days and then some, will be a perfectly legit picture story. Right now you can't see it because of all the family stuff. Take it from me, though, your father—there's no way I won't get great shots of him, a face like that, and the way he handles himself like he's his own prize invention. The camera doesn't care what you think of him."

"Listen, Mariah. That may be. Say he's the most photogenic doomed person this side of Garbo in *Camille*." He locked eyes with her. "Don't you think you're crossing a line, just gaily handing yourself a story where Lexa and I are mixed into it too?"

"You've never crossed a line into a story? Alaska?"

Even after the supper club, the house was not a welcome sight to any of them but Lyle. Mariah brightly said she had better get herself and her camera gear established in the bunkhouse, hadn't she, while Lexa felt the need to walk somewhere and

Mitch, still looking more fed up than fed, said maybe that's what he needed, too.

As if it was an effort but worth making, Lyle underhanded the keys to his pickup in a high lob from the kitchen steps across the driveway. "Head on out to the Bench, why don't you. Show missy the sunset from there." Turning to go in, he left them with: "Just remember, you're walking all on money."

Mitch drove west out of town, Lexa watching partly the tops of the mountains coming closer and partly him.

"I never should have let her climb off that plane, huh?"

"Lexa, I am not holding you responsible, can't you tell?"

"But."

"But why the hell couldn't you have warned me some way that she was going to want to take snapshots of my dear doomed father while he goes defunct?"

"When? How?" Lexa shifted defensively in her seat. Lyle's pickup was like a junk room calved off the house, the dashboard full of flotsam and the floor of jetsam. She pinned down a stray screwdriver that was threatening to bounce up and impale her. "Even if I'd managed to send you smoke signals or something, what were you going to do with them? You can't think it's your decision instead of your father's, whether he lets Mariah poke a camera in his face for what little is left of his life?"

There was a side of Mitch the size of Half Dome that did think precisely that, of course. But the more rational portion of him knew Lexa's argument had justice to it. If Lyle Rozier wanted to go out in his own form of sunset, kindled into blaze by the focus of Mariah's manifold damnable camera lenses, who could deny him that wish?

"She won't pretty him up any, you know," Lexa was saying. "If he goes out of life throwing up on his shoes, she'll shoot that, too."

"Gee, that's reassuring."

Reminding herself that maybe it was time to concede a point, Lexa granted: "For somebody dying, he is pretty lively."

Mitch stared ahead bleakly, to where Phantom Woman's browlike summit stood above the other peaks of the Continental Divide. "You don't know the half of it yet."

They parked atop the long ramp of ridge, a hundred miles of the Rockies awaiting them in the first dye color of evening. The sunset didn't stop with the rose-washed mountains; Mitch at once turned Lexa around by her shoulders to view the exquisite three rises on the northeast horizon of the plains; the Sweetgrass Hills, outlined in last minutes of golden light.

While they walked along the top of the benchland, which was oddly like a pebbly beach elevated into the sky, Mitch thought out loud about the medical siege ahead and a father who until now had never spent so much as a minute in a hospital bed. It fell to Lexa to do the private thinking about being back on a patch of earth like this, toe to toe with the old hungers.

There when she and Lyle were alone at the table, during Mitch and Mariah's circumnavigations of the salad bar, Lyle had favored her with a cagey grin and confided: "Glad you're on hand in this, what'll we call it, continuing discussion. I feel I can tell you anything, pretty much." Then inclined his head toward the front window of the supper club and the distant skyline framed there and said as if the thought had just strolled up to him: "You know what, though, Lexa? Mitch doesn't like to hear me say so, but those mountains do just sit there. So much of this country has always been locked up—the Bob and all that, up there. Finally along comes a way that land can be put to real use, some gas and oil drilling—not all that much, it's only a kind of dental work on a bigger scale, if Mitch would just think of it that way—and if gravel roads up into there," he nodded toward the mountains again, "are going to be part of that deal, they might as well be Rozier Bench gravel roads, hadn't they? I figure you ought to know how things stand, since you're sort of in the family and all."

The *sort of* had put her wary. "Leading to what, Lyle?"

He smiled the smile of a kindly trick roper. "Just that I believe I'll go ahead and dab my name on those papers that Mitch is still a little skittish about, is all. That way, if he happens to change his mind, that arrangement will be ready to go no matter what condition I'm in. You and Mitch haven't got so much money in life that you can pass this up, have you?"

It is something, how he can be so bossy and full of dickering at the same time, she had noted with what she was sure was poker-faced calm and simultaneously heard her best intentions go out the window.

"Lyle, I came to be any help I can on the household stuff, okay? The rest of it, you and I are pretty much going to be oil and water, shall we say. If Mitch asks me what to do with the papers on your gravel deal, I'll tell him to tear the fuckers up and throw them to the forty-eight winds."

Yet was it worth it, Lexa asked herself again now, even trying to keep country like this at arm's length from the dreams and schemes of the endless Lyles? ("You don't have to be in the family so much you sound like Mitch," he had ended up huffing to her there in the supper club.) North of here some fifty miles, the McCaskills had come and put in their century—homesteading, rangering, ranching, trying not to disgrace the land that held them. Maybe that was all that could be hoped for, one family canceling out the other in the world's ledger. She had wanted to keep it going in Alaska, her tribal line of people who lived by seasons instead of core samples. But it turned out there would be no kids; Travis was shooting blanks. It turned out short for her in a lot of ways, the sum of Alaska.

She realized she and Mitch had done the length of the ridge and back, and he was still restless. He reached over and cupped her shoulder as if to buck her up and kidded, "Never knew Easy

Street is all gravel, did you." It at least made her blink. *I thought I was the designated kidder.*

"Come on," Mitch said suddenly, "I'll show you the real family landmark."

Now he drove north and a bit east to the Donstedder Bench. The late spring's green blush was still on the slopes of that more arable benchland, although the grass would soon enough turn tawny. The road climbed the side of the bluff in a long swooping curve, and right at the crest Mitch stopped the pickup. He climbed out, Lexa following, and stepped through the plowed dirt to the last furrow of the field, at the very verge of the bluff. Under them now, the coulee leading down to the Soda Creek valley was a massive spill of stone, from junior boulders to the size that could be pitched with one hand.

"Lot of big mama rocks had their nest here, looks like," Lexa said.

"We picked rocks on all these benches that got farmed." Mitch dipped his head to each of the several long landforms around like a moored fleet. "Most truckloads ended up here. Some guys didn't want rock piles taking up the corners of their fields, but Donstedder didn't care about this coulee; we could fill it to the brim as far as he was concerned."

Mitch paused, seeming to think back as Lexa measured the rock pile with her eyes. "Dad had crews of us out every spring as soon as the fields dried enough to drive a truck on." He let out a bitter half laugh. "Sometimes barely dry enough."

"Dad? It's awful soft out here."

"A little mud won't hurt you guys," his father scoffing. The man with a war behind him.

In his mind's eye, they were fanned out in this field again, two boys on each side of the blue truck, ranging out to pick up rocks from the size of softballs on up. They began brighthanded, wearing cheap white cotton work gloves which by the end of the first day would be irredeemably soiled and by noon of the second day would be worn out. Every farmer whose field they worked pointed out that leather gloves might cost more but would last longer, and every boy resented laying out his own money and went on buying the cheap ones.

Those farmers were not happy to have to deal with Lyle Rozier on rock picking. They knew they could hire these same boys for the same dollar an hour he paid them, but overseeing a bunch of high school kids took too much time from everything else that needed doing on a place in springtime. So they scowled and paid Lyle two dollars an hour for every pair of hands (including himself, sitting like a duke in that truck cab) and gassed up the truck for him as well.

On that first day Mitch had been paired with Sharpless on the far side of the truck, and over on the driver's side were his other buddy from the football team, Loper, and some skim-milk kid whose name was lost now. In compound gear, the truck grumbled along at slowest speed. The truck tires cut alarming furrows, but Lyle had been right, rock picking was possible. Chilly and messy and clumsy, with mud built up on their shoes, but they could do it. The boys worked hard to keep warm, which doubtless was in Lyle's calculation too. When they met up with the most sizable rocks, glacier leavings the size of anvils or more, he might stop the truck and jump down to help the grunting pair of boys. Or he might not. He was breaking Sharpless and Loper and the no-name kid in on who was boss. Mitch already knew.

So it had come as a surprise, about an hour into the day, when they saw Donstedder and his hired man moving some mother cows and their fresh calves in the fence lane on the far side of the field and Lyle stopped the truck and called over the top of the cab to his four rock pickers, "Need to go ask Donstedder if the gate's unlocked to his coulee. Mitch, come drive the

Goose a couple minutes." He gave them a satisfied nod for the heap of rocks already in the truck bed. "There, didn't I tell you? Any prissypants can work in a dry field."

Mitch ascended to the truck cab and his father marched off across the mud. As he got the truck inching along, Sharpless promptly drifted around to the side where the other two boys were.

Sharpless called out, "Here comes a lateral, Lope." With both hands he lobbed a rock the size of a work shoe.

Loper caught the rock, tucked it to his middle like a football and, laughing, dropped back a few steps and passed it overhand into the truck bed. Sharpless and the skim-milker cheered and clomped around searching for rocks the right size to shovel-pass to one another.

Mitch watched several fancy flings of rocks, all three boys into the game now, before pulling out the throttle a fraction to keep the truck going, then stepped out onto the running board.

"Hey, Sharps, and you guys, bad idea," he shouted while keeping his hand on the steering wheel. "My old man's not going to go for that." He tried a forced laugh, already knowing this could be major trouble. "You're leaving rocks like crazy, he'll can your asses."

The trio giggled, took a peek across the field to make sure Lyle's distant back was still turned and kept on pitching and passing to one another, each rock that found its way to the truck leaving many others undisturbed in the mud.

Mitch rode there on the running board, in charge of disaster. The field that first day was full of fresh frost heave, rocks galore, rocks—

He stood looking at them again now, the filled vee of coulee like the comet tail of a glacier. One oblong rock, somewhere there, that his life had pivoted on.

"You never told me you had a rock collection," Lexa tried on him, slipping an arm into his.

He made the effort to laugh, but his eyes stayed soberly on the coulee of stone. "If you have to wrestle the country from the rocks every damn year, maybe that ought to tell you something about the country. But it never did Lyle Rozier, or these dryland farmers."

"You're not going to change him at this late date, you know."

"I do know, Lex, but I can't help wanting him to have been something else than what he was. Or for that matter still is." Mitch nodded violently across the corner of the valley toward the gravel-gray Rozier Bench. "Sonofabitching guy who is always out to make a killing instead of a living."

He gave Lexa a bit of a gaze, then away. "That's always been his story," he raggedly went on. "Always been a promoter. He got all excited when yuppies started swilling down mineral water. He and the town honchos sent off samples of the springs to the bottling companies—half of them wrote back that the stuff tasted too terrible, and the other half said it tasted too good. Another time, we were going to get rich on antique tractor radiator caps. Now it's branding irons."

"Mitch, he's up in years now, not to mention on his last legs. You're going to have to—"

"That's the latest thing he's trying to get away with. Time for sympathy for Lyle."

"And the worst part is, you're feeling some."

"*Yes!* Damn right I am, and I don't want to be." He was silent a moment. "I know it sounds cruel."

It sounded near criminal, her expression seemed to say.

Desperately Mitch delved for a way out of his divided state of mind. He knew he had to answer that look on her. But which was the real side of things? The Coast life, the fumble of marriage and the kids, the long devotion to a newspaper that was Bingford's plaything between mountain romps, the try with

Lexa, years now and still somewhere in the experimental stage? Or this born-into obligation, this confusing but unavoidable step back to—what do you even call it? Certainly it was no longer childhood, but it was offspringhood of some inescapable kind.

"He pretty much *was* dead, as far as I was concerned," he explained, if it was an explanation. "Had been since I left here, as little as we had to do with each other all those years. Now it's like he's popped back to life. Temporarily."

"And now you have to deal with him, and you don't like that."

"Both of the above, sorry to say."

Lexa shook her head, whether wondering about his mental fitness or her own he couldn't tell. She told him, "I came to try to help along the edges. But you're going to have to let me know when you and your father are in the here and now, and not back there wishing each other would turn out differently."

Rooted there at the outermost furrow of the field, Mitch did not say anything for several seconds. Then it all came.

"Lexa, I am a fifty-year-old unfeathered biped carrying too much weight. With a marriage behind me that I wouldn't wish on an alimony lawyer. And grown children who maybe are what they are because I didn't wage a fifteen-year war over them with their mother, and they don't care spit about me. The only occupation I've ever had is about to turn into street litter. Now I'm back here where I don't want to be, in Lyle Land. He and I have let each other down in ways we can't even spell out. Then there's you."

She blinked a quick semaphore of alarm at arriving on this list.

Mitch was surging on. "I know I torpedoed Travis and you—"

"Hey, that only took a cap pistol."

"—and I've only ever managed to be so-so at playing house

with you, I know that, too. Why don't you just walk out on the Roziers?"

"You are in a mood."

"You can, you know. Give this relationship the big haircut."

Lexa stood perfectly still. Around her she could sense dusk dropping degree by degree, the feel of the chilling field. All she knew was that she wasn't going to surrender here on the stony ground of Mitch's past.

"Come on, let's get you back to town," she resorted to. "We could both use some beauty sleep."

Sleep was not anywhere near either of their minds, though, the darkness still fresh by the time they drove back in. She gave him a try again as they came to the outskirts of town.

"So, fullback. Going to drive me by the old high school, see if they've put up a statue yet of you throwing your helmet into the stands?"

"Don't get your hopes up." She thought she could see the area around his mouth twitch a little.

"Tsk. Here you are, legendary, and I don't even get to see the blade of grass you first fullbacked all over, you, the Iron Tum—"

"Don't start with that!" he commanded, but now he definitely was suppressing a provoked smile.

She watched him watch her from the corner of his eye until he finally broke out with: "Okay, Smart Mouth, you want local attractions, I'll show you the one and only."

He swung the pickup down a side street and pulled over at Artesia Park. They stepped onto the neglected grass, Lexa turning her nose in the direction of the springs as if investigating an aroma that had no business in her kitchen.

"You still want walking," Mitch was saying, "four times around this mother is a mile."

"Let's just move our feet a little. Show me the sights, Slick." She put her hand in his side jacket pocket, causing him to put his arm around her as they began the tour.

Even by night it was a scabby park. In the harsh bluish glow from backyard lights behind most of the nearby houses, the crusts around the side-by-side sulphur springs looked deathly alkaline, and the timeworn gazebo appeared to have fallen off the forklift from a high school production of *The Music Man*. Trees had a hard life here.

Yet frolicsome touches had been tried. Sporadic picnic tables still were around, scattered like old survivors of a shipwreck, and over by the weatherbeaten *Artesia Park* sign was a plywood cutout where tourists could poke their heads through holes and have jokey photos taken.

When they reached the artesian swimming holes, Mitch shifted from one foot to another then back again, studying the pair of pools with surpassing interest. "Umm, Lexa? Want to go for a euphemism?"

Lexa gazed at him, then at the springs steaming gently in the night. "Is this the point where the shy maiden says, 'But I didn't bring my swimsuit'?"

"I was sort of hoping she'd say, 'Let's shoot out the blue sodium lights and go naked.' "

"Welcome to Yard Light City, all right. What do these people have that they think is so worth swiping?" Eyes creased against the acetylene hover of night-lights behind most of the nearby houses, she peered around the none-too-dark park.

"There's a corner of the big spring in behind the gazebo," Mitch issued like a bulletin.

"How do you know this?"

"Hearsay."

Lexa laughed down in her throat. "Her say, don't you mean? So who was she, Rozier? The cheerleader who was easy to score on? The 4-H Club sweetiepoo?"

Mitch enwrapped her, jolting her off her footing, seeming to stagger a little himself as he gave her a kiss that could have been felt in France. After the maximum visitation back and forth by their tongues, he pulled his head back and said thickly: "She wasn't anybody. You're it."

"In that case," Lexa heard herself say in a rush, so starved for him her throat wasn't working quite right, "you probably don't want any more years to go by before testing out that water."

There were a few scrawny tree shadows at the far end of the park for them to scurry to the back of the gazebo. On the spring bank there, hidden or close enough, they clutched and kissed some more. Clothing cascaded off. His large pale form loomed, her compact one emerged from a sudden circlet of blue jeans and panties. *The non-bride wore moonlight. If it doesn't suit the occasion, Mitch, I don't know what better I can do.* She steadied herself against him with an inquiring spread palm.

They plunged in, Mitch first, lifting her down. The water was coarse but warm as a zinc-tub bath. The sulphur odor might as well have been harem musk.

Hair wet, they were sleek as seals in a pocket of sea. When he lifted her a bit she rode on his thigh, rocking there, pleasure-clenched on the might of him; making love with Mitch was trying out a jungle gym, there were all these . . . *dimensions* to take into consideration, to play on. Her hand found him ready. She shifted, and his breath drew in. Openmouthed with need, they joined, surged together, the water of the spring lapping against the gray silver rim of bank.

"This stuff," Mitch panted and laughed urgently at the same time, "makes your hair stand up," he panted again, "in spikes."

"Break my heart some more," she growled and buried her lips into his.

·   ·   ·

"Mitch? Lexa? That you?"

"Everybody but." Bumping her way through the kitchen maze to the refrigerator, Mariah blanched at what she found when she opened its door, but shoved enough of it aside to stash her extra film. "Just keeping my camera food cool," she called to Lyle in the other room.

"Doing okay in the bunkhouse? Been a while since it had anybody in it."

"It's fine, no livestock or anything. Ta-ta."

Woop, Mariah. You're back dealing in American. Better go in and tell him nighty-night. She went to the living room door and saw him planted there in his chair, up close to the television.

In the ghostblue light from the screen he again studied her all he wanted to, his manners so rusty he didn't think to invite her to take the load off her feet. No immediate "good night" forthcoming from that quarter, either. She wondered what she was getting into, inserting herself and her camera into the last days of this ironbound old man.

As she was about to murmur "See you in the morning," Lyle nodded toward the TV screen.

"This Internet stuff is quite something. Found myself, on there."

"No crap?" She was unwillingly drawn into the room. Her body clock was still ticking in Eskimo or some such, but she could always put off being tired long enough to be curious. "Let's have a peek at you." She came and hunkered by his easy chair.

"First thing is, get rid of Dugout Doug here." Lyle peered down into the keyboard on the TV tray table, struck something, and General MacArthur and his corncob pipe vanished back into history. "So you just been everywhere. What was that like?" She was surprised he could make conversation as he hunted and pecked.

"That's what I'm trying to figure out. What fits with what, in the book I'm doing."

Peering up at the screen and frowning down at the keyboard with every stroke, Lyle mashed away at keys with two fingers stiff as drill presses. "Does that pay good, a book?"

"There's no telling."

"You're gonna be putting the whole world in a book, hadn't you ought to be able to charge plenty?"

"My stuff, you can't sell by the cubic yard."

We Who Were the Jungleers arrived on the screen, with the cartoon of a Sad Sack soldier wearing the patch of the Forty-first Infantry Division where Superman wore his *S*.

"Progress," Lyle announced, and stopped to take stock of the menu. He brought up onto the screen *Australia—the Queensland training*, frowned harder and zapped it. "That kid Matthew can squirrel around in this stuff like nobody's business. Takes me some hit and miss." He managed to find *New Guinea—the jungle war*. Mariah watching, he began a fresh search through *zones of combat*.

"The world." The word came from him as if he considered it an interesting affliction. "I've never much budged, myself. Not that you'll be overly surprised to hear so." He indicated the crammed room shadowed around them. She felt a bit guilty for equating his house with the quake-shaken museum, but the resemblance was still there.

"Had to go when they sent me to fight Tojo," Lyle said as if thinking it over. "But that was different. See the world from under a helmet."

Very much as if he had timed it, combat photography arrived onto the screen. Smudges of landing craft, and bomb geysers in the water. Dead bodies on a grainy beach.

Mariah was the third generation of McCaskill women tired of hearing about it from men who had gone to war, as if women's lives weren't some level of combat.

"That was my father's story, too," she let him know. "Came back from the Aleutians with his leg shot up. Then there was my uncle who didn't come back at all."

Lyle paused a moment over what she had said. "Don't know how, but the ones I went with all stayed in one piece."

His next stab brought them. The trio of young soldiers, himself in the middle. Helmets with camouflage netting, rifles slung on their shoulders, a bazooka in their possession, too; younger-than-springtime smiles at odds with all that. Central as he and his sergeant stripes were in the grouping, Lyle in particular looked convinced he was bulletproof. Mariah could tell it was confidence put on for the camera, but even so. A face like that came from the climate inside the person.

He must have been a heartbreaker when they came home in uniform, she thought to herself. War hero, or what passed for one, here. Mariah was veteran enough about men to know halo sheen when she saw it.

"This business of pictures for nothing," he was saying. "They can just put me up on there?"

"Seems like," she said, intent on the set of faces on the screen. "Good-looking bunch of devils you were."

"Yeah, well, two out of three isn't bad." They chortled together at the pug-faced bazooka man, his smile a bit lopsided and loose around the edges, posing shoulder to shoulder with Lyle.

"Buddies of mine," Lyle identified, even though their countenances were speaking for themselves on the screen. Fritz Mannion, prima facie dumb. Joe Ferragamo, noble as some statue in the middle of Rome.

"And then the next thing I knew," he said as if still caught off balance by it, "I was back here in the Springs, family man and all. You ever tie the knot?"

"You bet." Mariah grinned with fond scorn for the marriage to Riley. "Turned out to be a slipknot, lucky for me."

The old man sharpened his tone on that answer of hers.

"Divorce has gotten kind of contagious, yeah."

One thing Mariah never liked was sermonettes on marriage

from people who were not current in the field. By whatever hole card of fate, this man was a loner, she could tell, and she decided to call him on it.

"Your wife—what's that wimpy way they put it now—predeceased you some time ago, did she?"

Lyle jerked a fit-to-kill look at her. But of course she had no way of knowing about Adele, flying along on black ice until here came the bridge abutment. He sat there forcibly swallowing ire and memory, while Mariah watched him from only a few feet away. Women these days didn't give you much ground to maneuver on.

"A lot of time ago," he said and left it at that.

Mariah stood. "I'd better call it a night. Always have to get up early for good light for shooting. Thanks for the loan of the bunkhouse." She glanced again at the image of the three young GIs on the screen. Leaving, she wished him "Happy World War Two," seeming to mean it.

Alone again except for the tired feeling which was pretty much with him all the time now, Lyle had to debate whether to bed down here in the chair and have to justify that to Mitch and Lexa when they came in, or drag himself off to his bedroom. Dying wore on you after a while.

Yet it had taken all these years for the one with his name on it to catch up with him, hadn't it. This was what he kept finding intriguing, that he was being handed time enough to know he was a goner, to think through the disposition of things. Settle accounts.

Not that he was deluding himself about knowing how to handle death; he was still trying on the one brought back again by that "predeceased" crack of Mariah's. (She and that Lexa had the sort of mouths that needed holsters, didn't they.) He had been secretly relieved when Mitch's mother went out of his life—went out of life, period—in that car wreck. Secret didn't begin to say enough, about a reaction like that. A person could never admit to that kind of thing even to himself. But deep down Lyle knew that was what his feeling toward Adele's death amounted to, a lifting of what he had blindly brought on himself. He figured he might be particularly conscious of this because he was a man with only a few such things buried out of sight that way, and there had been his scare when one of those had half got out, that summer of Mitch's leg accident and all the commotion after.

Adele had been touchy. (Mitch got that quality from her. Mama's boy without a mama; maybe that accounted for Mitch breaking away from him, back there.) Any number of times she utterly did not want to go along with the program, his ventures to try to make something of the Springs country and this family along with it. It still burned him, Adele's lack of trust. Watch your chance and take a gamble every so often on a deal like the Rozier Bench and that was your reward at home, arguments. He had been amazed the first time Adele pulled out of here and spun gravel halfway to the Sweetgrass Hills. Then when she came back, that time and every time, and the household would settle down for a while, the word turned to more like *amused*.

It was Mitch they stayed together for, of course.

He hadn't known jack-squat about having a kid. Or even wanting one. Cravings a person never suspected before had built up throughout the war, though; had they ever. Kids poured forth, from the ex-sergeant Lyle Roziers and the ripe and waiting Adele Conlons. Like probably any number of people then, they had got themselves caught, barely started going together when Adele missed her time of the month. But she went up to her people in the Sweetgrass Hills to have the baby, and when Mitch was born a bit overdue, even the bookkeeping on that looked pretty close to balanced.

Lyle shifted in the chair in the semi-dark. It wasn't the life he'd thought he would lead. Whose is?

He hesitated, listening to make sure Mitch and Lexa weren't on their way in, then keyboarded back to the war-scarred beachhead on the Web.

New Guinea was a sonofagun of a place to go to war unless you had a taste for vines, mosquitoes, snakes, sopping horse-blanket heat, tropical diseases severe enough to make your bones rattle and the likelihood of Japanese snipers up every mangrove. Not even to mention being ushered in to the Guinea shore the way they were, aboard a disabled landing craft lying there on Tambu Bay like an engraved invitation to the Japanese air force for target practice. Some idiot on his last cigarette had crumpled the empty pack and tossed it onto the floor of the landing craft instead of over the side and the wad went into the sump pump like silk drawers up a vacuum cleaner. Sergeant Lyle Rozier's natural tendency was to suspect Fritz Mannion, but he lacked total evidence and besides there was the more pressing matter of the water leaking in fast around the landing ramp without the sump pump to draw it back out. Half a mile short of the beach, the coxswain had to dead-stop the already half-swamped vessel or risk driving it under the waves. And so there Lyle and his cherished platoon of Company C were, invasion-force soldiers bailing like madmen with their helmets.

Lyle still was proud of getting the men at the bailing without anybody panicking. In those little details that stick up in memory, he even now could see Ferragamo carefully rack his Browning automatic rifle in the side struts of the landing craft to keep it high and dry, and Mannion taking the same care with his bazooka, before starting to shovel saltwater. Most of the other guys were from the Montana National Guard and like Joe and Fritz they knew how to work. Meanwhile Lieutenant Candless seemed to think he could repair the situation by belaboring the Seabees who were trying to get the sump pump up and running again. The lieutenant was militarily doomed anyway on account of his name's resemblance to *candy ass*, but Company C's wariness toward ninety-day wonders such as him ran deeper than nomenclature. In young looeys whose only hand-to-hand combat had been with pencils at Officers Training School, they trusted not. Right there in that gap of trust between the enlisted men and the candy asses, Lyle figured, was where he had to operate. Even all these years after, he could bring back the bluff cozy sensation of acting as sergeant, like watching himself in a mirror shop. See himself young and on top of the job, giving the blessed order to drop packs and take a smoke or jokingly commanding, *Listen up, you modified civilians.* Then back off a little as his mind reflected, man by man, the precious complicated unit of soldiery assigned to him. Then savor to himself again the piece of authority that had come to him with that set of stripes on his sleeve. Back in the CCC camp, he had learned that he could put up with things better if he had a hand in running them. It didn't need to be everything; he didn't have to be total MacArthur. But in on the plan, some orders to give, dealing instead of being dealt to: this he liked very much. And was managing to live up to, here in their welcome party to New Guinea, at least enough to keep them all from drowning yet.

Finally the lieutenant quit profanely wasting breath when one of the Seabees yelled back up to him that they were ready to give the pump a try.

"Sergeant, have the men put their packs and helmets on again."

Dealing with this shavetail lieutenant was a matter of buying time. "Right away, sir, but just to be on the safe side, how about we give it another couple minutes of—"

They all heard the plane at the same time.

It was the lead Zero of three, and while the other fighter planes were farther back and a mile or more into the sky, this one was coming in at about a hundred feet. Coming with an odd laziness, as if the Japanese pilot had all the time in the world to look them over before starting to strafe the landing craft.

There was a mad scramble for their weapons, Fritz ridiculously trying to get his bazooka set up, Joe quickest with his BAR, but the plane was roaring in on top of them even by the time his finger was ready on the trigger.

"Ferragamo!" the lieutenant screamed as the Zero buzzed over them without strafing. "Get that BAR working!"

"Sorry, sir," Joe said, keeping watch on the two as yet uninterested planes. "I'm loaded with tracers. The other Zekes will see me firing, think I'm real ack-ack worth knocking out."

The Zero departed low over the water, wigwagging his wings as if to say *You look like you have enough trouble, Yanks.*

If it had ended there, that would have been the story brought home to the V.F.W. club—Lyle, drylander boatman, keeping them afloat while Joe, coolest head in the cauldron of the bay, kept them from being blown out of the water. But then came the patrol.

By now they were turning into jungleers, baptized combatants in the steamy and treacherous fighting as the Forty-first Infantry laboriously thrashed inland from the beachhead. Some more baptized than others. The night before they were due to go on patrol, dog tired from the first week in the forward area but on another level pleased enough with himself, Lyle filed along ahead of Joe in the first real chow line they had seen since hitting the beach. Mess kits in their right hand for the more or less hot food, and helmets held out in the other for the next week's worth of C rations to be dropped into, Lyle joked something to Joe about the two of them standing in a line that paid off twice as good as the CCC one for beans.

Ferragamo looked at him from under dark eyebrows, eyes shadowed with fatigue. Ferragamo's life had filled out handsomely in his years in the West, but the military with its ruthless pecking order reminded him of being back in the slum again.

He hunched up and soldiered and never said a word of complaint about lugging the twenty-two-pound automatic rifle and another twenty pounds in ammunition clips, but that didn't mean he liked any of the army rigamarole, as Lyle a little too obviously did.

"You can have this 'jungleer' good stuff," Ferragamo replied. Then added, giving it full Jersey accent: "Sawjint Rozier." He smiled at Lyle but only barely. "All's I want is to get my butt out of this war in one piece."

"Get with the program, Joe, your precious butt's already got a crack in it."

At the time Lyle just thought being shot at most days of the week was on Ferragamo's nerves. He couldn't do much about that, couldn't play favorites now that he wore sergeant's stripes. It would all pan out okay if he could keep dealing with Lieutenant Schwartz. (Candless was already a distant memory, picked off by a sniper the second day of the assault.) Keep an even rein on the men in the unit. Keep on keeping them from harm's way.

New Guinea was not the most cooperative country for that. The island's terrain was the goddamnedest tangle any of them had ever seen, mangrove swamps one instant and hellish shelves of tropical forest the next, and beyond those, some of the worst mountains in the world, the Owen Stanley Range. When their patrol set out the next morning to probe a spine of ridge along the Division's left flank, they first had to clamber on top of mangrove roots, one slippery muscle of wood to the next, to keep from going into mud up to their nuts. It took a couple hours of that to creep through a few hundred yards of swamp, but they came out of it not too badly situated, Lyle thought, hidden at the bottom of the slope. Somewhere on the ridge not far above them a Japanese heavy machine gun was firing bursts in the other direction toward the Americans' main advance.

The patrol crept up on the machine gun situation, the

Japanese dumb and happy there with their protection of a cliff behind them and the swamp below. With hand signals, Lyle sent Fritz and his bazooka to the brow of the ridge and a little behind the unsuspecting enemy. About any of the fine points of military life, Fritz could be stupider than snot. But let him get his mind set on something and a coyote cleverness took over. He had grasped that the bazooka was a job that spared a person from, say, being point man of the patrol. As if deer hunting with a blunderbuss, Fritz excruciatingly sighted in on the machine gun position and killed the gun crew with that first big shell.

That seemed a sufficient morning's work, particularly since the cliff closed off any reason to scout farther inland. With the men gathered around him at the former machine gun nest, Lyle looked at the jungle trail the enemy had been firing down.

"Careful on the road home," he said. "Let's fall back."

The sergeant part of Lyle was feeling good as the men lined out. They'd blown up some Japs, the patrol was all in one piece and they had this trail back to their lines instead of kangarooing among the mangroves. All the time after, running it through his mind again and again, shaping it for telling in the V.F.W. club, even now when memory was fed fresh by the pictures from the Web, he could not identify when and how he let his guard down.

As these things do, it happened too fast. Fritz tripped on a root and sprawled, the bazooka under him. Lyle remembered hoping the bazooka wasn't bent. He took a couple of quick steps to reach Fritz and help him up with as little commotion as possible.

Fritz was still down on all fours swearing under his breath when something rustled in the foliage. Without thinking, Lyle popped his head over a clump of green for a look. For a confused moment he thought the figure squatting there in the shadows, automatic rifle cradled in its arms, was Ferragamo taking a crap. Until he recognized the curved cartridge clip up top, Japanese make, instead of a BAR's clip under the gun. His own rifle not at the ready, he knew in that paralyzed instant he was dead, the whole patrol was dead, led blindly by him into the fusillade about to come as the enemy gunner began the scythe swing of that gun barrel.

Simultaneously a deafening stutter of shots dislodged that from Lyle's mind. It was Ferragamo firing, six BAR bullets a second cutting a strip across the Japanese soldier's shoulders and the base of his throat.

Lyle felt blood on his face and hands, could not believe this either. The Jap hadn't had a chance to fire. Then he realized Ferragamo's spray of bullets had blown the Jap's blood all over him.

Out in the night now, he heard the pickup pull into the driveway. Mitch and Lexa, coastal night owls, finally on their way in. Lyle sat up straighter and started zapping the traces of the war from the silent glowing screen. And laughed, not because he had any particular reason to be happy with himself, but at the way things turned out. He had far outlived Ferragamo, Hero Joe himself. And was at least tied with that old bastard Fritz yet.

Five

SO WHY DID I DO IT? In the time after, Lexa would work back at the puzzle of those weeks of the three of them and Mariah's nibbling camera keeping Lyle company as he gradually left life, frame by frame.

It's not pretty to have to admit, but I started at it all thinking that Lyle was a hopeless case in more ways than one. For Mitch's sake, I took on caring for his father as if I was pitching in on, oh, a sputtering tractor out there in the backyard mess. After all, that congregation of old odds and ends, at rest and yet somehow restless, was a lot like what comes with letting yourself love somebody. The debris field of the other person's family stuff. You can tell yourself until you are blue in the face that none of their history with one another concerns you, you don't care who put whose nose out of joint, way back when. But those are the things that make people the ones they are. That made Mitch, for better or worse. And Lord only knows, the makings of somebody like Lyle. So you do have to let yourself in for some of their weird family junk. Otherwise, you might as well go off by yourself in life and take up street mime.

The unknown weeks were still ahead of them when Mitch stepped out of the house yawning, rubbing his head and wondering why his hair was stiff. Then a remembering smile came, and he kissed at the air in the direction of the upstairs bedroom where Lexa was still under the covers. No sooner had he done so than he heard the instep of a boot come to rest on a nearby bottom pole of the jackstay fence.

"Mitch. I hope I can call you that?"

"Why not, it's my name. What's foremost on your mind this morning, Donald?"

"I wondered if you could give me any timeline yet on cleaning up your father's place. I have some clients I want to bring in to stay with me for some fly-fishing."

Mitch shook his head. "The flies in this country are pretty hard to catch, even with those little hooks. They don't fry up very good anyway."

Brainerd evidently was not to be dissuaded. "Your father has been telling me that the disposing"—Mitch shot him a look—"of his items in his yard is going to have to be up to you."

"He and I have been holding discussions about the place," Mitch confided. "We think we might turn it into a hog farm."

Brainerd tried that tight little smile of his. "I hate to have to bring this up again, really. But I've been here next door for some time now, and I haven't seen any improvement on your side of—"

The bunkhouse door banged open, and Mariah came out at full velocity, mane of hair richly red in the morning sun, well-filled lavender shirt with pearl snap buttons, blue jeans built for her. She threw a wave toward the two men and with her other hand slung her camera bag into the VW van, slid in like a Monte Carlo race driver and launched away in a crackle of gravel.

Mitch peered at Brainerd.

"Donald? Were your eyes green before?"

Mariah's eyes were thinking all the time, which maybe shouldn't have been news to me—sisters are expected to know each other microscopically, aren't they?—but still took some getting used to. Yet even Mitch, whose nerves she was primarily on, backed off some after she did the old Scotch preacher bit to say to him, "Forgive us our press passes, laddie." Me, I jumped out of my skin probably the first forty times when I'd be at something with Lyle, trying to get him to eat or at least slurp a milk shake between cigarettes, and out of nowhere would come the click. *I have to hand it to her, she was an utter damn genius at turning herself into atmosphere.*

The Great Falls doctor did nothing to conceal his annoyance at Mariah and her camera showing up with the rest of them for Lyle's medical appointment until Lyle sniffed majestically and said, "Can't hurt me much at this point, can it?"

Sitting there waiting for the mortal arithmetic of the latest medical tests, Mitch himself felt so rotten that he couldn't begin to imagine how his father must feel. Mitch's body was the over-size barometer of his mood, and the strain of trying to do right by unwanted bloodline obligations kept registering heavily. He could feel himself waning inside, turning to sludge. His every exercise-deprived muscle was yelping its conscience out at him. *Yo, Dairy Queenster, you want us to turn into rubber bands and suet?* He sat tense and tired and defensive against he didn't know quite what, as if his father's affliction were casting its shadow into him.

Lexa had been through this before, not that a person ever got used to visiting death's anteroom. Her mother sitting as Lyle now sat. *"I wanted to do this on Mother,"* Mariah had spilled in the sister session last night. *"Record the last of her. And I couldn't. Jick was having a tough enough time as it was. I'd probably have had to fight you on it—"*

"No 'probably' about it."

"—and so it ended up I didn't even try. I just didn't have the guts."

"Maybe some heart was involved there somewhere, Mariah. Give yourself a break."

"Vicinity of the insides anyway, okay. Makes me wonder about myself, though. A gut check telling me 'Huh uh' then, and 'You've got to' on Mitch's dad now."

From the look on this doctor, intestinal fortitude was going to be in demand for all of them before this was over, Lexa figured.

In the bull's-eye of the camera lens and the latest verdict being recited by the doctor, Lyle still was trying to resist showing how he actually felt. Scared. Scared as he had been only about three times before in his life, and two of those in New Guinea. The phase before this, when he had been the only one outside this office who knew he was dying, had been surprisingly like going away somewhere, traveling in solitary, being a tourist where nobody really knew him. Like on that visit of his to Seattle, watching people who had no idea he existed: in an odd kind of way, he couldn't help feeling he had that over them. Now Mitch and Lexa and Mariah and her camera had to be in on it all, but feeling scared was at least a sort of last privacy.

Mariah drifted around the room, not soundlessly but softly enough, consulting with her light meter until she gravitated to the shaft of prairie light coming in through the glass door to the office's genteel balcony. Eyeing the tableau of Lyle and Mitch and Lexa huddled next to the doctor's blondwood desk, she backed up against the glass door, tensed there, waiting, waiting, snapping a picture, waiting, snapping. When at last she was done and stepped away, a moisture outline of her upper body was left on the glass, fogged there from her body heat like a negative.

There wasn't any rehearsal available on any of this, most of all for Lyle. He reminded me of one of those big old hall clocks running down. Tired as he would get, though, he could still play sergeant. When that doctor finally coughed up the prognosis that he had better figure he at most had only a few months left, Lyle said right back to him, "I get to choose which ones, I hope?"

We all grew acquainted with leukemia in a hurry, through the symptoms that seemed to visit Lyle from day to day. Not that he would ever say so, but all of sudden one of us would notice that he was short of breath. Or sweating in a cool room. Or if he happened to bump into anything, it would leave a bruise on him dark as a plum. The healthy cells in him were gradually being overtaken by the others, we could tell. Looking back on it, living with Lyle and his affliction, and for that matter one another, was as complicated as bear-tagging camp. You try to watch your step and everybody else's as well, the whole crew of you tend to the chores and nobody gets any fingers nipped off, but in the end that's not quite all the danger there is. It goes beyond the actual griz. It's that clawprint on the trail. It's something just out of sight.

All of them but Mariah were at Lyle's desk, the latest gauntlet of paperwork spread there. Lexa was trying to be a buffer between the two men, not that buffing seemed to have much effect on either of them. Mitch by now looked as though he were undergoing the torture of a thousand paper cuts, having spent days on end with the Choteau lawyer clearing up the snarl of branding-iron niceties and along the way finding innumerable other loose ends, inevitably fiscally treacherous, from Lyle's lifetime of dealings. Lyle, on the other hand, notably perked up whenever he could corner Mitch into a business discussion.

"You see, though, the water rights on the banana farm"—
what Lyle had taken to calling the Rozier Bench in order to
piously hew to his promise not to mention the gravel deal—
"ought to be a whole separate kit and caboodle from the mineral. Who the heck knows how much of this country is, how
would you say, artesian?"

"Dad, it's a bone-dry glacial rock heap, okay? You'd have to
drill halfway to—"

"Drilling is a bad habit anyway," Lexa put in.

"Excuse me." Ever scrounging for the photographable,
Mariah was over by the sideboard examining the globe of metal
rods buoying out of the clutter there. "This has been bugging
the daylights out of me. What *is* this?" The thing had been nag-
ging her since the minute she first walked into this room; welded
together of pencil-thick rods, the metal tarnished with time, its
skeletal sphere shape reminded her of, of, of she wasn't sure
what.

Mitch glanced over, then flinched. Then unconvincingly
shrugged as if the item amounted to no more than, oh, say, a
giant dustball. "Just somebody's idea of a joke. Long time ago.
Should've thrown it—"

" 'Joke' nothing!" Lyle trumpeted in, then coughed hideously.
"It's his trophy. That's what they always called him in the newspaper, you know. When he was rolling down the field on all those
touchdown runs."

Feeling dumb for having looked at it day after day without
seeing it for what it was, Lexa blurted:

"The Iron Tumbleweed!"

"Well, well, well," said Mariah, a glitter in her eye.

"Hey, the whole bunch of you—do you mind?" Mitch gritted out.

"But I don't get it," Mariah kept on, Mitch appearing more
and more uncomfortable as she hovered there. "If it's iron, it
wouldn't roll like a you-know-what, would it?" She leaned down

lithely and fastidiously, puckered her lips a little and blew at the cross-strutted ball of metal. "I mean, you could huff and puff on this sucker until . . ."

Mitch gave her a glower. "Think about it, Mariah: newspapers are responsible for a lot of inane things."

Neither Mitch nor I wanted to admit it after all the fuss we'd each kicked up with my sister the self-invited roving photographer, but her picture taking seemed to do Lyle some good. Except when he wasn't the one directly in her sights.

"Let's try this, over here."

Set on getting a fresh picture of Lexa and Mitch together, and by now having used up virtually every backdrop at the Rozier house and a considerable distance around, Mariah had shooed them across town to Artesia Park.

Lexa unaccountably giggled at the venue.

To their surprise, Lyle had been determined to come along. It was one of his cranky days, but they figured he had every right, so Mitch with tight-lipped attentiveness bolstered him into the pickup and then over to a picnic table bench, where he could sit and light cigarettes and scowl.

Mariah had already circled the set of springs and the gazebo a couple of times, wrinkling her nose and muttering about what a thin excuse for a park this was. Now she came back for another frowning look at the plywood cutout. It was in the approximate shape of the zigzag mountain skyline, with the two whitish springs daubed in and the full-size figures of a male bather in a Victorian bathing suit and a female bather in a bikini about the size of a spotted bandanna and two leftover polka dots. Each figure was topped with a face-sized hole.

"Time to try crazy," she announced, twirling a different lens onto her camera as she coaxed her subjects into poking their heads through the cutouts, Lexa reluctantly and Mitch twice that. He still couldn't decide if Mariah was a genius with that damned camera or more like an idiot savant; instead of the fluke of rattling off what day of the week the Fourth of July fell on in the year 2099, maybe her mystifying capacity for calculation was all in her eye. Likely she was some of both, freakily inspired. Mitch could remember the fascination of watching Peggy Fleming in Olympic figure skating and taking to heart the commentator's remark that no one would ever skate more beautiful routines than hers, merely prettier ones. Mariah on a shoot had that same cool sense of highest possibility.

Glancing over at his father while she worked out the shot she wanted of Lexa and himself, Mitch saw that familiar figure at the picnic table now wearing an expression that was unmistakably jealous. One more side effect, Mitch thought resignedly, of Lexa's sister the ice maiden.

Meanwhile Mariah backed and forthed in front of the weather-beaten painted wood, still trying out lenses for the cracked-old-masterpiece effect she wanted. Mitch and Lexa, reduced to heads only, looked like carnival targets.

Lexa ogled downward. "The last time I had a figure like this, I was seven years old."

"You want to talk numbers, mine was twenty pounds ago," Mitch lamented.

"Don't smile, be yourselves," Mariah commanded, alternating long patient stares through the camera with flurries of firing away.

When she at last was through with that, Mitch ducked down so that only a void showed where the man's head was supposed to be. " 'Where's the rest of me?' " he delivered in the squawky fashion of Ronald Reagan waking up in the hospital bed in *Kings Row*.

"Quit," Mariah ordered, snickering. "Although you did give

me about half an idea. Switch, why don't you? Lexa, you stand in the guy's place. Mitch, be the bikini beauty."

"Not sure I'm required to sit here and watch that kind of stuff," Lyle huffed from behind his blue haze.

"No advice from the cheap seats, please," retorted Mariah, who by now could get away with kidding him. The camera glided to her eye and in the next instant she was crouching as if starting a run. Mitch as well as Lexa watched the balanced footwork and the delicate fingering, the athletic devotional moments, being clicked off now in hundredths of a second, that he recognized from football and she from barrel racing. And Mariah caught them as eternally as figureheads of vessels moored side by side in foreignmost docks.

"That'll do." She quit shooting, sounding pleased for once. Lexa proclaimed that what she was about to do was walk. But before setting out on her daily route up to the Bench, she hung on until Mitch had gone over to see how his father was holding up, then sidled to where Mariah was putting away camera gear.

"Umm, Mariah? Been meaning to ask you. If I show up in the newspaper, um, being with Mitch and all—what am I going to be called?"

"*Fiancée* is the journalistic style, sweetie," Mariah superinnocently provided.

She watched the determined figure of her sister, the walking woman in territory where people drove a block to the post office, recede past the slightly steaming springs; gave a little *tock* of her tongue against the roof of her mouth in salute to Lexa; and had to go back to her camera stowing. Then, though, it was Mitch's turn at her.

"Mariah? Do me a favor?" He looked highly uncomfortable.

"If it can be done pretty fast. I have to scoot into Great Falls yet and talk to the curator about how many walls I get for my museum show."

Mitch gandered down at this prestidigitator of newspaper,

book and museum wall. "You have three jobs? Am I counting right?"

"Well, sure, more or less." She shrugged those huntress shoulders at him.

He could feel the place in each week where "Coastwatch" had been. "It must be nice," he muttered. Then motioned with his head, ever so slightly, toward the bench where Lyle was perched, pensively fieldstripping his cigarette butt down to tobacco crumbs and a pea of paper. "Shoot this for me, would you? Him there at that picnic table."

Mariah only had to glance over there before telling him, "Mitch, it'd only be wallpaper, a shot like that. I've got a whole bunch of better ones of him today and—"

"It's one I want. For myself."

He had an expression on his face she couldn't read as she pulled her Pentax out of the bag again and advanced the film with a flick of her thumb.

"None of us had a camera here," he said as much to himself as to her, "the first time around."

Those weeks dragged and flew, both. I felt like I was running a visitor center, with a short-order kitchen on the side. The teenage ghost next door, Matthew, all of a sudden would crop up there by Lyle's chair and the two of them would go chasing around on the Web. Or old cronies of Lyle's from the town and around would drop in to say sorry for how sick he was, and about as many enemies would come by to make sure of it. He hadn't yet reached the point of being bedridden, but pretty much chair-ridden, when Mitch and I couldn't any longer put off taking turns at Seattle.

Imagine my surprise that the old burg had managed to feed itself in my absence. I took back my crew from Gretchen long enough to do a wedding and a non, remind everybody of my existence. Then just wandered for a day, sopping up the city. After Lyle's place and the Springs, Seattle looked like king-

dom come. And there was one bonus of showing up back there alone: Ing-valdson missed Mitch so much he was semi-glad to see me as a proxy.

The highway out of Twin Sulphur Springs was still warm from Lexa's zooming return when Mitch began making his miles to the Coast. It was a long drive, and he still felt as if he was in a troubled dream. Geography ruled time; driving limitless across western Montana and riskily above the posted miles per hour through the Idaho panhandle and eastern Washington, even so he had to call it quits for the day at a motel in the farming town of Ritzville.

The next morning soon enough brought the basalt gorge of the Columbia River and the freeway's roundabout approach to that surprise girth of water. At the rest area on top of the big ridge to the west of the river, still a hundred miles out from Seattle, he pulled in to look at the peak of Mount Rainier cresting over the horizon of the Cascade Range like an iceberg adrift in the sky.

As he drove down out of the Cascades, the honeycomb of suburbs began, then the glass stalagmite skylines of Bellevue and downtown Seattle appeared. Restless margins wherever he looked, here in the land of ZYX and other quakes not yet awake. The Springs back there on perfectly sound ground if you could live on a diet of rocks and sulphur water.

All the way on in to the *Cascopia* building he had the sense of returning to the known, yet with the edges of things not quite meeting.

Bingford didn't waste any time.

"You don't really want to hear me say 'the bottom line.' "

"My bottom and your line, you mean, Bing?" Mitch gazed out at the ship canal and the Fremont Bridge. The bridgetender waved at him. Mitch wondered if the guy could use an assistant.

He plinked a finger against the pane of the window and looked around at Bingford. "Last request before the blindfold goes on. Let me use a cube a couple days, do some phoning, E-mailing, downloading, upchucking, whatever. And I need to copy my morgue disks of Leopold and Marshall." Mitch smiled, with a bite behind it. "I may have to go up a mountain someday."

Bingford didn't even want to come near that. "Help yourself." He gestured toward the now underpopulated cubicles.

Mitch started out of the office, then turned. "Bing? What's going to happen to Shyanne?"

"Already out of here. She's a content provider at *Herburbia.com.*"

So we never were a household you would want to patent. Mitch and Mariah kept nipping at each other, although it was what each of them was trying to do that kept getting in each other's way as much as anything. That sister of mine could give the impression she had the attention span of a swizzle stick, but she was chronically working on pictures in her head. Busy as we all were, the comings and goings like those strings from finger to finger to finger when you play cat's cradle, there were times we tended to forget how many agendas Lyle had.

One of Lexa's self-appointed chores was to keep half an eye on Lyle cigarette by cigarette to make sure he didn't snooze off and set the whole place on fire. When she looked in on him now, he was leaning back in his chair with his eyes closed, but no smoke in the vicinity. An angled rectangle of sunlight from the bay window cast itself across his reclining figure from armrest to armrest, the cords and veins on the backs of his hands standing out like junctures of old wiring.

"I hear your folks were Forest Service people," he said, eyes suddenly half open. "Explains a lot."

Lexa's eyebrows lifted. You always had to remember with Lyle the element of surprise. A lot of bravado ago, this man wore the uniform of a jungle fighter.

"I can guess who spilled the beans to you on that." Mariah, absent this afternoon to shoot a ribbon cutting in Great Falls, sometimes gave away the oddest conversational tidbits to see what expressions they would bring onto the face in her viewfinder. "But you bet, the Two"—Lexa indulged in a look out the bay window at the Two Medicine National Forest along the face of the mountains—"had its share of McCaskill footprints."

"How far back?"

"Our grandfather was the English Creek ranger practically forever."

"Must have been one of his shavetail assistant rangers I built that fire tower for. Small world."

Lexa studied him. "And?"

"Nothing, nothing. Just thinking back over some stuff."

She came on in to his chair lair and put the back of her hand against his forehead, testing again for fever. By now he accepted such fussing over him, even seemed to expect it. For a relationship that had started off below room temperature, she reflected, the two of them spent a lot of time gauging how much heat was being given off.

"You're not scorching," she judged. "Better than this morning?"

"Was I supposed to be keeping track?" He followed that with a little laugh. He watched her, only his eyes moving, as she cleared away the latest filled ashtray from the arm of his chair. "You've got hands a lot like Adele's were, only hers weren't scarred up."

Lexa stopped short, meeting his gaze. She wondered what roamed in the gloom behind those eyes. The wife topic, Mitch's mother, he never once had brought up until now. More than sufficiently curious, Lexa asked:

"Lyle? How come you never tried again, after Adele?"

He didn't even blink. "I didn't want to be one of those people who's always got love trouble."

The loneliness in that about took her heart out. "When did the world ever work like that?" she started.

One of the chronic knocks at the door put her on hold. *If this is another sympathy casserole . . .*

Lexa opened the door to a man who stood there looking uncertain.

"I'm trying to find Blazing Brands Enterprises. I saw its sign on a fence post along Highway 89 but—"

"Sorry, this isn't—"

"Hey, no, missy." Lyle's voice, a little frantic, rose from the living room interior. "It is too."

Oh, right, the SOBing branding irons. Not that she knew what a typical customer for them was supposed to look like, but this man appeared likely to be in one of Montana's new lines of business, llamas or lattes. "Excuse me," she told him with a bright forced smile, "I have to check on our merchandising procedure. Meet you over there at the shed in a jif."

Lyle was straight up in his chair, bouncing his fist on the arm in triumph. "Wish I could get out there. You're gonna have to do the deal. Now, first thing is, don't be too eager to sell."

Lexa nodded.

"But don't let the customer start to lose interest, or—"

Lexa shook her head. "Let's do this." She moved his desk telephone to where he could reach it beside his chair, then went out to the van and grabbed her cell phone. She headed toward the machine shed and the puzzled man waiting.

Lexa flung open the shed door, then began punching numbers on the phone in her palm. "Uh *huh,*" she heard the man say at the sight of the Fort Knox of branding irons. "Well!"

They could hear the phone ring in the house. "We're going

to have to share this," she apologized to the man and tilted the
cellular so that he could put his ear alongside it across from hers.

"Lyle? Ready to deal iron?"

"You bet."

Lexa glanced encouragement at the customer and tipped
the cell phone for him to speak into.

"I'll take a dozen," the man decided. "They'll make fantastic
Christmas presents."

"No, sir," Lyle said at once.

The customer gave a businesslike smile, recognizing the time
to dicker. "Then what kind of lots do you sell them in? I suppose
I could use twenty."

"Nothing intermediate-size, sorry," Lyle's tone was firm.
"We're dealing in little lots or the whole collection."

Lexa took the phone for herself.

"Since the hell when?"

"Don't want to do Mitch out of what he has coming," Lyle's
phone voice explained patiently. "See, the collection is the real
jackpot here, and while it doesn't hurt to sell a few brands now
and then, keep the ante in the game, so to say, you don't want to
be selling off sizable chunks of your kitty, see what I mean?"

"Lyle, believe me, there are branding irons to spare out here!
You can sell this gentleman as many as he can load in his car and
still have—"

"Not the way it works, Lexa. Give the guy back to me."

She beckoned the frowning customer to the phone again.

"Mister? Naturally you can buy one for yourself"—Lyle
seemed to be counting off numbers on his fingers—"and I can
let you have one for the wife—how many kids you got?"

"Eh, two, but I want some for other—"

"Four family members, then. So there's four irons, if you
want, and Lexa will see to it you get nice ones. But you can't just
buy them like stuff for a charm bracelet."

. . .

That night Lexa was in Lyle's chair, fiddling with the RealAudio stream from the *On Rush* Web site she had managed to find and nodding time to Marian McPartland's slow balletic fingering at the start of "Twilight World." Jazz like a river of time flowing from the past. Back there in Chicago the first other of any significance: Foster, one of Mariah's classmates at the Illinois Institute of the Arts. Lexa had the week in the big city while the Stockyards Rodeo was on; Mariah was part-timing almost every night shooting accident photos for the City News Bureau, but still found ways to give her sophomore sister the world—terrific pictures of Lexa winning the barrel-racing finals at the Stockyards in record time, and fixing her up with Foster. A Loop date, deep-dish pizza at the Uno, and then music at the Do-Re-Mi Club on lower Dearborn. Whatever the jazz equivalent of a maître d' is, he took one look at the pair of them—Lexa with her prom-date chest and cowgirl freckles, Foster the finest young manhood Des Moines had to offer—and seated them up next to the piano, inches from the end of the keyboard. They each ordered a beer of a kind they had never heard of, and peeked around at the huge blowup photographs covering the walls. Krupa on his drums sounding the wake-up call at Carnegie Hall in the Goodman concert. Billie Holiday with eyes so deeply closed. And most of all the one of Louis Armstrong with his cheeks and eyes as big as his horn, and above him the dance of lettering of his creed, *We all go do-re-mi, but you got to find the other notes for yourself.* When Marian McPartland came on, slight woman in a velvet pantsuit, three-inch earrings dangling like dollhouse chandeliers, she sat down to the piano, glanced, a little startled, at Lexa and Foster and said, "Wow, music in the round." Then shifted slightly sideways toward the audience and began to play. Lexa breathlessly took it all in, vowed earrings into her life, vowed a life of high-wire grace. She watched the astonishing hands, already knobby on a couple of the knuckles, terrifically long spatulate fingers; and the music came and came, Ellington's velvet "Long Valley" and a Coltrane piece called "Red Planet" that indeed sounded from beyond the bounds of this earth and then one of McPartland's own, "Twilight World," of course. Came request time—Lexa definitely remembered this—and someone called out, "Love Supreme." McPartland scoffed, " 'Love Supreme,' that will be the day," but caressed into it, her fingers at the black keys and sliding down to the seams of the white. When it was over, Lexa and Foster sailed out of the Do-Re-Mi in a certain state of ecstasy that they both knew was going to lead to the next. Desire under the El. They kissed further and further in the swaying seat of the elevated train on their way back to campus and Foster's room—he had the collection of Rush Street LPs—and then made love that was pretty good for amateurs, if not yet supreme. She still believed you could do worse than lose your virginity to Chicago jazz.

The phone made her jump. She muted the music and picked up the ringing instrument.

"It's me, done with the dance of death Bing's putting the paper through." Mitch sounded a whole lot older. "Can you talk?"

"As they say in this town, yup indeed," Lexa tried to cheer him up with her own tone. "Your dad turned in early tonight. Mariah went to the bunkhouse to mark up her proof sheets because there isn't a flat surface anywhere in this house. I'm holding out against a solo swim in the springs. When you coming back?"

"Tomorrow late. I'm about to head out now, drive as far as the Columbia at least. How's he doing?"

"Same." She saved the news that Lyle was parceling out branding irons one per capita. "Mitch, I'm sorry as hell about no more 'Coastwatch.' "

"Lex, listen, I found something out. Called every old source

I could think of in the 'crat bureaus, the Forest Service, Interior, the bunch. And here's what: those reef leases are being put on a fast track. The big feds don't want to take any more heat on energy giveaways, so they've bucked the decision down to the supervisor of the Two."

"Then I hope he has a head on his shoulders," declared Lexa.

"It's a she."

Into the unaccustomed silence at her end, Mitch resumed:

"But here's the thing. I had our tax guy run all the numbers for me on Dad's so-called finances. No wonder he's got gravel and the Aggregate deal on his brain."

It was his turn for expressive silence. *Don't vague out on this, Mitch. The bastards don't need to pipeline-and-road this country next.* Standing there in the gloom behind Lyle's crammed desk, Lexa felt as if she was back in the tight confines of a fishboat. "You know, you don't sound like somebody happy to have a surplus of gravel."

"I'm not happy to give the world another gravel pit either, Lex," his voice came reluctantly, "but without one the Rozier family finances look like a black hole."

Bushed and, of course, hungry, Mitch pulled into the driveway late the next afternoon. The van was gone, Lexa more than likely downtown buying groceries, he figured, but Mariah was on the lawn trying to draw Rin's attention to his dog dish.

"Hi," Mitch made his manners, "at least to the one of you who can hear me."

"Yeah, hi." Without a camera swaying somewhere on her, Mariah looked oddly lost out there on the lawn.

"Where's Lex?"

"In Choteau."

"Big-time shopping?" He started for the house and whatever razzing greeting his father would have for his return from the Coast.

"Mitch, she's . . . she's at the funeral home."

He froze at her words. *Not even the hospital?*

Mariah took some steps toward him, long legs scissoring slowly. "Your dad didn't wake up this morning. Lexa went in his room and found him—" She didn't need to finish. Almost to him, she halted and crossed her arms on her chest as if squeezing out the next words. "Damn it, there just isn't a good way to say any of this. But I'm sorry, Mitch."

He stood looking at her, still trying to register what was over now and what wasn't. Absurdly he wondered what expression was on his father's face in the last picture she had taken of him.

"I hung on here," Mariah was saying, tone as wan as her face, "we didn't want you walking in cold on this, finding everybody gone when you came."

"Mmhmm"—the family load couldn't get more impossible than this—"I, ah—" after everything, he hadn't even managed to be on hand when his father died—"I'd better . . ." Dazed, he headed on into the house to call to the funeral home.

The evening was all but night by the time the three of them returned from Choteau and Mitch's making arrangements for his father to be cremated.

Lexa and Mariah quietly offered to fetch some fast food, giving Mitch a little time to himself, and he said that would be appreciated.

He flipped on the lights in the machine shed. The branding irons had not quite taken over every inch of the place. Here and there along the walls were tools and implements like sidelined players. He hauled out a sledgehammer about the weight of a small barbell. Next, found a steel fence-post driver, about twice that heavy. Then there was the anvil, big weight. He lined them up, stripped off his shirt.

In the rust silence of the machine shop, he began lifting.

"Mitch, help me get the Blue Goose ready."

His father's day-starting voice, that distant morning when they were to begin rock picking on the Donstedder Bench.

Out the two of them trek to the faded Dodge truck and take off the high boxboards used to haul grain. In place of those went a set of two-by-ten boards along both sides of the truck bed, enough wall to hold rocks on the truck but low enough to toss over.

By the time the truck was ready, Sharpless and Loper and the third kid showed up, managing sleepy grins when Lyle razzed them about how much work he was going to wring out of their sissy hides. The man wasn't kidding. Lyle considered that teenage boys barely had the brains of sheep, but you could stretch their day's work—twelve hours instead of ten if a field could be fin-ished by keeping at it until dark—in ways that would make an older man keel over.

Up until this point in life it had not particularly bothered Mitch to be the rock boss's son. His father made no exception for him in prodding all the work he could out of drifty teenagers, and whatever god is assigned to rocks knew that Mitch wanted no soft treatment—maybe there was something worse than your football buddies teasing you about being babied, but so far he couldn't imagine it. Consequently he could not believe the fix he found himself in by the middle of this first morning, deputized to drive the truck and having to hold forth on the running board while Sharpless and Loper and the other one insisted on sluffing off, his father due back any minute and sure to fire those three so fast their heads would swim.

Gulping, Mitch shut off the truck and jumped into the field. He aimed himself toward Sharpless, who was ahead of him in growth, filled out like a bulging grain sack.

"Sharps, come on. I'm telling you, my old man will kick your asses down the road if you guys don't get back to work."

Sharpless only laughed. And caught in the infection of goofiness, now Loper giggled, stutter-stepped over to Sharpless and faked a handoff to him, spun about, and lobbed an oval rock toward the truck in a pass that fell ten feet short.

"You're right out here with us now, Mitchmo," Sharpless crooned. "How's your daddy gonna fire us and not you?" Loper giggled again.

Mitch gauged the two of them. Then he jumped Sharpless, half wrestling, half mauling him, managing to land a couple of solid wallops before Sharpless could gather himself. When Sharpless did get his feet set in the loose soil of the field, he hit Mitch a painful whack on the side of the neck. Then as he drew back for another one, Mitch drove into him in a tackle stunningly perfect, his right shoulder into Sharpless's midriff and his lowered arms lifting and dumping him. Mitch and his momentum must have carried Sharpless a full ten feet backward before Sharpless pancaked to the ground on his back.

Sharpless lay stunned, no breath nor battle left in him. Puffing, Mitch scrambled off him and whirled around to take on Loper. But Lope looked at the heap that was Sharpless, swallowed and put up his hands only to fend off Mitch if he came; he offered no fight. Off to the side, the kid none of them knew that well looked as if he wished he had a hole to crawl into.

Mitch stepped back over to where Sharpless was struggling to sit up.

"Come on, Sharps," Mitch gasped and put a hand down to help him up. "Let's call it quits on this."

"Mitch?" His father came boiling around the truck to them. "What the devil's going on?"

"Little argument," Mitch panted. "School stuff, right, Sharps?"

"It's okay, Mr. Rozier," Sharpless managed to cough out. "I asked for it."

"The whole grab-butt bunch of you are asking for it here if you don't watch out," Lyle started in on them, laying it to Mitch especially. When he wound down, he made Mitch and Sharpless shake hands and go back to work together, a piece of Lyle sergeantry that his son took in silence.

The four boys rock-picked like good fellows, the truck soon filled and then the clatter and chain-thunder crack of the rocks being dumped in the Donstedder coulee. By then Sharpless and Mitch were exchanging sheepish smiles. What wasn't over yet, however, was Lyle's powwow with Donstedder. Soon into the second load he had to tromp off again and check whether the farmer wanted the patch of alkali just ahead in the field picked or ignored.

"See if you can not draw blood on each other while I'm gone," he instructed. This time he left the truck idling but pointedly did not tell Mitch to get in there and drive.

While he was at that, the boys scooped up the rocks in the usual span on either side of the truck, then stood around waiting, four cases of conspicuously good behavior there under the sun's eye.

Sharpless was confining himself to a baseball dream, tossing up little stones and taking swings, the *tlock* of his tongue the sound of the imaginary bat. Leaving well enough alone, Mitch moved around to keep warm, restlessly glancing over at the truck to see when his father would get things under way again.

He saw the rock caught between the dual tires. "Under the truck, Sharps," he called out the code.

"Sure thing," came back from Sharpless, unleashing another home-run swing.

Mitch crouched under the truck bed to work the piece of stone loose before mud built up behind it and clogged solid against the frame, making an even nastier mess to dig out. Oblong, about the size and taper of a bowling pin, the rock was wedged hard, and he dug in his heels, bracing to give it enough of a pull. No sooner had he done so than he heard the truck go into gear and his father's shout, "Okay, make those rocks fly."

Mitch slipped in the muck of the field as he flung himself sideways. The outside tire of the duals ran over his right leg just above the ankle with a disheartening sound of bone cracking. What flew through his mind was that this could cost him football next fall. Before the gouge of pain made his eyes clamp shut he saw Sharpless semaphoring his arms, screaming to Lyle to stop the truck, and he hoped the truck was not going to back up.

So there they were in bed for the rest of the summer, Mitch and his cast-encased broken leg. Doubly broken; the bone had been snapped at the ankle and the shin. And but for the softness of the mud beneath, the wheel would have crushed his foot and ankle as well.

The first week or more, his mother was dangerously silent toward his father, and constrained in how to try to handle a household with the chores of a nurse dumped on it. She could not go off to the Sweetgrass Hills with this situation. "Let me know," she kept saying to Mitch, wanting to do more for him than she had been able to think of so far. Her square-cut face, more striking than any kind of lovely, would knit in concentration as she tightened the sheets for him or brought him a warm basin of water and a washcloth for his daily bath. (Planted there in bed for those months, Mitch for the first time had the leisure to wonder about such things as whether his parents had got married because they looked like each other.) Then she would have to go back to life downstairs, and there would be the occasional sound of her at some kitchen chore or the murmur of her soap operas on the television in the living room.

Those first bedridden days, Mitch read the *Great Falls Tribune* for the baseball scores and roundups. Then, since you can read a sports page only so many times, he began reading everything else in the paper. Then everything in the house, and a good amount of the library at school when his mother arranged to fetch books for him.

Sharpless came around a couple of times, tongue-tied with apology, and so morose that Mitch immediately felt better when he left.

It was his father who registered on the million hours of that summer. From his service in the military he had some feel for the monotony Mitch was going to have to endure. The first morning of haying season he came into the bedroom, his work-stained straw hat already on, to ask:

"How you holding up?"

"Okay, I guess." Mitch smiled as best he could. He hadn't yet found what he could cheerfully say to the father who had run over him.

For a minute or two they talked haying, Lyle bluffly complaining about the shortcomings of his crew as he did every year, Mitch maintaining how much he was going to miss being out in the field. Then Lyle suddenly said:

"How about you keep the days, this summer? Give you something to do." With both hands he gave Mitch the cloth-bound daybook.

Surprised didn't say it, for his son. The daybook was the Bible of this household, holy writ and sacred accounts combined, as Lyle ritually sat down at the end of each working day to keep record of wages and expenses in the waiting pages.

Momentarily Mitch blanked on words. Then mustered the ones he had to, even wanted to:

"Sure, I'd like to."

With enough pillows propped under him he could see out to the machine shed where the haying crew assembled each morning, his father laying out their day for them. Dark good-looking Ferragamo, on vacation and downtime from the Black Eagle smelter. Fritz Mannion, the joker of the crew, bowlegged as a bulldog and as staunch if he wasn't drinking. Some new men every summer, this time Truax and Larsen with an *e*, and a young Hutterite man from one of the colonies that would cautiously hire somebody out if Lyle Rozier went to them and dickered just right. And others from around the area like Tom Tourniere, all carefully recorded by Mitch in the big timekeeping pages. Creamy paper, with a light green crosshatch of little squares. When each crew member worked a day, a *1* went into that day's square on the line with his name; half a day, interrupted by a toothache or some such, a slash across the little box. No work, such as Sundays or the Fourth of July or Labor Day or what his father called AWOA (away without alibi), that day's square was left empty—Lyle's system, although Mitch was mightily tempted to write a goose egg in there, as more apt.

Sitting up there in bed musing and bookkeeping, a clerk of ideas for the first time in his life, Mitch soon noticed what a jinxed summer this was turning out to be. The machinery was often as crippled up as his leg. Equipment was always breaking in the hayfield, but this year the power buckrake was chronic that way. With Mitch to be tended to, his mother couldn't make the runs for parts, so it would be his father who would have to dash down to the auto supply place in Great Falls, time and again coming in at night shaking his head as he brought the sales slips up to Mitch to enter expenses in the daybook: a carburetor filter, an epidemic of burst radiator hoses, new rotor for the distributor cap—the mechanical items became a casualty list down a page of their own, that summer of fractures.

But gradually the haying progressed, and so did the boy with the shattered leg. Came the monumental day, that week before the crew picnic in the park, when Mitch was at last up on crutches. He swung himself on them, learning how to get around on arm stilts, until his armpits started to go raw. "Mitch, don't overdo," his mother said more than once, and even his father instructed him to take things a little easy. But he was determined to be set for school. Truth be told, he did not at all mind that the crutches might make him a bit heroic there.

The last Saturday night, when his father was writing out the checks for the hayhands, Mitch made sure to be on hand outside as the crew said their good-byes. He took their kidding about his summer off from the labors of haying. Then one by one they were gone. Ferragamo's wife had come for him; Mitch's mother was delivering Truax and Larsen to the bus station in Choteau. Mitch went back in the house feeling a little lonely for the names he'd had in his care all summer. He was heading for the stairs and the still not easy climb to his room when he heard his father say:

"I can tear it up."

Then, his tone odd: "If you're dead-set that I have to."

"Hell, Lyle, you know how I hate to bitch against the kid's bookkeeping and all, but . . ."

Mitch swung into the living room on his crutches. "What's going on? Did I hear my name being taken in vain?"

Their work hats on the back of their heads, indoors style, the two men looked up at him. After a moment his father said:

"Little problem on Fritz's days, is all."

"What problem? When?"

Lyle hesitated. Fritz did not, laying it out pronto:

"Back there around the Fourth. I had it happen to me before, Mitch, on other jobs. A holiday comes around and maybe whoever's keeping the days doesn't get back to it right away after and something gets overlooked. It's understandable."

Mitch swung around to see where his father's capped fountain pen was tapping onto the daybook page. The white gap, amid the crew's steady crosshatch of days labored, where the squares stood blank. July 4, 5, 6: Fritz's three-day drunk. "Fritz, that's when you were—downtown. You remember, Dad. You were all steamed up about having to clean Donstedder's field of bales with only the buckrake and nobody to run the Farmall."

"Can't say as I do," Lyle said shortly.

"Funny summer that way," Fritz put in, keeping his gaze on Lyle. "Broke down as much as we were. Hard to keep track, what's what. Don't think I'm laying blame on you, Mitch, hell no. Just that a man hates not to get paid for what's coming to him."

"But—there *wasn't* any mistake. I *remember* what happened then, Fritz, don't you? You didn't make it back to work until the morning of the seventh. Dad, Mom would remember. She said something to you about Fritz showing up days later than the wrath of God and still so hungover he—"

"Leave your mother out of this, you hear?" Lyle said harshly. "This is a crew matter."

Mitch hung there in his crutches as if legless. Bewildered, he next ventured: "Then Joe—he'd be able to say, you can call down to the Falls and ask—"

"Ferragamo either," his father snapped. "Any trouble keeping the days, we don't want to ki-yi about to anybody out of this room."

The ugly silence that followed, Fritz finally broke. "I tied one on, the day of the Fourth, sure. Practically unpatriotic not to, right, Lyle? But I hauled myself back into the hayfield the morning after, I'm sure of it."

A little ripping sound came as Lyle tore the check in half. "These things happen, Mitch. I'm gonna give Fritz that couple of days, that'll settle it. We'll call it three months even."

Fritz bobbed his head as happy as if he had good sense, Mitch thought, and told them he appreciated fair dealing like this.

Mitch couldn't find anything to say after Fritz went out, fresh check in hand. His father came up with: "Hurts old Fritz's pride, I guess maybe. Besides, there's a fifty-fifty chance he's right, huh, son?" He rose rapidly from his desk chair. "Going to the Freez-out colony with the check for our Hutterite. Tell your mother I'll be back by supper."

As soon as he heard his father's pickup leave the driveway, Mitch swung himself around and headed back outside.

He crossed the backyard in a kind of wooden gallop, then maneuvered onto the low porch of the bunkhouse and grabbed on to the doorway. Reestablishing his crutches, he swung on in to the long bare-board room. Summers past, he had been in this bunkhouse hundreds of occasions, roughhousing there at the corner bunk that was Fritz's by seniority, listening to Fritz and Ferragamo and his father fight the war over again, speculating on the longevity of each year's new crewmen in his father's scheme of things. This was the first time he was the biggest fig-ure in the room.

Fritz peered up from rolling his bedroll. "Heard you coming. Sound like pegleg Siamese twins doing a jig."

Mitch said nothing.

"No hard feelings," Fritz said, eyeing him from across the stripped cot, "but I had those days coming to me."

"You know you're lying."

"Just ask your dad." Usually you could read the expression on Fritz in block letters: now he kept overlapping himself, right-eous and guilty. "There's different verses, Mitch, of just damn near anything. Sorry you had to be in the middle, is all. But this'll wear off."

"Why'd you pull this?"

"Goddamn it," Fritz said, his voice losing its rein, "any man'll tell you an even three months of wages beats two months and the rest days. It's like fishing. Filling out your limit."

"You didn't deserve those two days. You were downtown drunk."

"We're gonna have to not quite agree on that." Fritz hoisted his bedroll under one arm and picked up a battered metal suitcase. He stuck his right hand toward Mitch.

"See you next summer."

Mitch did not take the hand. He left Fritz Mannion the angry echoes of his crutches tapping away on the bunkhouse porch.

He knew it didn't amount to a bean hill, in the range of contentions hurled up by life. But Fritz's swiped days stayed with Mitch, smarting on and on, perpetually there at the edge of how he got along with his father the rest of that autumn. When he was able to cast off the crutches and begin taking laps around the park, walking and then gingerly jogging, testing the leg, he would be thinking about something that had happened at school or what he was going to do on the weekend, and out of nowhere those disputed days would return. Hadn't the proof been right down there in black and white? Mitch had thought the daybook was sacred, but evidently something else counted more with Lyle Rozier. Then came his mother's car wreck, and that unending winter, the man and the man-size boy without the woman who had been the lightning rod between them.

That next spring Mitch picked rock on his father's crew without question until school let out. Then he went to him with the word back from the Sweetgrass Hills, his great-uncle's letter saying yes, there was a summer job for Mitch if his father didn't care.

Lyle couldn't help but grin at the clumsy penciling of the letter.

"Rock picking all summer long? Doesn't that thick mick know you're supposed to stop and put something in the ground sometime?"

"It's on sod he just plowed up," Mitch defended. "What he wants is to get the worst rocks off before he plants winter wheat."

"Conlon can be kind of a hardbutt to get along with," Lyle said slowly. Mitch watched him, lips pressed against saying *Takes one to know one.* "Sure you want to let yourself in for a summer of him?"

"Sure I'm sure."

His father stood there, waiting him out.

"Uncle Alf'll pay me good," Mitch resorted to; wages were always a trump card in this household. "I can buy my own school clothes, that way. And my letterman's jacket."

"You're putting me on the spot, shavetail. I was counting on you to drive the buckrake now that you're back in one piece." This was news. The buckrake was the race car of the hayfield, a stripped-down chassis swooping and roaring out after the next load of hay; gunning it across the cropped fields was always the prize job on the crew.

"You always drive that yourself."

"Nothing good lasts forever, I hear." In all its capacity, his father's face looked rueful and oddly mischievous at the same time.

"Can't you put"—Mitch was not going to do Fritz Mannion any favors, ever—"Joe on the buckrake?"

"Ferragamo's not haying anymore, the prick."

Mitch blinked, shocked. His father hardly ever swore. Again he was puzzled at the way this was going, the mixed looks on his father—at the moment, he seemed both indignant and embarrassed at the matchless Ferragamo's desertion from his haying crew.

Lyle's expression took on further complication as he gave Mitch a looking over. Something shaded in, wanting to be said but evidently unsayable.

Then Lyle Rozier gave a frustrated shrug of his shoulders that no longer quite came up to his son's.

"And next thing, Conlon and his blasted rock-picking job," he all but spat. "Costing me my own kid for the summer."

It took a moment to dawn on Mitch that he had won on this, as surely as he had lost over the daybook.

He left in the morning for that solo summer. There, next to Canada, the trio of Sweetgrass Hills, actually small mountains aged down to the size of high-standing buttes, hovered on the plain like three competing tellings of the spyglass hill in *Treasure Island.* The west butte, whale-backed, Mitch watched make the weather for the area, clouds rising over its broad hump and letting down veils of silver-gray rain. Those showers would come and lightly test the thrust of the middle butte, shaped like a young woman's taut breast, in a way he would see again years later when he walked in on Marnie, zonked on postprandial pot and readying for sex, flat on her back atop the bedspread and bare from the waist up, brushing her own slow hand over her risen nipple. (Never after would Mitch scoff at yearning mountain men who dubbed winsome rises of peak "tetons.") Biggest and last, the eastern butte, where his mother's people, the Conlons, farmed on the skirt of soil. East Butte was the most complicated geographically and the most piratical: up on its circus-tent-like set of summits, squinty goldstruck miners periodically pecked away at the one named Devil's Chimney, and the entire steep-sloped promontory sat like a frontier walled city elbowing the Canadian boundary. Mitch's imagination quickly was fueled with the fact that on the far side of the butte lay Dead Horse Coulee, boneyard of the done-in steeds of the first Royal Mounted Police trying to make their way from Toronto to frontier Alberta. Raffish history. For that matter, he knew from hints dropped by his father that there were likely old reasons, originating in bootlegging times, why Alf Conlon lived with his back to the border.

Here Mitch's mother had grown up, townless, ward of relatives. As soon as he arrived to this prairie archipelago he was aware of her life here, the same wind blowing on him, the triple islands of earth standing up into the sky around him as they had for her, his shadow as virginal on this lonesome ground as hers. And Alf and Edna Conlon, dried to their roles in life like pressed prairie flowers, swung open the same wind-peeled farmhouse door. Their awkward hearts had rescued his mother time and again, and now they came through for him. Edna Conlon fed and pampered him in the auntish way of a woman guessing what a youngster might like. Alf Conlon turned him loose onto the Sweetgrass summer.

Eighty acres broken from sod, Mitch was to work on. The field newly undressed by the plow was geological chaos, rocks ranging from the size of grapefruit to as big as suitcases, a strew as if an avalanche had hurried through. His uncle lined him out with an elderly John Deere tractor to pull the stoneboat. After the first half hour, Mitch shut the tractor down; there was such an abundance of rocks to toss or wrestle to the stoneboat that he could have long periods of silence before he had to pull the equipment ahead another fifteen feet. His uncle appeared, to make sure the tractor hadn't quit of its own accord, then said nothing more all summer about Mitch's chosen rock-picking system, the brief stammer of the poppin' John and then the next radius of rocks.

He picked rock as if determined to rid the earth of it. The first day he believed he would die on his feet, the stoneboat a hopeless raft in the mocking wake of glaciers. Places in the field, it was a standoff as to whether there was more soil showing than rocks. The stone bit at his hands differently than that of the Twin Sulphur Springs country—these were igneous, fire-formed countless eons ago when the Sweetgrass Hills were dunes of lava. Gasping loads of air into himself and shedding an equivalent in sweat, Mitch time and again took a look around at the scattered tons of stone, and went back at it. He underhanded the football-sized rocks, hefted the larger ones with his hands under either end as if moving an anvil. His aunt's provisions saved him, the water jug wrapped in a wet gunnysack for coolness of drink and at noon the lunchbox glory of food, two thick sandwiches and a couple of pieces of fried chicken and a cinnamon roll and an apple. He ate then and every noon in the shade cast by the high rear tires of the tractor, around him the first fresh country of his life. As if in rebuke of the plowed ground, the prairie next to the field bloomed with Indian paintbrush, lupine and Queen Anne's lace. And there was the sweetgrass, thin golden whipbunches of it, lending its vanilla smell as the sun warmed it. With the flywheel monotony of the tractor shut down, the sweetgrass made a whisking rattle as the wind blew through it.

Some weeks of that June and July and August the field threw itself in his face, fine dirt blowing off the rocks as he lobbed them aboard the stoneboat, six days out of seven. (The Conlons determinedly rested on Sunday, watching preachers on television from Canada with the abstract gaze of obligation, and by the second sabbath Mitch was running the buffalo trails that zigzagged up the butte. Building up his wind for football, he labored into view after view, now the Rockies a distant low wall in the west, now grain elevators pegged into the prairie amid the strip farming. At the top of East Butte awaited the reward of color, everywhere around him from up there the farmed gold of canola, the green of spring wheat, the blue of flax.) And there were days he worked even though the field was muddy, the rocks coming up with a sucking sound, his footing slippery and his memory on the accident beneath the truck a year ago. But in any weather this was something to get hold of, to wrestle to a finish even if the result was merely a mound of rocks at the edge of plowed land.

As that summer deepened, the country around turned tawny, and Mitch along with it. He had his father's attribute of effortlessly tanning, and before long he could work with his shirt off, young cinnamon giant there amid the surprising pinks and blue-grays of the rock spill against the greater brown of the soil. He muscled up, thickened at the chest and thighs, his leg now stronger than new, his arms seriously powerful pulleys. The machine of his body became faster at the rock picking. There was an immense coarse beauty to this season of work, the huge days and the infinite shapes of the rocks, the peninsular solitude of the Hills so quietly clocking through him, the earned voyages of the stoneboat to the end of the field and back again, that he knew he was honing himself against. What he was on his way to becoming he didn't know, although he daydreamed version after version—pilot, Mountie, fullback for the Cleveland Browns. None of it his father's route, he was determined on that. But whatever his life turned out to be, the footprints of it started in these independent hills where the sweetgrass sang its song.

Lexa found him in the machine shop, sweating and weeping.

"Sonofabitching death, Lex. You have to cry your guts out at it. Anybody's."

The
Divide

One

LEXA STEPPED OUT OF THE HOUSE TO STRETCH HER LEGS and for that matter her capacity for any more odd jobs.

Whew. I'd forgotten. But when our mom went, we didn't have to dive right in to keep mountains of stuff from gaining on us.

How the past half week had evaporated, none of them could have recounted, but Lyle's death left in its wake a whirlpool of chores that blindly sucked away time. The deciding on what Mitch might want to keep—*no iron tumbleweed on the mantel in Seattle*—and what ought to go to the Teton County Historical Society in Choteau and what ought to be forthwith lugged to the trash; the wrestle with bales of newsprint; the disheartening daily discoveries of stashes they hadn't noticed before; the unending housecleaning—*that kitchen, unbelievable, that kitchen*—every time they turned around, some major duty was staring them in the face. She and Mitch had slaved steadily and Mariah pitched in whenever she wasn't inspired to photographically record this or that in the accumulation bought, bartered or long-term borrowed by Lyle. But this morning Mariah had bailed out early to scour the countryside for something fresh to shoot, stuck as usual at this time of week for the Sunday feature photo she owed the newspaper.

Time we all came up for breath. So, just to be out, hands in the top of her jeans pockets and her hat brim leading her on, Lexa strolled around to the open sunshine at the back of the house. The town was quiet, not attuned to anything except the welcome weather. Glad as she would be whenever they could clear their way out of here, she had to admit Seattle could use a little of this toasty torpor.

The clutter that greeted her in the backyard gave her pause, the truck body and the remains of tractors and three generations of haying equipment that she could recognize all fanned out across the rear of the property. "What people leave after them tells a lot," Mariah had insisted as she clicked away out here. If that was the case, Lyle must be an unabridged edition. Lexa picked her way past a much weathered stoneboat and stepped over an automotive axle lying in ambush. He had stayed contrary to the end, had Lyle. Mitch and she and the recording angel Mariah more than once talked over the dreaded hospital vigil awaiting them in Great Falls whenever Lyle's condition went into final fade. He'd made them promise there would be *no tubes, no jumper cables on me, hear?* but they fully knew that someone like him, stubborn to the last bone of his existence, could lie there for weeks as his rugged old body borrowed against itself. Instead, he checked out of life like an early-rising guest, while Mitch was on his way back from the Coast yet and Mariah out prowling the photographable precincts of dawn, so that she,

Lexa, was the one to find him there on his back in bed, the light of morning hitting him full in the face.

To have him so suddenly gone—which she at first thought would be a somewhat guilty relief, the last tricky chapter of Mitch's father over and done with—was proving to be not that simple. Good, bad, indifferent, better, worse, the confusing truth was she missed the old antagonist. Of course, about the damnable gravel or any of that, to the very end she still wanted to bat him across the ears. But the way he bit down and didn't complain about the leukemia: she had to give him full credit there. And littler things kept cropping up in the scatter that was memory. Lyle's incredulous bark of laugh, plainly the kind he hadn't let out in many years, when she once wised off to him with *Aren't you just more fun than a wet kiss*. Then that characteristic line of his, *I feel I can tell you anything, pretty much*, which she all along knew was horseshit but gallantly varnished horseshit. No, there was no quick disposing of Lyle Rozier.

She wandered on into the rust jungle. A time or two a day Mitch would come out here to stare at this derelict fleet, hands on his hips, then shake his head and go back inside. Lexa had to believe they were beginning to see progress on the long sorting of the antique from the antic. But in this situation loose ends seemed to proliferate. She could hear Mitch's voice start up again in the house. He had been tooth and nail at desk dilemmas all morning long.

Right now he was on his third round of tag with Jocelyn's voice mail, pining hopelessly for the dear gone days of face mail. (To wish to actually be standing there and see the living skin of someone you were trying to talk to, what a dinosaurian concept, Rozier.)

"Jocelyn, hi, it's your father again. Just letting you know we're still at it here. Done with the funeral home, so at least that's over. I'm getting to the picture sorting—there's some of your mother and you kids, the time or two you were ever here. Though maybe you were too little to remember? Anyway, I'll send them. If you'd divide them with Ritz, that would help. I hope the job is going okay."

He put down the phone feeling excessively tired between the ears. Picking up after the last generation was task enough; getting hold of the next seemed to him like trying to tweeze out slivers in the dark. The E-mail back from Ritz, cyber-regrets instantaneous and crimped, had begun without a salutation, merely *LRozier@Teton.net,* as if his grandfather still existed. Jocelyn's drawled phone-machine messages sounded just as distant and denatured. The old story of being so young, momentarily immune to parents, ailments, death. It occurred to Mitch he had never even heard Ritz's voice since it passed through puberty. If his twentysomething version had any of Jocelyn's conch-shell accent, somewhere this minute were Indonesians talking like a Tennessee Williams play. Was this a confusing world or what.

He sat back from the desk and took stock. Colorful little tongues of paper stuck out at him from the many heaps that still needed shuffling and winnowing. He supposed he ought to feel sheepish about slapping querulous stickits all over another person's lifetime, but how else keep track of any of this scatter? He rubbed his eyes, dry-scrubbed his temples, tried to put the main thing in proportion. His father, author of this household strew that went all the way out to the property line in the backyard, that intrinsic cargo load that was Lyle Rozier, now consisted of cubic inches of ashes. The beige box sat unmissable in front of its weary heir, on the shelf with the daybooks.

Shaking his head at it, quite as if the receptacle had asked to be taken out for a walk, Mitch pondered family ties and why the Roziers were full of attitudes like knots. For Lyle Rozier, of all people, to have wanted his final act to be a snowy sift across a sylvan resting place in a Forest Service wilderness, his son still found as galling as it was mystifying. One more time Mitch was highly glad that in saying he would perform the ash task up on top of Phantom Woman, he hadn't said when. (Maybe ballasting a deal with tricky footnotes was more of an inheritable trait than he had ever supposed.) And he felt uneasily relieved, if that was possible, that his father hadn't wanted anyone else to know about that carry-me-back-to-the-old-fire-tower conversation. Not that Mitch himself felt it deserved to be a secret, exactly. It just didn't need to be mentioned to anybody (Lexa, who had already had to put up with forty kinds of Lyle whims, for instance) until the right time. Eventually the smarting scab of his father's last-minute dickering for a wilderness place of repose would become only one more scar, the way he had it figured, and he could deal with the ashes then.

But *in the old girl's eye?*

Mitch drew in a deep distasteful sniff which would have done credit to Lyle's nasal capabilities, then coughed from it. The smell of cigarette smoke that stained the whole house while his father was alive was now the stale smell of cigarette smoke. Fresh air, maybe that's what the overtaxed filial brain needed, in all this. He got onto his feet and went outside to hunt up Lexa.

Stalking rocks, Mariah traipsed up yet another hillside. This was one of those days in a photographer's life when a desk job didn't sound nearly so ridiculous. The slopes of these lesser benchlands south of town were hummocky, covered with diminutive mounds where tough wiry grass sprouted and not much footing in between. She had been on her feet for hours out here, trying for some semirespectable shot to send in for Sunday but at the same time going back over Lyle. After every assignment, every photo subject, she had to shift gears and go on to the next. But the browy old man was turning out to be surprisingly hard to pull away from. Her set of photos of him kept ramming into her thinking even when she had plenty else to think about. Tricky matter, choosing how to show a person leaving life frame by frame. At least Mitch had worked up caption notes for her. Despite his less than charitable attitude toward her assignment, she was all admiration for how he had hunkered down last night and tapped out every needed word. Craft forgave much. It had been that way when she was married to Riley, who could get on her nerves just by walking into the room but whose style when it came to turning out words, she lapped up. *Typical. The guy and I, the only language we both speak is* job.

She stopped and blew for breath. With one thing and another, by now the best light of the morning was gone, her camera bag weighed on her like a mail pouch on catalogue day, the wind was starting to blow and she discovered she had left her close-up lens in the van. Nor were the damn rocks cooperating.

She was in search of the right rock face. Out in this lower end of the bench country the glacier leavings were big lone stones called erratic boulders, the size of Volkswagen Beetles, deposited by the ice sheet when it pushed out of the mountain canyons. Such rough old displaced chunks often were rouged with orange lichens, so that they resembled decorated Gibraltars on the prairie. Shoot the right one from up close against the wavery horizon of grass, and it would make an effect like crossing Weegee with van Gogh. She felt mildly guilty resorting to this. But you could slap anything inanimate on a Sunday page and readers would think it had more than everyday meaning. She knew a passable picture existed somewhere out here. She just hadn't found it yet.

Two rocks later, a distant upright shape caught her eye, off on one of the foothills to the west. More curious than convinced, she half trotted back down to the van and drove as close as she could get on a fence line road. Then she trudged up the hogback hill, skirting little stands of jack pine and switchbacking against the steep incline. She was going to be as pissed off as she was leg weary if the thing up top wasn't what she hoped.

It was, though. Not one rock but many, a cairn; square-cornered, tapering as it rose, fitted together like a stack of exceedingly thick jigsaw puzzles from the slatelike stones of a broken outcropping nearby. Amateur dry-rock masonry, as all these were, but done with divine patience. Already camera to eye, she was focusing in on the head-high sentinel mound.

It was a sheepherder's monument. These stood on the ridgelines and the shoulders of mountain pastures throughout the Two Medicine country where she and Lexa grew up, each stone stack the product of boredom or mania or whimsy or the need for a landmark or a grazing allotment boundary or simply the urge to build something well. Back in the times when the McCaskill bands of sheep were part of the wool tide on these slopes along the Rockies, their sheepherder might build one of these in a fevered afternoon to take his mind off a sudden terrible thirst for the attractions in the skid row bars in Great Falls. Another might fiddle around all summer erecting one or two, perhaps a puzzle-piece layer a day, the monument corners exquisitely joined (as on this one) with proper fit as the only mortar. On one of the camp-tending trips of their girlhood, their father was inside the sheep wagon in touchy diplomacy with the herder while she and Lexa proudly tussled up a sizable rock and crammed it onto the cairn the man had under way nearby. The herder came out, saw their achievement and threw a fit. "What's that doing on there? That's a bad leave!" After he quit raving and expelled their rock in favor of a smaller one that chinked into place more readily, the girls grasped that whenever stones were forced to fit together the way theirs was jammed in, it left trouble when the next stone had to be inserted. The "leave" was what you left yourself to start again.

I'm going to cry. I never cry.

There had been a cairn like this at Taiaroa, on the South Island of New Zealand.

Colin had taken her home to meet his parents; it reached that stage. He and she drove down from the Mount Cook country farther and farther south into red fertile hills, every so often Mariah dandling a hand over to his in ratification of the scenery but also as if to make sure of his wordless presence. Sheep raisers evolving into bed-and-breakfast providers, Colin's folks scrupulously put the two of them in separate bedrooms but adjoining.

Mariah entered into the occasion still having hopes for something lasting, still shoving the difference in their ages as far to the back of her mind as she could. Throughout her Fuji year of traveling, there had been the embassy types hitting on her with invitations to tennis and evening functions. The guides and taxi drivers in twenty countries asking, "Your husband is where?" (At which she would look them in the eye and say, "He is in a business meeting with your secret police.") Colin with his mountaineer grooves and his god bod was a more straight-forward proposition than any of those.

A home weekend with him, though, except for his too-short visit in the night, proved to be quite a length of time. After it dawned on him that Mariah had seen sheep before, and the fields of giant turnips they fed on were interesting for only so long, he took her to the coast, to a nesting refuge of royal albatrosses. To Taiaroa.

And there the stupendous birds, yachts of their kind, came swooping in from Antarctica, constant thousands of miles of glide on the circular air currents to bring food to their young. Those jumbo youngsters perched on the cliff brinks, like dodoes resolved to pass the evolution exam this time around, lifting their wings over and over again in the testing wind along the New Zealand coast. And in would come another parent albatross with its dozen-foot wingspread, sailing with the South Pole at its back. Mariah was enchanted, lit up through and through with this spectacle of wingspans beyond angels'. (If she was remembering her Brit Lit course right, Coleridge had to resort to serious drugs to reach this point.) To be out of the wind while she got her camera into action, she tugged Colin down onto a grassy spot behind the marker cairn of purplish stones on the crest of the headland. (Built by some fallen-to-the-bottom-of-the-world Scottish sheepherder?) Then she crawled out a little way into the blowing grass and settled down there in the tussocks, scoping the bear-cub-sized chicks through her long lens and turning her head upward to catch each whispered flight of the elder royals. She watched by the hour, Colin stoically bored behind her, the wind ruffling no feathers of aspiration on him.

Mitch found Lexa around back, where she had hopped up onto the somewhat-still-extant stuffed seat of the buckrake, lying back with her legs crossed on a random flange of the bare ruined chassis, hat down over her eyes as she soaked up sun. "Any luck?" she asked about his phone try on Jocelyn.

"The usual. Bad."

Mitch came on over toward the buckrake, passing the dog with its nose down among black-and-white feathers, dozing and digesting. He reminded himself to go next door yet today; Matthew over there might like to have Rin.

"Take five, why don't you?" Lexa murmured. "Can't hurt. Could help."

Wordlessly he agreed and sat on the low lazyboard of the buckrake, his head back against the seat cushion where she was ensconced. Without disturbing herself under her hat, Lexa reached down and cupped a hand around his shoulder as if he might fall off. He contemplated the Rozier backyard's maze of machinery carcasses, but drew no new conclusion.

"Mitch?" Lexa asked from under the hat. "I keep wondering, that whole thing yesterday where the funeral home gave you that package." Plainly they didn't often hand out modest contents for urns around here; Twin Sulphur Springs self-evidently had a bigger population of burial stones than citizens up walking around. And for that matter, McCaskills themselves were tombstone types, generations of them interred when their time came, their epitaphs incised a century deep in the cemetery on the hill outside Gros Ventre. So it had tantalized her that Lyle, of all people, would spurn a monument for himself and go the ash route. "How did your dad come around to that?"

"Hell if I know." Mitch treated himself to a sigh. "Cremation always sounded to me like a perfectly good idea, until he thought of it too."

"Quite something, though, for him." She tipped the hat back up away from her eyes. "Wanting his ashes spread over the Divide that way."

It startled a look out of Mitch as though she had caught him hiding a lewd item. After some moments he managed to say:

"He told you about that, did he."

"Naturally. We were alone here, after that guy got to buy four whole branding irons, and I guess your dad was all excited. Anyway, next thing I knew he sat me down and was going strong on—"

"—the disposing of ashes," Mitch finished tiredly.

"You know it. Made me swear not to let on about it to anybody else, keep his little last wish between him and you and me. It surprised the strudel out of me that he'd want the 'ashes to ashes, dust to dust' treatment. But I figured it'd be pushy to ask why."

"Wherever it came from, Lex, I couldn't get it out of him." Mitch got up off the lazyboard and walked a little circle in the yard. "He and a buddy drove some nails into the fire tower up there when they were CCC kids, but he never had a good word to say for the Forest Service from then on. Asking me to pack his ashes up there sounded to me like one of his V.F.W. club jokes, until I saw he really meant it."

"It'd be a week on the trail, I guess you know."

The way Lexa said it, he looked around at her.

"Three days hiking in. Another three out." She took her hat off, glanced at it, then back to Mitch. "And we'd want to spend one up there at the fire tower, take life a little easy for a day."

We. As relieved as he was to hear that particular word, the others added up to more than he wanted them to.

"What are we talking in miles?"

"Oh, about ten a day. That's plenty in up-and-down country like that."

He was idly wondering how many hundred football fields that amounted to when Lexa pressed on with:

"So, then. When?"

The turn of the century, maybe? Deliver my father into the millennium he was forever trying to get to with his deals? "I hadn't decided on the exact, uhm, getting at it." He knew she was itchy to head back to Seattle, and that would take care of putting off the ash chore for this summer. "Sometime when life lets up a little bit we can figure that out, don't you think?"

"What I was thinking is tomorrow."

Mitch made a skittish motion downward with his forefinger as if pressing a dreaded button. "*Tomorrow* tomorrow?"

"Why not? We're here handy to the mountains. We could use a break from this house, that's for sure." The way she was reeling off reasons, it seemed to him, she could have printed up the Lyle Rozier Memorial Hike as a brochure. "The streams are down some this time of year, when it comes to wading. It could snow up in there, anytime beginning in August. So I figure right away—like tomorrow—makes sense." She cocked a look at him. "Only a thought."

It inescapably was mental material, all right. Mitch tried to digest the notion of starting out up the pyramid slopes of the continent not all that many hours from now. Sixty miles of fresh air, some of it pretty thin.

"Just like that, though?" he objected to her hit-the-trail mode. Looming over him at least as significantly as those mountains was the fact that the more and more unignorable gravel deal needed dealing with. He kept away from that with Lexa now by indicating vaguely around the Rozier place. "I mean, there's still the upstairs to sort out, and something to be done with the ever-popular branding irons."

"Mitch, this stuff isn't going to trot off out of here."

"Mariah theoretically is. Weren't you going to get her and her wide world of belongings moved tomorrow?"

Lexa didn't even have to lift her hat to swat that away.

"No problem. She has that museum gig in the Falls she's been putting off. I'll tell her I have to run in there anyway this afternoon, she can get packed up and come along. That way I can pick up trail gear for us." She checked Mitch with something like dubious hope. "Do you have any at all, in everything else there is around here?"

"I'll have you know I have"—he had to think before defensively coming up with—"boots. And maybe socks."

"Right, Rambo of the Rockies." She patted her pockets and then his for something to start making a list on.

He provided her with a half-used pad of stickits. Then reached out and cupped her chin, bringing her face up to let this register. "You're revved to get into those mountains, aren't you."

To his surprise, she reddened in a shy way. She pushed both hands back through her hair, the sunlight warming its copper hue. "Really am." She glanced in the direction of Phantom Woman and the rest of the spinnaker pinnacles and blocky thrown-dice summits of the Rockies and spent a moment savoring the skyline congregation. Then laughed a little. "Been a while." Alaska, and the *Exxon Valdez* spill, and the crackup with

Travis, and the long mend with Mitch, all had happened since she had been into the mountains of the Two Medicine country.

Now she was gazing back at him with open curiosity. Half a dozen years with him and she still was trying to learn to read between his lines.

"Mitch? You okay with this?"

"Not particularly." He let it gust out of him.

Beyond that he felt it was too complicated for words: his father's absence seemed so prominent it was a stand-in for his presence. As though no inch of territory around Lyle, past or present, could ever be neutral: either Lyle was going to be hugely there or hugely not there, take your choice. Mitch felt Lexa's gaze still on him. The best he could give her was quirked bemusement with himself and his burden of ashes. "But flinch and bear it, right?"

Lexa's van entered the driveway with an eager washing-machine roar, Mariah returning from her photographic scavenger hunt.

When the van door slammed decisively, Lexa called: "We're around back, in the used-equipment dealership."

Mariah picked her way to them. "Hi, gang. Another mission of focus-pocus accomplished." She looked worn down to her socks but persevering. After the long siege of Lyle's illness and the emotional drain of being around death, all three of them must look something like that, Mitch reflected. He watched her put down her camera bag like a traveler at the end of an extended journey.

"When are your pictures of my dad going to run, do you think?"

Mariah gave him an odd look and said, "Some slow week. You know editors."

"Cover your ears, Lexa, I'm going to say something nice about your sister."

"Don't, you'll spoil the kid," Lexa warned with a grin.

Her arms crossed, Mariah stood and watched Mitch, looking medium wary.

"I never thought I'd be saying so," he brought out, "but your pictures *are* my father. For better or worse." Seeing the whole portfolio for the first time last night, he and Lexa both had exclaimed time and again at Lyle to the life: sniffing, sneaking that extra air in; or pooching out his lower lip, dubious of everything over the horizon; even when he was at his most parade-ground grand, watching himself go by, her shutter click caught him against the hard soil of age. Unsparing but heart-catching, Mariah's camera work. Mitch smiled congratulations at her. "You nailed him."

"Just about." She gave her head a shake that rattled her cut-glass earrings.

Mitch and Lexa glanced at each other. Her gallery of Lyles, they both figured, likely outnumbered Matthew Brady's of the whole Civil War.

"Kind of late to be second-guessing, isn't it?" Lexa pointed out, not unkindly.

"Yeah, really," Mitch began, "you bagged him in every conceivable—"

"I still need the right shot of you," Mariah was saying impatiently, "spreading his ashes on Phantom Woman. That's what he told me he wanted, you know."

TWO

IN AN ALMOST CRYOGENIC STATE OF COOL AT GETTING TO palm the wheel of the rattly retired Forest Service pickup, Matthew Brainerd had driven them to the trailhead next to Agency Lake earliest that morning, hung around restlessly while they checked over their packs, then took off back down the one-lane gravel in a road warrior's plume of dust.

"I hope he knows the meaning of a week," Mitch said, watching him go.

"Did you when you were sixteen?" was Mariah's contribution.

"He'll be back for us okay," Lexa said absently, tying on a Sierra cup with a little length of parachute cord so it would bang on her pack frame as a noise against bears. "I threatened to hack his home page if he screws up on the time."

Their packs were leaned against old stumps on the lake shore like bulging creatures after a meal. They had gear and more gear. Nice new nylon tents, a change of clothing apiece, extra socks, sweatshirts for warmth, rain jackets that would double as wind shells. Caps, dark glasses, sunblock, moleskin. Candle lantern and pencil-sized flashlight. Binoculars, smallest pair possible. Toothbrushes with the handles sawn off. Waterproof container with pitch fire starter and matches. Lexa's sleek little Bleuet camp stove and sufficient butane cartridges. Food, much food.

When they helped one another heft into their pack straps, Mitch in particular appeared laden, his pack threatening to tip him over onto his back like a beetle. Lexa had had to buy him an extra-large sleeping bag called the Big and Tall model, and since it was too bulky to ride at the bottom of his pack frame it had to be strapped atop. Now she took an inspecting look at him, top-heavy as a moonwalker, and for the first time in years had a pang for Travis and his nature-boy fit into the outdoors.

Mariah was going with what she insisted was an absolute basic irreducible minimum of photographic apparatus, which included a tripod and two spare cameras and enough film to send Fuji stock up.

Lexa resolutely reviewed her trail troops. *Could be worse. He at least left Lyle's desk home and she didn't bring her darkroom.* Despite her own hefty enough pack she could have charged off into the mountains at a high trot. This was always a moment she loved: the pumped readiness as she jockeyed in the saddle before the start of a barrel race; the palette of food made by her own hands gloriously ready to meet the partycomers; the minute before setting boot onto trail. Right this instant she felt something like a hum of delight circling through her, a neural scat melody that seemed to break out into the air when a redwing blackbird flew from the top of a willow near them, its chevrons bright against the limestone palisade of Jericho Reef.

She reminded herself to throttle down; there were three days of footsteps ahead to the Divide, along with one trail companion who was not exactly a lean whippet of the highlands, and another with about the same attention span as her shutter speed. Trying not to sound doubtful, she asked:

"Ready?"

"Red-*aye*," Mitch proclaimed, giving her a game little salute.

"Anytime," said Mariah, buckling the belt strap of her pack like a gunfighter.

There was a scatter of trails near the lake, a delta of footsteps before geography narrowed the choice. Jericho Reef steadily stood on its head in the lake's mirror of water, a perfect unwavering stalactite of itself, as they threaded along the shore, Lexa in the lead by unspoken vote. Shortly she was pointing left, where the trail turned up Agency Creek, and that quick they were into the first of the funneling valleys, the flumes of the continental drainage. The top flap pocket of Lexa's pack held three transparent waterproof packets, each with a U.S. Geological Survey quadrangle map folded with a day's traced-in-red route showing out. Today's crawl-line of trail angled behind the length of Jericho and led on into the mountains beyond the north rampart of neighboring Roman Reef, less arduous than tackling the canyon between the huge shields of stone straight on.

Even this junior valley, however, was so deeply cut that its walls dictated when the trail would be allowed on one side of the creek or the other. Not more than an hour after leaving the lake, they had to cross Agency Creek in water uncomfortably far up their thighs, water swift enough that to stay on their feet they had to lean into the current like slow, slow prowlers.

Seeing both Lexa and Mariah sit down on the bank, remove

their boots, and take out the insoles, take off their socks, then put their boots back on to cross the rock-bottomed creek, Mitch had followed their example.

When they booted up for real again on the opposite bank he felt almost pathetically grateful for the solace of dry socks and insoles.

Before resuming on the trail the three of them stood and gazed up at the formationed mountainsides virtually overhead, reefs and deeps like an ocean tipped empty and left on its side. Agency Creek, all the creek any of them wanted to have to tackle in one wading lifetime, skittered between these skyscraping valley walls.

Then the *clong* of Lexa's cup in rhythm against her pack frame was leading them onto the narrow table of trail ahead.

They forded the obstinate creek twice more that morning, wet blue jeans and clammy loins convincing them lunch was deserved at the last ford.

Packs were shed gratefully, even by Lexa. Mariah and Mitch chorused that the cheese and crackers, cherries and banana chips she passed around were easily the best food she had ever fixed. There was scenery to munch on, too. Drying out on the creek bank, they could see ahead through the turn of the valley to the mountains that carry the continent, dividing its waters and halving its scenery into the West and the rest.

Lexa zeroed in on the one that was central on the skyline.

"Phantom Woman," she said dreamily. "The great goat photo studio; Mariah McCaskill, girl proprietor."

"Career built on a golden stream, thanks to you."

"You're getting awful." Lexa laughed and flipped a banana chip at her.

"Did I miss a hairpin turn in the conversation?" Mitch wondered.

"Sister talk," Lexa told him as if it were higher physics, a flicker of commiserating grin coming his way from Mariah. This country was just west of childhood for them. Lexa the tomboy ranch kid then, and rambunctious big sister Mariah already halfway to another planet—Mariah maybe *was* another planet. Mitch hadn't a doubt that there were sibling zones no only child could penetrate.

"You brought *sheep* up in here, with your dad?" He had been trying to fathom low-slung wool-laden animals crisscrossing this creek that was close to hip deep on him.

"We weren't in through here." The explanation came from Lexa. "This was Primitive Area even before Phantom Woman and the rest ever got set aside and they started calling the whole thing the Bob Wilderness. No mutton conductors allowed, orders of the Forest Service. So we trailed in south of here, along Roman Reef, didn't we, my ridin'-double sister."

"Wait a minute. There's an easier trail?"

"Longer. Not as interesting."

"For wimpy tenderfeet," Mariah put in with a straight face.

"Maybe I qualify," Mitch proposed. "How many tender feet does a guy have to have to apply?"

"Company," murmured Lexa, sharpest outdoor eyes among them. Mitch was sitting across from Mariah, and when she went rigidly still at the word he did too.

Fifty yards upstream the four-point buck deer, horns in velvet, stared at them in poised surprise. Then was gone in dolphinlike leaps into the brush.

By early afternoon the creek was a wistful dabble behind and below them. The hike now was steadily up, across the shoulder of a high stony ridge. The Overthrust Belt, this sea of Rockies was called, a vast tectonic slosh that left behind rank after rank of tilted mountains, like frozen tidal waves aimed east toward the continental beach of plains. Cross one of these slabs of strata, and your reward was another of the alpine valleys raked into the geography by glaciers. But first you had to cross it. The three hikers now were spaced with great unevenness on the hard gray clay trail over the first of these mile-long upturns.

Mariah had taken the lead, launching off into a head start so that she would have time near the top to scope around with her camera. A couple of hundred yards above Lexa now and letting out anti-bear yodels every so often, she was pushing herself in long climbing steps that she would pay for in stiffness by tonight, but Lexa knew that was simply par for Mariah.

So, Lyle. Lexa allowed herself a little roving of her own. *I never would have bet you had it in you. To pass up a townwide funeral for a procession like the three of us strung along this mountain. How ever Phantom Woman did it, she got hold of you for good.*

Going up this sharply, Lexa loosened her bootlaces enough so her ankles could flex. That done, she concentrated on matching her breathing with her climbing stride, inhaling when she lifted her right leg, letting the breath out over the next step or two. How that rhythmic lungful of air within you could give the illusion of lift, she didn't know, only that it worked. Here on this high and starkly open section of the trail she had the same elevated feeling as being on horseback. The torso has memory, too. For one sweet selfish and quite guilty moment she let herself wish she was doing a high lonesome, up here. Solo, she could maintain the pace her exhilarated body wanted to reach for.

Mitch, though. A hundred yards behind her, and not noticeably keeping up. Apparently Mitch had not been put on earth to traverse mountains. Even from here she could see the dark wash of sweat on his shirt. Even as she watched, he sought a convenient boulder to sag onto and rest.

She half jogged back down to where he had plopped.

"Getting your second wind?"

"I'm already on about my ninth," he panted.

"You'll toughen in. First day is the hardest."

He devoutly hoped so. Too tired to crane around to see where Mariah had yo-yoed off to this time, he asked between breaths: "The roving photographer still roving, is she?"

"Yup."

"You're starting to talk like a backcountry guide, you know that?"

"Indubitably."

"Tell me something. You've got some excuse for being good at this, from tromping around Alaska those years. Where does Mariah get it from?"

"She got the family share of legs."

Sitting and blowing, he gandered around at the rock faces, the quilled forest below, while Lexa watched him.

"Lex? Everybody thinks I'm as strong as a Bibleful of oxes. I'm reasonably sure myself I don't have a leg in the grave yet. This country could not be prettier. Then why is this so hard?"

She patiently pulled out the quad map to show him. "We're climbing about, oh, a thousand feet an hour in through here. See these contour lines? Each of those is a forty-foot rise in elevation—that's not what you mean, though, is it."

"The guy on my back is what I mean."

At the bottom of Mitch's backpack sat the box of ashes.

Pulling into the Rozier driveway the night before with her Great Falls–bought trove of trail gear for them, Lexa had managed to not quite run down Mitch as he headed for the machine shed, the beige box in his hands.

"Caught me at it," he said. "Give me a hand with this, okay?"

Together they went into the shed and Mitch handed her the box, stepped on the antiquated platform scale and weighed himself, grimacing. Then he took the box and had Lexa do the weighing while he held it. She pushed the balance along with her index finger, a little a time. At six pounds more than Mitch's weight, it balanced.

He backed off the scale. "Then it's so. A person's ashes weigh about the same as a newborn baby. Trite and true."

Lexa held her tongue about any such neat arithmetic of life.

In the flurry of assembling gear for the hiking trip, Mariah crossed paths with them as Lexa was closing the machine shed door. Her eyes fastened onto the box Mitch held.

"Weighing in our distinguished hitchhiker," he joked lamely.

Without a word Mariah stared on at the box. In India she had witnessed a public cremation. Fire on the Ganges, the funeral pyre floating. One of maybe fifty funeral pyres: she'd had to choose among that flotilla of conflagrations, fire rafts of souls she had never known. Several summers before when the big fires swept Yellowstone Park, she had spent weeks shooting on the firefighters' lines, had seen every part of nature burn, lone trees suddenly aflame, the persisting lick of fire on a charred buffalo, entire mountains red in firestorm. Yet it had not prepared her for what came into her viewfinder at the eternal and filthy river: that the flames of a person were like any other. Maybe that was what had made her hands shake when she took that picture of human fuel flaring into the universe and again now as she looked at Mitch and all that remained of his corporeal father.

Now Lexa flexed the straps of her pack off the front of her shoulders by thrusting her thumbs under the strap pads, as if to unloosen Mitch from his rock perch, too. "You're still on that? Your dad going woo-woo in his last wish? What happened to 'flinch and bear it'?"

"Goddamnit, I can't help having trouble with this ashes idea. It feels operatic or something."

She did not want this trailside repose to go on too long. Periodic brief stops, a few quick deep breaths were better than a long leadbutt sitdown. "Mitch, not to get on your case or anything, but we ought to keep moving."

"That's one opinion."

"As we say in the barrel-racing profession, giddyup."

"Minute more."

"Come on, town kid. What'd they tell you back there in UW football practice—'Roll on, Iron Tumbleweed'?"

His head snapped up. "They did not!"

"Or, oh ho ho, I bet I know. Those coaches of yours knitted samplers of this one from pairs of their old white socks, didn't they. The one that starts off, 'When—' "

"Lex, don't. Not that old crap, okay? Honest, I'll—"

" '—the going gets—' "

"Lexa, I'm warning you!"

" '—tough, the tough get—' "

"Look, I'm on my feet. Holy Kajesus, you'd have made a hard-ass coach."

They dry-camped that first night, high but shelved out of the wind, they hoped.

Their only company at the timberline campsite was the crests of the gigantic reef formations and the portals between. Jericho, its bowed palisade the nearest to them, appeared to arch its back in everlasting surprise as the plains butted into its bedrock. Across a deep thickly forested gulch from Jericho, Roman Reef stood higher and a mile longer, its rimrock crest as regular as the frieze of a vestal temple but incalculably more ancient. Grizzly Reef, true to its name, seemed to threaten on into eternity with its half-turned slab face targeting north toward the flanks of the other two.

Moving stiffly as marionettes, Mitch and Mariah had gone

to their packs to dig out sweatshirts, hours of dusk yet ahead here under the timbered shoulder. Lexa already was setting up things for supper. Loaf of heavy dark bread, tough nourishing stuff. Uwajimaya noodles, a good carbo load. Thuringer sausage, protein supreme. A menu that would have set off prepare-to-waddle alarms in them all down on the flatlands but would be welcomed by digestive systems up here.

"What can I do to help, cookie?" Mariah inquired as she came back over tugging down a sweatshirt which read across its front, *Mount Cook Guide Service—Glaciers are a kick in the ice.*

"Firewood for later," Lexa recited. "Tents. Roll out the sleeping bags. Dig a potty place over there in the trees."

"That'll teach me to ask." Mariah cast a look in a pertinent direction.

"I heard, I heard." Mitch headed off into the timber. "I'll do the woodsy stuff."

Squatting to untie Lexa's tent packet, Mariah grimaced. "My legs ache in every pore."

"No shit, ridge runner."

"Aren't you tired at all?"

"Sure. But it's a good tired."

Mariah looked up at her sister standing there against the sky as she stretched, arms out and fists balled, at ease after earning this mountain.

The freshest of fresh air woke Mitch in the morning. Only inches of him were outside the sleeping bag, from his nose on up, but those were thermometer enough. He saw there was frost on the outside of the tent. He lay looking at it a minute, then reluctantly risked an arm outside the down bag and put a finger up to the tent fabric. The frost was on the *in*side of the tent, too.

There was scrabbling at his tent flap.

Lexa came scooting in. Shucking her unlaced boots, she slid

inside the sleeping bag with him. "Came to check out the rumor on you—cold feet, warm heart?"

"Good morning, Nanook. You didn't tell me this was going to be a polar experience."

"Brisk, is all." She puffed an experimental cloud of breath toward the frost motif on the tent ceiling. "Think of it as not snow." She snuggled in on him some more. "Having any fun?"

"Through all these layers of clothes?"

"I meant the hike." Nonetheless she kissed the place under his ear in incendiary fashion. Tempting as it was to continue on each other from there, murmurs between asleep and awake were emanating from the neighborhood of Mariah. Lexa gave him a promissory *later, sailor* wink and they stayed almost nose to nose to transmit warmth. From such close range she noticed Mitch's face was starting to look seamed. As if Lyle's generational markings were already shifting to him. The twinge that this gave her reminded her to ask: "How's every little muscle this morning?"

"Letting me know they spent the night on the ground," Mitch admitted. "Stiff, is all—nothing really shrieking."

"Hey, then"—she sounded pleased—"you're in not bad shape, considering. When's the last night you slept in a tent? Boy Scouts?"

He went still.

Coldwater Ridge. One other fine bright conscienceless morning, amid mountains with lodes of time up their canyon sleeves. Juanita Trippe another relentlessly cheerful morning type, surely out there on the ridge smiling in Mount St. Helens' direction when volcanic hell cut loose.

"What's the matter?"

"Nothing." Nothing anything could be done about. "The tent and I? A big while ago," he said huskily.

The current mountain, which had been so early to go into dusk, now made up for it by being the first to catch sunshine. The orange tent fabric began to give vivid light. "Looks like a sweetie of a day," Lexa reported to Mitch, propping onto one elbow to check on the dawn's progress. Moisture pearled on the ceiling of the tent, and she swiped away the worst of it with a bandanna. By now the frost on the outside was melting into plump globules, and she and he lay there watching the beads of water blip around on the grid of the tent pattern, like some outer space video game screen. Taking turns poking under a poised glob to make it run, they giggled and estimated that each one of these raindrop races knocked a point off their IQs.

"I better get to work on breakfast," Lexa finally called this off. "What can the chef put you into ecstasy with this morning, the soup du jour or the bread of life?"

"I like either, so I'll have both," Mitch declaimed with a stretch and a grunt, coaxing his body into the day.

Mariah was fumbling a fire into being, and before long they were breakfasting on steaming pea soup and pumpernickel and hot chocolate.

This day's hiking had a reward only an hour into it, the talus shoulder of the mountain and downhill ahead. Now they were in the Bob. Up here in the interior peaks and the supple valleys under them lay its million acres of designated wilderness. And up ahead, on the skyline, the Continental Divide the guarding rim of it all.

At the marker amid the rockfield on top, Mariah insisted on posing Lexa and Mitch like summit conquerors, their packs leaning nonchalantly against the tin yellow *National Wilderness Area* sign wired around it. While she fussed with her camera setting, Lexa telling her she would eventually get the hang of it, Mitch sneaked peeks back down at the Two Medicine National Forest land they had come through, ever since Agency Lake. Oil and gas pocketed in those geological folds. *Just remember*—Lyle

Rozier's memorial gravel handy for roads to them—*you're walking all on money.* He faced around to Mariah's camera with not his best expression.

When they set out again, the trail zigzagged down and then flattened across a broad scoop of valley, meadowed where it wasn't forested, a stretch of miles they accepted with silent gratitude after yesterday's more vertical ones.

It was only midafternoon when they came to the clear rush of water. Aspens pintoed the opposite bank, their leaves exquisitely trembling in the least whiff of breeze. From not far upstream poured the more industrious sound of a waterfall, twenty or thirty feet high, a toboggan of white water. The rocky sidehill around the waterfall broke up through the valley floor, like the mammoth root of a mountain surfacing, strewing the streambed and the slope down to it with stones the size of small flagstones. In the broken mosaic of it all, the water pooled and then tumbled down rapids like glass over marbles.

"Ledge Creek," Lexa announced off her map. More than evidently she was on the ledge, a low smooth sedimentary span that led like a little dock to where the shallow stream could be crossed on other flat stones. She had close company there: a rough-mounded cairn, no taller than she was, had been built on the ledge near the water's edge. Standing there absorbing the glorious surroundings, she clapped her hat on top of the monument and ran her hands through her hair.

The other two trailed up onto the vantage point next to her and the compact tower of rocks.

"Why one here, I wonder?" Mariah kicked at the cairn's base a little, as if wanting it out of the way.

Absorbed elsewhere, Lexa simply gestured around. "Duh. Where the rocks are."

"Thank you for sharing that, Ms. Einstein," Mariah said none too mildly. "But you know what I mean. Up along the Divide or back at the Two boundary, sure, you expect these anywhere there. But not directing traffic at a creek crossing." She squeezed past the cairn, still seeming to take its presence personally.

"What, are you allergic to monuments all of a sudden?" Lexa said absently, still gazing around at the waterfall, the chorusing creek, the nimble grove of aspens. "Probably it was one of our bored sheepherders."

"Duh yourself. The old Primitive Area here, remember."

"Jesus, Mariah, *I* don't know how it got—"

"I believe, as an expert on the behavior of rocks"—Mitch stepped in to head off sisterdom's sudden propensity toward civil disturbance over anything mineral, vegetable or animal— "that these, how do you say it in America, *dogpiled* onto each other." He ran a hand over the uneven but effective dry-stone construction. "It's standing up okay, but it doesn't look like anybody put in all their time on it."

"Well, it has some scenery," Lexa said as if this spot on earth needed her defending. "Good-looking campsite."

Mitch was watching her hopefully, and so was Mariah.

Lexa chewed her lip, calculating.

"It'll make a humongous day tomorrow, but we seem to be ready for this." She plucked her hat off the monument. "Okay, gang? Let's go unload."

As soon as they were on the other side of the creek, they saw they were not the first to think of it as a camping spot. A canvas tepee gray with age poked up not far downstream, on a nice high dry place handy to the water. No one around, though, when they approached it, and the campfire ashes were not recent. Inspecting, they whistled appreciatively at the amenities: dragged-up logs to sit on, a fire circle of blackened rocks, even a rusted but serviceable cooking grill that gladdened Lexa's heart. Mitch zeroed in on the tepee, walking around it in admiration.

"A tent tall enough to stand up in? Wouldn't that be too bad. *Woop!*" He nearly fell over a bundle in the grass at the rear of the tepee.

The others joined him and stared down at a rolled-up sleeping bag that had a foam mat wrapped around it for protection. The protection had not much worked; the foam had been vigorously gnawed through, shreds of bag fabric and tufts of down oozing out through the mauled mat.

Lexa shot a look toward the tepee, Mitch and Mariah an instant after her. Muddy pawprints at shoulder height showed where the animal, evidently up on its hind feet like somebody nearsighted feeling along a wall, had patted along the canvas of the tepee until deciding to rip its way in.

The trio stared at the claw-cut slash, big enough for a grizzly to walk through.

"We can assume the griz isn't in there anymore," Lexa deduced.

Their combined six eyes frisked the low brush along the creek.

"So then, where is he. It." Trying not to sound nervous, Mitch wanted to know with some urgency: "Don't we want to clear out of here?"

"Minutes ago?" chimed Mariah, her head swiveling back and forth steadily as a radar dish.

"Probably not," Lexa figured out loud. "The bear has been and gone. If we're careful to make noise and build a fire, generally announce ourselves, it isn't likely to bother back here again real soon. Zweborg used to say each grizzly bear has a hunting territory bigger than Rhode Island."

"Lexa, Rhode Island is the most microscopic state."

"Mitch, if a bear wants to come visiting, it *could* come visiting if we were camped out on the trail somewhere."

"I'm not for that either," he conceded.

"Okay, then," Mariah voted, shucking off her backpack. "If we're going to be eaten, let's be eaten in comfort."

They banged cooking pots together and whooped and hollered for some minutes, a racket that they felt would clear any self-respecting grizzly out of the valley. Then turned to the night's hostelry, unsnugging the tepee flap and stooping in like cave explorers. Strewn in there were other sets of mat-encased bedrolls, tossed around by the bear after some sample bites.

"Fishing camp." Mariah pointed to the rod tips sticking out of the ends of a few of the foam rolls.

"Hunter-gatherer time!" Lexa exulted.

"His clan's tools of the trade, right here," Mariah happily seconded.

They could form alliances quicker than he could turn around, Mitch too late realized. "Sexism," he protested. "Fishermanism. How about if I spread doilies around in here while you two go kill fish?"

The McCaskill sisters only snickered. "What's the use of having an alpha male along," Mariah was asking Lexa rhetorically, "if he won't get out there and alph?"

Lexa knew another formula. "Fried trout for supper," she cooed in Mitch's direction. "Golden brown. Just crisp enough you can eat them with your fingers, like corn on the cob. If only some big strong mansie would go catch them."

"You are the Bobbsey Twins from hell," Mitch observed.

A bit of soothing came from Mariah, who said she might as well come help slay trout after the tepee was kicked into shape, while Lexa said she wanted the leisure of setting up a camp kitchen in style for a change.

Armed with rod and pocket-size box of lures that had been tucked into the middle of a mat bundle and a few angleworms he'd scouted from under rocks, Mitch headed up the creek. Past the crossing and the cairn was water which he thought either should have fish in it or be impounded for false pretenses. It was a classic pool, dappled with shadow and blue, while an apprentice waterfall about two feet high spilled in over a terracelike ledge. Snags abounded in the brush roots and fallen trees along the faster water that riffled out of the lower end of the pool, but he thought he could do something with the shade-quiet eddy along the edge of all that. Knowing there was going to be a lot of rust in his casting, he decided to stick with tin fishing—lures—instead of trying to deposit worms or grasshoppers delicately across thirty feet of pool into skeptical fish.

Just when he had been at this long enough to get into the fishing mood, halfway between boredom and fascination, he heard willow branches thrashing.

The crashing in the brush had familiar red hair. "How's fishin'?" Mariah called across the pool in more than passable Bacall huskiness.

"The fishing's great. The catching isn't worth a crap."

Rod already at the ready, she glanced up and down the stream at the lay of the water. "Mind if I sneak in here and try the riffle?"

"Just don't catch any of the ones I'm slowly hypnotizing."

Mariah made a respectable but not great cast. "It's been about forever," she self-critiqued her technique. "Since my ex. Last person you'd expect to find up to his brisket in the Clark Fork, whipping the water with this stuff. But there he'd be, so I did some with him. Never got as good at it as he was," she mused into another toss of her line, "so at least our marriage wasn't done in by that."

"Anything worth doing is worth doing so-so," Mitch attested. He aimed, flicked the first cast yet that felt right, bounced the lure off a half-submerged tree trunk, and it plopped squarely into the eddy he wanted.

"No fair," she protested. "You didn't warn me you've got coordination."

"It's all in the—*yow!*" The hit of the fish dipped the end of his fishing pole.

"Don't horse him!" she shouted as he instinctively yanked the pole back. "You'll lose him. Play him in slow!"

"Right right right. Okay, I'm playing him, *no, not under the log, you bastard,* there, right this way—"

Mariah was so busy laughing she let her line drift into a snag. "Oh, horseshit."

"What's this I hear, nasty talk in the vicinity of my meal?" He had the trout, about a twelve-inch rainbow, on the bank.

Mariah eyed toward her branch-snarled line, which was on Mitch's side of the creek, and then at Mitch.

He smiled vengefully. "Don't even think it, lady."

She puckered and blew a raspberry at him, then surged into the water. To reach the riffle she had to wade along the side of the pool, in almost up to her waist, and then clamber among the submerged rocks until she could bend down and get hold of the snag to snap it off. Mitch watched every moment of it, not least because of how interestingly her wet Levi's were plastered on her. Finally holding up the soggy black branch with her hook and line still tangled in it, she turned and gave Mitch a baleful little grin. Then outfished him six to three.

They came rolling back into camp like old whaling chums, showing off their catch on a willow stringer apiece, the trout lovely as jewel-dusted jade.

Lexa got busy on supper. The campfire smoke behaved beautifully, twining straight up like a mystic rope trick. In daylight's last act at this spot, aspen shadows danced on the creek water. The waterfall drew silver from the air. She kept marveling around over her shoulder as she pottered the meal together.

She was frying the trout when she heard the sound of a keyboard in use.

Mitch was hunched on a jack pine log, tapping away at the laptop across his knees.

"You packed that?" Lexa stormed. *Skreek* of the frying pan's bottom as she yanked it across the campfire grill to inspect the golden-brown fish. "No wonder I got stuck with carrying all the cooking gear and most of the food, too."

"I had to. Any of my Bob Marshall stuff is on disk." Looking caught, he chucked back into his pack the extra batteries he'd brought, away from her counting eye. "The guy was a hiking machine," he alibied lightly. "I thought I'd pick up some tips."

Silence met that.

"Habit, Lex, okay?" he came clean. "Even if I don't have anyplace to write for anymore."

Supper in them and the fire pleasant, they sat watching a placid sunset, the last light raying like golden spokes through the tree-tops on the rim of the valley. The minute the sun went down, Mitch dug out his laptop again with a wary glance at Lexa.

"Play 'April in Paris,' " Mariah requested dreamily.

He vamped a run along a piano keyboard, and even Lexa broke up.

"All right, techie gear freak," she said in resignation. "What's with our man Bob?"

"He was a strange one." Mitch shook his head. "Maybe saints in any trade are. Marshall was a kind of bean-counting poet." He hit a few keys and peered close to read off the small screen: " '*First snow on the Lolo Trail, September 6, 1928. The path was too muddy to show white so soon, but the grass along the sides and the sur-rounding trees were already blanketed. Under this cover flowers, berries, mosses, highly pigmented rocks, everything that made the forest warm and colorful, had vanished. In a few hours the season had jumped from late sum-mer completely over autumn, and had landed frigidly in January.*' "

Mitch bopped the side of his head with the flat of his hand in admiration.

"You get that from him one minute, next he's geeking

around counting every sonofabitching thing. Literally. *'Conversation between lumberjacks today: God 38, damn 33, Jesus 16, Christ 13,'* on down through *bastard, hell, ass, fart* . . . you get the picture." He joined the others' laughter at the Hallelujah Chorus of swearing.

"How was he on *'Sightings of bears'?*" Mariah went facetiously wide eyed. "Like, how many guh-guh-guh—"

"Don't start with that." Mitch glanced into the coming dark.

"Nobody in the history of Rhode Island," Lexa pitched in with a lecturing tone, "has ever ended up as a hide on the floor of a grizzly's den."

"Miles on the trail," Mitch adamantly steered his topic past theirs. "Marshall kept track of every one of those babies. I'm up to nineteen thirty-eight in his notebook and here's the kind of thing, over in the Flathead: *'8 day totals: miles, 288 . . . feet climbed, 54,000 . . . number of peaks ascended, 20.'*"

As she heard this, the back of Lexa's neck prickled. She, too, had the impulse to always tally the distance she had covered, calculate the outdoors into herself incessantly. The same mainspring that drove her to measure herself against the clock in barrel racing, perhaps. Whatever installed it, ever since the first time she set foot into these mountains and took off up a grassy mountainside with Mariah while their father dealt with a sheepherder, she would run through her mind a sweet-sad estimate of the amount of time ahead, how many more years of hiking she had left if she lived to be such-and-such. Who knew, Lyle maybe had some such soul calculus when he was up here at eighteen.

"Jesus," Mariah let out in a way Bob Marshall would have given her extra points for, "what'd he do, *run?*"

"Pushed himself like crazy," Mitch confirmed. "That probably was what killed him. Remember, all he was doing in the Forest Service in the meanwhile was installing the whole wilderness system, against every old bull of the woods who figured trees are there to be chopped down. So there he was, dead at thirty-eight. Makes those of us who are too old for drugs and too young for

Alzheimer's wonder what the hell we ever spent any time at."
Broodily he heaved a piece of wood onto the campfire, sparks
taking to the air. "Spooky last chapter for you," he told the
women watching him in the firelight. "The obits say Marshall
went back to Washington from one of his high lonesomes out
here and right away died on the train to New York. Conductor
found him in his sleeper when the train pulled into Penn Station."

"Lead us not into Penn Station," Mariah said reflectively in
preacher tone. Lexa seemed to be appraising every scuff on her
veteran hiking boots.

They talked on for a long while, held by the fire and a
demon hiker who believed mountains made the difference in the
world.

The wind came up in the night, the canvas walls of the tepee
flapping as if wanting to sail away. When the canvas commotion
woke Mitch he rolled over, listened to Lexa breathing in her
sleep as regular as a swimmer and Mariah in the minor key of z,
then went out and built up the campfire. For once he was up
first, the next morning, starting the oatmeal and coffee by the
time the women ducked out under the tepee flap.

Lexa kept them on the move all this day. One step, another,
rhythm across the hours. Up Ledge Creek the country rough-
ened into abrupt little gulleys with muddy bottoms. Then at the
head of the creek a boggy area lay in wait with clouds of mosquitoes. Amid three sets of voluble swatting, they doused repel-
lent on their necks and the backs of their hands and cuffs and
collars and slogged through. When they came out into Big Elk
Meadow, over them stood the crag with an outcropping that
resembled a nose of delicacy, its placement of eyes a lucky accident of symmetry by winsome sockets of rockslide. Phantom
Woman lived up to its name in its bearing, comely at first glance
but then oddly withdrawing; at the mountain's hem, the timber

began green-black and luxurious, then gradually silvered away upward on its slopes where forest fires of old had left a coarse shawl of snags. Wordlessly Lexa pointed out a certain pocket of rock, and Mariah whipped out mini binoculars but could discern no goats.

By noon the tightly bunched trio of hikers was edging toward the mountain through Flathead Gorge, with Yosemite-like rock thrusts browing in above them on either side. The trail here was no more than a ribbon across a talus face, with a clear creek plunging along sometimes two hundred feet below them. At what passed for a wide spot in the dizzying trail Lexa decided it was the time for the reward of lunch, and had it backfire when they heard the sound of rocks avalanching somewhere not far behind them. They ate on the go until they were out of the gorge and at the base of the trail up Phantom Woman.

They climbed the mountain slope in perfect sunshine and a ripping wind. It caught at their packs absurdly hard, the three of them leaning into the cloudless gale swearing and laughing. Around them the wildflowers, lupine and Indian paintbrush and daisies, tugged against the tethers of their stems. Dandy day for a picnic up here, if you didn't mind a hurricane as a guest. Over the force of the wind Lexa yelled that she was going to have to shed her hat. Mariah complained that her eyes kept watering up so that she couldn't see to sight in her camera. Mitch said little, just trying to cope against this air avalanche down from the mountain. He was taking the rest steps Lexa had tutored him in: step—pause a moment—another step.

They plodded, swayed. Dusk came to their side of the mountain. Lexa knew they were cutting this pretty fine. She had them gobble granola bars and raisins and keep trudging.

They made it to the top as the setting sun was washing the fire tower in light, peaks and valleys stroked into heavier outline. Straddling the summit of the mountain and windowed all around, the tower faced four directions at once. Its stilty legs were a bit spraddled, built to angle all possible support to the sky-riding cabin at their precarious top. The sunset ran through its gradations, yellow to gold to pewter, as Lexa, Mitch, Mariah made for the tower with the last exertion they had left. Drifting over from the west were small puffy clouds all the same size, as if being turned out by an ice machine. Ridiculously on cue, as the trio reached the base of the tower the last of the light set the clouds glowing red, like coals of the sun. The done-in hikers trooped up the steep flights of stairs, their bootsteps tattoos of sound in the mountain silence. Did hurried housekeeping to the lookout cabin, sweeping mouse droppings into the stairwell with a broom worn down to its nub. Feasted on the hot meal Lexa conjured in record time. Then slept, slept, slept as night came to the Bob.

Mariah's sleeping bag was empty when Lexa sat up in the first of light the next morning. Rolling her shoulders a little to unstiffen from the night on the floor and vaguely combing her hair with her hands, she blinked around at the aged cabin, elemental in its furnishings and decidedly not built for three. Their packs and cooking gear and Mariah's movable photographic emporium were strewn as if everything had been dumped out in the dark. Which, she reflected, had pretty much been the case. She peeked past the rickety old table in the middle of it all to see how Mitch was faring in his share of the cluttered space. His sleeping bag, too, was vacant.

Her every motion stopped. Silence, heartbeat heartbeat heartbeat . . . Now she heard a cough from out on the railinged platform that cupped around the cabin on all sides. "Mitch?"

"Taking a whizz," he warned her against coming out. "Care-ful-ly. Got your choice up here, claustrophobia or acrophobia." After a minute she heard him zip up. "Okay, the scenery is undiluted again. Come see."

She stuck her feet in her boots but didn't lace them, pulled on a sweatshirt and clopped to the open door to the deck.

She came out yawning, and then simply stood catching her breath at the view. The lookout tower was aptly placed; you could see out over a dozen watersheds and headwaters, out to the dark pelt of pine on a hundred mountains, out into supple valleys, out all the way to the half-mile-high walls of stone that fronted the mountain range. Up here the continent was tipsy with mountains. Three ranks now stood between them and the trailhead at Agency Lake, and throngs of peaks to the west. And of all these, the beadline of gravity rested here on this stony brow. Down Phantom Woman's back, the snows and rains of the seasons ran off into the west-going rivers that culminated in the Columbia and the great gate to the Pacific at Astoria. Those trickling off its front streamed away to the Missouri River and thence the Mississippi River and at last into the vast delta catchment at the Gulf of Mexico. Inclines of the continent under her in both directions, Lexa moved to the railing beside Mitch and went up on tiptoes, seeing all the way back to when she was a girl with her first horse.

After a while she said, "No wonder this place stuck in your dad's mind."

"It should have." Mitch bounced a fist on the railing as if testing the tower.

She glanced sideways at him. The fatigue lines in his face made her remind him, "Day off."

"Going to use it, too. Catch some more sleep. Then maybe have a nap. And after that, relax with my eyes closed."

He seemed to be serious. *Can anybody be that tired and still be breathing?*

But then he gave her a difficult little smile and admitted: "Need to collect my thoughts. Today isn't anywhere on what I thought was the graph paper of my life." He arched his head partway around toward the cabin and his pack with the box of ashes in it. "Or what I thought was the guest of honor's."

"You want mental health time, you've got it," Lexa bestowed. "Let's get some breakfast in us, and I'll go see what Mariah is burning film on."

Mariah did not know—who ever does?—how she had arrived at past forty and still had to figure out her job every cottonpicking new day. Wouldn't you think the act of taking a picture was essentially the same each time: camera, lens, film speed ought to add up to abracadabra, no? This picture, this morning, no.

She rambled around the summit of the mountain, trying from here and there in the early morning light she adored (not for nothing were television commercials for cars shot at dawn in front of the Tetons or the Rockies, after all) and each time she sensed with the click of the shutter that the shot was a throwaway. *Too bad you don't believe in the Zen Zone,* she tweaked herself, *and just leave the lens cap on all the time.* In Grenoble she'd had a battle royal with one of the old lionesses of photography, a portly presence who had been in the Magnum agency with Capa and Cartier-Bresson. "I no longer anymore *need* to take the photograph," the grande dame insisted. "I see it, and it stays forever in my mind." Mariah went at her from every which way, arguing that whatever was in her mind, it was not a photo. (She had got into a similarly intense debate, but full of bowing and ducking, with her host in Kyoto over haiku. Why always a seventeen-syllable poem? What if an eighteenth sylla-ble would make it better? What if sixteen sounded just right? Her host's reminder that sonnets too had a set form did nothing to change her mind. Mariah was not your sonnet type.) She hoped she never reached the point of scorning the photo for the shadow in the brain.

"How's it going?" Lexa called as she cut across the mountain's topknot of meadow to her.

Mariah made a face. "As we high-toned photographers say, I seem to be trying to polish a turd here. Hoped I'd get a book shot out of this"—she nodded toward the fire tower—"to pair with the Bell Rock."

"Nothing wrong with that idea." Lexa deeply meant it. Their grandfather's mountain-topping tower for his lookouts, one of the string he caused to be built across his English Creek ranger district after being handed the wounded district—the inferno of 1929 had burned on for nearly a month up here, a generation of trees charring away, Phantom Woman madly determined to wear black. *His* great-grandfather's lighthouse on an impossible smidgin of rock off the coast of Scotland—stonemasons, Alexander McCaskill among them for three years, plying their tools on granite at low tide and fleeing in boats at high. Marks against the sky, Mariah and Lexa both knew, in their family history.

"But it doesn't hold up in the viewfinder," Mariah lamented. "Old lookout tower here just won't compare to a granite lighthouse. I've shot it from every fancy angle I can think of, and it sits there like a stack of toothpicks and says—" Mariah gave a chorus director's downbeat.

"Duh!" the sisters chimed together.

"Anyway, it'll do to slap on a Sunday page," Mariah concluded. "So that's my day so far. What've you been up to, a little ten-mile hike?"

"Mariah? You know your trouble?" Lexa told her with narrowed eyes, startling the daylights out of her. "You don't put your munchies where your mouth is." Lexa whipped a bag of trail mix out from behind her back.

"Breakfast? I've heard of that. My sister the foodie, what will I do without you?"

Mariah wolfed into the trail mix, Lexa taking an occasional

handful herself as they kept track of the morning's tones of light on the mountains around. Through most of a mouthful Mariah asked: "You and Mitch heading back to the Coast as soon as we get down out of here?"

"*I'm* going to have to, or turn the business into Ex-Do-Re-Mi Catering."

"Mmm, know what you mean. I need to haul butt into the Falls and that museum residency, or change my name to Absentia." With a ghost of a grin Mariah turned to face Lexa. "Three more days of each other's unforgettable company, then, kitten. If our guide knows how to get us back."

"Nothing to it." Lexa grinned back. "All you have to do is roll downhill for thirty miles."

They gathered on the observation deck just before dusk. Mariah positioned Mitch at the railing in the best light, scenery galore behind him for the ashes to cascade out into. "It's going to be so good," she crooned of the picture-to-be. Then frowned around the deck. "Wish I could get higher."

"You came into the world wishing that," Lexa told her. She gestured at the mountains everywhere below Phantom Woman. "There *isn't* higher."

"Actually," Mariah mused, "there is. Up by the lightning rod."

The other two could see, as she did, that the shingles didn't amount to much anymore, but the roof boards looked sound. She strode over and tested the board rungs up the side of the cabin to the roof. "They'll hold me. I think." And began to climb.

Grimacing, Lexa watched her progress. "Mariah, you fall off there and we'll have to scoop you up with spoons."

"Yes, little mother." She did, though, lodge herself firmly above the stanchion base of the lightning rod.

It was time, Mitch knew. Lexa waiting with her patented get-on-with-it expression, Mariah up there like a sniper in heaven. Nerved up as he was, he approached the railing of the platform as if it lipped out over the Grand Canyon.

"Mitch?" Lexa's tone was light but meaningful. "Figure out where downwind is, then don't be there, okay?"

Feeling silly, he licked a finger and held it up for a minute, the drying telling him the direction of the barely perceptible breeze, and moved so that his body was between the whisper of air and the box clutched to his middle. Then he balanced the ash receptacle on the gray wood of the railing, his gaze fixed on the rock brow of Phantom Woman below. *We take you now to the tomb of the known soldier. My father, the sergeant of the Continental Divide.* For a crazy moment all he could think of was his father's habit of sniffing deeply, as if trying to snare air in from this most distant horizon of the nowhereville where he led his life. *If he had such a taste of this country the summer he was up here, then why . . .*

One more time Mitch reminded himself this was a *how* occasion, not a *why*. He made sure that he had the ashes in a firm enough grip to be shaken, sprinkled out in prescribed fashion, except—he was determined—not in the direction that would carry them toward the eye of the mountain. Gathering breath, he tried to find the words to commend his father to this wilderness, the peace of pine valleys and windsinging mountains.

What came out was:

"This is too weird."

He took the box off the railing, holding it cradled as if not to let it squirm away.

"My father never cared a whoop about any of this"—he spoke as if to the surroundings—"one way or the other. No, I take that back. He wanted it carved up into money. Just never quite managed to figure out how."

Lexa gave him a careful looking at. This was not the send-off Lyle had in mind, pretty surely.

Mitch met her eyes. "I'm not going to do it. His ashes don't belong up here."

"Mitch, very, very funny," Mariah called down from where she was sprawled on the roof with camera cocked and ready. "You gave my chain a real yank there for a moment. The rest of the kidding later, though, okay? My light is starting to go."

"For real, Mariah. No performance." Mitch stepped away from the railing, then thought to say in the direction of the cabin roof: "Sorry about your picture."

"Oh, come on, you've got to." Peering at him over her camera, Mariah appeared perfectly diplomatic except for those two perturbed indents between her eyes. "You can't haul—carry—someone's ashes all the way up here and then not go through with it."

"You're seeing it."

"*God* damn," Mariah emitted. She came down the ladder in nothing flat and over to Mitch at least that swiftly.

"We hiked three days to do this! The light is right, the setup couldn't be better, you've got the ashes right there in your hands the way your father *asked* you to. All you have to do is open the box and"—Mariah gestured as if madly salting soup—"*shake!*"

Mitch shook only his head, at her.

She stood planted there, looking at him with whatever is beyond disbelief. "Lexa, you could pitch in," she said through her teeth.

Lexa made a despairing noise in her throat, then managed: "Mitch, you did promise him—"

"It saved a fight while he was dying. What choice did I have?" Mitch retorted. "But I can't believe he lived up to his end of this, either. Here's a man who told forty thousand stories in his life, everything that ever happened to him, and he never once mentioned this." He nodded emphatically downward. "So where did it come from all of a sudden, his big notion that this fire tower owes its existence to him? That he ever did anything for country like this?" The expression on Lexa went even more pinched. Mariah still looked purely furious. He felt bad that Mariah was taking it this way; here went being bosom fishing buddies and all that. But this was his to contend with, him and the mischief merchant boxed up in his hands. "The whole thing doesn't sit right," Mitch stubbornly maintained to the two women. He swept a hand out toward the earthly kingdom of Marshall, the wilderness, then whapped it against the side of the box. "My father didn't earn his way up here in the least; he worked against the Bob every chance he could."

The instant he stopped, Mariah launched again:

"Your father didn't know me from a can of paint when I showed up and asked him to do one of the hardest things you can ask of a person—let me stick my camera in his dying face. Whatever else you think about him, that took guts for him to say, 'Sure, shoot away.' Why is it so tough for you to go through with what he wanted as his last shot?"

"His last *wish*," Lexa put in, her tone equally exasperated.

"His last fast one," Mitch insisted, "that he was trying to pull with this. I don't know why, I don't know straight-up about half the cockeyed deals he cooked up. But this is another Lyle special—I can feel it. Something for nothing, if he can just punch our buttons right."

Mariah bit her lip, her eyes snapping around at the dissipating light and her foot tapping the platform floor with the sound of an impatient woodpecker. "I'll tell you what let's do: how about we take a vote?"

"We are not going to goddamn *vote!*" Mitch moved farther away from the railing. "He put this on me. And I'm not going to let him get away with it—going out of the world in some phony fancy way."

"Never mind his sake, then," Lexa's turn came. "I think," she said in a voice struggling to stay even, "you ought to throw those ashes and get him out of your craw."

"No can do. I—"

"Which? *Which?*" Lexa blazed. "Toss those into the wind, or get over your father? Mitch, which can't you do?"

"Lexa, will you just let me handle my own family matter?"

She gestured angrily to what he had in his hands. "You don't seem to want to handle it."

"*Want* to, no. But I'm trying." He gave her a beseeching look, to no apparent avail. "He's the one who dumped all this on us." Mitch shook the box as if to demonstrate his father's shifty nature. "Turn what little we've got into a gravel pit, sell every yuppie a brand for his llama and oh, by the way, 'Sprinkle my ashes on the Continental Divide, the country of my heart although I never gave any least indication of that in my previous seventy-five years.' Lexa, it's one whole hell of a lot to get over. It's too much."

He looked from her to Mariah and back again. "He's going back down with us."

Supper was snappy in more ways than one.

Lexa, giving off about as much heat as the camp stove she fired up, whipped together a pot of Uwajimaya noodles with carrots sliced in and flung in flecks of basil for flavor. (Mitch tentatively: "Can I help?" Lexa: "No. Yes—stay out of the way.") Mariah had stormed down the tower stairs at breakneck pace and stood out on the rock brow fuming at the graying light until the food was ready, when she charged back up the stairs. The three of them ate in silence except for the angry clatter of utensils. Then found themselves in another furious go-around.

"You can't get back at him—"

"I am not getting *back* at him."

"—after he's dead. What good does that do?" Lexa showed no intention of waiting for an answer to her hotly put question. "Why can't you blow off the past stuff?"

"For the same goddamn reason you still won't gas up at an Exxon station. Do things back somewhere *count,* or don't they? It turns out this does, with me."

"But you're making it count, as you call it"—Mariah trying on a voice of reason none too successfully—"on somebody who can't even know you are. Your dad isn't around to have the errors of his ways corrected, is he."

"Fine, then he won't be bothered about not being up here, will he."

Through it all, Lyle reposed again in the bottom compartment of Mitch's backpack.

As soon as dark arrived they turned in, Mitch and Mariah all but wordlessly acquiescing to Lexa's suggestion that they get an early start in the morning, down out of here. Marching orders on the trail were hers, she reflected as she angrily snuggled into her sleeping bag. It was only everything else about life that she couldn't herd in any given direction. *How do I keep getting hooked up with the wars of the Roziers?* The cabin was a contest area of tossing and turning. She could hear Mitch lie on one side and a restless minute later revolve to his other. She could practically feel the shock waves when periodically Mariah reared up to punch her rolled-up sweatshirt into shape as a pillow, then slam her head back down on it.

In the crow's nest of the continent, Phantom Woman the topmost mast of mountain between Halifax and Astoria, the three rolled through the night.

By midnight or so, Mitch finally was in half sleep, the notebook of his mind open but woozy material creeping in, *right in the old girl's eye* slurring around in there with *not without your telling me why* . . . He heard the dry rustle of a sleeping bag, then a pause. Lexa or Mariah, needing to go down the stairs to do the necessary and obviously reluctant about the three-flight trip in the dark. A miniscule flashlight clicked on resignedly. He started to settle back into drowse, not for the first time in his life taking satisfaction in the male anatomical arrangement. Then heard the scrabbling at the packs. Mice were to be expected, but why didn't Lexa or Mariah as the case may be step over there and scare off the persistent little—

With an explosive grunt, Mitch reared up, the sleeping bag cocooned on him. He fought at the zipper, floundering at the same time toward his backpack and the pencil beam of light there.

"Quit!" he shouted. "No you don't! Put that back—"

Finally managing to shed the sleeping bag, Mitch closed in on the figure at the stack of packs. He couldn't make out her face in the dark, but how many photographers were there on this mountain incensed because the devious last wish of Lyle Rozier had not been honored? She was holding the box of ashes with both hands and the tiny flashlight clamped against the box. Faced off against him in the darkened tower, she feinted with the box to one side and then the other, Mitch recalling with dismay that Mariah had been a standout ball handler in high school basketball.

"Just put it down, okay?"

The answer was a palmed move, the box moving down behind her in the dimness while the flashlight hand flicked back and forth in the other direction.

Trying to read her in the dark, Mitch shuffled his feet in a stutter-step fake, but stayed poised just where he was.

The box came back together with the flashlight in a protective clutch and the hands hesitated for an instant. He leaped in and grabbed.

"Keep the damned stuff, then." Lexa's voice was resigned.

"I intend to," Mitch said, taking a righteous step backward from her while cradling the box tightly.

"What *is* going on?" The groggy sounds of Mariah from the direction of her sleeping bag mingled into his surprised plaint as he confronted the downcast pencil light of Lexa. "You were going to spread these off of here, weren't you. Let me wake up in the morning and that father of mine would be blowing around out there. Is that it, Lex?"

Her silence was all too much answer.

"Well, no way," his tone still high and hurt. "These," he spelled out into the dark to her, "are going back down with us," taking another step for emphasis. Backward into the stairwell.

He fell like a full keg, one thump after another after another, noises alone loud enough to bring out bruises, tumbling and tumbling down the steep chute of stairs and railing until he hit the top landing, sprawling there on his back like a flattened prizefighter. His breath knocked out of him, he lay in an aching heap waiting for the stun to go away and air to return. The box of ashes was still in his gripping arms like a recovered fumble, mashed but not leaking. Every whomp against a stair step had left a place on him that hurt. He managed to come to a bit more. Toward the base of his body, he realized, was something that did not feel right.

"Mitch!?"

Lexa's voice sounded almost in awe, in the dark at the top of the stairs. "You okay? Say something."

"My leg. Broken."

Lexa swore impressively and came clattering down the stairs to him.

"I know what I was going to do, and didn't." Mariah's voice and footsteps following her down. "Take that first-aid course."

"M-Mitch, I'm sorry. Am I ever sorry." With care Lexa lifted his head and shoved her sweatshirt under as a pillow. "Don't move, don't move," she keened, although he showed no signs of doing so. Her mind raced to what it was going to take to get him off this mountain. "You couldn't have brought a cell phone instead of that laptop, could you." She shined the pencil light in his eyes, checking his pupils for shock.

"Do you mind," he gritted at her, "if I don't be blind," clamping both eyes shut, "as well as half dead?"

She turned her head toward Mariah tensely kneeling beside her on the landing. "It's too chilly here. We've got to get him moved."

Mariah thought so too, but glanced dubiously at the long sharp flight of stairs to the tower cabin. "Up or down, do we?"

That brought Mitch's eyes open again. "If it's between griz country," he panted out, "and up with you two, I'll take you two. Although it's not a real clear choice."

The women were stymied for anything to splint his leg with until Mariah thought of the shingles she had encountered on her photographic excursion to the roof. Together they raced up and out onto the platform. In the open dark, the stars up there with them, it seemed miles down to the ground.

"Careful."

"I *am* being—oof!"

"I've got you. Take your time. Just don't—"

"I'm not going to—"

"—fall."

Mariah crept up the ladder until she could stretch from the waist and feel around on the roof, Lexa two rungs below her holding her legs in tightest clasp against the ladder boards. Pawing around up there for loosened shingles, Mariah broke several to the accompaniment of an equal number of swearwords, until she at last managed to wrest enough off.

Mitch's leg wrapped in the shingle splints from thigh to heel, they now had to maneuver him up the stairs. It was like slaughterhouse work, his agonized grunts hurting their ears as they tried to help him lift himself. Finally onto his good leg, he teetered against the railing of the landing, gasping that he was as ready for the next as he was ever going to be.

Lexa staggering under one of his shoulders and Mariah

wobbling under the other, they supported him up each stair in a perilous series of lurches. Mitch, close to passing out on every tread of the way, remembered hoping that whoever installed the steps did a solid job of it, with the weight of all three of them on each one.

Like tangled contestants in a three-legged race they made it to the side of the cabin nearest the barrel stove; Mariah fretfully propped up Mitch, whose every breath now was a ragged shudder, until Lexa could drag his sleeping bag and foam pad over and they could work him down, splinted leg causing him harsh toothsucks of pain no matter how careful they tried to be, into resting position on the floor.

Lexa was still tucking and zipping him into the bag when he blurted: "The ashes. I don't want you to—"

"All right, all *right*, we won't touch them, right, Mariah?"

"Speaking for myself," Mariah ground out, "I never have, never wanted to, don't intend to and won't."

She flung into starting a fire in the stove but Lexa didn't wait, lighting the butane camp stove and hurrying water on to heat. Seeing what she was at, Mariah went to her pack, felt around in all the gear she had in there and handed what she found to Lexa, who turned it over in the light of the candle lantern to read its label. "Can't hurt." In a minute she was pouring hot water and stirring and then kneeling to Mitch, Mariah holding his head up enough that he could drink from the cup she held steady for him in both hands.

"What—what's this?"

"Black cherry Jell-O, hot. With airline brandy in it, courtesy of Mariah."

He took a dubious swallow. The mixture was luscious. He needed no coaxing for the repeated swigs Lexa urged on him while the drink was still hot.

Gradually his breathing settled down. He felt himself going into a kind of daze, haze, combination of shock and the dark glow of the drink spreading through him. As he slipped under, the women backed off quietly.

Now that she had time, Lexa was crying. She grabbed her backpack, brought it to the table and dumped everything out.

Mariah saw she was sorting to travel light. She caught Lexa's wrist. "Why not you stay with him and I go?"

"Because I'm faster on the trail," Lexa raged in a rushing whisper. "Because the last thing Mitch needs right now is looking at my face for the next two days. Because I was the bucket head who thought I was doing everybody a favor with the ashes. Because . . ."

"Those'll do," Mariah murmured, swallowing. She didn't let go of Lexa's wrist yet. "*Two* days. Coming in it took us—"

"Alone is always faster." Lexa wiped her eyes with her free hand. "It better be two days, a leg like that—"

They both checked Mitch, lying with an arm over his eyes. They hoped he was conked out and not hearing their diagnosis.

"It won't be any cinch here with him, either," Lexa pointed out softly.

Mariah let her go back to readying her pack. Lexa chucked back in one change of heavy socks, her wind shell and rain pants, a share of trail mix, her water bottle, container of matches and fire starter, the smallest cooking pot and a Sierra cup, package of noodles and, after hesitation, the last of the sausage. "Hate to, but I'll need it." Without a word Mariah dealt her a swatch of moleskin for blistered feet, drawing a rueful glance from Lexa as she stood there ticking off items in her head. "Let me have your sweatshirt, okay? Mine is Mitch's pillow."

Mariah crossed over to her sleeping bag and tossed the sweatshirt to her. She strenuously kept from saying anything until she saw Lexa stand the pack ready by the stairwell with neither sleeping bag nor tent strapped on.

"Lexa, think about this," Mariah whispered furiously. "Hypothermia when you have to sleep out won't help this situation!"

Lexa turned around expressionless. "That fishing camp," she reminded in a murmur. "I don't dare aim for any farther than that anyway tonight—do myself in too much." Now tried for a reassuring look to give Mariah. "Maybe I'll be lucky, meet somebody on the trail even before then."

They both knew this was the start of their fifth day with no other people than themselves.

The first hard thing was to wait for light beyond question. Stumbling in the dimness getting off the rocky summit of Phantom Woman, Lexa over and over told herself, was very much to be avoided.

At dawn plus a little, Mariah went down the lookout tower stairs with her. Mitch was asleep or passed out; they hoped one was as good as the other. Mariah's eyes glistened as she kissed Lexa. "Don't make me sisterless," she instructed with a jumpy attempt at a grin. Lexa tucked in the bottom of the *Glaciers are a kick in the ice* sweatshirt under the belt strap of her pack and wordlessly went.

Watching until the top of Lexa's pack disappeared beneath the brow of the mountain, Mariah checked west for the change of weather she could feel coming. She hoped Lexa hadn't seen the telltale thin streaks over the farthest mountains, mare's tails before more serious clouds.

Mitch, damn, why—

He jumbled in with every thought she tried to put to the day she had ahead of her, the mountain's severe shoulder, the gorge, the corrugated valley before the Ledge Creek crossing. The weather. If the clouds closed in up here, it could take a week to get him out. That invited complications on a broken limb, she knew that much medicine. Gangrene, her boots pounded out the syllables. Blood clot—break loose—hit the heart. Complications and worse beat upward at her from each jarring footstep.

Watch your own bones, she fiercely counseled herself as the trail steepened down from Phantom Woman's brow. The downhill trick of hiking. She stopped and tightened her laces so her boots were firm on her ankles and kept the toes from jamming. Then set a steeled careful pace, not to pound herself too much on the trail yet make steady time.

Her mind jittered back into the night, to the ashes, to the hours of furious thrashing. Lot of mental coin flips you have to do in life, and hers to throw Lyle to the winds for Mitch was one she would grab back out of the air of time if she could. Not that Mitch, damn him, hadn't flipped out, too. She knew it wasn't right to be as mad at him as she was at herself. But why couldn't he have just scattered those ashes, let Lyle blow away if that's what the old poot wanted? Lyle Rozier wasn't the first dubious choice to mingle into the earth. And likely not the last. Who appointed Mitch to be the decider?

She knew in the heart of her despair that he'd have said they all did. The old holies of earthwatching, his laptop tribe of wordslingers. Muir. She breathed in as her right foot lifted. Leopold. Rhythmed the exhale to the stride of her left. Stegner. Her boot dodged a fist-sized rock in the trail. Abbey. The other boot set a firm mark into the dust-filmed ground. Bob—

—Marshall jounced down the identical shoulder of Phantom Woman, his bootprints an everlasting instant coinciding where hers were alighting in the dust of the trail, the bulging canvas pack on his back gray-shadowing her Kelty, she and he together breathing the thin air of not enough time.

Now that he was down out of sight of the fire tower and could write without setting off the nervous young ranger, he made himself stop. He batted a persistent horsefly from the vicinity of an ear, then creased open his notebook to this day's page, *June 21, 1939*. Poor old notebook, nothing but interruptions today; lunch to smooth the ranger's feathers, and then that doozy of a close call on the stair landing. Shortcut to the parlor, of the funeral sort. But didn't happen. It will when it will, and until then, he would get away every chance he could, up here away from the swarm.

He did his sum of the miles hiked to the fire tower from where he had started that morning. To his category *Marker cairns observed on the Divide*, added a final three and their locations. Flipped through to the page where he kept his lingo tally, for a moment impishly pursing his lips at how the tower crew swore no stronger than seminary girls: half a dozen *golly*s out of the ranger, Eliason; three uses of *sonofagun* by the blocky boy.

Done with those, he tucked the notebook in his shirt pocket and resumed his mile-eating pace. Three days earlier he had set out from Marias Pass, straight from his sleeper on the *Empire Builder* to the trail up from the depot. He had wanted to follow as much of the Continental Divide as he could in the short week left to him before he had to go back to office life, to call it that. Reports to be written on this Western swing and be seeded among his allies in the alphabet agencies in Washington. Life was this, the high lonesome; the other was obligatory existence. The chores of paper and committee. And then he had that trip to New York to make, its canyons the dead opposite of these wild passages.

At the gorge, Lexa made herself stop and drink from her water bottle. Hat off, to let the sweat dry. Handful of trail mix to munch while she willed herself to rest briefly. The wind gusting with wicked swirls through the gorge for some reason brought back the time on the Anaktuvuk River. How, for the eight days of toughing out hunger in the sleeping bags, it had blown in the Brooks Range, coursing over her and the others in its running start north across Alaska through—

—the Gates of the Arctic was his first entry in this summer's well-creased notebook, and since then the California mountains and the Cascades up through Oregon and Washington, and now the old loved Rockies, all of it to take the miles and words back with him to what passed for civilization.

He shifted the balance of his pack to the inward side of the trail, away from the drop of the gorge. Already he could taste missing this, the continent's center of gravity, the high wild equilibrium in these mountains. An earth all lowland, entirely gentle and cliffless, invited engineering and the tame patterns of residence.

He hiked on, the flavor of the day a little off, weary already of the next scrap ahead when he returned East. The old bulls in the regional offices resented him and the Primitive Area designations his division was pushing on them, he knew that. Bob Marshall needs more seasoning, they kept writing in their reports at every point of his hopscotch career through the Forest Service. But country like this was worth pushing for. The swarm didn't need it, couldn't even make much use of it, yet would manage to riddle it with needless roads, peckerpole logging, the maws of mines, dry-hole wells, if it wasn't set aside.

Hard to get the wilderness idea across, though. It was only fifty-fifty among even the CCC lads up there on Phantom Woman, where you could see mountains all the way to kingdom come. In the look on the Italian kid he had caught a schoolboy reflection of himself, back in Adirondack summer vacations when he and his brothers were scampering up every peak. The other boy, nothing doing. The top of his world was not the Divide.

"Hey! Yo! Anybody?"

With some daylight to spare but not much, Lexa came within sight of the fishing camp. At the top of her voice she tried again:

"Hello? Anybody here?"

Of course not. Where were fly fishermen when they could be some actual use to someone? She tromped toward the creek. Alone. No help for it.

Her mind was operating desperately as she reached the ledge, jetty to the creek crossing, the cairn there. At her last glimpse of the Divide before coming down into the valley, Phantom Woman wore a fox fur of cloud. *Why don't I keep going? Grab a sleeping bag here and make some more miles. Screw the weather, it'd just be one night.* Half panting, she stood by the stack of stones, the constant tumbling sound of the waterfall and the murmur of the creek at her weary feet holding her for a minute, long enough to realize those thoughts were breakneck. Catching her breath and herself with it, in forced calm she checked downstream toward the tepee. She'd almost have sworn she could feel someone else around, but the camp stood there empty. Funny how she didn't want to let go of company which all too plainly wasn't there. That was what she had given Mitch hell about over Lyle, wasn't it. Nobody said life is all one straight line. Resolutely she put her mind into list form. She was going to have to rest, get a strong meal into herself, crawl into one of those mauled sleeping bags and spend the night under shelter. As soon as there was any light at all in the morning, get going on the long last lap down out of here.

There. Back to sanity. Revive herself before pitching camp and she had it made.

She knelt to throw water on her face.

The grizzly rose in the upstream brush not a hundred feet away, out of her line of sight but less than a minute from her if it decided to charge.

Mingled human smells came to it and the dark rounded ears were alert, instantly triggered to territorial threat. Behind the great jaws a low steady *urrr* sang in the throat. Standing to its full height to peer in her direction, the bear moved its head, size of a man trap, from side to side. Eyesight was the bear's only sense that was not powerful. Almost lost in the wide furry head, the eyes tried to bring in the puzzle of shapes at the edge of the water.

Constrained by her pack, Lexa shrugged out of it, put it beside her against the monument. Remembered she would need water to cook with over there in camp, and still on her knees, dug into the pack to retrieve the cooking pot and save a trip back to the stream. Then put herself around to the rushing water again.

The other creature watched, only the fur on its humped back moving in a ripple of breeze. There at the water it discerned more than a single form, then one, now more than something alone again. The shifting shapes confused the grizzly.

Lexa stripped off the sweatshirt, chucked it up onto the cairn. Stuck her hat up there with it. Now rolled her shirtsleeves partway up and dabbled her hands and wrists in the water. Bracing herself, she dipped water onto her face, the cold against her skin making her gasp.

To the bear, the standing figure had grown, the other mysteriously moved close to the ground. Now the smaller shape was up, merging against the other; they became a single large form in the bear's field of vision.

In ancient instinct of ceding ground to the unknown, the grizzly dropped to all fours and vanished upstream. Lexa kept at her water chores, shielded by the standing stones.

Mariah woke in the night to a sound like a sandstorm sifting hard against the outside wall.

She lay there trying to get her bearings. Couldn't be, she tried telling herself. Not again. The grit of Mount St. Helens' ash cloud hitting the siding of the house she and Riley had at the time in Frenchtown, west of Missoula, a full thirty-six hours after the eruption.

Spooked and blinking, she wildly sat up and sorted dream from darkness. Not St. Helens. Not Riley. The sting of rain, this was, and Mitch prone as a chopped log over there, the other side of the cabin.

She listened to the rain, which sounded as if it was here to stay awhile. No drippedy-drip pattern onto floor or table yet, but she didn't dare have much more faith in the elderly roof of this place. She got up and stoked the fire, undid the tents from Mitch's backpack and her own, spread one over him to make sure he stayed dry, did the same for herself. Then lay there to wait for dawn, knowing any more chance of sleep was shot.

"What time did she go?" Mitch right away had wanted to know when he came out of his stupor. By then he had slept so far into the morning that she had about chewed the inside of her mouth out, waiting for him to come to so she could see how he was.

"Five, a little after." And right away she had told him Lexa intended two days out, to try to take at least some of the long chore of time ahead of them off his mind. He said nothing to that.

She'd had to spend much of the day down out of the tower scrounging firewood. As she kept making trips up the stairs with armloads, he caught on that she was stoking in much more than two days' worth.

Played out from packing wood but satisfied that whatever else happened they wouldn't freeze to death up here, she managed to cook a noodle meal with much frowning at the instructions on the package. Mitch ate out of duty rather than enthusiasm, she saw.

She was braced for it when he said the next.

"What got into her?" Tone as haggard as the rest of him.

"Lexa was trying to . . . close the book on your dad for you." Mariah picked her words carefully. "You have to admit, Mitch, there's a lot more than one side to that argument. I mean, you and I had it out with each other in the worst way yesterday."

"Job stuff, that was. You just wanted your picture. That I can live with—if our situations had been reversed, you know damn well I'd have jumped all over you for the story I thought was coming to me." His face was set in a wince. "But she wanted to let him go ahead and be the archangel Lyle. Write his own ticket into ever after. Fly off over all this, like his ashes were Gandhi or somebody."

"Take it a little easy, okay?" she said nervously. Elevated blood pressure entering into this already not great medical picture, she did not want.

"Where did she ever get the idea it was up to her?" He didn't sound toned down.

"Sort this out with her later, can't you? After we're down out of here."

"I don't see how."

Now she could hear the first drops of a leak, direct hits on one of the packs from the sound of it. *Right,* she thought wearily, *all we need next is for those ashes to get wet and dribble out on the floor.* She went over and moved the packs to the other side of the cabin, then poked the fire to life again. While she was at that, a fresh drip started on the tent spread over her sleeping bag, so she dragged everything there under the far end of the table. "Leak like a fucking sieve," she told the tower under her breath; "see if I care."

Enough gray daylight had come that she could look out at the swirling curtains of rain and tell that Phantom Woman was weathered in for the day. Sometimes these squalls merely played along the Divide, didn't gravitate into the valleys, out toward the plains. Sometimes, but not most times. Mariah's mouth was dry with worry. It was going to be a scummy enough day in the shelter of the cabin. It would be liquid misery for Lexa out there in miles of mud and wet scree, already bone chilled when she'd have to wade that creek behind Jericho Reef. And wade it again. And again.

Mariah tried to think of something she could be doing. Yesterday her dance card had all too much on it; the firewood supply, figuring out food, alternately tamping Mitch down and trying to cheer him up. Today looked like it was going to be Zombie Junction around here. Mitch was still heavily asleep; that was fine, that was good, just so long as his chest kept rising and falling. She put her head down on the table to try to nap.

She would have sworn it was no time at all later, a few swift thoughts tangling in and out of places on the trail and the rain falling onto the cabin and into it and streaming off Lexa's hat if she was okay and up and going, when she lifted her head to check on Mitch. And jumped a little when she saw he was awake and had been watching her.

"I'm falling down on the job here." She stretched to unkink herself and tackled breakfast. "How do you like your oatmeal, one lump or two?"

"I'm not very hungry anyway." Nothing he could have said would have worried her more.

But after she coaxed, he ate some and came to life enough to uncomfortably shift what he could of his body, which seemed determined to kill him of backache if the rest of this didn't get him. "Prop me up some more, could you?" he asked with a groan.

She rolled up her sleeping bag and mat together and lodged it for him to rest his back against. That done, they sat and looked out at the dishwater day.

"Not doing us any favors today, is it," Mitch offered.

"None that I can see."

"Know what?"

"What?"

"Whiskers are a terrible invention." He fiercely scratched his facial stubble.

The start of a grin wouldn't stay off her lips. "You'll never make Hutterite."

"Yeah, well, another career advancement shot to hell." Making talk, Mitch did not look quite as much of a wreck. Mariah had the impression that, whatever kind of medicine words were, keeping up the conversation was having a bracing effect on her, too. And then it came. One thing led to another and something else and back around again a little closer to the heart of matters each time until they found themselves spilling to each other in earnest. Colin made it into the conversation *(But all his smarts were from the neck down)* and Jocelyn *(The only gene we seem to share at all is the shape of a Rollerblade wheel)* and Ritz across his chosen oceans *(Jakarta! Hey, I dropped a bundle of Fuji expense money on interpreters there. I wonder if . . .).* War stories of work, past *(Bingford, the ship that left us sinking rats)* and imminent *(So now with the museum residency and the book and the* Montanian *I've got three sets of deadlines people want to kill me over).* He stared at the ceiling as he put together his rendition of his father *(There just was never any halfway, with him. You either sided with him in chasing his next rainbow or you hit the road).* She leaned forward with a sad smile to deliver herself of her ex-husband *(If I lived to be a thousand I could never be as sure about anything as Riley was about everything).* Crusoe and Friday. Lara and Zhivago. They talked away the rain, talked away the tremendous hours. The only inflection that fell flat between them all that day was Lexa's name.

And that night, Mitch asleep at last, before crawling into her own sleeping bag Mariah stood by the stove, her crossed arms hugging her chest as if clinging to herself. The sum of this day was complicated enough to make her cringe. Perturbed as she was about the alarming new feel of this between Mitch and her, she was also dizzied with it in a way she wouldn't really have traded, intrigued as a person can't help but be by an unexpected avenue of the heart. The oldest contrary symptoms. (The whole while repeating to herself that this was stupid. Nursie in the tower and her patient swooning for her because that was all in the world he had to occupy himself with. *Stupid squared—there are two of us.*) She absolutely would have rather eaten dirt than cut in on Lexa. But everything about this was doing its utmost to cut in on Lexa.

She looked over at Mitch's pack, where the box of ashes rested. *You monumental old SOB.* Whatever Lyle had had in mind, his grasp at Phantom Woman was jerking everybody's strings in unintended directions.

Morning three was clouds lapping at the summit of Phantom Woman like an inconsistent tide.

Cork on a white sea, the lookout tower was riding atop a lid of weather. At moments Mariah could see the filled-in expanse, cottony and thick, with only the topmost shards of other peaks sticking through like offshore sea stacks in fog. The rest of the time a milky haze teased around the tower and she couldn't even see down to the ground.

Give us a break, she thought, not confining the command to the cloud lid.

She checked on Mitch again. Rise and fall of his chest, the

helpless grandeur of his big face in sleep against Lexa's pillowed sweatshirt.

Mariah puffed out her cheeks in exasperation at the prospect of another set of hours like the past forty-eight, then told herself to get with it, feed the fire, feed Mitch whenever he woke up. She was about to turn from the window and its panorama of murk when she heard the noise.

Lexa's cruddy blue jeans, soaked onto her three times in fordings of the last creek, felt to her like she'd been born in them, had she been born in a barn. Her feet, plastered with moleskin, were like toothaches at the wrong end of her. She had never been so tired in her life and at the same time never so wired.

The noise inside the helicopter was a constant chopped-up thunder. She was belted in behind the copilot, where the fourth member of the Malmstrom Air Force Base rescue team usually rode; she was the one who knew Phantom Woman.

Out on the observation platform Mariah craned her neck, trying to glimpse the source of the blade noise, which sounded close enough at times to cut the roof off the tower. Now came the loudspeaker voice:

"We don't have enough visibility to land. Medic Gorman is coming down to you on a line. When he has the patient ready, we're going to lower a basket sling and bring the patient up in that. Stand by."

A hideous groan erupted out of Mitch. Mariah whirled to him.

His eyes were wide and staring. He asked:

"How much does a piano weigh?"

•   •   •

The medic sedated Mitch and jockeyed the stretcherlike basket down from the helicopter with a stream of talk into his helmet mike. "I've got to go up next and see to him," he shouted to Mariah over the helicopter roar. "Then we send down the sling harness for you. Buckle yourself in good and tight, understand? Then give us the high sign and we reel you up."

Mariah looked abstracted, hunched, staring off into the field of fog. The medic frowned. "Are you all right?"

"Tip-top," she said wearily. "I have to get my camera gear together and a box from his pack. I'll be ready by the time you get Mitch lifted."

Lexa was kneeling by Mitch in his medical cocoon, the medic fussing over him on the other side. She did not want to babble, so she let her hand do the talking in its steady grip on his. With the sedative in him he was dead to the world, a phrase she could face now.

Beside the copter's open bay of door the copilot was controlling the sling bringing Mariah up. "What's she doing? Hey, lady! Pay attention up here, can't you?"

Mariah did not look up. She clasped the camera to her eye, shooting and shooting as the sling reeled her up, below her the lookout tower on its base of rock standing forth, reeflike and beaconlike, out of the layer of cloud that looked like ocean.

Three

WAKING UP EACH MORNING AND REACHING BACK TO THE knob on the bedpost that exactly fit his hand, remember- ing to be careful of his lower half as he pulled himself up to half sitting, he had the weird impression of being a parade balloon of himself when he was sixteen. Moored to his boyhood bed by the same leg.

The sun was already pouring in the window and he closed his eyes again for a minute knowing it wouldn't help much. He believed, along with Hemingway (his one resemblance there), that some people's eyelids were thinner than other people's; light was harder on fellows like them. When he once told that to Lexa, she looked at him and asked, *How do you guys* know *that?*

Reluctantly he opened his eyes now, and nothing had changed overnight or maybe since 1962. Out the window, the rust museum of dead equipment in the backyard was indistinguishable from earlier machine generations that his father had used up and left parked there for eternity. This too-silent house, then as now the domain of disappointed schemes. Mitch edged out from under the covers, the leg with the cast on it first. At least medical fashion was different, the lightweight black fiberglass bootie rather than the plaster anchor of the first time around. He balanced there at the brink of the bed, putting his clothes on the way he'd had to do everything, factored around his leg, in the three weeks since the helicopter took him from Phantom Woman like a cracked Easter egg in a basket.

For two of those weeks now, Mariah had been roaring out of here daily to her gig at the museum in Great Falls and Lexa had been licking her wounds in Seattle.

I still can't believe how three-way stupid we were. Better get used to believing it, though. They're there, I'm here.

The front half of her mind could bargain, no problem, for the pick of little tender spears of asparagus with one of the growers who had more than likely negotiated his way out of Vietnam on a refugee boat. She always shopped the low stalls at Pike Place Market, where there were homegrown vegetables and faces like this man's, while the high stalls farther inside have California crops and the glossy bins that magazine photographers love so much. Today the bargaining was a hard go, the Vietnamese man insisting she had to take some of the big woody stalks that would sit like beaver food on the table at the party she was catering that night. As she haggled, her hands went through considerable gestures. It took her a little to realize the Vietnamese was following her wrists with his eyes, judging the scars there. "Barbwire," the word came right out of her as though the two of them had been comparing the fence lines in their lives, and he looked at her from his mask of crinkles. He nodded, one sharp up-and-down, to say she had a deal.

Lexa carried her string bags of vegetables down the hill of steps behind the Market, to catch the waterfront trolley to where she always parked at the north end of the piers. At least trying to hang on to a sense of humor, on her Walkman earphones she was listening to "I Cover the Waterfront," the rare Shelly Manne and Andre Previn pussyfoot rendition. She was resorting to the Walkman a lot.

"Mitch. I'm thinking I should clear out," she had said.

"Can't blame you there," he had said.

Even before he left the hospital she knew something was up between him and Mariah.

Mariah. Why, with all the DNA in the world, couldn't she have been somebody else's sister?

At first she had tried to write if off as that kind of endless-reunion air that survivors of a major accident have toward one another. No way could she share in that; she had been too busy racing down the trail trying to save his damn life. (All right, to be fair, she with her little midnight raid on the ashes had been the one who put him in the position where his life needed saving. Sort of.) But after he was home in the Springs and starting to get around, and the strain between him and her showed absolutely no sign of letting up and Mariah had that look on her like her heart was in quicksand, Lexa packed for Seattle.

"I know when I've been cut out of the picture."

"Lexa, none of the tower trip was my idea, was it."

"You're still going to have to get over what we wrestled about up there, you know," she had tried one last shot on him. *"Dispose of the disposing of."*

"How about giving me time to get used to being a cripple again first, okay?" he had fired back.

Then there had been the confrontation with Mariah,

another pathetic breakup scene that she had not had any luck drowning out with the Walkman.

Up the street toward the Space Needle now she spotted another of the ubiquitous billboards for a new bottled water, every one of which reminded her of the nonbottled variety and taking the plunge together as Mariah and Mitch no doubt nightly were in the steaming dark of Artesia Park. Such scenes of the two of them kept adding up in the back of her mind like chalk all over a blackboard.

Mariah was trudging back to the museum after speaking to the Great Falls Rotary Club and showing some of her slides. She was in a powder blue pants suit that she'd had to buy for such occasions during this museum gig, and she felt like a rodeo princess who had stepped in the droppings of the parade horses. The person running the projector had filled the carousel with every slide upside down. Nor had it been such a sharp idea to douse the lights and have the slide show right after everybody was stuffed with lunch; more than one Rotarian had caught a little sleep.

Taking the longest way back to work, she veered off into the neighborhood of big leafy trees and old houses north of downtown. The day was hot and sticky, and she tried to glide from one pool of shade to the next, wondering if she was timing this right to be ahead of the thunderstorm. Great Falls seemed to receive a lot of pent-up weather, clouds that started off with white innocence in the mountains boiling themselves black by the time they reached here.

Weather was the least of grievances. The hike into the Bob, the quakelike rearrangement of Mitch and her and of Mitch and Lexa and of Lexa and her: *We all three walked into this one, did we ever.*

She came to the river, the museum at once in sight on a bluff of the Missouri. Between her and there, though, commotion in the air. The thunderheads were pushing agitation along the river ahead of them, and at the Tenth Street Bridge fork-tailed swallows by the hundreds were swooping and drifting back and forth over the bridge and then under its archways to start looping their restless loops all over again. Mariah downed her camera bag and in the next motion came up with her Pentax. It allowed her one click and then was out of film. Swearing succinctly, she reloaded and cupped the camera to her eye again like a sentry habitually hoisting binoculars and found her picture of the storm of birds within the wild weather. Sunday taken care of, at least.

The droopy-eyed houses with their shades half down in the summer swelter watched her make her way on along the river. Long ago, it seemed now, Great Falls had been literally the place in the distance that she aimed at in life. The smelter stack when it still stood across the river on the rise called Black Eagle she could recall like the mast of a ship pulling in for her, drawing nearer and nearer when, at sixteen, she had won her first photo competition, and she and her folks, proud and a little mystified at having produced a photographer, were driving down here for the ceremony at the *Tribune*.

The long ago. She quickened her pace as if prodded. Growing up on the ranch, in all the weathers there were. By each January the gleam on the snow began to tarnish, and there were a hundred days yet until spring. Then came summer, and was gone as if the first nice breeze along Noon Creek shook those months off the calendar. Was that what turned her toward seasonless work, she wondered, the camera lens its same fresh day every time? But Lexa with the identical starting point had taken to horseback, to running the hills; somehow she was cut out for kid life on the ranch and the rhythm of chores taken in stride from then on.

There seems to be a lot I'm not cut out for. She still was cringing at what had been said between them before Lexa bailed out for Seattle.

"*Mariah, what is it with you—a sweet tooth for newspaper guys?*"

"*Damn it, damn it, damn it, Lexa. I didn't intend any of this. Please don't think I did.*"

"*I am so slow on this. Now that it's over, I can see it happening.*"

"*Nothing is over, and not that much has happened.*"

"*Hasn't it? If you have anything to do with it, it will.*"

There had been occasions before when *sibling*, as practiced by the sisters McCaskill, became an active verb. Mariah had given Lexa a hard time about splitting up with Travis and, worse, been wrong about it. Lexa had given Mariah unshirted hell for getting back together with Riley and, worse, been right about it. But this made those look like warm-up bouts, and Mariah winced again at how sistering had turned tooth and nail.

Outside a neighborhood drugstore just ahead, Lyle's face looked at her, same as from every corner in the city today. The *Montanian* photo editor had chosen one of the shots from Artesia Park for the lead-in, Lyle in command of a weathered bench at a picnic table, his hat the only thing that still fit him in his gauntness. The first big raindrop blotch hit the plastic window of the newspaper box, trickling down his untouchable visage, as Mariah hastened by.

Rounds of the park were their next chore, him and his leg. This was another thing medical opinion had done a 180-degree turn on, how long Mitch Rozier was assigned to lie around when he went through life breaking that leg. That summer-long bedtime after the truck rolled over him wasn't prescribed nowadays. As per doctor's orders this time around, he had been up and hobbling on crutches the first week and since then just grimly hobbling.

So now he stumped around Artesia Park the given number of laps, watching other people's weather—in this case, a thunderstorm over there dumping on Great Falls—and speculating on today's temperature of the smelly springs, then drove back to the house. There was that about the soft cast; he could manage it into a car and then use his good leg for driving. Not that there was anywhere much to go.

He went in to resume what he had come to think of as non-housecleaning. Ever since the interruption by their hike into the Bob, the Rozier place had actually accrued a fresh top layer of clutter—Mariah's photographic gear all over the house and bunkhouse both. He supposed this was like dwelling with Picasso, if Picasso had happened to use film.

Mariah. Plenty to be sorted out there yet, too.

At the moment, the only thing in the world he felt he could do justice to was a cup of coffee. He hobbled into the kitchen and put the pot on, then propped himself in the doorway to the living room to wait out the perking and figure out a next step in the minefield of his father's belongings. At least there was one less stack of paper on the desk across there. As though the distance across the room lent the perspective he had been looking for, he contemplated the bare little bay of desktop where the Aggregate deal had rested. The non-deal, now. Making the call this forenoon to say that the Rozier Bench was not for sale at any price had not come easily, but it had come.

Passing a hand over his face, Mitch once more wondered what a crippled-up debt-saddled ex-newspaperman could do for a living: lean out of a car and change the pointers on those Forest Service *Fire Danger* signs, maybe? Yet there was a corner of peace in him, now that he had torn up the Aggregate paperwork, and he just wished it didn't have to be such a lonely one. Mariah naturally was out of here, working her job or three, from can see to can't see. Lexa, he knew, would have stood here applauding him to the skies for not letting loose of those megatons of gravel if Lexa had not gone out of his life because he would not let loose of a few pounds of ashes.

The pot gave a final *blub*, then added to the silence of the house. He poured a cupful of coffee and plucked up the newspaper for the dozenth time. When Mariah came in late last night from handling the photography class at her museum gig, she had left the early edition of the *Montanian* on the kitchen table. Those eyes drilling up through the newsprint were the first thing that met Mitch when he limped downstairs this morning.

Now he took the paper to the big chair in the living room and sat there staring at it. From a working lifetime as a word jockey fighting for space in the narrow confines of news columns, he could take photojournalism or leave it, preferably leave. But this was like a family album known by heart. In one of Lyle's moments caught by Mariah there was cigarette smoke around him like the haze of his life. Another, he was talking and you could tell that this man had a tongue in him like a clapper of a bell. Looking down at that face of his father, Mitch could all but hear him sounding off to his rockfield platoons. Sharpless and Loper and the skim-milk kid. His annual army of hay makers, Fritz and Ferragamo and the three Swensons down through the years and one-armed Eddie and the mute Hutterite and Truax and Larsen with an *e*; it was as if the ghost legion of them was mustered out of the daybooks and crowded from wall to wall in this room where Lyle Rozier had handed out their paychecks.

All that was a long way back, yet it was in no way gone. It sat there on the daybooks shelf in a somewhat beat-up beige box.

Mitch gazed over there a considerable while, mulling the ledgers of his father. Then hauled himself out of the chair and over to the desk and the phone. He looked up the number in the not very many pages of the Teton County phone book. Across the driveway he could see Donald Brainerd in his bay-window office whip a small cellular device to his ear.

"Donald? It's Mitch Rozier. Could I borrow Matthew over here for a while this evening?"

Four

Versions of earth changed and changed along his route the next day, as though the car windows were thin-sawn prisms. Soon freed of the benchlands around Twin Sulphur Springs and the Soda Creek valley, the highway streaked straight across an elevated plain of tanned grass and then roller-coastered down to the fanned-open bottomlands of the Sun River. Onward south from there the land puckered into steep castellated buttes, crisp-edged inland islands of the sort he had liked ever since being around the Sweetgrass Hills.

Except for the excessive company of his cast, Mitch was solo in the Honda. It felt strange, after everything, not to have the vocal jury of Lexa and Mariah along. But witnessing himself at this was going to be hard enough.

Beyond the buttes the Missouri River took charge. Concentrated and curving, it cut its way through the bent hard-candy colors of Wolf Creek Canyon. On past the course of the river lay the long valley at Helena, knotted by the freeway interchange.

And here he made the turn onto the MacDonald Pass highway, the paved and banked route up to the Continental Divide.

The road crossed the Divide in a yawn of summit meadow and wound its way down into pockets of hayfields and small ranches before becoming a tributary into the rush of Interstate 90. In minutes came the Deer Lodge exit sign on the freeway and the unforgiving walls out at the edge of the town limits. "Our graduate of Penn State," his father always would say, just out of hearing of whatever occasional member of his haying crews happened to have served time here in the state pen.

He pulled in at Deer Lodge to the Hasty Tasty, which didn't look either one. The place was churning out food to a standing-room crowd, though, apparently keyed to weekly visitors' hours. Lots of ways in life to end up penned up, Mitch thought to himself, covertly assessing the bleak faces here to do their visiting-room duty. This town and the even smaller old ones south down this valley had been at the front of the line, back in the state's earliest history, when institutions were being handed out. Besides the penitentiary here, the insane asylum had been awarded to Warm Springs at the far end of the valley, and halfway between here and there, Hydropolis had the Montana National Guard pensioners' facility known as the Vets' Home. He fortified himself with a cheeseburger and two refills of watery coffee to try for the voltage of one decent cup. Then drove the last dozen miles south down the valley of the institutionalized.

. . .

The Vets' Home resembled a grade school of the 1950s, low and flattish, built of the elongated squashed-looking material known as ick brick. It sat a block back from the brief main street of Hydropolis, an aging patch of storefronts and a bar aglow with a green sign redundantly declaring itself the Oasis. At the Vets' Home itself nothing much was going on, so far as the reportorial eye of Mitch could see, except the kaleidoscopic turns of colors on television screens through the windows of several of the rooms.

But the source for what he was after was not likely to be in there at this time of day glued to *Jeopardy*, was he. How to deal with the source. Always the trick on any story. He drove around the block twice. Then headed for the lone motel in Hydropolis, to wait for morning.

The sun was already delivering a little too much warmth when, a few minutes before eight, here came two of them down the street from the Vets' Home, not together but not very far apart either in their race to the Oasis. The man in the lead, World War II vintage, was toothless, his caved-in mouth making him look constantly concerned. The next one, shaggier and slouching, flapped along in an unbuttoned Nam field jacket. Each of them, Mitch could see as they passed where he was sitting in the parked car, was wearing loafers. Too shaky to tie shoelaces.

He kept watch in the rearview mirror. It took only another minute. Number three of the morning brigade, purposefully gaiting down the sidewalk now, had the remembered bulldog build.

Serial number 20929162, private, Montana National Guard, activated to Forty-first Infantry Division. Service in forward area New Guinea. Occupation duty in Japan. . . .

DWI conviction, Yellowstone County, 1947 . . .

Disturbance of the peace, three months suspended sentence, Gallatin County, 1948 . . .

Reenlistment during Korean conflict, 1951, disability discharge . . .

DWI second conviction, 6-month license suspension, 1956 . . .

Those and other buffets of life that had brought this man here where the pensioned lived alone with their wars ancient and current, Mitch's laptop now held, thanks to Matthew's ransacking on the Web.

As rapidly as he could maneuver his cast, he climbed out of the car.

"Fritz, hi there. Mitch Rozier, remember?"

"Mitch, old kid!"

Fritz Mannion instantly sounded like the closest pal imaginable, honorary uncle in the bunkhouse. Midway through the handshake he already was peeking down in wrinkled concern at Mitch's walking cast. "You look kind of bunged up."

"Missed a step," Mitch said minimally, waiting for the conversation to go the way he knew it would.

Fritz didn't disappoint, shuffling into a stance as if appraising a historical tapestry. "Don't I recall one other time you were hobbling around with something like that on?" He all too solemnly wagged his head. "You don't want to let that get to be a habit."

The inevitable about the weather and how different this country around here was from Mitch's neck of the woods. Then as if on cue Fritz gave a lopsided chummy smile. "How's that dad of yours, how's Lyle?"

Dead but still making trouble, Mitch wanted to say but didn't. "Passed away, about a month ago."

"No! Hate to hear that. What of?"

Mitch told him, watching the face that had aged so radically yet had the rubbery lineaments of those past summers. The old man listened as if he knew how to assess death; New Guinea had given him at least that.

"That's hell, when that happens." Fritz shook his head at leukemia. Then nodded over his shoulder toward the Vets' Home and said confidentially: "See people go to the marble farm every kind of way in that place."

Mitch said nothing, waiting him out.

Starting to fidget, Fritz nonetheless hesitated before asking: "What do I owe this pleasure to?"

"Brought something to show you." Mitch reached in the backseat of the car and drew out the daybook from 1962, spreading it open on the hood of the Honda.

Fritz glanced toward the Oasis, where the door had opened and the earlier two thirst cases had charged in, then peered uncertainly down at the daybook pages. "Been goin' through your dad's stuff, is this? Get my cheaters on." He fumbled reading glasses out of his shirt pocket.

The penmanship caught his eye instantly. He glanced up at Mitch as if they were allies against forgery. "Too nice a writing for your dad. What, Mitch, did your mother keep the days some? Funny, I never knew her to handle any of the book side of things."

This was like pulling hens' teeth, but Mitch recited with patience: "That was my bookkeeper summer, because I was in bed with a cast on, wasn't I."

"Oh, yeah. Dimly remember."

His forefinger a slightly shaking guide, Fritz examined the names of the crew and the crosshatched record of their hayfield days as if it gave him every pleasure to do so. "Hadn't thought about some of these guys in years." After a little, his finger found its way across the page to what the mens' labor ultimately added up to, the tonnage of the bale stacks.

"We were fiends on that haying when things'd go right," he vouched. "Godamighty, look at this run of days—two hundred tons put up, that week. That's going some."

"The week of the Fourth of July," Mitch prompted. "Take a look at that."

IVAN DOIG

With due deliberation Fritz turned the page and studied the three-day gap. "I see I got docked some days, in there. Must've been laid up some way."

"Actually you hung on to those days," Mitch came back with, "but it wasn't because I didn't try."

Every wrinkle on that face wrote out innocent amazement. "What, did we have some kind of little disagreement? Old stuff like this, it's hard to bring back."

Not for one of them, it wasn't. As distinct as a recording Mitch could hear his younger self saying, *You know you're lying,* and this man saying back, *Just ask your dad.*

Mitch went through it all like a prompter feeding lines to a soured actor, how Fritz's spree began on the Fourth and lapped over the next two days when the rest of the crew was back in the hayfield. "I marked you for showing up for work again on the seventh, and when everybody got paid off at the end of the summer you bitched like crazy on those two docked days. And my father backed you on it instead of his own kid. Sat there and lied right along with you. How come?"

Fritz moved his bowed shoulders an inch apiece. "If Lyle'd wanted you to know, he'd have told you."

"Fritz, *I* want to know. He had thirty-five years and never got around to it. I didn't come here to jump on you about whatever you were up to, okay?" Mitch watched the face in front of him, but not even the eyelids moved. What did it take to make a mark on these old men? "But it played hell between my father and me when he let you screw over the daybook the way you did and then told me your word on it was better than mine. Everything went wrong between us after that. Help me out on this, Fritz. Just tell me what that was about, back there."

"Wish I could help you out."

From somewhere in memory another saying of his father's came to Mitch: *That Fritz, he'll fill you so full of it it your eyes'll be brown.*

Mitch kept watch on the old man, then closed the buckram cover on the daybook. "Tell you what. Climb in the car with me, let's take the load off our feet. We can drive around a little, while we catch up on those days."

"Another time maybe, Mitch. Been nice, but I got something needs doing downtown."

"Really? Not much open this time of day except the cafe and the Oasis. And I imagine they give you breakfast there in the Vets' Home, don't they?" He gazed down at Fritz's feet. They were in sandals.

Watching the flushed old man, desire for the first drink of the day hanging out all over him, Mitch hardened himself to say:

"Come on, let's get in the car, Fritz."

Fritz was chattering out the not many sights of greater Hydropolis when he noticed that Mitch had turned onto the access road that led back out to the freeway. He clammed up, but the looks he gave Mitch out of the corner of his eye said worlds.

Controlling his voice, Mitch said like the least time-conscious of tour guides: "I thought we'd just see some country. Mosey over to Billings and back, maybe." He punched the cruise control, the speed set at fifty. It didn't take a minute before a bread truck passed them as if they were parked. Billings and back would be an all-day trip at this anemic speed.

"You're meaner than Lyle ever thought of being."

Mitch clenched his teeth, on the hope that if it was true it was temporary.

"This car has got reverse in it," he said. Then forced the next sentence out: "Help me straighten out that daybook, and we'll turn around."

Fritz's eyes were watering.

Mitch did not know how far he could bear to push the man or his own revulsion for this. But he was determined to see. He had played by the rules of their generation, back then, and been run over by his headlong father and blindsided by this remorseless liar as his rewards. *Do things back somewhere count, or don't they?* Time stalled on Interstate 90. Each in his own way, the old hayhand and the boy now middle-aged sat there in the slowly gliding car sweating it out. They rode five miles in silence, fence posts creeping past, before Fritz Mannion used his hands to lift one leg over the other, the way a cripple would. Hands, legs, knees still twisted together, he said with a wince:

"Ferragamo's wife."

Immediately Mitch punched the cruise control off and whipped the Honda around on a highway patrol crossover, aiming back toward Hydropolis. But he put the car on fifty again to remind his passenger not to get too relieved.

"Say more."

Fritz rubbed the veiny back of a hand across his mouth.

"Those trips Lyle kept making into Great Falls—remember how much we was broke down all that summer? Radiator hose kept blowing out on his buckrake. This'd happen, that'd happen, time or two a week away he'd have to go to the Falls to get parts, wouldn't he. What he was mainly getting was sack time with Janine."

Fritz glanced nervously across the car. "Mitch, I don't know that your mother ever found out. If she did, not from me. I made sure she wasn't even around when we got into it over my days."

Mitch kept his eyes fixed to the road ahead, as though down its unrolling lane of time he could see them form again, the people at that picnic—the creamy Mrs. Ferragamo, and his father with that sergeant stare, and his mother whose life was all potluck, and the good Joe: picnickers and more. "I caught on," now Fritz swallowed audibly, "I don't even remember how. It started out as kidding, was all. Just me saying something to Lyle about it sure being a hard summer on a certain kind of hose. He reddened right up, you know that way he would? And next thing gave me one of his goddamn winks." Fritz paused. Wiped an eye, then his nose. "I just wanted him to know that I knew he was getting his dong polished regularly by Janine, those little trips down to the Falls for 'parts.' "

Then climbing upstairs to his son who was keeping the days, to hand him the expenses of cheating.

"Ferragamo"—Mitch put a voice together—"he was always the one in that story—"

"—spotted the Jap in the bushes, saved Lyle's life, yeah, yeah. He did that. More than likely saved mine, too." Fritz stopped again to gather his next words. "Your dad came out of that with the notion he wasn't as much of a man as Joe, is what I think. And when he couldn't be, he . . . what would you say? Tried to whittle Ferragamo down. Those summer jobs, bossing him around with the rest of us. Sneaking off and laying Janine."

And last of all, getting it into his head to smudge away the man's time on a mountain, sift himself into that place. *In memory of Ferragamo, let's just say:* back there in the running-board conclave, Lyle Rozier saying it as though it were just the epitaph of a Divide summer. Mitch gripped the Honda's steering wheel as unrelentingly as if he had the box of ashes in hand again.

"I always figured Lyle was getting set to fight it out with Joe over her, that next summer. Your mother gone, Janine'd have to choose, wouldn't she?" Fritz's voice had loosened, soft with gratitude at the sight of the Oasis now. "But right before haying, Ferragamo took her and moved to Oregon. Never said a word to Lyle, just up and did it. That's what really got to your dad. Joe dropped him like he was just nothing."

Five

THEY WERE EATING IT UP, THE WEDDING-GOERS, WHUF-fling right through the hors d'oeuvres and munching, munching, munching onward into the big food.

Nervously she circled off from the groom a little, wanting the reception to be perfect, the most mouthwatering page in nuptial history.

"We're out of the salmon pâté, Lexa," Jaci of her crew came up and whispered.

Lexa pulled out the couple of emergency fifties she always kept in the pocket under her apron. "Run over to Gretchen's and beg some, quick."

She monitored the room trying to recognize the next incipient emergency. Now groom and bride were whooping it up with another champagne-brandishing phalanx of friends. He owned a chain of sunglasses shops and she was concertmaster of a chamber orchestra; they had met in one of the *hiking/biking/caring/sharing* chat rooms on the Internet. Lexa nibbled her lip. Those champagne glasses were emptying fast, and she swung around to check on the level of traffic over by the bar and Mitch.

Mitch?

She was over there in a flash. Absence and the heart and all that notwithstanding, she was purely panicked by his materialization here.

"Where'd—what're you—"

Giving the roomful a broken-field runner's alert scan, he appraised the wedding reception: "Not bad as these things go, hmm?"

She couldn't say the same for him. Unshaven for a couple of days, clothes that all too obviously had been slept in for at least that long, the giant black glob of his cast sticking out alongside the bar table, he looked like something a very large cat had dragged in off the road. To her outrage, he was perusing her companionably. There he loomed, a winning grin hung on him, damn him. As much as she wanted to whale into him with her fists for this derisive bye-bye or whatever he thought it was, she had to keep frantic watch over her shoulder for the mother of the bride, big mama of the universe at these events. All it would take was enough disturbance of the peace to bring the Matriarch of the Day over with the pronouncement *You'll never fix food in this town again.* In a fierce whisper Lexa demanded to know: "What did you do with Brad?"

"He slipped out to his car to listen to his Kenny G instructional CD."

"How'd you find—" She shut up and stood in front of as

much of Mitch as she could while he dispensed champagne into
the next covey of thrust glasses. When those guests moved off, he
turned to her as if surprised she had to ask.

"Went to the house for some things and read the refrigerator
door, how else?"

That was it, then. He had come for his stuff. Packing it all
up, to add to the permanent houseload in the Springs. Roziers.
A penchant for mess ran in the family. For almost three weeks
she had been fuming about having to live with his belongings
and now she found herself equally ticked off that the house
was going to look half empty. One pang after another going
through her, she tried to keep her mind on the point that he had
no business playing around with her business.

"The house is one thing, but where I'm trying to do my work
is another. Why'd you bother to slip in here?"

"Thought it was time I did a little shopping." He studied the
reception room again. "Might need one of these someday."

"You really are determined to be a sonofabitch about this,
aren't you. Mitch, I don't care how terminally peed off you are
at me over the ashes and what happened at the tower and whatever else you've managed to come up with to add to the list. I
don't deserve this. You and Mariah can go off into the wedding
sunset if you goddamn want, but—"

"Lexa—"

"—I don't have to have that picture painted for me." She
stood there seething at the future. McCaskill family reunions
were going to be a real case of the jollies, weren't they, with him
on hand as Mariah's hubby and Lexa's ex-you-name-it.

"Lexa, listen—"

"And I don't have to listen to any of your—"

"Lexa, Mariah and I are not in the marrying picture. We've
never even tried the sample of that."

She shot a suspicious gaze at him all the way up. True, his
hair was not standing up in sulphur spikes.

He caught her look and smiled. "Think about it. How could I go in the water with this cast?"

By then it didn't take thinking. It only took erasing the blackboard of her mind, and then their bodies were colliding in a desperate hug and more.

Coming into the empty house, Mariah deposited the sack with a Dairy Queen hamburger in one direction and her camera bag in another. How damnably quiet. *Price of peace,* she told herself, and went to the kitchen for one of Lyle's beers to help prop up supper.

When Mitch had come back from Hydropolis yesterday with the goods on Lyle and told her he was going right on to Seattle, he'd asked if she didn't think she should come along and start making her own mend with Lexa. "How convincing is that?" she had pointed out. "We come trotting into Seattle, joined at the hip, to tell her we're not an item together? You go alone. Give her me to be mad at."

Mitch had touched her on the shoulder. "We are an item together. Just not the household kind."

"Second thoughts. Story of my date book."

Standing there, they drew new assessments of each other, a daily occupation since their time in the fire tower. He saw a woman who cut trails through life as brisk as a comet, and as unfollowable. Steady eyes on his, she was looking back at a route not taken, not takable, running as it did between the sisters McCaskill. She and he traded those appraisals with self-conscious attempts at grins, and Mitch went out the door.

Someone at that door now. She opened it to a pair of men all in black, including hats and beards, who peered at her as if a beautiful redheaded woman in a *Hard Rock Cafe—Beijing* ball cap and a bottle of beer in her hand had not been their expectation.

"Is t'e mister here?" inquired the older Hutterite.

"We're fresh out of misters. Can I do anything for you?"

"T'ose brands of Lyle's, ve vant to buy vun." The older Hutterite locked eyes with her to avoid the temptation of straying into the rest of her scenery, then decided to confide, the other man nodding grave accompaniment: "Ve are hiving."

Mariah stepped back a little. "Is that a fact." It took her a few seconds to recall the Hutterite custom of hiving off into new colonies, entire families resettling on the next communal farm whenever an old one reached a certain population. A new dairy herd would need a new brand; maybe Lyle's iron menagerie was worthwhile after all. "Congratulations, I think. Come on out to the shed with me."

The branding irons appeared to have been busy learning from their clothes-hanger cousins how to multiply in the equivalent of a closet. There were angular heaps of them, wall-climbing squads of them, corner congregations of them. Mariah gestured at everything with what she figured was businesslike aplomb.

"Help yourself, gentlemen."

The Hutterite pair looked at her. The elder one said:

"Ve vant a T Cross."

Mariah blinked. Half of the iron in the known world, wrought into fancy combinations of who knew how many kinds in this shed, and they wanted a specific one? "Well, we can look, I guess. See if you can find it burned into the wall there while I scout around in the irons themselves."

The Hutterites read along the wall while she tried to figure out any system Lyle might have had to this. It wasn't numerical, it wasn't alphabetical, it wasn't even brandabetical. Under no approach did it seem to want to divulge an iron stem with a **T** and a cross on the end of it. After much murmuring from the men and much clattering from her, Mariah announced:

"Whoa, here you go." The Hutterites looked at the swoop-necked branding iron she was brandishing. "The U Cross, next best thing," she maintained.

"Ve vant a T Cross," the two Hutterites said in chorus.

"If you don't mind my asking, why the f—heck does it have to be a—?"

"Ve go the alphabet."

"Could you sort of spell that out for me?"

"Ven ve hive a colony, t'e new colony gets t'e next letter for its brand," the elder Hutterite explained. "T'e New Alberta colony, t'at vas our first, its brand is t'e A Cross." His beard lifted a little like a preacher coming to his favorite part of Deuteronomy. "T'e next vun, Kipp Creek Colony, t'e B Cross. Right up the alphabet, ve go. Now ve vant a T Cross."

She gave up and rummaged some more. "Look, this is as close as it gets—an ET Cross. Must've been Spielberg's his very self."

The Hutterite men looked at her. "Nein, t'at is Ernie Toomey's old brand."

"Never mind. See, all you have to do is cut off the **E**." She cast a wild glance at the tools here and there along the wall. "I'll throw in that hacksaw and a blade, even."

The Hutterites conferred with each other in German, and with a great show of reluctance snapped up the deal.

Wedding-goers gone, bride and groom on a floatplane whirring to the San Juan Islands, the Do-Re-Mi Catering crew was cleaning up. The crew, which looked a little hurt at having to get by with less than usual bossing, left a space around the bar, where a great amount of public kissing and earnest vowing was still going on.

"So he had love trouble in spite of himself," Lexa digested his account about Lyle.

"It used to run in the family," said Mitch, and reached for her again.

Back in the living room of the Rozier house, Mariah stood over the pages of the *Montanian* spread out on the desk, eating her thoroughly cold hamburger with one hand and running the other critically over the sheets of newsprint, trying a tighter cropping on one image, tracing and retracing the angle of perspective through another. Finally, more or less satisfied, she balled up her napkin from one hand to the other. *All this time on a newspaper and I still don't know why the ink has to come off on a person's fingers.*

The still unvanquished face of Lyle gazed up at her from the dozen incarnations on the pages. All at once she was reminded of his habit of E-mailing Ritz about each triumph in selling off a branding iron. *Last favor, you old handful* and in the general cyber-direction of Jakarta, *One from beyond the grave, kid.* Turning on the tired-looking old set and connecting to WebTV, she plopped into the big chair, keyboard cradled in her lap, then went to E-mail and typed out the message. When she came to the designation of the brand she tapped a capital T onto the screen and then the plus sign, pleased by its resemblance to a cross so that Ritz would have a nice evocative **T+** for his E-mail equivalent of a scrapbook. She clicked on *SEND*, but that didn't seem to want to be the end of it. Something still tickled at her, back up there in the vicinity of the plus-sign key. For curiosity's sake she tried its nearest neighbor, the minus sign, then typed another capital T. Sure enough, the **-T** there on the screen nicely approximated another brand, the Bar T.

Doing away with the minus sign, she shopped further along the row of keys, to the caret sign. **T̂.** Recognizably the Rafter T.

She took off the caret and moved over a couple of keys to the asterisk. **T*.** A pretty presentable T Spur.

Faster now, she deleted the asterisk, held down the shift key and tapped the colon key, twice. **::T.** The Dice T. Dumped that and put a pinky down in the lowest right of the keyboard. **/T.** The Slash T.

Mariah stared down at the keyboard. She wasn't even into dingbat options, circles and boxes and triangles and hearts and spades and diamonds and the whole computer zoo of other graphics. Nor had she started to go the alphabet, pairing twenty-five more letters and combinations thereof with each of these keyable mutations.

She lunged for the phone book, pawed out the number, waited impatiently for response at the other end.

"Donald, is it? Could you send Matthew over here to the Roziers'? I've got something on the screen I need to have him check out." Then she called Seattle.

BlazingBrands.com, as quick as they got it on-line, billed a junior fortune in orders its first week. Brands went from being the return addresses of cows to the latest must-have as PICs—personal identification codes—in the cyber frontier beyond PINs, and the Webspeak equivalent of monograms transposable to everything from tech team T-shirts to personalized steaks sizzling on barbecue grills at company get-togethers. From ZYX headquarters arrived a fine fat offer to buy all three of those letters, in all permutations.

Wouldn't you know, Mariah set her sights on the world again. This time, with her cut of our cyber gold rush, she figured she could poke the planet in the ribs with her camera for as long as she wanted. Before she could take off, Mitch and I asked her to perform the photo honors the day Lyle's ashes were dealt with.

She was circling around the site, restless as a jay, her camera bag bumping on her hip, when Mitch and Lexa pulled up.

The box clutched to him, Mitch ducked into the lee of the

BlazingBrands.com corporate Chevy Blazer, Lexa and Mariah already huddling there.

"This place is going to miss him," Mariah mused.

"But it doesn't need any more like him, either," Mitch said with equal meditation.

"Watch your footing out there," Lexa warned.

"Where was that advice the last time I needed it?" He sent her a flit of a grin, then looked soberly at Mariah. "Got your camera angle scoped out?"

"Always got that."

"Then here goes."

The two women watched him transport the ashes the last little way, carefully edging himself into position.

"Lexa?" ventured Mariah in a lip-biting tone. "No hard feelings?"

"Oh, yeah. But other kinds too. We're still sisters." She gave Mariah a reflecting smile. Then gently gave her a push, fond but a push, out into the wind.

Mitch stood at the edge of the Donstedder benchland where the coulee cut in. The pile of rocks below still seemed oddly concentrated here in this one place, like a sac of glacier stones. Lexa stood off to one side a little, upwind. Mariah went around to the brow of the coulee on the other side of them and cocked her camera.

"Maybe in error, but never in doubt—that was my father." Mitch's voice steadied against the wind. "He read himself wrong there at the end. He thought he could make himself add up to all that he wasn't, with these"—Mitch raised the ashes a little—"and Phantom Woman. If he figured he had to have a monument, there is nothing shameful about this one. This one he earned over and over."

He opened the lid of the box, undid the plastic liner inside it. Hands high, he leaned out over the coulee and carefully turned the box upside down, shaking the ashes. They were the consistency of sand, and of the same color as the rocks they fell among.

In a mountain valley as old as the visit of glaciers, the hiker stopped to drink out of the swift stream.

He gazed around with care as he walked out onto the low smooth outcropping that led right to the creek. Upstream, a waterfall slid with a pleasant little roar, and then water that looked as if it had fish in it pooled against the parentheses of bank before riffling off down the valley. *Pretty sonofagun of a place* occurred to him with a small smile. And it had the lookout tower beat for calm instead of commotion. All in all, he supposed he could tell himself he had come up in the world by coming down from Phantom Woman. But tired, Lord, he was tired and thirsty after the hot pace on the trail; it had been a long time since that fortifying can of tomatoes at lunch.

Taking off his hat and wiping away sweat, he looked for somewhere to set the hat and his things while he watered up, but there was nothing of the kind on the bare ledge of the creek crossing. He backtracked off the dock of rock and put it all, his Stetson on top, against the nearest aspen. Then came back to the stream's stone edge. He drank from his hands, wiped his sleeve across his mouth, and stayed squatting on his haunches a minute, simply looking around. No matter how old he lived to be he would never cease to be captivated by the green tingling leaves of aspens. Everywhere under them, flat rocks from a sedimentary ledge vastly larger than the creek's namesake where he hunkered. The spill of rocks out of the mountainside was like a flow of stone joining the creek. A lot like flagstones. Tempting. It wouldn't take much to pile them.

Running his eyes over the palette of rocks he mulled whether to put up a cairn, mark this place for the kick of it. Didn't really have time. Another hour, maybe two, he could pound on down the trail before calling it a day. But the trail would be there in the morning, too. The monument this spot of solace seemed to want would not, unless he lent a hand to those rocks.

Leave it up to gravity, he decided. He stood up and dug into his britches pocket for the good-luck piece he carried, a Liberty head silver dollar. If the toss came up heads, camp here and work with the rocks until they mounted up in monument form. Tails, then—he chortled at the play of words, starting to feel like himself for the first time this day—hightail on down the trail.

Bob Marshall poised the silver dollar on his broad thumbnail. Then flipped the coin high, the lucky piece spinning its arc of tails and heads up, up, into the mountain air.

Acknowledgments

Bill Tidyman for gallantly refurbishing my memory of rock picking; John Maatta for circumnavigating the Sweetgrass Hills with me; Lynn Korman for skillfully threading me through San Francisco's Friday-night weave of Rollerblading; the Bancroft Library at the University of California, Berkeley, for access to Bob Marshall's notebooks; Laird Nelson and Sarah Auerbach for tuning up my ear to techies and their music; range scholar Hank Mathiason for tutelage in livestock brands, and Dave Walter for his inimitable role as interlocutor; Bud Moore and George Engler for readily sharing their decades of experience on the trails of the northern Rockies; Cheryl Oakes and Pete Steen of the Forest History Society for fire tower data; Mike Olsen for stimulating observations on the Baby Boomered West; Bradley Hamlett for Montana haying lore, and Rebecca and Joe Brewster for sharing their thoughts on going home again to where they and I came from; bush pilot Scott Reeburgh for the unforgettable Anaktuvuk flight; Lennart Lovstrand, whose

WebTV I poetically licensed dingbats to; Gloria Flora, Lewis and Clark National Forest supervisor, for acting as Bob Marshall would have toward the Rocky Mountain Front; Ann Nelson, Sarah and Nile Norton, Jean and John Roden, Linda Sullivan and Marcella Walter for cheerfully cross-examining wayward scenes for me; Richard Maxwell Brown, Linda Bierds, John and Katharina Maloof, Sarah Nelson, Margaret Svec, Walter Walkinshaw, and Mary Jane and Andy DiSanti for bits of inspiration that they made the mistake of letting drop within range of my notebook; the Avenue of the Americas bookmakers, Nan Graham, Susan Moldow, Carolyn Reidy, Brooke Zimmer and Brant Rumble; Rebecca Saletan, in at the launch; Marshall Nelson, without whom I would do I know not what; and companion on our high lonesome in the Bob Marshall Wilderness and the other geographies of love, Carol Doig.

A SCRIBNER PAPERBACK FICTION READING GROUP GUIDE

MOUNTAIN TIME

DISCUSSION POINTS

1. Discuss Lyle, Mitch, Lexa and Mariah's differing relationships to the natural world. How do the characters' childhoods and career choices reflect or shape their connections to the land? How do their attitudes toward nature serve as both barriers and bonds in their relationships with one another?
2. Discuss Doig's use of flashbacks. What effect does he achieve by offering vivid glimpses of his characters' pasts?
3. Mitch wants to safeguard the environment while his father Lyle seems bent on exploiting it. Do you view Mitch's environmentalism as a filial rebellion, a conscious departure from his father's lifestyle and choices? Or, do you think it reflects a generational shift from considering the earth an inexhaustible resource to viewing it as endangered?
4. Does Mariah use her camera as a way of connecting with the world or of keeping it at a distance? What do you think of her pairing of "earthly resemblances" to document the "natural family of forms"? Does she photograph natural and historic sites as a means of protecting or preserving them, or simply to achieve an aesthetic end?
5. Mitch decides not to honor his father's dying wish. Do you think he is courageous and his action defensible, or is he wrong? By defying Mitch, is Lexa primarily defending Lyle's decision, or trying to help Mitch let go of his bitterness?
6. Mitch "had the terrifying suspicion that he was beginning to understand extinction, from the inside out." In the course of the book, Mitch is faced with several endings: the dissolution of his first marriage, the end of the "Coastwatch" column, and the end of his father's life. What does the novel suggest about the significance of endings, and of our chances for beginning anew?
7. In pondering the past, Mitch asks: "Do things back somewhere count, or don't they?" Find examples of how Doig explores the past

and its effect on the present. Is it wise for Mitch to find Fritz and dig for the reasons behind the old daybook controversy? Is he better off knowing what he finds out?

8. Doig alternates accounts of Lexa's climb out of the mountains for help with Bob Marshall's last hike along the Continental Divide, the "high lonesome" of wild passages he so loved. What effect does Doig achieve by pairing these characters in this way?

9. What do the cairns, those stone monuments erected in the mountains, symbolize? What do they reflect about our need to alter the natural world, leave reminders of our presence and create things that may outlast us?

10. Bob Marshall is invoked several times in the novel, which ends with a scene of his stream-side reverie. What significance does Marshall's legend lend to the choices and struggles of the four main characters? Why do you think Doig ends the book with the image of Marshall tossing a coin to decide whether or not to build a cairn?

11. Ivan Doig has said that he uses the places he knows to write about that larger country: life. Do you think that the themes of *Mountain Time* could successfully be set in some other place?

12. Who do you think is the strongest character in the novel? Which one is most sympathetic to you? Provide examples that help explain why you think so.

NOTE TO READERS FROM IVAN DOIG

No one is likely to confuse my writing style with that of Charlotte Brontë, but when that impassioned parson's daughter lifted her pen from *Jane Eyre* and bequeathed us the most intriguing of plot summaries— "Reader, I married him"—she also was subliminally saying what any novelist, even one from the Montana highlands rather than the Yorkshire moors, must croon to those of you with your eyes on our pages: "Reader, my story is flirting with you; please love it back." Our books come to you with bright-cheeked hope, but before you take the time to get to know them you might well want to know: where do these suitors in their printed jackets and composed pages come from? What, as Ms. Brontë would grant that you have a perfect right to ask, is their parentage? My own literary "begats" now add up to nine books, and a biographical browsing of me customarily brings up such phrases as these:

"Ivan Doig was born in White Sulphur Springs, Montana, in 1939 . . . grew up along the Rocky Mountain Front where much of his writing takes place . . . first book, the highly acclaimed memoir *This House of Sky,* was a finalist for the National Book Award . . . former ranch hand, newspaperman, and magazine editor, Doig is a graduate of Northwestern University, where he received bachelor's and master's degrees in journalism . . . he also holds a Ph.D in history from the University of Washington . . . in the century's-end *San Francisco Chronicle* polls to name the best Western novels and works of nonfiction, Doig is the only living writer with books in the top dozen on both lists: *English Creek* in fiction and *This House of Sky* in nonfiction . . . he lives in Seattle with his wife Carol, who has taught the literature of the American West."

Taking apart a career in such summary sentences always seems to me like dissecting a frog—some of the life inevitably goes out of it—and so I think the more pertinent Ivan Doig for you, Reader, is the red-headed only child, son of ranch hand Charlie Doig and ranch cook Berneta Ringer Doig (who died of her lifelong asthma on my sixth birthday), who in his junior year of high school (Valier, Montana; my class of 1957 had twenty-one members) made up his mind to be a writer of some kind.

At the time, my motivation seemed to be simply to go away to college and break out of a not very promising ranch-work future in Montana. Jobs in journalism followed—as an editorial writer in Decatur, Illinois (where I truly grasped Keats's meaning of "amid the alien corn"), and as assistant editor of *The Rotarian* magazine in Evanston. Then, starved as we were for mountains and ocean, Carol and I left the Chicago area in 1966 and came to Seattle, with the notion that I would get a Ph.D in history as background to bring to journalism teaching.

What graduate school taught me, though, was that I wanted to write more than I wanted to teach. I was continuing to freelance magazine articles during grad school and I also began, to my surprise, writing poetry, which I had never even thought of attempting before.

My eight or nine published poems showed me that I lacked a poet's final skill, the one Yeats called closing a poem with the click of a well-made box. But still wanting to work at stretching the craft of writing toward the areas where it mysteriously starts to be art, I began working on what Norman Maclean has called the poetry under the prose—a lyrical language, with what I call a poetry of the vernacular in how my characters speak on the page. (In *Mountain Time,* for instance, one of the McCaskill sisters says of a set of neighbor kids who were hard to tell apart: "All the faces in that family rhyme.") One of my diary entries, midway through the half-dozen years of effort on *This House of Sky*, shows me trying "to write it all as highly charged as poetry." Twenty-five years and these nine books later, that's still my intention.

One last word about the setting of my work, the American West. I don't think of myself as a "Western" writer. To me, language—the substance on the page, that poetry under the prose—is the ultimate "region," the true home, for a writer. Specific geographies, but galaxies of imaginative expression—we've seen them both exist in William Faulkner's postage stamp-size Yoknapatawpha County, and in Gabriel García Márquez's nowhere village of Macondo, dreaming in its hundred years of solitude. If I have any creed that I wish you as readers, necessary accomplices in this flirtatious ceremony of writing and reading, will take with you from my pages, it'd be this belief of mine that writers of caliber can ground their work in specific land and lingo and yet be writing of that larger country: life.

Discover more reading group guides on-line!
Browse our complete list of guides and download them for free at
www.SimonSays.com/reading_guides.html.